A FIELD OF RED

A FRANK HARPER MYSTERY

GREG ENSLEN

GYPSY
PUBLICATIONS

Published in 2013, by Gypsy Publications
Troy, OH 45373, U.S.A.
www.GypsyPublications.com

First Edition, Second Printing

Enslen, Greg
A Field of Red / by Greg Enslen
ISBN 978-1-938768-23-1 (paperback)

Library of Congress Control Number
2013944938

Edited by Diana Ceres
Cover Design by Pamela Schwartz
Cover Photo © Eric Cherry, 2008
Flickr/Getty Images used with permission

For more information, please visit the author's
website at www.GregEnslen.com

PRINTED IN THE UNITED STATES OF AMERICA

ACKNOWLEDGMENTS

This book was, like my others, a collaborative effort. If it weren't for the immeasurable assistance of some amazing people, this book would never have crawled its way out of my brain and onto the printed page. This book took about two-and-a-half years to complete, going through several rewrites and revisions until something emerged that I could be happy with. Anything great in this book is probably as a result of a suggestion one of these people made, whereas all the mistakes and miscalculations fall squarely on my shoulders.

I'd like to thank the following people for their hard work to help make this book a reality:

• My wife Samantha, who had to listen to me talk on and on endlessly about Frank Harper and the other characters;

• My parents, Mary and Albert Enslen, for reading and rereading this—along with my father's attention to timelines and details—and marking it up until it was perfect;

• My editor, Diana Ceres, who vastly improved the book by giving it a rigorous edit and bringing up a lot of questions that made me think;

• And the wonderful folks of Tipp City, Ohio, upon which the fictional town of Cooper's Mill is based.

A FIELD
OF
RED

PROLOGUE

The man sat in his car, waiting.

Other cars passed his location, but Tyler was parked far down the alley and no one could see him.

He spent a lot of time parked in his car, usually in plain sight. It was in the job description. On those occasions, other cars would pass him, and the drivers would glance over at Tyler; often, they smiled and nodded, or threw him a quick wave. Tyler could tell it wasn't out of friendliness. They feared him, or respected him, or both. It didn't really matter; the result was the same. Deference.

Tyler checked his watch again. He didn't like being out here for the world to see. Even half-hidden in the alley, he was parked just off one of the busiest streets in Cooper's Mill. At any moment, some idiot might decide to take a shortcut and use this alley, which ran between Hyatt and Seventh Street. He had parked far away for a good reason, but he still felt exposed.

But there was no other option.

When it was time, he opened the heavy door of his car and climbed out, straightening his uniform. Tyler was dressed perfectly, as always. He was tall and lean and carried himself with an air that some people found haughty. He liked to think of it as confidence—and he knew he earned it. Tyler was always working the angles, coming up with new plans.

Tyler smiled and walked down the alley to Hyatt. Large houses lined both sides of the wide, suburban street, fronted by huge lawns and driveways dotted with expensive cars. Big yards, the kind that required riding lawnmowers or, better yet, a lawn care service. The richest people in town lived on this street. They could afford it.

He turned and began walking south, down the street, taking his time. Tyler watched the front of a house far down the block, a huge brick home with a circular driveway. The girl was running late. He stopped at the corner of Hyatt and Broadway and waited casually, taking out his phone and pretending to talk on it, keeping one eye on the house and the other on any witnesses who might appear.

Hopefully, this whole exercise would come off with no problems. Of course, the kid would never make it home—she would know his face—but other than that, things should go smoothly. It was all set up, and the others were ready. And, if things worked out, all of his money troubles would be solved.

A Louis Prima song drifted into his head while he waited. It was "Bona Sera," another of his mother's favorites. She'd sung it obsessively around the house when he was young, back before she went out on a Thursday morning and never came back.

A car passed Tyler, and he glanced away. The fewer people who could identify him, the better. But it was a good plan. The others were—

The young girl came out of her house.

Tyler watched, still "talking" on the phone. The little girl walked down the long driveway and turned, waving back to the front door, where her mother, Glenda Martin, was standing, waving. Tyler remembered Glenda from school: brunette, tall, beautiful. Now she was in her mid-30s, a pillar of the community. She'd been too good to talk to Tyler in high school—she'd ended up with Nick, the football player, of course.

The young girl, Charlene, hitched up her pink backpack and started up the sidewalk that ran along Hyatt Avenue, heading his way. Suddenly, from behind her, there must have been a shout, unheard by Tyler, because she stopped and turned and waited, looking back at the house.

A second girl—a young Hispanic girl with a plastic bag instead of a backpack—ran down the long, leaf-covered driveway and joined the first. Together, they started up Hyatt.

Two girls.

Shit.

That wasn't the plan, Tyler thought, his mother's song dying in his head. It was only supposed to be the Martin girl, walking to school by herself. Tyler was supposed to walk her to his car, and they would drive away. Now, Tyler would have to take Maya as well. That complicated things greatly.

He shook his head. It was too late to call and get instructions. Everything was rolling now. The train had already left the station. Things were all set up; beep beep, these girls were going on a trip. Not to the moon, like in the song. But a trip, nonetheless.

Tyler didn't want to take them both, but he didn't want to make a scene. The second girl would be able to identify him if he left her behind.

And it was too messy to kill her here.

Tyler made up his mind. The two girls walked up Hyatt toward him and made the turn onto Broadway, kicking through a pile of fallen leaves. He waited. They giggled at some private joke. Two hundred yards behind him, Tyler could hear the shouts of fellow students arriving at Broadway Elementary, the boxy brick building that took up an entire block of Broadway Avenue. Crossing guards were directing kids across the street. He was exposed—anyone could see him. He glanced in the direction of the alley where he was parked.

The two girls looked up from their conversation to see the man standing there, leaning casually against a low fence. For just a moment, their faces filled with wary curiosity. But then they smiled.

Of course they smiled. They recognized him.

1

Frank Harper sat in a dark corner of Ricky's, a dingy bar in the downtown historical district of the rural Ohio town of Cooper's Mill. He was nursing a beer, looking up every time anyone entered the establishment. It was a habit he couldn't break.

Frank was a solid man in his mid-50s; not old, but not young anymore. He had the trim and sinewy frame of a man who worked out regularly, if only out of habit. The short, dark hair atop his head suggested a police or military past, but was longer and shaggier than any cop would have worn it. His age was betrayed by the weary lines on his tired face. He looked worn, spent, his face darkened with five days' worth of dark stubble. He also looked like the kind of man who knew how to throw a punch and how to take one.

The bar was bigger on the inside than he'd expected—a wide space filled with low tables surrounding the central wooden bar, with seating on all four sides. Several televisions hung from the walls, amid a collage of bar decorations: neon signs, pinup girls and other pictures of scantily clad women advertising something or the other, posters for local sports teams, and beer and liquor advertisements. Above the bar hung purple and green pennants, remnants from some long-forgotten Mardi Gras celebration. He was probably the only person here to notice the familiar colors.

The floor was dirty linoleum, the lighting low and dingy, and every window was covered. From the outside, it had looked like a strip club. Brisk air from outside occasionally wafted in as customers came and went, breaking up the smoke. It was a non-smoking restaurant, as was every other restaurant in Ohio, evidently, but it looked like Ricky's and its patrons hadn't gotten the memo.

Frank Harper had arrived in town only hours ago and settled into the Vacation Inn by the highway. He had needed a shower after traveling, and the drive up from Birmingham had been a long one. It had been ten hours of boring, with the radio broken in the Taurus; he didn't have the money to get it fixed. The jury-rigged CD player, hooked into the car's speakers, and a stack of jazz and blues CDs had to do. Benny Golson and Earl Hooker, Coltrane and Ervin had kept him company, with a little Pinetop Perkins thrown in for good measure.

After a shower, he had left the hotel and climbed in his car to drive around a bit to get the lay of the land. He'd gotten the Taurus on the cheap from the ABI, one of those "retired vehicles" the Alabama Bureau of Investigation and the Alabama Department of Public Safety were always trying to get rid of. After driving it a week, he figured out why. It was a piece of crap. Almost nothing worked.

Cooper's Mill was located right on the highway, just north of Dayton, Ohio. The small town had a busy commercial area near the highway and, a mile to the east, a quaint historical district by the river. The grid of downtown streets had great, old-timey names like Plum and Elm and was dotted with little shops and restaurants—they even had a toy store—and a few bars. There were only three traffic lights and, as far as Frank could tell, the entire downtown consisted of this one strip of old buildings and shops, surrounded by blocks and blocks of old homes.

Frank sipped at his beer. He'd been in a lot of bars, dives to high-end places. This place had all the ambiance of a beer tent at a state fair. The place was a dump, and it suited him perfectly. He just wanted to be left alone.

It looked like half the town was here. He had no idea how big Cooper's Mill was, but Ricky's was packed. He'd been sitting at a table by himself for nearly two hours and was working on his fifth beer. He preferred whiskey, or bourbon, when he could get it, but tonight it had to be beer. The empties were still lined up on his table. The "waitress" hadn't been around for a while. The sticky floor and cheap tables told him he'd probably pass out before the help came around to bus the table or bring him another round.

He pretended to be oblivious to the bar fight that was about to start.

Frank didn't think anyone else had noticed yet. The two women behind the counter had their hands full, handing out watery beer as fast as they could and taking wads of wet bills. Customers lined the bar, three deep. Around the perimeter of the room, every one of the low wooden tables was filled.

It was a Saturday night, October 8, and the bar was slammed. And now things were getting louder. Everything had been fine for a while, but now there was some college football game on, and people were getting excited.

Frank was trying to ignore the people around him, but the tension in the place was growing thicker by the minute. It was chilly outside—a light rain was falling—but in here, it was hot and humid. Frank pushed it out of his mind and concentrated on the Bud Light in his hands. It was getting warm and tasted horrible, but at least it was something.

He ignored the tall guy at the bar and his six friends.

They'd been bickering off and on with another group, three guys sitting at a table next to the bar. They'd been shouting at the game on the TV and exchanging words for the last hour. The more they drank, the braver their words became. Frank knew the type—he'd seen a million of them, big talkers after three rounds. He'd been in enough bars in his life to know you didn't get involved, unless your life, or the life of somebody you cared about, was involved. And it wasn't his place to get involved, not anymore. Two years ago, he would've separated the two groups before things got worse, or at least got them to take it outside.

Tonight, he didn't really care. Frank was only in town for a week to talk to somebody, someone he hadn't seen in a long time.

The whole situation had gone in the shitter years ago, after Trudy had left him. Maybe driving up here to Cooper's Mill could help fix some of that. Or maybe it wouldn't. Who knew how Laura was going to react. At least on the phone she'd agreed to see him. That was something.

Frank wanted a bourbon so badly he could feel the shape of the bottle in his hands. Bourbon and whiskey were essentially the same thing, bourbon being a specific type of whiskey made in the good old U.S.A. The good stuff, like Maker's Mark, was made in Bourbon County, Kentucky, and aged several years. His hands started to shake just thinking about it.

Ben Stone, one of Frank's old partners, had liked Irish whiskey. Frank had been on loan to the Florida State Police for a temporary counterfeiting assignment. Frank had been thinking about Ben a lot lately, wondering how his family was doing. Ben's wife had always been nice to Frank. She'd been one of those solid, no-nonsense cop wives. Frank remembered fondly one occasion he'd been over at the Stones' house for dinner. Ben had somehow convinced Frank to take a night off from bar-hopping for a "good, home-cooked meal." His wife had made bruschetta and chicken saltimbocca. She'd said that "saltimbocca" was Italian for "jump in the mouth," and she'd been right—it had been damn good.

That had been a nice evening. Frank didn't socialize as much as he should, and his partners had always razzed him about that. Ben, too.

Poor Ben. Killed by stupidity.

Frank looked back down at his beer, wishing he had something else. Ben used to say there were three kinds of whiskey in the world—good whiskey, OK whiskey, and shitty whiskey. At this point, Frank really wouldn't have refused any of them. He couldn't afford to be picky.

All he knew was the beer was doing nothing to settle his nerves.

He hoped this meeting with Laura would go well. He'd been thinking about her a lot lately as well. Frank was just glad she'd agreed to see him. Frank was good at reading people, but you didn't have to be a crack investigator to hear the reluctance in Laura's voice. Of course she was wary. She had every right to be.

But she'd said "yes," and he'd gotten himself to this little town in Ohio. Frank wasn't sure if it was going to be a good meeting or a bad meeting. All he knew was that she had allowed him to come up to Ohio and chat with her. And after he talked to Laura, he'd be heading back to Birmingham. She couldn't see him until Tuesday at noon, but he'd driven up early anyway to get his bearings.

Once a cop, always a cop.

Frank's thoughts returned to the Maker's Mark. He didn't have much money coming in. The retirement checks were thin. He was retired from the force after 21 years with the New Orleans Police Department. Good years, most of them. A few investigations that had gone south. A couple really bad ones, kidnapping cases he'd worked that had turned out horribly. But, all in all, a good career, right up until Katrina in 2005. After that, Frank had barely held on until retirement. Now, he was working part-time in Birmingham for the Alabama Bureau of Investigation, or ABI. Crappy little temporary cubicle, working their "cold cases" that led nowhere.

The job didn't really matter to anyone, especially the ABI, and it didn't pay much. The good money was saved for people doing field work, busting bad guys. Frank was stuck in his cubicle, working a never-shrinking stack of their cold cases. Half the time, Frank thought the only reason some poor sap was assigned to these cases was so the ABI could honestly tell reporters and family members that someone was still "looking into the old cases."

But money was tight. Most of the other retired cops Frank knew picked up freelance work to make ends meet. They usually did private investigations, or worked security, or "consulting," as it was better known. Frank didn't have the taste for that sort of work—chasing down bail jumpers or tracking husbands stepping out on their wives. He'd taken a couple jobs for other "consultants" and hated it—taking orders from some wet-behind-the-ear kid in charge of security.

But the money was running thin. Birmingham to Dayton had been a stretch, and the Taurus was a gas guzzler. He needed to be careful with his limited funds; the hotel, some meals, and gas money home, that's all he had. Not the best time to splurge on a bottle of Whistle Pig Rye.

They didn't have any good bourbon or whiskey in this place any-way. In fact, they didn't have any bourbon at all. Most bars at least had a wall of bottles of nice alcohol behind the counter, "aspirational bottles," as Ben had always called them. Fancy bottles with fancy caps, sitting on little shelves like trophies. Bottles for the folks drink-ing cheap swill to stare at and admire and dream about. But no fancy trophy alcohol in here—all they sold in Ricky's was beer, and only in bottles.

Above the bar was a big sign: "Welcome to Ricky's. Stay Classy, or You Get the Boot." Frank smiled at the ironic use of the word "classy" and wondered where they kept the shotgun. Every bar in America had a shotgun somewhere behind the counter, but this four-sided bar would make it harder to hide.

Suddenly, the voices in the bar got louder, shouting back and forth between the two groups Frank had noticed earlier.

He ignored the raised voices. It sounded like these two groups of men had a history. If Frank stepped in and stopped them tonight, they just beat the crap out of each other next week or the week after or the week after that. There was no need for Frank to get involved, not anymore.

"Hey, sit down, or I'm gonna ask you to leave," the taller barmaid yelled, pointing at the tall guy at the counter.

"Rosie, calm down," the tall guy said, laughing and shaking his head. "Don't get your panties all in a wad."

One of the men from the adjoining table stood and got in the tall guy's face.

"Derek, can it. She's having a rough week. Her niece is the one that's—"

"I don't give a shit," Derek said, shaking his head.

The shorter guy's eyes went wide, and Frank knew what would come next. It was nice that the guy was defending the woman behind the counter, but it would be better if he knew how to diffuse a situa-tion instead of throwing punches. Of course, there was always a time and a place for violence, but not in a crowded place like this, if it could be avoided.

Rosie looked around the rest of the bar for help. Probably looking for off-duty cops or any locals who could help her.

Her eyes settled on Frank.

Maybe she sensed in him something, an air of muddled authority, a history in law enforcement. He was getting up there in years but still had the body for it. Sometimes, when he wasn't deep in his cups, he could project a menacing air.

Maybe it was his facial expression, or maybe he was the only one watching the fight—everyone else in the bar seemed to be studiously ignoring the two groups of men.

Whatever the cause, Rosie looked directly at Frank, and they held each other's gaze for a long moment before he looked down at his beer. After another moment, he heard her speak up.

"Look, take it outside. Jake, thanks for sticking up for me, but I don't need the help. And Derek—back off."

Derek climbed off the stool and began to fall. One of his friends grabbed him up, and between him and Jake and another guy, they got Derek through the doors and outside. Through the closing doors, Frank could hear more raised voices outside. It sounded like the fight had only been delayed or relocated.

Frank sipped at his warm beer.

He should've been angrier at himself. Instead, he just tried to remember his place. Frank looked down at his left arm and ran his fingers along the thin scar that ran from the palm to disappear under the sleeve of his jacket. Getting involved wasn't always the smartest thing to do. Or the safest.

A few minutes later, Rosie came over.

She walked up to the table next to his and wiped it down, glancing over at him. She was shorter than she looked behind the bar. The floor was probably raised back there. When she was done, Rosie walked over and collected Frank's empties.

"Hey," she said, looking down at him.

He nodded.

"I could've used your help back there," she said, smiling. "I know those guys. They're going to get into it tonight, at some point. It was just good luck that Derek had had one too many."

Frank looked up at her.

"Sorry, but it's not my problem," he said quietly. "I don't know them, and I don't know you."

She looked at him for a second, taken aback.

"Oh, really?" she asked.

Frank nodded again, looking at the TV.

"I don't get involved in that kind of stuff. Not anymore."

He gave her no further explanation, resisting that human need to fill the empty, awkward space hanging between them. He knew how hard it was to just let the silence linger. Dead air. Frank had done it before, a thousand times. Suspects and witnesses alike rushed in to fill that space with something. More information, a confession, whatever. Anything to fill that pregnant pause. He could tell she wanted more information.

Instead, Frank looked at her, held her eyes, and said nothing.

After another long moment of awkward silence, the woman shook her head and walked away.

2

Kyle Park was an expansive stretch of grass and baseball diamonds and soccer fields on the eastern edge of Cooper's Mill. One of several parks and green spaces operated by the town's parks department, the massive park was built in the extensive floodplain east of town in the 1980s. In contrast, the old downtown City Park, located on north Third Street, was small, almost claustrophobic. It was filled with large, thick trees, playground equipment, two tennis courts, and the famous Round-house building. It was the perfect park for a picnic or a small get-together, but there wasn't enough open space to hold even a pick-up softball game.

But Kyle Park stretched as far as the eye could see, from the remnants of the old canal that paralleled south First Street all the way to the line of dark trees that lined the Great Miami River two miles away to the east. Most of the area east of the old canal was a floodplain—flat, muddy, and fertile—and it made for great soccer fields and rich, dark baseball fields.

It was a perfect use of the space, as the floodplain belonged to the Ohio Conservancy and most types of construction was prohibited anyway. In 1913, the Miami River had flooded, wiping out everything in Cooper's Mill east of the canal and destroying parts of Dayton, ten miles to the south. After the floods, construction east of the canal had been outlawed.

Glenda Martin wasn't thinking about construction restrictions in Kyle Park, or the fact that where she was sitting had been twenty feet underwater a hundred years ago. She was thinking about Charlie, her daughter, and a conversation they'd had last week.

Charlie had wanted to come to Kyle Park, but Glenda had demurred, saying it was too cold. It hadn't really been that cold—early October was a weird time. Unpredictable weather. But Glenda hadn't felt like coming to Kyle and had told Charlie no.

Now it was cold. And Glenda knew that Charlie could be out somewhere in it, alone. Or with Maya. No one knew anything, it seemed.

Glenda Martin was a beautiful woman, but her face was strained and unhappy, lately drawn into a semi-permanent scowl. The gusting breeze whipped her long brown hair around her face. She pulled the sweater tighter around her.

Six days since that horrible morning, October 3rd. She would never forget that date, no matter what happened. No calls, no ransom demands. Nothing from any kidnappers.

The cops weren't even sure there were kidnappers.

Glenad thought the cops were working from a much darker assumption; the girls had been abducted and were out of the area completely. Three Amber alerts had gone out over the past six days, but nothing had come of them.

Yesterday, Glenda had heard a subtle change in the way the police spoke to her and to each other: they were starting to assume harm had come to the girls, either by accident or at the hands of someone.

She sat on a park bench in Kyle Park, next to the baseball fields, waiting. It was early on Sunday morning and chilly.

Glenda heard voices and looked up. The group of volunteers was straggling back in. They were returning from searching the southern side of Kyle, an area of the park made up of wetlands and large stands of poplars and other trees that separated Kyle Park from the farmland to the south. The volunteers had covered the low areas and fields now stripped of their crops, the old corn lying in twisted, irregular patterns on the ground. It could be easy for a kid, or kids, to get lost in the fields where the dead corn hadn't been plowed under.

She could see that several of the volunteers had gotten muddy and dusty, and now they walked past her, back to their cars. A few stopped to say something comforting to her, or to take her hand for a moment, but most of them simply walked past her without making any kind of eye contact.

They probably felt bad.

Part of her was glad they hadn't found the missing girls. These searches were strange. She wanted them to find something, evidence of what had happened, so at least they would know something. But, on another level, she tried not to think about what they might find. Her mind resisted even going there.

Little Charlie had been born too early, her skin so pink and wrinkled. The nurse had brusquely shown her to an exhausted Glenda and then raced the little girl away to another part of the maternity ward. Glenda remembered watching as the preemie doctor and nurses worked to keep her alive. And finally, weeks after the little girl's birthday, the doctors decided to take Charlie off the tiny ventilator and let her try to breathe on her own.

And that moment, that wonderful moment, when the doctor had looked up and smiled behind his mask and Glenda had relaxed for the first time in months.

The young cop approached, his face grim. She remembered his name was Peters, Deputy Peters—all the cop's names and faces were starting to blur together in her mind. Glenda knew every cop in town was working the case, nights and weekends, and she was grateful for the help. Seeing the grim look on his face, her insides erupted with a sudden, intense fire that made her feel like she was about to explode.

He's got bad news, she thought suddenly. And only a few of the volunteers had looked at her.

"Oh, God, did you find something?" she said, pleading, her hand clenched in a fist at her chest. "Please tell me you—"

The deputy shook his head.

"Nothing, Mrs. Martin," Deputy Peters said, shaking his head. He'd taken his hat off and was scrunching it up in his hands. "We didn't find anything."

She felt herself relax. Like in the hospital, in that magical, heart-stopping instant after the preemie doctor had smiled. After she'd known Charlie would pull through.

"We're setting up another search of City Park in a little while," the deputy said, not looking at her. He was looking away at the parking lot, nodding at the group of volunteers who waited by their cars. "The volunteers are heading over now. And another group is going to cover the soccer fields again," he said, gesturing to the massive open stretch of grass to the north that ran nearly all the way to Route 571. "Hopefully, we'll find something."

She looked up at him, and he shook his head and mumbled quietly under his breath.

"Something good, I mean," he said, grimacing. He walked away and nearly tripped over the curb before climbing into a Cooper's Mill squad car and driving away.

Glenda nodded to herself and pulled the sweater tighter around her. The weather was turning colder, and rain was expected tonight. That was one reason the volunteers were searching all day, before the bad weather hit tonight.

Her little girl wasn't here at Kyle—that much was obvious. At least they hadn't found her somewhere, hurt. Or worse.

Her cell phone rang, making her jump.

That would be Nick, checking in. She didn't even need to look at the number on her phone. Glenda wished her husband had stayed with her for today's searches, but he was giving yet another police statement and helping the FBI and CMPD go over the family finances again. Glenda just wished there was someone here to take her by the shoulder and tell her that things were going to be all right. She didn't care if it was a lie.

It was the not knowing that was the worst part.

Nick had told her to stay busy, to get out there and search. She wished he would stop trying to distract her. She didn't need to be distracted; she needed to feel like she wasn't in this all alone.

She held the phone up to her ear.

"Nick?"

There was a weird clicking on the line. For a moment, Glenda thought the call had dropped.

"Mrs. Martin? Mrs. Glenda Martin?"

Her eyes went wide. Her stomach did a sudden, nauseating loop. She pulled away from the phone and saw that the number was blocked before putting it back to her ear.

It was a voice she did not recognize.

"Yes?"

Another long pause.

"We have your daughter," the voice on the other end of the line said— it was odd, metallic. Glenda felt her world shrink down to just her and the phone and the cold bench she was sitting on. Nothing else mattered. Her hands went cold. She glanced up in the direction of the police car, but it was long gone.

Glenda was alone.

"Charlie and the other girl are safe, for now," the voice continued. "They are being taken care of. We will call this number tomorrow at noon with instructions. Comply with our demands, or the girls will die."

The line went dead.

3

The water was rising. Frank was floating on top of it, with nowhere to go.

The white ceiling tiles were only inches above the top of the brackish, rising water. Frank could tell from the rising water that he didn't have much time. All around him, in the water and on the surface, floated the detritus of the flooded hospital—IV bags, surgical gowns, medicine bottles, and trash. He splashed around in the water, trying to stay on the surface, but the gunshot wound in his shoulder made it hard to swim. He felt with his feet, deep under the water, trying to find a surface to push on, or submerged furniture or something, but all he could feel was empty, sloshing water. Frank grabbed at the ceiling with his left arm, catching a loose hold on a piece of the ceiling. He tried to pull himself up, but something sharp and metallic—an exposed shard of the metal grid that held up the ruined ceiling—ripped at the skin. He felt it tear but tried to hold on. But his hand was wet and kept slipping, and he felt weak. He was losing a lot of blood.

He wasn't going to make it out.

And there was no backup. The National Guard had moved on, and he'd stayed to clear St. Barts, but that was before the gang bangers. And the floating patients, with their dead eyes. More dark water splashed in his mouth. It tasted like swamp water. Brackish, gritty, full of dirt. Like the bayous of his youth. Frank struggled to keep his head above the black water and suddenly realized, deep in the heart of him, that he was trapped in this abandoned hospital, where the patients had been left in their beds to die, surrounded by rising black water. And, like them, Frank was trapped. He was going to die.

He sat up.

Frank was in his hotel room, not back at St. Bartholomew's.

He looked around—he'd fallen asleep on the bed watching TV. Frank relaxed a little and shook his head, setting down the empty glass in his hand and checking his cell phone. No calls or texts from Laura. No calls from anyone else, for that matter.

Frank glanced back up at the TV. He hadn't been paying attention to the show—it was something to do with animals—and had dozed off.

He tried to stand, but his legs were shaky. It was Sunday evening, and he was hungry and needed to go back out again but didn't feel like it.

He'd needed a little hair of the dog, after last night and Ricky's, so Frank had gone out early Sunday morning and found a local grocery and stocked up. He'd driven past the only wine and spirits store listed in the phone book in Cooper's Mill, but it was closed on Sundays.

Frank wondered if all the package stores in Ohio were closed on Sundays, another throwback to the old "Blue Law" days. It was the same in Alabama—the government limited alcohol sales on Sundays. Sometimes, Frank wondered if laws like that stayed on the books out of some kind of forward momentum—the law had always been there, and no one had gotten around to changing it.

He'd ventured inside the grocery store and found an extensive beer and wine area, along with a few harder liquors. The whiskey and bourbon had been out of his price range—even the cheaper stuff—so he'd switched over to vodka. After two excruciating minutes dealing with an overly-happy clerk who wanted to ask him all kinds of questions about his Louisiana driver's license, Frank had carried two bottles of vodka out to his car.

Now, one bottle was half gone now, the other waiting its turn. The buzzing in his head was solid and pleasant and familiar. The whole of Sunday had been a blur.

The curtains stood wide open. It was getting dark outside. He suddenly wondered if Laura would call and cancel the Tuesday lunch meeting. Frankly, he was surprised she hadn't already begged off their family reunion. She probably knew it was doomed to failure anyway. Frank wasn't good for anyone anymore. He only had one hobby left, and, although he was very good at it, he couldn't make it pay. Being a drunkard never helped anyone, and it certainly hadn't helped Laura, or Trudy, for that matter. Once she got one look at Frank, she probably wouldn't want him around little Jackson.

He stood, shaky, and walked to the window, leaning on the bed and then the TV for support. His hands were still shaking. It had been quite a bender, but with a day to kill and nowhere to be, it didn't matter. He had a hotel room and free cable and plenty of cheap booze.

Frank stumbled to the window and leaned against it. His forehead felt good on the cold glass.

4

Charlie had no idea where she was.

The house was cold and drafty and smelled old. She could hear the rain starting up again outside, and there was wind, and tree branches were scraping on the window—at least, she hoped they were tree branches. They sounded like fingernails.

Across the hall, it sounded like Maya was sleeping. Charlie hadn't heard any crying for a while.

It was a dark, old bedroom, with big, dusty furniture and a tall mirror hung on the wall above a long dresser. Every surface was covered with dust. A window, framed with dark curtains, took up half of one wall, and she could see shapes moving against the glass. Ugly wallpaper decorated all four walls, that weird, thick kind of wallpaper that her father had shown her in some of the old buildings he sometimes bought and fixed up. They always removed that kind of wallpaper, and it came off in big yellow sheets.

The room smelled old and musty, like a wet basement. She knew that meant it had been shut up too long.

Charlie shook her head. She had been so stupid.

Daddy had always warned her about getting into cars. She and Maya knew better. They knew all about "stranger danger" and all of that stuff. But he hadn't been a stranger. He'd simply offered her and Maya a ride around the block in the car, and they had only hesitated for a moment.

She'd never been in a police car before. They'd gone up the alley and turned, walking to his car. Then he'd asked them to sit in the back, because it would be fun, and suggested they take a little drive before he took them to school. They drove away from her school, and she started to say something, but thought better of it. It might be cool to have a policeman drive her to school – they worked for her Dad.

He'd driven out of town, heading north and then east, saying they were taking a quick drive past the river. Charlie remembered driving past the new pool and then over the river, passing the canoe livery where she and her Dad had gone for a canoe ride last year. The police officer had driven them out just past the river and stopped, pulling the car over onto the shoulder and down a slope, then along a dirt area and stopping by some trees.

The doors had unlocked, and he asked them to get out. He said there was something he wanted to show them, down by the river.

She should have figured it out then.

She and Maya had looked at each other, but when Maya shrugged, saying it would be fine. Charlie gave up the tiny argument in her mind and agreed. They climbed out, leaving their backpacks. He took longer—he was doing something in the front seat, something funny that she couldn't see, before climbing out and following them.

They were near the river, near the City Pool and close to where the canoes were put in the water. Charlie could see the river through the trees, down the thin path that snaked alongside the road. Tall grass edged the path to her right, and she ran ahead, wanting to see the water. She followed the slope down to the river. As she'd approached it, she'd heard a rustling behind her and turned and the policeman was holding Maya strangely. Charlie thought for a second that maybe Maya had stumbled, and the policeman had caught her in one arm. But he was holding something funny over her mouth, a small white square of fabric that looked like a napkin or a towel.

Something was wrong.

In a moment, Maya seemed to fall asleep. Her eyes fluttered closed, and the man dropped her roughly into the grass, then turned and looked at Charlie. He'd grabbed at her, and she'd pulled away, screaming, scrambling into the tall, wet grass. But his hands were too strong, and he'd grabbed her legs. Something white and soft was stuffed over her nose and mouth. It smelled horrible—like a doctor's office, she thought for a moment, and then the world had shimmered around her, and her knees felt weak, and then everything turned black.

She'd woken in this big, creepy room, her clothes still damp from falling into the tall grass. It had only taken her a moment to realize she was tied to the wooden headboard of the big bed. She wasn't handcuffed, like the criminals in old movies. Instead, her left wrist was hooked to the headboard with two thin black plastic ties, like the kind she'd seen used to tie together electrical cords. Zip ties, she thought they were called. One around her left wrist, and that tie went through another zip tie that was looped around one of the thick wooden posts of the headboard. She could stretch out and lay down, but it wasn't comfortable, or she could roll off the bed and stand.

Charlie wondered about Maya. She was younger than Charlie and always a little more scared. Maya's mother didn't speak much English and worked for Charlie's mom. The two girls got along great. Sometimes, Charlie pretended that Maya was her sister. They went to the same school and played together. Sometimes they would play dress-up and paint each other's nails, when they were allowed.

Charlie could hear Maya start crying in the other room, and the crying quickly grew louder and louder, until it was half crying and half angry shouting. Charlie had never heard Maya cry like that. They'd lived together in the same house for almost two years. One time, Maya had fallen down in the park near their home and had gotten hurt pretty bad. Even that time, Maya hadn't cried like this. And there was nothing Charlie could do except listen to her cry.

It worried Charlie that a policeman had taken her and Maya. Charlie had always thought the police in town worked for her father—he'd said that once. He was one of the seven people on the City Council. But if the policeman had taken her, would the other policemen in town be looking for her and Maya? Or were all the police friends?

Charlie wasn't sure, but she hoped someone was looking for them. It made her feel better, but only slightly. Charlie had spent the first six hours straight trying to wiggle free, but the zip ties were too tight. After that, she'd joined Maya and cried until she fell asleep, tired and alone in a bed far too big for her.

5

Frank Harper stood by the window of his hotel room again, looking out at the highway. It was Monday morning, and his head hurt. A lot.

Beer always did that to him—he was good with whiskey and bourbon, even the cheap stuff, but the headaches that came with beer stuck with him, sometimes for days. When the vodka had run out, he'd switched to cheap beer, knowing he would pay the price. Yesterday had been a fog—he'd spent most of it looking out this window, staring at the highway and thinking about Tuesday and Laura. And St. Barts.

Really, what was the point of it all? Things probably weren't going to improve with Laura. She'd take one look at him and kick him out. Or they would start to talk, and he'd say something stupid, like something about her mother, or about how they had left, and she would politely ask him to leave.

But he didn't want to go back to that cubicle in Birmingham. It didn't matter if Frank was sitting there or not—exactly the same amount of progress would be made on the cold cases. Just getting out of there felt better. Maybe he should skip the meeting with Laura. It was destined to fail, anyway. Maybe he should just climb into his crappy car and leave. Start driving in some random direction and never look back.

The Vacation Inn was just a few yards from Interstate 75, a wide swath of concrete full of speeding trucks and cars. He could take it anywhere, maybe find someplace where he could be useful again. The road, if one were interested in following it, stretched north all the way to Canada and south to Miami.

Ben Stone had been from Miami.

The guy was a crack shot, always topping Frank at the sandy Florida shooting range where they practiced. They would go almost every week, and Ben would always kick Frank's butt, never letting him forget it. They'd gotten along okay, and their competition at the range had been a nice diversion from the counterfeiting case, even if sometimes Ben would keep the used paper target silhouette of his shots and leave it in their car just to piss Frank off.

But Ben was also a hot head and prone to occasional bouts of stupidity. One day, Ben decided to return to investigate a lead on the case on his own—without Frank or department approval—and got himself killed in a back alley in Coral Gables. His gun was still in its holster.

Fat lot of good his range rating ended up doing.

Frank looked out at the highway and wondered if the weather would be as miserable today as it had been yesterday—cold and wet.

He'd tried to sleep in, but Frank had never been really good at that—too many years of rising early. First the military, then the NOPD. Too many early mornings, early meetings, early drills.

But early mornings were good for some things. He liked the quiet stillness, before everyone else was up. He'd heard an old-timer once sum it up nicely. The elderly black man only had two or three teeth, but smiled all the time, nonetheless. Worked at one of the restaurants in the French Quarter, an area of town Frank had frequented as much as possible. The old man had loved the early mornings because he could "enjoy the day before some idiot screwed it up."

Frank turned and looked around the hotel room—it was looking pretty shabby. He thought about tidying up but then remembered no one was coming to visit him, and he really didn't give a shit.

His brain felt sluggish, out-of-sorts, with nothing to work on. Frank had also spent much of yesterday thinking about Saturday night and his inability, or more accurately his unwillingness, to step in and help with those drunk guys. Frank felt impotent, a caged animal straining to get out, but knowing that he should do the right thing and just stay in his cage. The cold cases weren't as interesting as his old work, and conversations with his old cop friends were few and far between. And the drinking wasn't helping as much as it used to.

It was all Trudy's fault. She should have stuck with him, after St. Barts, instead of taking Laura and leaving. He'd needed help, and she'd bolted. Of course, it was hard to blame her. He'd been a class "A" prick to her.

Frank shook his head and decided to run through an abbreviated workout to loosen up the kinks. Maybe it would work some of the alcohol out of his system.

He turned and sat on the edge of the hotel bed, turning on the TV and flipping through the channels. There was nothing on but the "Today" show, so Frank tossed the remote on the bed and got down on the floor in front of the TV to do crunches. The room swam when he moved too fast, so he slowed, rocking up and down, counting methodically. Frank concentrated on the crunches, trying to push everything else out of his mind. He willed the alcohol to burn through his system and evaporate out through his pores.

He hated the "Today" show. He hated all the morning shows, full of dumb news segments and canned interviews and staged interactions. He always felt sorry for the guests, who seemed rushed through their seg-ments. Why invite people onto your show, fly them all the way to New York, clean them up, and put them on TV, and then just talk over them and interrupt them for the whole segment? Why invite them on and then hurriedly kick them out the door? Some smart producer should come along and tell the folks on these morning shows to just slow down and breathe.

The "Today" show covered a little bit of news, leading into an inter-view with some teeny-bopper celebrity—the young woman on the TV was a movie star and had had multiple run-ins with the law. She had once had a promising career, but now in her twenties, she was caught up in a downward spiral of bad career moves, embarrassing paparazzi photos, and too many bad choices.

To Frank, doing crunches on the floor, it sounded like she needed rehab. Or maybe just someone in her life that wasn't always enabling her every stupid move. These people were usually surrounded by "yes" men, all part of an enabling entourage working hard to keep the gravy train on track.

Sometimes, all you needed to pull your shit together was someone in your life who was willing to say "no."

The show broke for commercials, then cut over to the local Day-ton news. Dayton was interesting. It wasn't the kind of place he would choose to live, but it wasn't as "Midwestern" as he'd been led to believe. The people were nice, so far, and they had Starbucks and Target, just like anywhere else.

The anchor came on, a woman with large hair and a chipper, coffee-fueled attitude that made Frank's beer headache kick back in.

"Welcome back," the woman said on the TV, grinning. "Coming up is an update on our top story, the two missing girls in Cooper's Mill, along with Scott Bumpers for the forecast. But first, an update on the news. A fire broke out in the 400 block of Tipper Avenue in Dayton last night, and investigators on the scene are suspecting arson. Let's go to Dale Scott for the report..."

The TV station cut to an impossibly fat man standing in front of a smoldering home in what looked like a rundown part of Dayton. The home had been reduced to rubble, and, as the fat guy fidgeted, he explained what had happened. The guy was so large, it looked like he was trapped in one of those puffy sumo wrestling suits. A few seconds into the story, the station cut away from the man to taped footage, filmed earlier, of the house still burning.

Frank stood up and started doing arm curls. He didn't have any weights, so he used the ice bucket. All the ice was melted, and all that was left were a few renegade cubes floating in cold water. He worked to keep the bucket steady, lifting smoothly, not wanting to spill.

"As you can see, the home was fully involved when the first firefighters arrived," the reporter continued over the footage, sounding winded. "Little could be done to save the home."

Thanks, Captain Obvious, Frank thought.

Frank had never investigated arsons or fires, but he'd known people who did. A nice black guy named Williams in Birmingham who specialized in arsons. The guy was like a savant. He knew all the subtle signs of accelerants and scorch patterns. That man could walk into a fire that had burned out a month before and say immediately whether or not it had been lit. It was amazing.

Williams sat near Frank in the Birmingham office and would, on occasion, bring over pictures of horribly burnt victims and vacant buildings.

Frank would always say the same thing:

"Holy shit, Williams."

Why did people enjoy sharing their shock? It happened a lot in the offices where he'd worked—NOPD, the field office in Florida, and now the cubicle farm in Birmingham. Investigators would run across a particularly gruesome photograph in whatever case they were working on and walk it all around the room, sharing them like baby pictures. Frank had done it too, a few times. Somehow, sharing the stories and the indignity helped make it seem less real, more tolerable.

But there were cases that Frank could never joke about. Like the little boy in Atlanta and the cardboard box. That one had gotten to Frank, more than the others. He'd never felt comfortable talking about it. Certainly never would have walked any pictures around. He hated the images he had in his head from that day, images that would never go away. And sharing them with others—well, he wouldn't wish those pictures, if they existed, on anyone.

Frank lowered the ice bucket and glanced at the clock. Time to go. He went into the small bathroom, brushed his teeth, and combed some water through his hair. His wife had always liked his hair—ex-wife, that is. After another glance in the mirror, he decided to spend a few minutes and shaved the beard and goatee from his face. Being clean shaven always made him feel more presentable. Normally, he didn't care, but tomorrow was different.

He left the hotel room and pulled the door shut behind him, then headed down the long, carpeted hall and took the stairs down to the lobby. He skipped the elevator; after St. Barts, Frank wasn't a fan of enclosed spaces.

In the lobby, he passed the front desk and nodded at the young kid working behind it. Frank couldn't recall his name, but he remembered clearly that the boy—he looked about 14—had sounded like a mouse when he talked, his voice high and squeaky. Good luck hitting puberty, kid.

Outside, the rain had let up. That was one thing he didn't miss from growing up—it had rained a lot in Baton Rouge. It was always humid, all year round, in the BR. Wet and steamy, they used to say. Birmingham was better, but it was even cooler here in Dayton, and Frank wasn't used to it. The sky was peeking out from behind the October clouds that covered the sky from horizon to horizon.

Frank started across the parking lot to the Tip Top Diner, where he'd already eaten a couple times. He glanced at the beat-up Taurus to make sure it hadn't been stolen. Unfortunately, it was still sitting there, hulking in the spot, exactly where he'd left it.

6

"Georgie!"

She was calling again, from inside.

George stood and wiped his muddy hands on his pants. He was surrounded by tall, bushy plants planted in long rows that stretched off toward a distant fence line and trees beyond.

He liked working in the mud, working with the plants. It made him feel like he was doing something real with his life, instead of wasting time in a jail cell. He'd had enough of that. Now, he truly appreciated the outdoors. The morning was warming up, coming up over the trees that lined the river, which ran along the eastern side of the property, beyond the tall fence. The plants liked it sunny and dry, and this crop was almost ready to take in. But it had rained yesterday and again this morning, and you had to watch it—too much water was bad. So he was out here checking on them.

They were growing like weeds.

He smiled to himself. He made that joke a lot and always thought it was funny. The marijuana plants were almost as tall as George, marching away in long rows toward the fence.

Chastity never laughed at his jokes. She was much more likely to roll her eyes and say something dirty under her breath. She didn't think he was funny. When she did laugh at his jokes, George got worried—he got the feeling she wasn't really laughing with him. More like at him.

At least she laughed. George had never gotten up the nerve to tell any of his excellent jokes to the boss.

George picked up his tools and started for the house—she'd be calling again. Once she started, she never let up. And it always seemed like she needed something.

He looked up at the house. The back yard, more like a field, was fenced on all sides with high planks of pine. Beyond the fence stood the big old farmhouse, two stories and a large side porch that wrapped partway around the front. Old wooden shutters hung from each window of both floors, mixed with the ivy that grew up the west side and had nearly taken over the south side, too. There was even an attic huge enough to play basketball in.

George liked the house. It wasn't his, but the boss let him stay here, as long as he kept things up and took care of the crop. Even though they were way out in the country, and no one ever came snooping around, the boss didn't like things to get too run down.

It was the closest thing George had to a home in a long time.

George walked to the tall gate and exited the field, turning and dead bolting the gate behind him. With the lock and the twelve-foot fence, no one could see what they were growing, not without a helicopter.

He turned and crossed the small yard. There was a rusty old play set with swings and a back concrete patio with ratty furniture and a sliding patio door. He was headed for the house but then remembered what he was carrying and veered off, walking to the back door of the large red barn that stood across the gravel driveway from the house. He undid another deadbolt and went inside.

The old wooden barn was huge on the inside, lined with old wooden rafters that framed a dusty central area. For some reason, the inside of the barn reminded George of the inside of a church—high ceiling, quiet, dusty. But this was unlike any church he'd been to—from the rafters hung hundreds of marijuana plants, drying in tight bunches and wrapped with brown twine. The plants cured in the dry heat of the barn. It had been a good summer, hot and dry, and the yield had been high. Between what was in the barn drying and what was still in the field, it had been an excellent summer and fall. The boss was very happy.

Pot came in two varieties. The narrow leaf, like what George was growing, was supposedly more potent than the wide-leaf variety, typically grown in humid and artificial environments. The broader leaves produced less resin per ounce of finished product, and the more resin, the better. At least, that's what the boss had told him once.

Of course, growing outdoors had its own share of problems—weather, weeds, insects, and prying eyes. That was why this farmhouse was perfect—surrounded on three sides by forest, with a backyard and the field beyond. The fence was only three years old and still looked new. The boss had it built after picking up the property in a Sheriff's real estate sale.

"PUDDIN'!"

Jeez, he hated it when she called him that.

It had all started out as a joke. "Georgie, Porgy, Puddin', Pie," when they'd first hooked up, but now Chastity called him that all the time. She almost never called him George anymore.

A dozen tables and other work surfaces ringed the perimeter of the barn. George tore himself away from looking at the drying marijuana and set down the tools, then picked up a large bundle of green plants he'd brought in earlier. The tables and benches around him were set up with production equipment: twine and hooks to gather up pot for drying and hang up the bundles, bundlers and a boxing machine for making bricks, and boxes of baggies and scales and anything else he might need to prepare the merchandise for sale. Using the twine, he tied the ends of the plants together and hung the bundle from one of the few open areas in the barn.

In the middle of the barn, also used as a garage, sat two vehicles: an old Mustang and a beat-up old white Corolla, parked under a grouping of work lights, surrounded by the tables and work surfaces. He looked at the new car taking up a good portion of the open area of the barn. It had appeared overnight, as if by magic, and would be gone soon. George would be driving it, as soon as they heard about the ransom. He wished he could keep it. He'd asked, but the boss said no.

George had always been into cars. He'd started out as a mechanic and sometimes wondered what would have happened, if he'd stayed at the dealership, busting his nut working on other people's cars. After he'd been released from prison, he'd gotten on with the boss and George had been able to fix up some of the old farm equipment around this place. But he missed working with cars, trying to figure out what made them tick, trying to fix them.

He ran his hands along the clean lines of the stolen Mustang. He assumed it was stolen. The boss hardly ever let him in on anything. All George knew was the plan required a fast car that couldn't be traced back to any of them, and so a car appeared.

The other car in the garage, the beat-up, old, white Corolla, George had found wasting away in a back corner of the garage, when he'd moved in. It hadn't worked at the beginning, but he'd fiddled with it for a few months and had gotten it working. Now, he used it when he needed to run into town. It was too bad they couldn't use the Corolla tomorrow and abandon it. He hated that useless car. It rattled like a deathtrap on the highway. He hadn't been able to fix the body panels, which, had swollen with rust and, in places, pulled away from the chassis.

The back door swung open, bathing the inside of the garage with sudden sunlight, and Chastity walked inside.

"Where have you BEEN, Puddin'?" Chastity asked, exasperated. She got exasperated a lot. "Leave that car alone and get inside. You know you can't keep it."

Chastity looked good.

He'd appreciated her from the moment they'd met, and thanked his lucky stars for every day that she put up with him. Even if she was mean to him. She was thin and blonde and gorgeous. And she knew it, too. One time, she'd told him that she hardly noticed anymore when men were admiring her. "I'm like a pretty painting," she'd said at the time. "They just like to look."

Chastity was wearing a tiny pair of blue denim shorts he liked and a tight, yellow shirt that showed off every curve of her figure. It made George happy to be a man, anyway. Just looking at her was worth putting up with—

"They won't shut up," she said, stopping in front of him and putting her hands on her hips. "The crying and the whining. Puddin', I'm getting sick of it!"

He loved those hips but pulled his eyes away and looked at her eyes, nodding.

"It's okay, Chas. I'm coming," George said, nodding. "I just had to finish up."

He left the garage, locking it behind him and walked to the house. She shadowed him, starting in again with the complaining. They were too far out in the country, there wasn't anything to eat, they were out of beer. You'd think with as much money as they were going to see from this job, she'd stow the whining.

"It's the little Mexican one, she's the worst," Chastity said, walking behind him. He wasn't looking at her, but he could tell she was shaking her head. "I can hear her up there, whining and talking away in her Spanish."

"Maybe, if you went up there—"

"I'm not going up there," she screeched. It reminded him of the owl he'd once found in the barn. It had taken him weeks to get rid of the thing.

They got to the patio doors at the same time, but Chastity stopped and just looked at the closed doors, her arms crossed. He knew she was waiting for him to pull the door open for her. Sometimes George wondered how she got along when he wasn't around.

He pulled the door aside and followed her into the dining room, which took up the back corner of the house. Sunlight slanted into the windows that lined the back wall of the kitchen and dining room, windows that looked out into the backyard.

To his right was the kitchen; every flat surface was covered with dishes or empty pizza boxes or other takeout trash. She didn't like to cook, and he couldn't make much except Mac and cheese.

She smiled and walked over to him with that bounce in her step that drew men's eyes wherever she went. "What about the plan?" she asked. The boss had been by earlier to talk to George.

"He gave me a cell phone," George said, patting his pocket proudly. "And he wrote down when I'm supposed to call and what I'm supposed to say. Then I'm to 'take the phone and break it and throw it in the river,'" he said slowly, repeating what he'd been told. He wanted to make sure he got the words right.

Chastity nodded.

"Good," she said. "We need to get this show going."

George looked up at the ceiling. He could hear someone crying upstairs.

"I'd better go up and check on them," he said.

Chastity nodded and went back out, carrying her cigarettes and lighter. George walked through the kitchen and then down the hall, passing other rooms—a large formal dining room, bathroom, the living room/parlor—and into the big foyer by the front door. He turned and started up the staircase.

The girls were in different rooms. There was no real need to keep them quiet, out here so far from town. But the boss had said not to put them together, so George had got them set up in two of the four upstairs bedrooms, on opposite sides of the hallway. As he climbed the stairs, he could hear them both crying.

George didn't like it, but he wasn't in charge. The boss was, and George did what he was told. There was a big payday coming, maybe even enough money for him and Chastity to finally head west. George wanted to see the ocean, the mountains, and the Golden Gate Bridge. Mostly, he just wanted to get into a car—even that old Corolla—and start driving. All he wanted was for him and Chastity to see the ocean, walk in the surf, get away from Ohio.

The boss had him and Chastity under his thumb, but this job was supposed to put things even. Once the pay came in, the boss had said that George and Chastity were free to leave. The boss was working with someone else, a guy George had never met, and this other guy was calling the shots on the schedule and the ransom. Between the mystery guy and George's boss, they had a whole plan all worked out.

George and Chastity were watching the girls. That was their job, their part of the plan. But Chastity wouldn't have anything to do with the girls, except complain about them. Sometimes she made the meals, but she wouldn't deliver them or talk to the girls. She sometimes helped let the girls out of their restraints to use the bathroom, but only at night and only after turning out all the lights. George thought Chastity didn't want the girls to be able to identify her.

So it fell to George to care for the girls, keeping them fed and relatively happy until the situation was over. Then Chastity and him, they'd be off. When this was all over, they'd be together in a car, driving the open roads on their way to San Francisco. They'd be together, with no one bossing them around. Chastity could ride in the car with the window down and her bare feet sticking out, like she liked to do. And when they got to the ocean, spread out flat in front of them, he and Chastity would park the car and take a blanket out of the trunk and sit on the wide, sandy beach and count their money. Count the stacks and stacks of cash from this job. She would love the ocean. Chastity had never seen it. Neither had George, but it didn't matter. They just needed to get away, a long way from here, where they could be together and happy.

Or, at least as happy as she could get. It seemed like Chastity was always cross about one thing or another.

The ransom money would come in soon. But he worried about the little girls. At one point, George had asked about what would happen to the girls after the ransom money came in, and the boss had said he'd "take care of it." He didn't even want to think about what his boss meant.

Even George was smart enough to know that didn't sound encouraging.

7

Heading inside the Tip Top Diner, Frank was struck again by how the place was "decorated." It literally looked like he'd stepped forty years back in time. The large restaurant was filled with wooden booths and square wooden tables, and the walls, and every other flat surface, were covered with old, faded wallpaper, broken up only by paneled, dark wood.

To go along with the season, the walls and booths and the crane game next to the entrance were decorated with paper pumpkins, crepe paper spiders, and dozens of other Halloween decorations. Next to the door stood a mannequin decorated to look like a mummy. Behind the counter, near the cash register, was perched a sad, old-looking stuffed witch, her pointy hat sagging. And, while the servers and greeters were costumed as well, sadly, all the spider webs in the corners were 100% genuine.

Nevertheless, the food was excellent and the wait staff friendly. They had Frank snugged away in his favorite booth with a mug of fresh coffee in no time. The coffee here wasn't as good as the numerous cups he'd enjoyed at the Café Du Monde in the French Quarter—so far, he'd never found a better cup anywhere—but the coffee should, at least, chase away his hangover.

Everywhere he went, it seemed he was attracted to these types of restaurants—quiet, family owned, the decor needing a massive update. Never a chain place, ever. And the crazy thing was there were places like the Tip Top Diner all over the nation, little hole-in-the-wall greasy spoons where you could always get a great meal and a hot cup of good coffee. And it didn't hurt that this particular restaurant was thirty feet from the front door of his hotel.

In Birmingham, he had a half-dozen dives and family restaurants like this one that he frequented, much to the chagrin of his partners. They always wanted to eat somewhere a little more "upscale." But places like this one were the backbone of the restaurant industry, and, to Frank, they just felt more "real." You knew that when you ordered something off the menu it wasn't just pulled out of a freezer somewhere and nuked. It was one of the reasons he never went out for Mexican food. He loved the cuisine, but it seemed like every Mexican restaurant's food tasted exactly the same, like it all came on the same delivery truck. Maybe it did.

The other thing he enjoyed about dives was that they left you alone. His wife had never understood his need for solitude and eventually had been happy to grant him a permanent supply, unfettered by her presence. He had always preferred going somewhere quiet to eat, usually bringing along a case file or something else to read.

He sat in booth #3, which had already become his favorite. Over the last few days, he'd been in here so often that the waitresses had learned his name and which booth he liked. And he had settled into a standard breakfast order after sampling about every breakfast plate on the menu.

Frank liked where he was sitting. The booth had nice view of the entire place and the door, and his back was to the wall. Situational awareness—it had been drummed into him at the Academy and was another old habit he couldn't seem to shake— meant choosing the seat with the best view of the room.

Frank just hoped he could go the whole meal without anyone talking to him. Frank had been told before that he was an introvert, but he didn't buy it. He just hated people, sometimes, and needed to be left alone to recharge his batteries. His partners had all tried, unsuccessfully, to get him to go out after his shift for drinks, but he'd never been into social-izing.

His wife had hated that, too.

Long before she'd left him, she'd bitch about them never going out. But then Laura had come along, and Trudy had found a new hobby that didn't involve complaining to him about her life. He should have seen what was coming next. Now, looking back on it, he wondered why it had been a surprise at all.

But so far, the best part of retirement was the quiet meals by himself: no one to entertain, or interrogate, or need to smile and nod while they blathered on and on, talking about whatever stupid thing had happened to them.

Frank had the Dayton paper spread out on the table in front of him— he'd grabbed a free copy of the *Dayton Daily News* from the hotel front desk—and was enjoying his OJ and coffee and a ham and cheese omelet. His doctor back in Alabama had said to back off the carbs, so he'd switched out the buttery hash browns for some fresh tomato slices.

But one thing he wouldn't give up was his eggs.

Frank remembered his one and only trip to Paris. In the mornings, waking in one of those truly tiny European hotel rooms he'd been warned about, he'd craved any kind of protein for breakfast. But this being Paris and all, all he could find were dainty little croissants and chocolate-covered pastries. For all the decadence of the food in Paris, he'd have traded all of it for a nice omelet. There was no meat at any of the breakfasts, just pastries and breads, everything drizzled in chocolate.

Trudy would've hated him for that. Of course, she never went on travel with him, on any of the occasions his work had taken him out of New Orleans. Maybe if he'd taken her with him, even once, things would have worked out better. But on the rare occasions they had taken trips together, it seemed the vacations were always more exhausting than they should have been.

"More coffee?"

He looked up. It was Gina, one of the waitresses, smiling at him. She had smoky eyes and wore too much makeup for his taste but seemed like a good sort. One of her eyes sported an ugly bruise.

"Yup. Thanks."

She smiled and leaned over the table, topping off his cup of coffee and setting a few creamers down, all in one practiced motion. He reached for the coffee, and she rested a hand lightly on his elbow.

"I just wanted to thank you, Mr. Harper," she said quietly.

Frank glanced up at her again and nodded.

"No problem. Did you change the locks?"

She nodded.

"Yeah, and I put all his stuff out. Took pictures, too. Everything I put out by the driveway, like you said."

Frank nodded. "That's good—he can't say you have anything of his?"

"No, no, everything left is mine," she said. "It's all from before we got married." She was rubbing her arm as she spoke, probably the site of an old bruise inflicted by her "loving" husband. Frank wondered if she was even aware of rubbing her arm like that.

"Good," he said. "What kind of pictures?"

"Pictures of the house and all my stuff," she said. "Like you said." She leaned in a little closer. "I also took those other pictures you talked about, the ones of me—my face, arms, legs. My sister took those, actually."

"Good, that's good," he said, his voice low. "Cops?"

She nodded.

"I filed the report, like you said. And gave them the envelope with all the photos of our property and me, so there was proof, if he ever hits me again," she said, glancing around. "Not sure how that's going to work, though. His buddies might protect him. But my sister's staying over, and things are already a lot better."

Frank nodded slowly and looked her in the eyes.

"Keep an eye open," Frank said, frowning. "Things will get worse for a while—a lot worse—before they get better."

She was taken aback.

"Are you sure?" she asked, glancing around comically, as if her ex-husband were hiding behind the crane game machine that stood near the front door.

Frank nodded and resisted saying anything else. He looked at her and nodded again, then turned back to his breakfast. After a long moment, she walked away, decidedly less chipper than she had been before.

Why did he do that? Frank knew he should say something to her, something more comforting, but he couldn't force himself to bullshit her.

He'd had enough bullshit in his life. Too many lies, too much death. He liked to keep things simple now, truthful. Maybe he'd been too truthful too often. Maybe that's how he'd ended up sitting in this random diner alone, eating breakfast in a small town he'd never heard of.

Sugarcoating things never worked. Trudy never wanted to hear about his work or the troubling things he saw. She only wanted to hear the good stories, and there weren't many of those. Frank must've started repeating himself somewhere along the line, because she'd lost interest. First in his career, then in him, and then their marriage.

Gina, the waitress, had asked for advice on his first visit, and he'd given it to her. Why had she asked? Maybe he still looked like a cop. That barkeep Saturday night had said the same, so maybe Frank still gave off the appearance of someone who cared. Or should care, at least.

But Gina had asked for his advice, and he'd given it, freely. He'd walked her through the steps, and she'd jotted them all down on the back of her ticket book. She asked intelligent questions, questions that told Frank she might have a chance of extricating herself from the situation.

He'd seen it enough to know the chances weren't good, but he thought she might be able to pull it off. Of course, it was up to her to follow through, to make it work. Either way, he didn't really care—he'd seen too many people in bad situations to assume it would work out. It usually didn't.

He resisted the temptation to call Gina back over and say something comforting, like "oh, you don't need to worry," or "he's probably moved on." Instead, Frank slipped out his flask, added the last of his vodka to the OJ, and went back to his paper.

There was trouble all over, he knew. But, reading the paper, the news in the Midwest seemed less dire than it had in other places he had lived. The Dayton paper was full of stories about unemployment and petty crimes and the occasional murder, but there were also a fair share of upbeat items. As he ate, he read about some new construction going on at the nearby Wright-Patterson Air Force Base, the large military installation in Dayton and a major local employer.

There was also ongoing construction on the highway heading down to Cincinnati, and the paper had included complicated maps to avoid the area and the traffic. And there had been several shootings in Dayton. Evidently, there was some kind of ongoing turf war over drugs, and several young men had been killed over the past 48 hours.

But there were several charming stories, too, something he didn't remember from Birmingham or the big Atlanta papers. Chili cook-off's and fundraisers and animal rescue stories might not save the planet, but they broke up the gloom and doom.

Frank heard the jingle of the bell on the front door.

He didn't look up.

He'd been trying to work on relaxing, on avoiding the temptation—or the habit—of monitoring every situation down to the "nth" degree. Instead, Frank forced himself to continue reading.

But his mind wandered, falling back into the old habits. He could hear two people. One spoke to the greeter, who led them to a nearby, empty booth. Frank managed to read the whole rest of the newspaper story before he gave in and glanced over at the pair.

It was an older man and a young woman, looking at menus. The man was in his late forties, dark hair, nice boots. Clean boots, too, not the kind you saw on the farmers around here. These boots were for dressing up, not shit-kicking or mucking out stalls or taking care of horses. He was probably a lawyer or a banker. Maybe a dentist.

The woman was younger, early twenties, brunette, her shoulders and face down and pointed at the table. Her hair hung down in wet tangled clumps. Frank knew immediately that there was something wrong with her.

He looked back at the paper and tried to ignore it. It wasn't something he needed to get involved in—she was probably just a depressed wife, a sad traveler. Maybe they were crossing the country, driving for long stretches. The man looked chipper and well-rested, but the woman looked like she'd just seen a hundred miles of hard road. Husband and wife or, more likely, father and daughter.

"Get ya something?" the other server, Donna, asked the pair.

The young woman glanced up at the waitress. Frank saw the young woman was one of those kids who liked piercings; she must've had a dozen in her lips, nose, and up her earlobe. She was also wearing dark makeup and had a streak of blue in the front of her otherwise black hair. He'd run into a bunch of Goth kids in the bigger cities—Atlanta had a whole area dedicated to spiky collars and tattoo parlors—but he hadn't seen a member of that honored crowd in a while.

"Got any Red Bull?" the girl asked, mumbling.

Frank saw Donna's eyes go wide. "Oh, no, but they have it at Speedway," Donna stammered, indicating out the windows at the gas station across the road.

"Please excuse my daughter," the man said, smiling. He was cool, collected, taking it all in stride. "She's not in the best of moods. We'll both take coffee."

Donna scooted away, and Frank went back to his paper, relaxing. It looked like the dad had it together. The daughter was busy rebelling, and the father looked like the sort of person who knew how to handle it. If Frank had to guess, it looked like the father was retrieving his daughter from some all-night party or rave.

Frank wondered idly if Laura had gone through a phase like that. She was 24 now. It had been years since he'd seen her. He'd missed out on so much of her life—actually, only the last five years, but it seemed like a lifetime. She'd moved to Ohio, gotten married, had a kid, had her husband walk out on her.

Trudy, Frank's ex-wife, had made it clear—Laura had wanted her own life, away from her father. He'd respected that for a while. Trudy had said that Laura had moved to Ohio but wouldn't tell him where. Of course, a few calls to the right people, and he had found out. People he used to work with, work for. They tracked down the name and passed it along to Frank, along with a small town in Ohio that he'd never heard of. And he hadn't used the information for two years, not sure what to do with it.

Now he was here.

Frank continued reading, trying to not eavesdrop on the whispered conversation between the man and his daughter. He was retired now. Other people were in charge, other people were making decisions. Trudy didn't want Frank around Laura, and even though it pained him, he'd left it alone.

It sounded like the father was trying to get the pierced girl to order some food, but she just wanted coffee and to antagonize him.

Frank shook his head and eased the small flask out of his pocket, adding another splash of vodka to his OJ. Trudy would have loved that, drinking this early.

Maybe if Frank hadn't pressed Trudy all the time, they would still be together. Happily married, a family, all that jazz. And he wouldn't be trying to reconnect with a daughter he hadn't seen in years.

Frank finished his meal and the coffee and paid, heading out. He was depressed after seeing the father and daughter; it only reminded him of his lost time away from Laura. Frank walked back across the wet parking lot and climbed into his Taurus. He flipped angrily through the CDs, picking out some Pinetop Perkins and starting up the car. Before this trip was over, he'd probably listen to every CD in the stack a dozen times.

Frank had errands to run. He checked his phone again, but there were no messages, as usual.

Exiting the parking lot, he turned right onto Main Street and crossed over the highway, heading downtown. He passed the gas stations and two strip malls, one on either side of the road. The one to the north held the liquor store, and, seeing that it was open, he swung off the road, parked, and went inside.

It was a typical liquor store, but they had a larger selection of wines and other spirits than he'd expected. Rows of wines marched across the store and ended near a large walk-in beer cooler. To the left of the beer cooler was a smaller area stocked with liquor, stretching all the way to the ceiling. Gin, bourbon, whiskey, and a hundred other shining, beautiful bottles catching the sunlight. It looked like the magnificent stained glass window of some lofty cathedral.

"Hi," a young man smiled from behind the counter, breaking Frank's reverie. "Can I help you find something?"

Frank shook his head and walked around the counter and into the colorful aisle of bottles, heading straight to the bourbon. They had an excellent selection—too bad it was all out of his price range. Dozens of bottles, imported and domestic, all sizes. Brands he'd never heard of, with prices that would break his budget. Frank shook his head and looked lower on the wall, settling on two bottles of cheap vodka from some region of Europe he'd never heard of.

"That going to be it for you?" the guy asked from behind the counter. He was still trying to be friendly. Frank wasn't sure why he bothered.

Frank just nodded and grunted and handed the man enough cash, then waited for his change. The guy wanted to talk about the weather, but Frank just nodded and mumbled, not taking the bait. Sometimes he just hated dealing with people.

As he left, Frank heard the young man say something like "have a good one," but the rest was cut off by the closing door.

Outside, Frank got in the Taurus and opened one bottle, transferring some of it to the flask and taking a long tug on the bottle. It wasn't good vodka, by any stretch, but it settled his stomach. After a minute, he climbed out and put the bottles into the trunk. No need to get arrested for open container, not in a little town where no one knew him.

Back out on Main Street, Frank turned and continued east, enjoying Pinetop and the warmth in his belly.

Cooper's Mill was a cute town, small and pretty. There was the busier area near the highway, with the McDonald's and hotels and chain restaurants. He passed several more shops, including a CVS and a Burger King, before Main turned into all residences. He passed a strip of smaller homes and stopped at the next intersection at Hyatt Avenue. This intersection sported a Dairy Queen, a fire station, and another small strip of businesses, including a laundromat. On the fourth corner sat a beautiful memorial park, which included a gorgeous white gazebo and a maze of paved brickwork that looked to be dedicated to veterans and fallen soldiers.

Beyond Hyatt, the houses on Main became much larger and more ornate: Victorian homes and brick mansions marched along both sides of Main. Beautiful old homes, with porches and tall trees and a few old wrought iron hitching posts for long-gone horses. The homes all looked well-maintained. One particularly ornate Victorian home, now a funeral home, featured a massive front staircase bedecked with white columns.

He continued on Main until he reached a set of train tracks, which he remembered marked the start of the small historical downtown. Passing over the tracks, he began to understand why the waitresses had wanted him to visit in the daytime. He'd been down here on Saturday night, but it had been dark, and he hadn't noticed how nice the buildings looked.

The small downtown was spectacular.

On either side of Main, four blocks of quaint shops and restaurants lined each side of the road. People were out walking, enjoying the break in the weather, and Frank saw they had a good variety of stores downtown—antique stores, restaurants, a bank, a toy store, and a dozen other shops. He could tell immediately that this was a real downtown and not one of those "fakes" he'd seen other places. These authentic buildings were a mix of exteriors, brick and wood and plaster. The sidewalks were lined with trees of differing sizes and benches and bike racks. None of the storefronts matched, and it appeared that all the buildings were different heights, a sure sign they'd been built at different times. Trees lined the streets; some had dropped all their leaves, but others still held on to wild colors that ran from green to flaming red. He'd been to newer "downtowns," and outdoor malls designed to look like old-timey downtowns. They always looked fake, like they'd been airlifted in and dropped into the middle of an open field.

Frank found the corner barber shop and started searching for a parking spot, finding one nearby.

He took a pull on the flask and tucked it under his seat, then climbed out and walked back up to Main Street, turned, and made his way to the intersection of Second and Main. The corner seemed like a busy destination. All four corners were taken up with stores and shops—two restaurants, an art gallery, and the place Frank had been looking for,

Willie's Barber Shop. It looked like one of those places you saw in the movies: there was even one of those old-style barber poles on the wall outside. When he pushed the doors open and headed inside, a small bell above the door rang, just like something out of Mayberry.

Of course, he shouldn't have been surprised. This place was as well preserved as the rest of the downtown. It was an authentic old barber shop—wood paneling, two large metal chairs in the middle of the wide, tiled floor. A row of metal seats by the front window for waiting customers, flanked by low tables piled high with old magazines. On one wall, above a doorway that evidently led into a back room, was a mounted deer head with a sign below that read "The Buck Stops Here." Toward the back, faded pinups from the 1980s decorated the walls. Racks of dusty shelves held rows of dated hair care products, a few of which Frank thought probably weren't even on the market any more.

But the place was busier than he'd expected. Two barbers were on duty, and both of the big swivel chairs in the middle of the room were occupied by customers. Next to the windows, three other men were waiting. Frank nodded at the older barber, a black man with graying hair at the temples. He wore a nametag that read "Willie."

"Be with you in a couple minutes," Willie said to Frank, nodding at the other waiting men.

Frank nodded and sat down to wait. He glanced at the magazines on the table and grabbed an issue of *Field and Stream*—it was seven years old—and began thumbing through it.

A conversation, probably interrupted by Frank when he entered, started up again mid-stream.

"But that's what I'm saying, Willie," the customer in the left chair said to the older barber. "It's just not right."

Willie nodded, continuing to trim. He didn't answer for a moment. The only sound was the scissors chopping at the customer's thinning hair.

"I know, Bill. I know," Willie said finally. "Whoever is doing this, they must hate the Martins, or want something out of 'em. But we got good cops in this town. They'll figure it out."

The man in the chair, Bill, laughed, a short squeaky bark that sounded almost like a seal.

"Not likely," Bill said. "I've been in all the meetings. Chief King came before the City Council and updated us Friday night at that emergency meeting. These cops are in over their head. He sat right there and said 'Mayor, we've never had a kidnapping,' like that explains everything."

The other barber spoke up. His nametag read "Chuck." He was a younger man, white, both of his arms and the back of his neck heavily tattooed. Frank knew immediately that Chuck was an ex-con. But working here, working under Willie, it looked like the guy was trying to go straight.

"I don't know about that—these cops can dog you," Chuck said. "I should know. They don't ever stop watching. And didn't Chief King help on a kidnapping case 'couple years back down in Dayton?"

Willie shook his head. "Don't remember that."

"Doesn't matter," Bill said. "He did help out, but he wasn't the lead. No one knows what they're doing. That's why they called in that idiot from the Cincinnati FBI. But he's just a kid, and he's just made things worse. Anyway, they ain't gonna find those girls. Been too long."

"Six days?" Willie asked?

"Seven, counting today," Bill answered, nodding at a calendar on the wall from some place called Maple Hill Nurseries. "Girls went missing last week, Monday. Like I said, Chief King is optimistic. But I can read people. And I heard somewhere they almost never find them when they're gone that long."

It got quiet in the barber shop. Frank guessed that, along with him, everyone in the shop was listening to the conversation. It was a conversation Frank had heard, and been involved in, a hundred times before. He tried to block it out—it wasn't any of his business.

Chuck, the younger barber, finished up his customer, and the young man stood up out of the chair, thanking him and paying. The ex-con nodded and waived over one of the other men sitting next to Frank. The new customer sat down in the empty chair, using his hands and quietly describing what kind of cut he wanted. Chuck nodded and got started, then looked up at the others.

"So the FBI, they're not gonna be any help?"

"Doesn't look like it," Bill said, shaking his head. With the movement of Bill's head, Willie pulled the scissors away and waited for his customer to stop moving before starting again. "The kid is wet behind the ears—that tells me Cincinnati doesn't think there's much that can be done. Or else they would have sent somebody who knew what the hell they were doing, not some fool who's only been on five or six cases," Bill said. Frank could hear the man was angry. "Anyway, sounds like they're working on the phone call. The kidnappers finally called yesterday to set up another call."

Frank looked up, intrigued. It was odd to have the kidnappers wait that long before making initial contact. Usually, you heard from them in the first 48 hours. Or there were no kidnappers. Or the victims were already dead.

Willie shook his head.

"Ain't gonna matter now," Willie said, grimacing. He had Bill leaning his head forward, trimming the short hairs on the back of his neck. "I hate to say it, but it's gotta be true. Been too long."

"I don't know—why would the kidnappers call?" Chuck asked. "They want money, so they'd keep the girls around, at least until they got their money from Nick Martin, right?"

"I'm not sure," Bill said, his voice muffled, his face pointed at the floor. "None of us on City Council are confident. Nick is hopeful, obviously, but the rest of us aren't holding our breaths. That briefing this morning was depressing. Ransom call is today."

"Two calls?" Chuck said.

"First call was yesterday, to let the mom know the girls were alive, though they didn't let Glenda talk to the girls," Bill said. "Next call is today. Supposed to get the ransom demands."

Frank nodded and went back to his magazine.

"Don't matter," Willie said. "They still ain't gonna find them girls."

"Nick is a mess," Bill said. "It'll ruin him. His marriage was already shaky enough, and now—"

"What?" Willie interrupted. "I didn't hear about anything."

Bill nodded his head. Willie was just finishing up with the razor on the neckline, so he paused the trimming until Bill's head stopped moving.

"They've been having a lot of money problems," Bill said. "From what I hear. Before this. Now it'll just be worse."

The others simply nodded. To Frank, it sounded like this Nick Martin person was having a tough month.

Willie pulled the barber cloth from Bill and shook it out. Bill stood and regarded his hair in the mirror, touching it with his hands. The man then reached into his pocket and pulled out a thick roll of money, peeling off a crisp $20 bill.

"That's too much," Willie said.

Bill shook his head.

"You're worth it," Bill said. "Always are. You take care, Willie."

"You take care, Mayor," Willie said, repeating it back to him with a smile.

Bill left, shaking hands with the other men in the waiting area on his way out, smiling at each of them except for one young kid who had his head buried in his hands. The Mayor even stopped and shook Frank's hand. The guy was clearly a glad-handing politician, perpetually running for office. Someone used to smiling and nodding and working behind the scenes to get his way. The little bell rang on his way out.

Willie took a minute, beating at the barber chair with a towel and sweeping up the hair on the floor around it. When he was done cleaning, he turned and nodded at Frank.

"Your turn, son."

Frank glanced at the others waiting, but they shook their heads.

"Don't worry 'bout them," Willie said to Frank. "They waiting for Chuck."

Chuck smiled. He was missing several teeth.

"Yup," Chuck said. "Gotta love those loyal customers, right?"

Willie scowled and shot him a look as Frank settled into the empty barber chair. Willie tied the barber cloth around Frank's neck.

"What we doin' today?" Willie asked.

"Needs to be tidy," Frank said curtly. "Short on top. Trim it above the ears and along the hairline in the back."

Willie nodded, clearly sensing there would be little or no small talk. He got to work trimming Frank's hair, occasionally squirting with a spray bottle to get the hair to lay flat. After a few minutes, Willie settled into a quiet routine.

"So, you from around here?" Willie asked Frank.

"No," Frank said.

Again, Frank heard the silence hanging there and knew he was supposed to fill it. He practiced his patience, concentrating on the clicking scissors working to tidy him up.

"Where you from?" Willie asked after a long, quiet minute.

Frank sighed.

"Just up from Birmingham for a couple days."

Willie nodded.

"Oh, Alabama. Nice down there?"

"Yeah, I guess," Frank said. He didn't volunteer anything, and after a long pause, Willie nodded again and set in to cutting.

"They ain't gonna find those girls," Chuck said, starting the other conversation back up again. From this angle, Frank could see more tattoos on the back of Chuck's neck, running up into the hair. Jail tattoos, roughly applied with handmade tools. Painful. Chuck was nodding, as he talked, his eyes on the customer in his chair. "But I've known a few bad folks," Chuck continued, his voice suddenly quiet. "I bet the girls are already dead."

Frank heard a low sound, like a sob, but couldn't see where it was coming from.

Willie nodded, working on Frank's hair. Frank had let it get way too long in the back, and Willie was taking off hunks with loud snips of his scissors. He was working quickly, with the practiced, quiet efficiency of someone who had been doing this for a long time.

"No, not yet," Willie said. "They need the girls for the phone call. Prove they alive still."

"But you heard Bill, and he's on city council," Chuck said, shaking his head. "The FBI isn't helping, and Chief King isn't confident. Why wait so long for that first call? It doesn't make sense to wait almost a week to call the parents, let them know you got their kid, right?"

Willie shrugged. Frank could see they were using the mirror on the wall to glance at each other. Next to the mirror hung a pinup of some blonde actress. The photo looked at least twenty years old, tattered and yellow around the edges.

"Well, nobody knows for sure, right?" Willie said. He turned and eyed Chuck intently, then nodded at one of the waiting patrons.

Frank followed Willie's gaze to the waiting patrons seated by the window. One of the people waiting was a young man, and he appeared visibly shaken by the conversation. Evidently, no one had noticed how upset the conversation was making him, and now the teenager had buried his face in his hands, crying quietly.

Chuck saw the young man sobbing and swallowed so loud Frank could hear the click in the man's throat.

"That's right, Willie," Chuck said, louder and more deliberately than he should have. "Nobody knows anything for sure."

The kid started crying louder, loud enough for everyone to hear.

"Now, look what you did," Willie said to Chuck. The shop grew quiet, except for the sobs of the young man.

Frank sighed. He knew it was a mistake to even open his mouth.

"They're still alive," Frank said quietly.

All the eyes in the place turned to him. Willie stopped and looked at Frank in the mirror.

"What do you mean?" Chuck asked.

Frank glanced up at him in the mirror.

"In most cases, they don't eliminate the victims," Frank said slowly, loud enough for the crying kid and the others to hear. "The kidnappers want their money, and they'll do anything to get it. Anything. Getting a call is good news—six days without a phone call usually means it's not a kidnapping. Usually means something much worse."

The barber shop somehow grew even more silent. Frank could hear traffic passing outside, and the ticking of the clock on the wall.

Chuck spoke up again. "But, why two calls?"

Frank shrugged.

"Not sure. But a second call, set up like that—that's a good sign," Frank said. "Kidnappers know they're going to be taped, so the girls are probably still alive. At least, the phone call greatly improves the chances of them being alive."

Willie nodded, eyeing Frank differently.

"That's good," Willie said. "You know about this kind of stuff?"

Frank could hear the curiosity in his voice—and the concern. Frank knew immediately what the old black man was thinking: Who is this stranger? And why does he know so much about kidnappings?

"Yeah, I do." Frank sighed. "Unfortunately. I'm an ex-cop. Used to investigate them."

"Really?" Chuck said.

Frank nodded.

Willie started back on Frank's hair, but he was going slower now, taking his time. After a minute, he spoke up again. "OK, what's going to happen next?"

"Not sure," Frank said. "But if the Bureau's involved, they will help with the ransom demand. Work with the family, pull the money together. People usually can't lay their hands on large amounts of cash quickly, so the Bureau assists." Frank could see Willie listening intently.

Frank turned to the young man who had been sobbing. He was quiet now but still had his head down.

"Then there will be an exchange of some sort," Frank said. "After that, hopefully, the girls come home."

"Huh," Willie said, laughing. "Not sure about that, my friend. I don't think they're coming home."

Frank looked up at the reflection of Willie in the mirror. Willie stopped trimming for a moment and looked at him.

"You're serious, aren't you?" Willie continued. "You really investigated stuff like this?"

Frank nodded.

"What are the chances the girls are OK?" Chuck asked.

Frank glanced at the sobbing kid again.

"Well, I'd say 80-20 right now they're alive."

The kid glanced up, his eyes red.

"Really?" the kid asked.

Frank nodded.

He should've never opened his mouth.

"Yeah, I think so," Frank continued. He thought about it for a moment. "But I have to be honest. Based on my experience, those numbers will start to drop quickly, as soon as the ransom is delivered."

The kid smiled. It wasn't really a smile, more of a grateful nod.

Frank expected more questions, but the barbers both moved on to another topic of conversation—some kind of big downtown construction project that was coming up next summer or the year after that would shut down the whole downtown. After a few minutes, Frank was done. The hair was trimmed and tidy, and he looked ten years younger. Combined with the shave from this morning, he was looking almost presentable.

When Willie removed the barber cloth, Frank stood and fished in his wallet, taking out enough money to cover the haircut and a tip. Frank thanked Willie, but he could feel all eyes in the place on him. They were all probably wondering if Frank would say anything else about the kidnapping case. But Frank didn't have anything to add. He wasn't involved and didn't want to be.

So, instead of bullshitting them or giving them false hope or making something up to make them all feel better, he did what he'd been trying to do lately—not lead people on. Frank nodded to Willie and Chuck and the others, and left.

On his way out, the little bell above the door jingled brightly. The sound was out of place, not matching in any way his somber mood.

8

They were in the Martin's living room.

Chief King looked down at the legal pad on the ornate coffee table in front of him. He always took all of his case notes on the pads. Yellow, lined. Not that big legal size but the regular, 8 1/2 by 11 size. It was a habit he'd picked up early in his career: write it all down, no matter how trivial. You never knew what detail would break a case open.

But Chief King wasn't feeling too confident about this case.

Agent Ted Shale, the kid from the Bureau, had gotten here early and set up the phone-tracing equipment, although Chief King had needed to step in and help with some of the connections. Clearly this was the first time the young agent had set it up on his own. He was "book smart," as they used to say, usually about someone who didn't have a lick of common sense.

So Chief King and the others sat in the Martin's expansive living room, waiting. Large framed photos of beautiful landscapes decorated the walls and, above the huge fireplace, a heavy wooden mantle was covered with photos of the family in a variety of exotic locales. In most, little Charlie could be seen at various ages, enjoying a day at Cooper's Mill Pool or riding a horse. In one frame, Charlie wore an oversized hard hat, jauntily tipped to one side; she was evidently visiting a construction site with her father, who smiled in the picture with her.

Glenda's cell phone sat in the middle of the ornate coffee table, cords running from the bottom of the phone for power and into the FBI equipment, ready to run the trace. Everyone in the room was seated and staring at the cell phone, except for the FBI kid, who'd wandered off somewhere. He'd probably gone off to find a bathroom in the Martin's huge home and gotten lost. The house was ridiculously large.

Or he'd been mesmerized by something shiny and King wouldn't find him for hours. Either way, Ted was out of his hair.

Not that the kid was making things worse. He just wasn't helping out at all or bringing anything to the table. King had expected more when he'd finally taken the Dayton PD's advice and called in the Bureau.

King glanced at his notepad. He had four pages of notes just from this morning. That went along with another hundred and thirty sheets of notes, reports and assessments and interviews with half of the town of Cooper's Mill.

So far, the case just didn't add up.

This was a great family, known by everyone in the community. Friendly, good neighbors, good people, with only a few enemies.

Nick Martin was a local high school football hero. He ran one of the most successful companies in town and was on the City Council, for Christ's sake. Glenda sat on a half-dozen charity boards and volunteered at the local farmers' market.

As far as King could tell, they had very few enemies. They were rich, of course, and that made them a target, along with Nick's recent actions on City Council. He'd been voted in on a budget-cutting platform, and he'd taken to streamlining the city's finances. And some people had been let go. But those folks had been interviewed, along with everyone else the cops could think of. A few hurt feelings, sure, but nothing criminal. It just didn't make sense.

It was how the girls had disappeared that really bothered Chief King. He'd been a cop in Cooper's Mill for twenty-two years, eight as the Chief. He'd risen up through the ranks from a dumbass patrolman. He'd seen a lot of small-town crime, most involving domestic disputes and petty drug charges. Being close to Dayton, he'd seen some bigger cases as well, mostly drugs passing through here on the way to somewhere important. Cooper's Mill had only two murders over past the two decades, but plenty of drug arrests and OVIs. Last year, the department even shut down a rinky-dink escort service some local couple had been running out of their apartment.

But this was the first kidnapping. They'd had false alarms before, but they'd always turned out to be some kid sneaking off to go to a party. This was a real kidnapping. The girls had been taken in broad daylight, walking to school. But there had been no witnesses.

None.

In a town the size of Cooper's Mill, it just didn't seem possible. It seemed like the switchboard got twenty calls a day from "snoopy neighbors," the cop's best friend: somebody "suspicious" was walking in front of the library, or a car was weaving in and out of their lane on the stretch of interstate highway that ran through the city limits. Once a week, someone called in thinking they'd heard a gunshot. Cooper's Mill was a small, close-knit community, and that meant people had their eyes open all the time. Some were looking out for others, and some were simply vindictive neighbors, quick to "tattle." Either way, it helped the cops. And people from outside of town stood out like sore thumbs, and any wrongdoing, or even the suspicion of wrongdoing, was quickly reported. In fact, most of the crime in town involved OVIs at the local bars, and the majority of those cases were drinkers from other local towns, like Troy or Vandalia or West Milton.

Someone must have seen what happened that morning. It was broad daylight, on a school morning. So why hadn't anyone called?

King shook his head and wondered what he should do about the FBI. King had called the FBI for assistance but, for some reason, the Bureau had decided to send a less-than-senior special agent. To King, the kid had looked like he was fresh out of the Academy and wasn't yet sure which end of the gun was dangerous.

But Ted had arrived and redirected some of the searches, redeploying the volunteers and police officers. Not knowing a thing about Cooper's Mill and the surrounding terrain, he'd gone by the book and started from the middle, working his way out. King didn't have the heart to tell him he'd already searched all those areas in the first 24 hours after the girls had disappeared. If the Bureau wanted to follow procedure, he didn't want to confuse the kid with a little thing like logic.

Ted had also sat with Nick Martin and poured through their finances, but King didn't think it had helped. The kid was too green to catch anything the CMPD would've missed on their investigation. But now that it had gone from a missing persons case to a kidnapping—yesterday's call to the mother's cell phone had been brief and to the point—King was wishing they'd sent someone with a little more experience.

"Will they call?" the mother, Glenda, asked. She was sitting on the couch, one hand gripping a pillow in her lap. The other hand was clenched in a fist at her chest. "They were supposed to call."

"They'll call," Nick said quietly from the other side of the room. The Chief noticed again that the husband wasn't sitting next to his wife, comforting her. It was the third or fourth time King had noticed the distance, all during earlier interviews. Interesting. He jotted it down—you never knew—and stood, walking around the room again. It felt like he was spending all of his time in this room, with these people, instead of out working the case.

He looked around the room—there were many pictures on the walls and expensive stuff sitting around. The entire home was also decorated with stuff for Halloween, down to the pumpkins on the front porch.

"Where's the nanny?" the Chief asked.

Glenda looked up at him. Her eyes were puffy and red.

"She was really upset," Glenda said. "We gave her the day off."

"Has she called to check in?" the Chief asked.

"No," Nick shook his head. "I told her I would call her if we heard anything."

That was interesting—the nanny had already been interviewed, of course, but Chief King would have thought the nanny would have wanted to be here for the call. He was making a note of it when there was a knock at the front door.

Deputy Peters, one of the patrolmen stationed at the house, left the room to answer it. King heard mumbled voices and then Peters came into the room and called the Chief over.

"Chief, it's Ken Meredith."

Great, King thought.

"I got it." King went to the door and pulled it open.

Ken ran CM-TV, the local public TV station. People were always confusing it with CMTV, the country music TV station on cable, and Ken could be very sensitive about that, and about the town not supporting the local station enough. He was always trying to put on interesting programming, usually to no avail.

CM-TV broadcast out of the third floor of the Monroe Township building downtown, a building that used to hold a downtown theater until it had been converted to offices in the 1970s. Current tenants included the local Chamber of Commerce. The broadcast facilities for CM-TV sat in the old balcony. In fact, there was a particular door, hidden behind the set of their semi-monthly local news show, which opened onto the cavernous space above the offices thirty feet below.

"Hey Chief," Ken asked quietly, leaning in and almost hitting the Chief with his camera. Ken's voice was low, conspiratorial. King noticed his face was sweaty. "Can I film the ransom call?"

Behind him, across the lawn in the driveway, were three satellite trucks from local TV stations. Chief King saw a couple of the reporters talking, including that rotund fellow from Channel 4, Dale Scott. Chief King recognized him from the escort case last year, which had made the local news for almost a week straight. He'd gotten a lot of practice giving press conferences and had gotten to know a lot of the local press. Another reporter was working on her makeup in the side mirror of one of the trucks.

Chief King shook his head.

"Ken, we talked about this," King said. "You can't film that, or the family, unless they want to do interviews or speak to the press. And you have to stop sneaking into the police station. It's completely inappropriate for you to be—"

"It's public information, what happens in the station," Ken answered, adjusting the camera on his shoulder.

"No, it's not," King said. "We're conducting an investigation." King could see that Meredith was completely wired, shaking like one of those little dogs that shakes all the time when they're cold.

"After the call, you're just going to come out and tell the media what happened," Meredith said, his eyes red. "Wouldn't it make it easier to just have me film it?"

Sergeant Graves, King's third-in-command, walked up the sidewalk, passing Meredith. Graves smiled at King and made a face that said something like, "I'm sorry for what you're having to put up with," then headed inside.

King looked at the man with the camera and shook his head.

"No, Ken. You can't film the phone call," King said, as forcefully as he dared. "It's sensitive, and we'll probably be negotiating."

Ken's face fell. He wasn't good at taking rejection. The same thing had happened last year, when Meredith had wanted special access for the escort case, and King had said 'no.'

But then Meredith had a thought and started literally jumping up and down.

"OH! Can I film this part, where we're talking?" Ken lifted the video camera and flicked it on, but the Chief put his hand on the lens and pulled the camera slowly back down.

"No, Ken," King said. "You need to calm down. Back on the Red Bull?"

Ken started to say something but looked at the other reporters.

"I just wanted an edge."

King shook his head. "You know how you get."

Meredith nodded.

The Chief patted Ken on the shoulder. "It's okay, just do your best. Look, I gotta get back inside. I'll let you know what we learn," he said and turned, shutting the door behind him.

King walked slowly back through the expansive foyer, shaking his head. This town was full of "interesting" people, that was certain. He took his time, looking at a collection of photos in frames on a long, low table that ran along one wall. When the call came, if it ever did, they would let him know.

Many pictures of Nick and Glenda and little Charlie, along with a few more: Nick Martin being sworn in as a city councilman, his hand on a Bible with the Mayor, Bill Hendrickson, administering the oath. Nick and Glenda on a vacation somewhere snowy. Nick and another guy golfing; it looked like Matt Lassiter, Nick's business partner. Another one of Nick and Matt, this time in Vegas.

There were several of Nick with different groups of serious-looking people in suits, posing at groundbreaking ceremonies. They all had those ridiculous golden shovels you always saw, digging into little fake plots of dirt. Glenda in New York with a group of friends, holding a beer and grinning in front of a limo. And one of Nick and Glenda on a beach, much younger. They looked happy.

King walked back into the living room. He'd seen all those pictures in the files, of course, but looking at them on the table and how they were arranged, it told you how important they were to the family. And that wasn't conveyed in a simple stack of copies that he'd been through. Maybe he needed to rethink some of their procedures.

The Bureau guy had returned and was fiddling with the wiretap equipment again. King hoped that he didn't mess something up or accidentally unplug an important wire.

Sergeant Graves had found a chair and was waiting. He nodded at King again. Graves was good. King wanted him to sit in on the call—the man never missed anything.

The Chief nodded back and walked over to the chair in the living room and, just as he sat down, the cell phone on the table in front of them rang loudly, making Glenda jump.

The Bureau kid hopped up and flicked on the equipment. The Chief was glad to see he'd returned in his absence. The guy was trying, at least. But Chief King was also certain that, when this case was over, the kid would have contributed exactly nothing to the outcome.

The cell phone rang again—wires were sticking out of it, leading to the Bureau equipment and two other phone handsets, which allowed the call to be monitored. It was also being recorded. King ran his eyes over the phone recording setup to make sure nothing had gotten put out of place and to verify the recording had started.

King nodded at Nick Martin, who picked up the cell phone, being careful to not dislodge the wires, and put it to his ear. Chief King picked up one of the other handsets, and he and Graves leaned in to share it. Glenda was perched on the arm of the chair next to Nick. They were both looking at the Chief, who nodded at Nick.

Nick pressed the button.

"Hello?" Nick's voice was nervous, tentative. That, as much as anything else King had seen over the past few days, told him that Nick wasn't involved in the kidnapping.

It was a hard thing to consider, but in most of these types of cases, it was a family member. King grabbed his legal pad and started taking notes. He'd be able to make notes on the call later, from the recording, but he wanted to jot down his initial impressions, including what he'd just decided about Nick.

"We have your daughter and the other girl," the gruff voice on the other end said.

To King, the voice sounded male, late 20s, smoker. King wrote it all down. The caller got right to the point, with no preamble. That would make negotiation more difficult.

Sergeant Graves leaned forward, listening intently—they were so close that King could smell coffee on his breath.

King jotted down:

THIS GUY KNOWS WHAT HE WANTS

and showed the note to Graves, who nodded.

"Um, okay," Nick Martin said. Next to him, Glenda burst into tears and then stifled them quickly, wanting to hear the exchange.

The kidnapper spoke again.

"We want $1,000,000. By tomorrow evening."

Every eye in the room turned to Nick, who slowly nodded.

"OK, OK. I want...I can get that for you," Nick said slowly. King had told him to take his time and not rush. "Just don't hurt her, OK? Don't hurt them."

Nick glanced up at King, who nodded, encouraging him. This was going to be the hardest part, getting the Martins to demand proof of life.

"But...but before I do anything," Martin continued, "I want to hear my daughter. To make sure she's OK."

The room was silent. Deputy Peters, standing behind the Martins, looked at the Chief. Agent Shale looked worried; he was actually biting his nails. Graves just stared at the cell phone in Nick Martin's hand. King knew it was a gamble that might piss off the kidnappers, but exercising a little control was rarely the wrong call.

On the phone, there was the sound of rustling. Finally, another voice came on.

"Daddy?"

Nick looked like he might drop the phone. Chief King smiled and leaned over and steadied the man's hand. After a moment, the father answered.

"We're here, honey." Nick said.

King could see that his hands were shaking.

"Are you OK, honey? We love you." Glenda said quietly into the phone, leaning close to her husband.

The little girl's voice came back.

"Yes, I'm OK," Charlie said, sounding distant, weak.

"Did they hurt you?" Glenda asked.

That got him thinking, as Charlie answered that she and Maya were okay. King jotted something down and held up the yellow pad for Nick to read. It said:

ASK HER TO IDENTIFY HER FAVORITE FOOD — HER VOICE COULD BE A RECORDING

Nick's eyes went wide, but King nodded. Nick turned back to the phone in his hand.

"Um, honey, I need to ask you a question. What is your favorite food?" Nick Martin asked, his voice tentative.

The phone rustled again.

"Hey, what's going on?" the gruff kidnapper barked.

Nick stood his ground.

"I'm talking to Charlie," he said. "Asking her a question. I just need to know if it's really her or some kind of recording."

King heard the kidnapper curse under his breath. The phone rustled again. Charlie came back on.

"Um, my favorite food is spaghetti and meatballs," she said quietly. "You know that, Daddy."

Glenda started to cry. Chief King nodded.

"Okay, honey," Nick said again. "Just do what they say, and this will be over soon. Put the man back on."

The phone rustled again, and the kidnapper spoke again.

"Okay, here's the deal," the kidnapper said. "I'm not calling again. You will put the money in a black satchel or briefcase. You know the Old Hotel, across from O'Shaughnessy's?"

Nick Martin nodded, then must have realized the guy on the other end couldn't see his nod. "Yes, I do."

"Good," the voice on the other end of the line said. "Put the briefcase in the trash can outside the Old Hotel Thursday at exactly 6:06 p.m. And no cops. Or the girls die."

Glenda's clenched hand went to her chest, an expression of panic that King had seen her make a few times.

"I'll call you back when I have the money and get away safely," the voice on the line said. "And if you or anybody else tries to stop me from picking up the money, or from leaving with the money, the girls die."

The phone went silent.

9

The bar at O'Shaughnessy's was Nick Martin's favorite part of the restaurant. Many people only sat in here while waiting for a table in the restaurant proper.

But Nick loved the feel of the long, narrow space and preferred it to the rest of the restaurant. The beautiful shelving and glassware behind the bar, the long, flat surface of the vintage wooden bar top, the frame around the doorway leading back into the rest of the restaurant—it screamed traditional bar decor. And the entire west wall was old, exposed brick, broken up only by framed historical pictures of Cooper's Mill and the old canal that had been the lifeblood of the small town for so many years.

Now, the canal was an empty ditch, and the town had long ago moved on, but, at least in the black and white photos, the canal was alive and well.

Nick knew that the owners had spent a pretty penny converting this place over from the old Natty's in 2004, and you could see where all the money had gone—the space was beautiful.

"We're all pulling for you, Nick. Let me know if you need anything."

Nick Martin looked up. It seemed like every single person coming through the bar was stopping at his table to say something. He'd been hugged and drinks had been sent over. One woman, who had worked hard to keep him from getting elected to city council, leaned in and gave him a heartfelt kiss on his cheek. She seemed genuinely upset about what had happened to him. He appreciated their thoughts and concern, but Nick really just wanted to be left alone.

Nick nodded to the speaker. It was Jake Delancy, a downtown resident. Good guy. Nick had used him on a couple jobs. The guy was a bit of a craftsman and tinkerer, but an odd one. Jake made his own cheese, for God's sake. But Nick had brought him in to do custom cabinetry on a few projects, and the man was a true artisan.

"Thanks, Jake," Nick said.

Jake nodded and headed off. Nick went back to his beer.

A few minutes later, Nick's partner, Matt Lassiter, walked in, and Nick waved him over. Matt was tall and thin and well-dressed, a longtime friend and popular in town, even though he wasn't from around here. Several people nodded and said "hi" to Lassiter as he walked through the bar to Nick's table.

Nick had known Matt Lassiter for years. He'd moved to town and immediately gotten involved in the local commercial real estate market. And the man had acquaintances everywhere, probably from his years out west in Vegas. He'd made a killing on real estate out there in 2002–2006 and still had the connections. Nick also considered Matt his closest friend. Nick was sure that Matt would help him out.

As Matt passed the bar, he slapped another patron on the back good-naturedly and smiled at the bartender, holding up two fingers. The bartender nodded and turned, starting a drink.

"That's impressive," he said, as Lassiter sat down. "You got some kind of signal?"

Matt nodded.

"For Spence? Oh, yeah," Matt said. "I have four drinks that I order regularly. He knows them so well, I just have to let him know which one when I come in." Lassiter turned and greeted another person as they passed the table, then turned back to Nick. His face turned serious. "How are you doing?" Matt asked.

"Not great," Nick said, running his hand along the beer glass. Beads of condensation ran down the glass and dripped onto the coaster. "We got the ransom call today."

Matt's eyes went wide.

"Jesus," Matt said. "But that's good, though, right? Now you know what's going on and that at least someone has her. Better than…better than she's just gone. Now, at least there's a plan. To get her back."

Nick nodded and took another long sip of his beer.

"So," Matt continued. "What do they want?"

"$1,000,000. By tomorrow evening, around 6ish," Nick said to his beer. "I don't have that kind of cash. Not on hand, anyway. It's invested in all my projects. I've closed out of a couple already today."

Spence, the bartender, brought over a drink and set it in front of Matt. It was blue and fizzy and Nick didn't even ask. He knew Matt was always trying new drinks and developing new favorites. Spence turned to Nick.

"You need anything, Mr. Martin?"

Nick shook his head. After a long silence, the bartender turned and left.

"Well, how can I help?" Matt asked quietly, sipping at his cocktail.

Nick sighed. "Not sure yet. But I spent the afternoon with the cops, trying to figure out how to raise the cash. I will need to close my partnerships on another deal or two and wanted to know if you want them."

"Anything I can do to help."

Nick looked at him.

"I hate to do it, but I guess I'm pulling out of the Dragon's complex downtown. I figured you might want to buy my shares."

Matt Lassiter nodded thoughtfully.

"I don't want in on the Dragon's location. I think it's too heavily leveraged," Matt said. "And I told you that when you got in," he said, pausing to take another drink before continuing. "If you are interested, I would be happy to buy you out of the Holly Toys building. The Holly Toys loft project isn't going anywhere, and even if the economy turns around, the renovation costs are going to eat up any profit. But I've always liked that property."

Nick smiled and looked up.

"You made that same offer a couple months ago, right?" he asked, nodding. "I know, the project took forever to get off the ground, and it will probably never make money. But even if it takes years to get finished, I really have a good feeling about that space," Nick said, looking at his beer. "It's probably because I grew up right there on Plum. I remember walking by that old building every day on the way to school. Back then, it was humming with activity."

"And now it's an empty shell," Matt said, looking at his blue drink and the umbrella that floated in it. "The only person making money on it right now is the security guard. Tell you what, sell me your half, and I'll give you $600,000. That'll get you half-way there."

Nick thought about it. It was a fair deal, more than fair. And Matt was good for it. After a second, Nick nodded his head.

"It hurts, but I can do that," Nick said, shaking his hands. "I had plans for that space, but now it looks like you're getting your wish—but at that price, you'd be overpaying."

Matt started to argue, then nodded. "I'm okay with overpaying a little."

Nick nodded, relieved but also saddened. Nick hated selling properties. It was like an admission of guilt, taking a loss. "And I'm gonna sell that Dragon's property," Nick said. "Another guy in the ownership group wanted to buy me out anyway."

Matt started to say something but went back to his drink.

"Thank you," Nick said to Matt. "And thanks for stepping up. I hate the idea of selling. But between the Lofts and the Dragon's project, I should have nearly enough."

Matt nodded, smiling. "Yeah. But I'm happy to help. I'll get you a cashier's check in the morning. Or do you need it tonight?"

Nick shook his head. "No, the morning is fine. I need to get word to the Dragon's people to set up the ownership transfer in the morning. And Shale, the FBI agent, said that if the money were in the account, he'd be able to facilitate converting it into cash."

Lassiter sipped at his blue drink as Nick took out his phone and started dialing.

10

The phone rang on the small table next to the bed.

Frank was watching TV and looked up at the clock—it was just after 10pm on Monday night. Only three people knew he was staying here at the hotel, and Frank quickly ticked them off in his head: it wasn't his daughter—she would call his cell, if she were delaying or canceling their lunch meeting tomorrow, something he'd been half-expecting all day. The staff at the Tip Top Diner next door wouldn't be calling—the place was closed up tight. And no one in Birmingham had the number of the hotel—they would call his cell, same as his daughter, if they needed him. That left only the front desk.

Frank muted the late local news and picked up the phone.

"What?"

"Hi, Mr. Harper," said the high, squeaky voice on the other end. Oscar at the front desk. "Sir? Umm…there's a policeman here, asking to speak to you..."

Frank sat up and shook his head.

"Fine," Frank said. "Send him up."

He knew what this was about. Gina, the waitress, had mentioned that her husband was a cop. And cops usually stuck together, especially in small towns. His name was Stan, or something like that. Frank had given her some advice on how to get clear of the guy, and now Stan had showed up here at the hotel to scare Frank off, or at least get him to stop putting ideas in Gina's head.

Frank felt sorry for Stan. It didn't matter to Frank if the guy was a cop. Stan was used to pushing his wife around, and Frank didn't have any use for those types of guys. And if Stan was here to scare Frank off.

Stan would find Frank hard to frighten. Frank had fought cops before. Plenty of times.

He shook his head and glanced around at the messy hotel room. Frank stood and started clearing away the bottles and beer cans. There was no need to give the guy an excuse to search the hotel room. As he picked up the empty glasses and tidied up, he shook his head at his own stupidity.

Ben Stone had gotten himself killed by taking chances, trying to do things without backup. Getting involved in stuff that didn't really matter, like this Gina situation. Why hadn't Frank learned his lesson? Don't get involved. Frank felt like he should get it tattooed on the back of his hand, where he could always see it. Or get it tattooed along the scar on his left arm, where he would see it every day and never forget.

When he was done, Frank opened the hotel room door and stood in the doorway. He heard the steps on the stairs before he could see the cop, who emerged from the stairway and turned up the carpeted hallway, looking at the room numbers.

He was a big sucker.

Frank didn't like it, but there was nothing he could do now except stand his ground.

"Hi, Mr. Harper?" the policeman said, as he approached. At least he appeared friendly.

Frank nodded.

The man stopped about eight feet back, well out of grappling range. Smart.

"I'm Sergeant Burwell," the burly cop said. He nodded at the hotel room behind Frank. "Can we speak for a minute?"

Frank nodded slowly, curious. This guy didn't look mad, or spoiling for a fight.

Frank stood back and held the door open, allowing the policeman inside. Deciding to take a casual approach to this "meeting," Frank closed the door, then nodded and crossed in front of the cop, taking a seat in one of the two chairs that flanked a small table by the window.

The cop stood by the television, even after Frank motioned him to sit. The cop's hands rested on the gun and container of mace located at each hip. Frank wondered if the cop even noticed what he was doing with his hands.

"How can I help you?" Frank asked, already knowing the answer.

"Well, Mr. Harper," Burwell began. "Chief of Police King asked me to come out and see you."

Frank looked up, not surprised.

"Oh? Why? Need me to keep out of it?" If this wife-beating cop already had his Chief involved, things could go south for Frank in a real hurry—

The cop looked confused. "What?"

"I know what this is about," Frank said, shaking his head. "You've got a cop that likes to use his wife like a punching bag, and you're here to tell me to mind my own business. Or you're the cop—I wouldn't know, since I haven't met the guy."

Burwell continued to look more and more confused. Frank started to feel less confident that the cop had any idea what Frank was talking about. Finally, the burly cop shook his head.

"I'm not sure what we're talking about," he said. "Are you talking about Stan and the restraining order? How do you know about that?"

Frank looked at him. "You're not Stan?"

"No, sir. He's been suspended," the cop said. "Too much going on right now for the Chief to look into it, so Stan's riding the pine."

Frank nodded, then shook his head.

"Okay, sorry about that. His wife works next door, and she wanted some advice about how to proceed. Sounds like you guys are handling it."

Burwell nodded.

"Okay, so how can I help you?" Frank was genuinely curious.

Burwell shuffled, looking at the ground. "Well, Chief King thinks you could help with a case we're working. It's the kidnapping, been going on for a week or so, and we got word you were a cop—"

"Ex-cop," Frank interjected.

The police officer looked at him.

"What?"

"I'm not a cop anymore, Sergeant Burwell." Frank said, looking out the window. "I'm retired. I'm part-time now with the Alabama Bureau of Investigation. Me in my cubicle, working nothing but cold cases."

Frank saw the officer's head nod in the reflection in the window.

"That may be the case," Burwell said. "But we're not trained for this kind of thing. We heard you worked these kinds of cases before, had some good insights. The Chief had me run your file, mostly to make sure you weren't somehow involved in the case. New faces in town can make people nervous."

Frank nodded.

"A few of us have had some training in this area," Burwell continued. "Detective Barnes worked one years ago in St. Louis. He and the Chief are the only ones with experience. But not a lot."

Frank turned and nodded at the muted TV. The large-haired anchor was back, her lips moving but no sound coming out.

"Sounds like you're doing the right things," Frank said, nodding at the TV. "I just saw the coverage—searches, talking to the family, looking for people with grudges. And the ransom call today—that's always good. Keep the bad guys talking."

Burwell nodded.

"That's right. But nothing is coming up."

Frank hated kidnapping cases. They almost never turned out well.

He turned and looked at the cop for the first time, really looking at him. The abrupt change in expectations had clouded Frank's view of the man, but now he could see that the sergeant was quiet, hat in hand, just looking at Frank. Frank didn't know what to say. This sounded like a genuine cry for help, not an invitation to come help them cover their asses with this investigation.

"No luck yet?" Frank asked.

Sergeant Burwell shook his head.

"The family checks out," Burwell said. "Both families, actually. The housekeeper has been with the Martins for years, and the girls practically grew up together. The Martins have money, although they might not have enough. The ransom call came in today. They want a million by tomorrow evening."

Frank nodded but didn't say anything.

The cop waited for a response from Frank, but none came. After a moment, Burwell continued.

"We were treating it as a missing person's case and worked it a while, before the Chief called in the Bureau. The kidnappers called the mom's cell phone yesterday, first call. The FBI representative up from Cincinnati will take point on that. I'm not sure…well, Chief said not to say much about Agent Shale, the FBI liaison. Anyway, it's been days, and you know, better than anyone, the statistics on kidnapping and child abductions. Most of the kids recovered alive are found with two days of the initial abduction."

Frank nodded.

"Yeah, after 48 hours, the percentages drop off," Frank said.

Burwell nodded and took out a small notepad and pen, taking notes, but Frank did not elaborate. After a moment, the cop looked up.

"And?" the cop said. "The percentages drop off, but not always, right?

Frank sighed. "The drop off severely. But those are in the cases of abductions."

Burwell wrote it down, then looked back at Frank. They both waited for the other to speak, but nothing came.

"Look," Burwell finally said. "I get that you might not trust us because of the Stan situation. But we have an active investigation going on here, and you're in our jurisdiction. If you know anything that can help—"

Frank shook his head.

"So, you're going to bring me in because I can't solve your case for you? What's the charge, officer?"

Burwell seemed taken aback by Frank's outburst.

"That's not what I meant, sir," Burwell said. "But I'm sworn to uphold the law, same as you were."

Frank nodded. "Emphasis on the past tense."

The room grew quiet. Frank wondered if Burwell had figured out Frank's little system of staying quiet to let the silences grow. Maybe Frank was getting a little of his own medicine.

Finally, Frank sighed again. "It's true, it's more likely in abductions that, as more time passes, it's more difficult to recover the victim. But in kidnappings for ransoms, the timeline doesn't matter as much. It can drag out over weeks or months."

"Oh," Burwell nodded, jotting it all down. "I hadn't thought about that. But we were relieved when the kidnappers called. Chief King wants you—"

"I can't," Frank said, shaking his head and cutting Burwell off. "I'm not getting involved. I told you what I know, and what I think about your prospects, but I'm not helping with the case."

Burwell looked up from his pad.

"Why?"

"It doesn't matter," Frank said. "But...any dialog with the kidnappers is good," he said, changing the subject. "Just give them what they want, keep them engaged."

The cop paused for a long moment.

"Yup, okay," he said. "Chief is working through all that with the Bureau. They will handle the ransom and the drop. But our investigation is going nowhere."

Frank thought about it for a minute to let the cop think he was considering it. But his mind was already made up. His mind had been made up since the conversation started.

"Look," Frank said. "I'm done with this kind of stuff. I...I'm done. And it sounds like you're on the right track. The Bureau is involved, now, so you don't really need me. Just follow the money, and it should work out."

Sergeant Burwell didn't answer.

"Have the Chief look into everyone's background that has regular contact with the family," Frank continued, suddenly feeling weary and old. Frank knew he should stop talking, but the cop looked like someone had just shot his dog. "It's often a family friend or accountant or someone like that, someone with ties to the family but without the loyalty of being part of the group."

The cop jotted down what Frank was saying. But just talking about it made Frank start to feel weary, remembering all the cases he'd followed and how few of them ended well. He remembered the kid in downtown Atlanta, buried in that cardboard box by the highway. Frank had gone through all the steps, done the work, just like he was telling this sergeant to do. Follow the leads, check the family. Cross the "i's", dot the "t's," as Williams, the arson investigator, liked to say with a wry smile.

But if this case was like the one in Atlanta, they could do everything right and still not get there in time. Frank remembered that poor little boy—

The sergeant stared at Frank, waiting for more words of wisdom, but Frank had none.

The room grew quiet.

"So, you're not going to help—" the sergeant began.

"No," Frank said.

"Why not?"

"You don't need me," Frank said, his voice coming out harsher than he wanted. "Just investigate the case and everyone involved. The kids will turn up."

It was cold. And a lie. They both knew it. The chances of recovering the girls alive diminished with each passing hour. But Frank didn't want to go down this road again.

Ever.

Another long moment of silence, with the burly cop staring at him, hands on his hips.

Frank shook his head and stood slowly. He always stood slowly when he was around angry, armed men. Frank walked to the hotel room door and pulled it open.

The burly cop hesitated and then shook his head and walked toward the door.

"You know, I would think you would want to help," Burwell said as he passed Frank. "Two young girls' lives are at stake," the sergeant said, stopping on the carpet out in the hallway and looking at him angrily.

"Don't you even care?"

Frank looked down at the carpet at the man's feet. Boots, clunky, good for running through muddy fields. Cop boots.

Frank resisted the overwhelming urge to say something nice. To get involved. To get back on that horse and have something in his life that didn't come out of a bottle. But he couldn't. He was here to see Laura and that had to be the only thing in his life right now. Laura, and Jackson, and getting his shit together. Not getting involved in another messy case that would probably end badly.

Frank looked up at Burwell.

"Sorry," Frank said. "But I can't help you."

Burwell looked at him. His face was hard, disappointed.

"Those girls are going to die," the sergeant said quietly, just between the two of them. Two professionals, standing in a hotel hallway late at night and assessing the case and the likelihood of a positive outcome. To Frank, it sounded almost like a plea.

He nodded somberly.

"Well, it's always something," Frank said, and slowly closed the door.

11

It was Tuesday morning, and Frank was back in his booth at the Tip Top Diner.

He was trying to read his *Dayton Daily News*. There was a big article on the front page about the ransom call and the kidnapping case and another article out of D.C. about an assassination plot to kill the Saudi Arabian ambassador to the United States.

He'd tried to read both articles three or four times now, but his mind kept wandering back to the conversation last night with Sergeant Burwell. Frank knew that not getting involved was the right thing to do, and yet, it still bothered him.

The restaurant door jingled again. Frank forced himself to keep his eyes on the paper. Situational awareness was overrated.

Plus, he had his gun, just in case.

Frank suddenly remembered another one of his old partners, Steve Furrows, who had just up and one day decided to quit smoking. The guy had acted like a class "A" prick for about three months, but Steve got through it and never smoked again. Frank just needed to get past the need to always know everything that was going on around him. He needed to relax, make "not looking" his priority. If Frank could stick with it, like Furrows, maybe he'd break the habit.

Frank's breakfast was gone and now he was having a piece of pie and finishing up the paper. Pakistan and Afghanistan were going at it again, according to the International section of the *Dayton Daily*, arguing and threatening to invade each other over some random patch of dirt. That region, along with the Middle East, had been in bad shape for millennia, and nothing that had happened over the past twenty years was going to make anything better.

Frank knew the region well. During his six years in the Marines, he'd never been deployed overseas, but it had been the focus of all of their training.

And 1983–1989, the years he'd been in, had been a tense period in the region: Iran and Iraq were duking it out along their border, bombing pipelines and shooting down aircraft. Lebanon was undergoing "difficulties," and Libya was on the warpath.

Incidents came to mind: 220 Marines killed when Hezbollah bombed the Marine barracks in Beirut in '83; the USS Vincennes shooting down an Iranian passenger jet; 270 people dying when that flight went down over Lockerbie, Scotland. Too much killing. Too much death.

Reagan and the U.S. stood by, tensely monitoring the situation and getting involved when necessary. Frank had trained for a war in the Mideast, a war that didn't come until after he'd gotten out in '89. But he knew lots of people who ended up in Kuwait, rolling into Iraq with Desert Storm in '91.

By then, he'd been back in the bayou, getting on with the NOPD and trying to forget his time in the military. He hadn't enjoyed his time in. He'd felt like an instrument of death that was never used, a weapon that had been loaded and aimed but never fired. It made him feel even more helpless, useless, to be fully trained and seeing all of the things that were going on in the world, and he couldn't do anything about any of them. It had been a big part of the decision to become a police officer.

Trudy hadn't been behind the idea. They'd married in 1985, and by 1989 she was happy to get out of the service and move back to Louisiana. But she'd fought him on joining the force. She wanted him home, safe, especially with Laura being only two at the time.

Frank shook his head and went back to the paper.

In Afghanistan, the Soviets hadn't been able to fix it in the '80s, and he doubted that the current U.S. war in Afghanistan would end any better. A hundred tiny fiefdoms, overseen by a hundred leaders, all squabbling to get a little more land or—

"I don't CARE!" a male voice shouted, breaking the quiet of the restaurant. Frank looked up.

Gina, the waitress, was standing behind the counter near the door, where customers paid their bills on the way out.

So was her soon-to-be ex-husband.

Stan was a short man with a thick neck and big arms, wearing civilian clothes. But Frank could tell by the haircut; the man was definitely a cop.

Gina had been Frank's waitress the first time he'd been in here, and he'd had most of his meals either here or at the Bob Evans across the way. She'd been crying that first day, and he'd asked about it. And Frank had heard the whole story.

He knew it was a mistake, as soon as he'd considered opening his mouth, but he hated to see a nice woman swinging from the gallows.

Of course, he should've left it all alone.

Stan was, according to her, an idiot. He drank and stayed out all night. And routinely and regularly kicked her ass. Frank had heard the same story a hundred times.

Instead of leaving it alone, he'd called her aside the next day and given her some advice. Stan and Gina were separated, but she was having trouble getting him to stay away. She'd been worried about his temper. Frank's list was easy, non-confrontational. But it looked like the husband had found an opportunity to discuss it with her.

"Stan, you have to leave," Gina hissed at him. "This is where I work—"

"You won't talk to me anywhere else," Stan said loudly. "You got me SUSPENDED!" His face was red, flushed—either the guy was embarrassed to be talking to her in public, or, more likely, he'd been drinking. Liquid courage, Ben Stone had called it.

"We don't have anything to talk about," Gina answered, standing her ground.

"Yes, we do," Stan said, his eyes wide, and lunged at her. Gina stumbled backward, knocking a paper calendar off the wall. Stan's hand swiped the air where she had just been.

Frank was on his feet.

Gina moved to the side and backed up against the window that looked out over the parking lot.

Stan stepped around the small counter and grabbed at her, latching a beefy fist onto her thin arm.

Frank knew he had two choices.

One, he could step up to the counter and chat the man up, try to get him to back off. Or, two, he could skip that and attempt to incapacitate the man immediately, though that would be difficult. They were in a very confined space. And Stan was a cop. And probably armed.

Frank decided to take option one.

"Hey, man," Frank said from across the counter. He kept his voice light, happy, non-confrontational. "The lady doesn't want any trouble. What do you say you let her go?" Frank said, smiling.

Stan turned and looked at Frank.

"Screw you, man," Stan said, spitting his words at Frank like bullets. "This is none of your business."

Frank pointed a thumb over his shoulder.

"They've got excellent coffee here," Frank said, smiling, keeping it light. A part of him was screaming to walk away, let it go. "I was enjoying a cup—actually, my fourth cup—when I heard you. It sounds like you're mad about something."

"Damn straight I'm mad," Stan yelled, gripping Gina's arm tightly. "She's leaving me!"

Frank caught the smell of alcohol on his breath and noticed the man's bloodshot eyes. Stan wasn't drunk, but he'd had a couple. Ben Stone had been right. He'd gotten an early start, kinda like Frank, but this guy obviously couldn't handle it.

"It's OK," Frank said calmly. "Sit down and have a cup of coffee with me. I've got some free time—tell me what's going on."

Gina piped up at that moment. And she managed to say the exact wrong thing.

"Let go of me, Stan," she said, struggling to break free of Stan's grip. "You're hurting my arm. This is Frank. He's been helping me figure out what to do."

Frank turned slowly and looked at her, shaking his head slightly. Seriously? Was she just trying to escalate this?

"So," Stan shouted, really looking at Frank for the first time. "You're the one that's been telling Gina to leave me, clear out my stuff?" Stan shouted at Frank. "I'm a cop! And now she had the locks changed. My keys don't work anymore! She's just not listening, and she's still my wife!"

Well, maybe it was better this way. At least Stan was mad at Frank now, focusing all of his anger on him. At least his grip on Gina seemed to have loosened.

Frank decided to take a gamble. He changed tactics midstream.

"Yeah, Gina is a peach," Frank said, smiling and turning to look at Gina. He ran his eyes up and down her body, smiling appreciatively, then nodded at Stan. "We've only been out a few times. But I'll tell you, she knows how to treat a man—"

Stan's face turned red, faster than Frank thought possible. Stan let go of Gina and turned, charging around the glass counter, coming at Frank like an angry bull seeing red.

Krav Maga was not a complicated martial art to master, but there were certain moves that worked better in tight, confined spaces, such as this one. Much of Krav was designed for fighting multiple foes at once, but some of the more acrobatic moves were centered around spinning. In fact, the martial art was similar to the Brazilian "capoeira" style, which involved so many spins and acrobatic moves that it looked like dancing.

Frank had trained others in Krav Maga for over ten years.

As Stan came around the counter, Frank stepped back to make room. It came as second nature, running through the checklist in his head. Assess the threat, verify the space requirements, check for bystanders. He'd taught it so many times, the patter of words was as familiar as an old song.

In just under a second, he grabbed Stan's arm and pivoted, backing away, using the man's forward momentum to spin Stan around, then using his free hand to grab Stan and shove him downward. In one smooth motion, Frank spun around and dropped the man and landed a knee square in the middle of Stan's spine, pinning him to the floor.

Stan screamed, probably a combination of surprise and the sudden pain from the twisted arm and hand. He struggled to turn over, kicking his legs and trying to buck Frank off, but the weight of Frank's body held him down.

"Settle down, now," Frank said quietly. He leaned in a little more, digging his knee into the man's spine, feeling the bones grind.

Stan let out a loud shriek, and the struggling ceased. One of Frank's hands was on the back of Stan's head, pushing his face down into the carpet. Frank's other hand was pulling upward on Stan's wrist, twisting it.

Frank let go of Stan's head and felt around to the back of his belt for where the cuffs should be, where they'd been for so many years, kept in a little pouch next to the gun on his belt. He felt at his belt for a moment, before he realized they weren't there anymore. It had been years since he carried cuffs, but the habit was hard to break.

Frank shook his head and looked up at Gina, who was staring down at Frank on top of her incapacitated, soon-to-be ex-husband.

"You better call the cops," Frank said.

It didn't take long before Frank could hear the sirens—this was one of their own, suspended or not. Frank waited patiently, one knee on Stan's back, until the police car and EMTs arrived.

Sergeant Burwell walked in, gun drawn, and assessed the situation. Frank nodded at him and put his hands up, then slowly stood up off of Stan, who rolled over loudly and began complaining to everyone within hearing distance.

Burwell looked from Stan back to Frank, who waited. Burwell escorted Stan outside—the man was rubbing his wrist and cradling one arm.

After a few minutes, Burwell came back inside the restaurant, his firearm back in the holster. He glanced in Frank's direction and then began taking statements. Frank had been talking to Gina, comforting her, but Burwell soon led her outside to get checked out by the EMTs. After Burwell got Gina settled in the ambulance, he waved in the window at Frank to come outside.

The parking lot of the Tip Top Diner was a hub of activity. The ambulance was treating Gina, and Stan was strapped to a stretcher inside the vehicle. Burwell directed Frank over to a patrol car, while another cop, a young deputy, was waving traffic out of the parking lot and keeping the area clear.

Stan saw Frank passing the ambulance and sat up, apologizing loudly. The fight was gone out of him, evaporated. Now the man was just flustered and sorry. Frank had seen it a thousand times—the fight was gone now, the fire in his blood quenched.

Gina didn't look like she was buying Stan's protestations and apologies. Another waitress stood with her, as the EMTs wound a bandage around her bruised arm. Her skin was already starting to turn blue.

Burwell stood by his car, working on the report.

"Did you have to break his arm?" Burwell asked.

Frank shrugged at the burly sergeant.

"He was making trouble," Frank said. "If I hadn't stopped him, he might have hurt the woman, or bystanders." He glanced up and saw Gina was sobbing while she talked to the female EMT.

"Stan's a cop," Burwell said defensively. "So technically, you've assaulted a police officer. That's a year, at least."

Frank nodded, thoughtful. He thought he detected a hint of bemused camaraderie in the man and took a chance.

"Yeah," Frank said. "But the guy's a real dick."

Burwell looked up, and a grin broke out on his face.

"That's true," he said.

Burwell went back to the paperwork, writing up the report. Frank watched, unsure of what to do next. He didn't want to be involved, of course, but it was true – he'd assaulted a cop, and in front of witnesses. While he wanted nothing more than to turn around and walk away, he couldn't afford to get thrown in jail, even for the day. Nothing could get in the way of his lunch with Laura.

So he said nothing.

Burwell glanced up. "Reports, huh? We're already spread thin, getting ready for the ransom drop later today."

Frank nodded. "My boss used to say the department was just like an outhouse – it didn't run without the paperwork," he said.

The burly sergeant nodded, and Frank thought he saw the hint of a smile.

"It's just that I don't really have time for this shit."

Frank nodded. "Sorry about that. But I couldn't just stand by and let him hurt her."

Burwell looked him in the eye. "So, you're happy to get involved in this, but you can't lift a finger when it comes to two kidnapped girls? Sorry, I'm having trouble figuring out your priorities."

"He got aggressive," Frank said quietly.

"Doesn't matter," Burwell said. "You call 911, or clear everybody out, or just draw down on him. I know you're carrying. But the assault charge – I can't make that go away. If Stan presses charges, it'll be up to a judge."

Frank shook his head. "I should have stayed out of it."

"Right."

"But he's a cop—he should know how to hold his temper. Don't you guys get trained?"

Burwell looked up sharply. "Of course he should have known better."

Frank shook his head.

"I don't think it would stick—too many witnesses saw him come in and push her around," Frank said. "Yelling like an idiot. Besides, I've been coaching her, getting her to take the steps she needed to take to get away from him. She told me a long story—sounds like everyone was on his side."

Frank looked at Burwell, the implication obvious. Had the cops been covering for one of their own?

Burwell nodded. "Yeah, maybe we shouldn't have taken his stories at face value. He said she was a crazy bitch."

Frank turned and looked at the ambulance, as they closed the back doors and prepared to leave. Gloomy rain clouds smudged the horizon.

"I don't know. I only know what she said," Frank said, nodding at Gina. "And I can tell when a woman is scared for her life. I told her what to do—change the locks, take a bunch of pictures, get his stuff out of the house. Any judge in the world will see him as the aggressor, coming to where she works."

"I know," Burwell agreed. "Gina came in a couple days ago and filed all the TRO paperwork. Surprised the hell out of a lot of people. That takes nerve, when your husband works there. Was that your idea?"

"Yeah," Frank nodded. A few drops of rain began to fall from the darkening sky above them. "I gave her my opinion. Once they start hitting…well, you know."

Burwell nodded.

"Like you said, he's a dick," Burwell conceded. Clearly, the man was starting to warm to Frank. "Always has been. But now I've gotta do a report and write everything up. He can press charges, but I doubt he will. I'll get statements."

Frank looked up at Burwell. Any normal person would thank Burwell. This could have been an ugly situation, a run-in that ended with a cop in the hospital. But Frank's mind was already on other things—getting disengaged from this situation, concentrating on his meeting later with Laura, leaving town. He didn't want anything to do with Burwell or anyone else. When Frank opened his mouth, Burwell was probably expecting a "thank you," or at least a kind word, from one cop to another.

Instead, Frank nodded curtly. "So, can I go?"

Burwell nodded, the half-smile fading from his lips. "You really are a piece of work, aren't you?"

Frank was taken aback.

Burwell leaned forward, his face turning red. "You aren't worried at all about this, are you? And you don't care at all about those kidnapped girls. You don't even care about Gina, either. So why get involved?"

Frank glanced back at where the ambulance had been, but he refused to get pulled into the debate again.

"We done here?" Frank asked quietly.

Burwell looked furious, but the man was a professional. After a long moment, he nodded.

"For now."

Frank nodded and walked back inside, not looking back. It was starting to rain. Out of the corner of his eye, he saw the ambulance leave.

He sat back down at his booth, ignoring the eyes of everyone in the restaurant. He picked up the paper again and started reading. After a minute or two, Frank picked up his drink and sipped at the half-empty mug. The coffee was cold.

12

Charlie shook her head. She had been so stupid.

After a few hours, a young man came to take care of them. He brought them their meals and untied them so they could use the bathroom a few times a day. Sometimes, at night, another person would come to let them use the bathroom, a woman with that screechy, horrible voice that sometimes echoed through the house. Charlie had never even seen the woman's face.

Other than that, she'd been on this bed for days and days. Charlie hoped it would all be over soon.

There was a scrape on the stairs—she'd seen the staircase railing through the open door yesterday, so she knew the bedroom was on the second floor—and she knew someone was coming. She'd heard the young man talking to two other people, the woman with the high, squeaky voice and another, older man, but only the young man talked to the girls. It was probably him.

The door unlocked and swung slowly open. The young man entered, carrying a tray.

"Do you need to use the restroom?" he asked, setting the tray down on a side table next to the bed.

She nodded, and he cut the zip tie around her wrist and let her go into the attached bathroom by herself. As she'd done in the past, she'd done her business and turned the water on to wash her hands. While the water ran, Charlie spent a short amount of time searching the bathroom for anything that could help her escape but found nothing. She climbed up onto the sink and peeked out the window, but only saw a roof sloping away and a tree. It looked too dangerous to try and escape that way. The window would be a tight fit as well.

She climbed down, shut off the water, and went back out into the bedroom.

"OK?" the man asked.

Charlie nodded.

"My Daddy is on the city council, you know," Charlie said, climbing onto the bed. "The police work for him. I'm sure they're looking for us."

The young man nodded. "I know. And don't worry—as soon as we get our money, you and Maya will be going home."

"Money?"

The man nodded again and set out the lunch—bologna sandwich, coleslaw, apple juice. Simple food. "It's called a kidnapping—the people pay a ransom, and then they get you back."

She thought about it a moment and picked up the sandwich, taking a bite.

"You asked for money for me. What if you don't get it?"

The man looked away.

"Have I told you about the ocean?" the man asked smiling.

She nodded. He'd told her before about San Francisco, a town that she'd heard about but never visited. This time he talked to her while she ate, telling her about the Fisherman's Wharf and an island jail in the middle of the harbor called "the Rock." And something called a Coit Tower.

13

Frank sat in her tiny living room on Tuesday, nervous.

It was just before noon. He'd gotten there early. She'd smiled and let him in and directed him to the threadbare couch and gone off to make coffee.

It was awkward, stiff, but at least she'd invited him in.

They hadn't seen each other in six years and had only spoken two or three times since. Laura had seemed very surprised by his call and that he was willing to drive all the way up to Ohio to have coffee.

Maybe it was because he was finally making the effort, or maybe enough time had passed. Or maybe it was Jackson. Perhaps she wanted her little boy to finally meet his grandfather. Frank had spent most of the drive up to Ohio from Birmingham thinking about that short phone conversation with his daughter, thinking about her words and the long spaces between those words. Trying to figure out what they meant.

Either way, she'd given him the address. At least it was a start.

It wasn't much of an apartment. He wondered if she would refuse if he offered her money, not that he had any to give. She had done what she could with the place: there was a small television near the front window, and a chipped coffee table separated the couch from an armchair that had seen much better days. In one corner of the room, a child's drawings and paintings were tacked to the walls above a second-hand dining room table that was piled with stacks of folders and paperwork. Fighting for room on the table were a pile of colorful construction paper, a box of crayons, and a toy robot.

But the place had the colorful, worn look of a house with kids—around the rest of the space that he could see, there were pictures and toys scattered about and drawings by Jackson in little frames.

Laura walked into the room—she was pretty, more than he remembered. Tall and blonde and pretty, like Trudy had been the first time he'd met her at that random "casual cotillion" in Baton Rouge during the summer of 1984. Trudy had breezed into the room and caught his eye with no effort. What had ever happened to that young girl, willing to date an impulsive military man and move away from Louisiana? Somewhere along the way, Trudy had changed into a person he didn't like anymore.

Or maybe he had changed.

He smiled at Laura. She was five years older than he remembered and much more independent. He could tell she had changed. Now she was a mother, and on her own, working a career and navigating life all on her own.

It made him suddenly sad. For her and for him. He'd missed so much.

He watched her walk across the room, carrying a small tray.

"I couldn't remember how you liked your coffee," Laura said, smiling at him.

"Just a little cream. Thanks."

She handed him a cup and set the tray down—on it were small, mismatched bowls of cream and sugar, along with a sleeve of sugar cookies. She took one and plopped down in the old chair, sitting back and nibbling on it, as he made his coffee. One thing he'd noticed about this new Laura was an air of confidence, out in the world, doing her thing, working hard and raising a child. He liked it.

Frank added the cream, then took a sip.

"Umm...that's good," he said, sitting back.

She smiled. "Thanks."

The room got very quiet again—each of them was probably waiting for the other to start. He looked around at the drawings and noticed a grouping of pictures on the table next to the TV. Two of Laura and Trudy and several of Jackson—he was at preschool right now—and Jackson with his mother. They were cute together.

None of Frank. Or Kyle, her grease-ball ex-husband, Jackson's father. The man had skipped out last year, leaving Laura to raise their son on her own. So Frank was in the same club as Kyle.

Frank nodded to the drawings and paintings tacked to the walls above the dining room table.

"Are those his?"

Laura followed his eyes and smiled.

"Jackson's really taken to preschool. He's enjoying learning his letters," Laura said. "The teachers are great, and he's getting along great with the other kids." Laura looked up at him and shook her head. "Kyle was nothing but trouble for me, but the move also delayed Jackson's start at kindergarten. But he's catching up, and loves learning."

Frank nodded.

"You were always good in school," he said.

She nodded and nibbled her cookie, waiting.

He turned and looked at the clock on the wall. It was an old clock, a white face with blocky, black numbers. He suddenly remembered the clock—it was from their old home in Louisiana, back before Trudy had moved out and taken Laura. It had always ticked too loud for him. Trudy had taken it with her, along with so many other things. How could he have not recognized it?

"You still drinking?" he heard her say.

Frank nodded, not looking at her. "Yeah, but I'm working on it. How's the job?"

"Good, good." Laura smiled at his obvious changing of the subject. "I'm at the new salon downtown, A Cut Above. Dumb name, I know, but they're very nice. I get plenty of customers and good shifts, and they give me nights off for Jackson."

Frank nodded. "Sounds like you like it there."

"It's okay. Not using my accounting degree at all, but it's work," she said, shrugging. "They just remodeled one of the buildings downtown," she said. "It used to be a little grocery store. These new owners fixed it up. Plus, it's next to DMs, the only pizza place downtown."

Frank smiled. He suddenly remembered that pizza had been her favorite food growing up. Was it still? How much had he missed? How much had changed?

"You like working there?" he asked. He needed to keep her talking. Listening to her talk was infinitely better than listening to that ticking clock on the wall, loudly counting down the seconds until this precious conversation was over.

"Yeah, it's better than down in Cincinnati," she said. "My last place, she nickel and dimed us about everything and charged us late fees if we didn't pay our chair rental on time. Plus, she would sit on our commissions for a month before handing them over."

Another pause began and threatened to drown the conversation. He hated these fits and starts, but he didn't want to do all the talking. Frank didn't want to come off desperate, even though, on some level, he wanted nothing more than to connect with this mysterious woman his little girl had become.

Frank leaned forward, setting the coffee cup down, and looked at her.

"Look...look," he began, looking at the tray on the table between them. "I just have to say this much, at least: I'm sorry. Sorry for the way things were. I know things were hard when you were growing up." The words raced out of him, escaping. Rats from a sinking ship. "You and Trudy—I was never around, and I wasn't always in the best shape when I was. I can't go back and fix any of that. But I'm...I'm trying to make up for it now, in my way. If I can."

It might have been the longest speech he'd ever given. It felt good, just getting it out there.

She nodded thoughtfully but didn't say anything.

"I know you don't want to hear about all of it," Frank said, looking at her. "You were there, even if you don't remember. But I was always off working, trying to close cases or investigate something or drink away the stress," he said, looking at her. "Anyway, it wasn't good for Trudy, or you, and after Katrina it got worse. A lot worse. Maybe if things had been different—"

"It's okay," she said quietly.

Frank stopped and looked at her, then slowly nodded. He wasn't sure if he was agreeing with her or encouraging her to keep talking or both, but he treasured those two words. He wasn't sure if this conversation would ever get to those words. And so quickly...

"Trudy...well, she hung in there," Frank continued. He felt like a person in church, giving confession. "Longer than anyone could expect, really." He couldn't remember the last time he'd said something nice about Trudy, or even thought something nice. He'd blamed her for so much—"

Laura just nodded and leaned forward.

"I mean it, Frank," she said. "It's okay."

He sat back and smiled.

"Thank you. Thank you for that," he said, then looked up at her, curious.

Laura smiled at him, and he saw a glimmer of the small girl she had been. "Too easy?"

He laughed. It sounded strange in his ears, a rare sound that he was not used to hearing. Frank was not the laughing kind.

"Maybe," Frank said, taking a sip of coffee. "You need to make me work harder."

Laura looked around at the art above the dining room table.

"Two years ago, I would have," Laura said thoughtfully. "But Jackson changed things. I'm...less angry, I guess. You hurt me, a lot. You hurt me and Mom—put us through a lot of mess. You made Mom so angry, for so long, that she doesn't even like to talk about it anymore."

Frank didn't know what to say.

"And you hurt me," she said quietly, not looking at him. "You were never there near the end, like you said, but I remember a time before, when we were close. We talked and had fun, and you and Mom and I used to go places. I remember a trip to Six Flags. Do you remember that trip?"

He nodded. He wasn't sure of the year, but he remembered the trip. The park was east of New Orleans, out near the Bayou Savage. It had been a good day—roller coaster rides and laughing on the merry-go-round. Amusement park food, greasy and wonderful.

"Yes, I remember," he said.

She nodded. "That was a good day. Things were okay. But then you got more and more into work, and things got bad between you and Mom. Fights, arguing. And then Katrina came, and you changed. You were different, and Mom was different, and everything fell apart. Just like the park."

He looked up at her.

"What do you mean?"

Laura laughed. "You don't know about it? That Six Flags is famous—the park was flooded during Katrina and abandoned afterward. There are pictures all over the Internet from people who have snuck in there in the years since. Creepy broken rides, tall weeds grown up through the boardwalks, rusted clown faces. Now it looks like the set of a horror movie. I think it's more famous now than it was before, when it was open."

Frank didn't know what to say. He still had fond memories of that park, and he'd been there many times. He didn't want to think about it abandoned, moldering into the ground.

"But people make mistakes, and things get screwed up," Laura continued. "That was my point. Look at me and Kyle. We went through a lot, and I have absolutely nothing to show for it, other than Jackson and a box of photos. And a lot of bad memories. That's one of the things I had to figure out—people make mistakes, even parents."

Frank nodded, not wanting to interrupt her now that she was talking.

"You know," she continued. "The whole time you're growing up, these people seem like rocks of stability. Your parents and other 'grown-ups.' And then, at some point, you figure it out: they're just people. Fallible, thick-headed. Even petty. It's a difficult realization, but freeing at the same time."

Frank didn't know what to say. His little girl had turned out to be a thinker. He'd always known she was good in school, smart. But this was a whole new level of insight, brought on by careful thought and experience. Brought on by time and introspection and maturity.

"You seem surprised," she said, smiling.

"I guess I am," Frank said, picking up his coffee and sipping at it again. "You just seem so…grown up."

She nodded. "Yeah. That happens."

Frank smiled and looked around at Jackson's drawings.

"I can't believe he's four," Frank said.

Laura nodded and grabbed another cookie. She sat back in the chair and folded her legs up underneath her.

"They have him in the three-times-a-week class," Laura said. It's more than I can afford, really. I'll have to figure out what to do next semester. But the schedule works really well with my job—lets me pick up extra shifts and appointments."

Laura was still staring at her son's picture.

"I'm glad he's at school," she said quietly. "It makes me feel safer. Every parent in town is freaking out because of the kidnapping. At least they haven't canceled school."

Frank frowned. He'd figured this would come up

"The missing girls?" he asked. "I've heard about it. I'm sure they'll find them."

Laura looked at him, her eyes shiny.

"You're sure?" she said, her voice suddenly sharp. "The girls were snatched on the way to school, right in broad daylight. Just a few blocks from here. And nobody saw a thing. A few of the parents are keeping their kids home."

"Most of the times, these situations turn out OK," Frank lied. He wasn't sure where this was going, but he didn't like—

"You worked a bunch of kidnappings, right?" she asked, looking at him. "How many came out OK?" Her eyes were so sharp, eyes like Trudy's, boring into him.

He couldn't look away and nodded slowly.

"OK, look, I'm not going to lie to you," Frank said. "There's been enough of that, and I'm looking for a fresh start. I'll tell you straight up, if that's what you're asking. Are you?"

She nodded soberly, her eyes wet.

"Okay," he said. "Look, they don't all turn out well. Most of them don't. But it's only been a week."

"Did you investigate a lot of kidnappings?"

Frank nodded carefully. He and Laura had never talked about his work before. With Trudy, this had always been dangerous territory.

"I don't know how you dealt with that," she said. "It's so sad and scary. I can't believe it's happened, here in this little town."

"Kidnappings like this are usually about money," Frank said. "so they can happen anywhere. It's actually better than an abduction. The recovery rate for kidnappings for ransom is much higher."

She nodded, listening.

"And there is a dialog going on," he continued. "The kidnappers are talking to the family, which is very good."

"Mom said the kidnapping cases were the worst for you," Laura said, surprising Frank. He couldn't imagine the two of them, sitting around the kitchen table, discussing Frank and his work. Talking about him when he wasn't around, debating what bothered him. But of course they had talked—they'd had no one else to talk to. Laura continued. "She said you would go days without talking, after they ended...badly."

He wasn't sure what to say. His new policy of complete and absolute honesty faltered when he looked at her—he could see she was frightened and unsure.

"Those cases were bad," he agreed. "But others ended well. I worked quite a few," he said. "New Orleans was a big city. We never lived in town, so you probably never really experienced all the hustle and bustle. There were many cases a year, and it was one of the things I specialized in."

"Until Katrina," she said.

He didn't answer. Frank wasn't really prepared to talk about that. It took him by surprise, but it shouldn't have—certainly she would want answers. Just like Trudy had wanted answers. But he had none to give. After a minute, he just nodded.

Another long, awkward pause threatened to settle over the room, and Frank didn't want to let the conversation lapse into silence. He'd had years of silence, and it felt like they were connecting, really starting to talk. He wasn't going to let St. Barts ruin this new opportunity. It had already ruined so many things.

Frank considered it for a moment. He didn't want to come off sounding prideful, or like he was bragging. But he needed to roll the dice—to change the subject and, perhaps, raise her opinion of him a tad.

"Actually, the local police have approached me. They asked me to help with the investigation," Frank said.

Her expression changed—a hint of a smile appeared.

"Really?"

"One of the officers came by my hotel room last night," Frank said. "He laid out the case for helping them. Not sure how they knew I was in town. It was nice to be asked, but I passed. Not a lot I can bring to the table."

Laura's face changed—she'd been smiling, but now it had morphed into a combination of confusion and anger. Not the emotion he'd been expecting. Or hoping for.

"You're not going to help?" she asked sharply.

"Ummm, no, I wasn't going to—"

"Why wouldn't you help them? They're just two little girls, out there somewhere. Scared," she asked, her eyes shiny again. "If you could do anything to help, you should. What if Jackson was missing?"

He was taken aback, confused by her sudden anger.

"No, that's different," he said, shaking his head. "Of course, if it were Jackson, I'd want to help."

"So what is it?"

"I'm not getting involved," he said, shaking his head. "I did enough of these types of cases, and I don't think I'd be any help anyway... besides, they have a Bureau guy, up from the Cincinnati office. What could an old retired cop add to the mix?"

She shook her head.

"I read the papers—we've got great police here in Cooper's Mill," she said. "Except for DUIs, crime is practically nonexistent. They wouldn't have asked you if they didn't really need the help."

He nodded. Frank had gotten that impression too, from Burwell. Laura looked at him, and he suddenly remembered a school play that she'd been in in elementary school. Her hair seemed similar, swept back and tied up in the back.

"I figured...I'm really just here to see you," Frank said, looking at her. "I don't want to get distracted. And I don't do these kinds of cases anymore." He could hear the panic starting to edge into his voice. He was losing ground, losing her.

"But if you can help out at all, people around here would appreciate it," Laura said, leaning forward. "People are scared, really scared. A couple of the officers' wives come into the salon. The case isn't going well."

He thought about what she was saying, then decided on a different tack.

"I'm surprised," Frank said quietly. "I figured you'd be happy to hear I was staying out. Didn't it drive you and your mom crazy, me being out in the world, all the time, in harm's way? I know Trudy hated it. She told me enough times."

Laura sipped at her coffee and nibbled another cookie before answering.

"I don't know," she said. "I guess it's different for me, now. When I was growing up, you were always gone, out helping other people. Even after we left and moved to Cincinnati, you stayed in Louisiana. Mom said you didn't get the hint."

Frank nodded slowly.

"But now that I have Jackson, I understand how helpless I would feel if he disappeared," she said. Laura was looking at the art on the wall again, and he felt his eyes drawn to them as well. "It makes me happy now, to know that you helped those people, people I never even met."

"I'm glad to hear it," Frank said. "But still, I don't think I would add anything to the case. Too many bad memories."

Like that kid in Atlanta, buried.

Frank and Ben Stone had worked together for almost a year and had traveled up from Florida to help out on a kidnapping case with connections to a counterfeiting case they had been assigned. Frank did the work, followed up on a weak lead, and broke the case wide open.

They had found the empty lot—reconstructed from a photo taken by a driver passing a suspicious vehicle. Frank had figured it out. He found the empty lot and dug up the buried cardboard box and opened it.

Frank would never forget that dusty, abandoned patch of dirt. According to the coroner, Frank had only been a few minutes too late.

"Too much history," he said, mostly to himself.

"Well," Laura said quietly, "if it were me, I'd want your help."

He looked down at the carpet and thought about it. Thought about her asking for his help—if it were Jackson, he wouldn't hesitate. Frank shut out the memory of Atlanta and tried to focus on the good cases, the ones that had turned out well. He had saved people, made a difference. After a moment, Frank nodded and looked at her.

"I guess…I guess I could think about it."

She smiled and put her hand on his. It was the first time she'd touched him.

"I think you could be more helpful than you think," his daughter said. "You can put all those skills to work, and if you can lend a hand, all the better. I remember a few of the things Mom told me. Didn't you work like fifty kidnappings?"

He nodded.

"Fifty-two solved. But each case was different," Frank said. "Some of them ended badly. Catching the kidnappers didn't always lead to a good ending. Sometimes the kids…they didn't make it. Or we never found them, and the kidnappers disappeared. Getting the groundwork done quickly was the key to keeping the victims alive."

They sat, chatting for a few more minutes, drinking coffee and eating cookies. He told her about some of the cases he had worked, good and bad. Of course, he held back some of the details. But it was nice. Just sitting here with her, talking, without her mother getting involved, or having their whole history dredged up again. It was all in the past, anyway.

"So, you really think I should do it?" Frank asked, after they had been talking about his past cases for a while. She had asked lots of good questions and not shied away from the ones that ended badly.

"Definitely," she said. "They are just scared little girls. Somebody has to help them, right?"

Frank nodded.

"OK, I'll think about it."

Laura nodded and handed him a cookie.

"Good," she said with a smile.

14

George carried the trays downstairs and into the kitchen, setting them on the large island that seemed to take up half the kitchen. Most of it was covered with old containers from takeout Chinese food. Chastity was at the dining room table, reading a fashion magazine.

"Well, at least they're eating," he said, putting the plates into the sink.

Chastity looked up.

"I don't care if they're eating or not. They can starve. When are we getting paid?"

Starting in again.

"I don't know, Chas. We'll get the ransom tonight, then leave it at the airport for the boss. He's got a whole plan. But the other guy's in charge. Him and the boss will work it out."

She shook her head and stood, walking over. He tried to ignore the fact that she was only wearing a pair of panties. She loved going around the house in next to nothing. It could be very distracting.

"You see what's going on here, Puddin'?" she said. "They're gonna get the money, and we'll be stuck here with the girls. How do you think this is going to go down?"

George nodded.

"Please don't call me that, Chas," he said. "You know I hate that."

She smiled as she approached, leaning into him.

"I know," she said.

"I know what you're thinking," he said, backing away from her. "But they're working on wrapping things up. That's what the boss said."

Chastity stood in front of him and crossed her arms, covering up her ample chest. It made it slightly easier for George to concentrate on what she was saying.

"You're an idiot," she said sharply. "What's to keep them from taking our money? Or what if they call the police anonymously on us? We're in jail for life, and they get away. With the money. No, I think we should just bail."

"And leave the money?"

"There ain't gonna be no money!" she screeched, exasperated. The barn owl was back. "We're gonna get screwed out of our money anyway, so why not take some of that pot and what money we do have and leave?"

George thought about it for a minute, looking down at the ground. It was hard to think, staring at Chastity. She was so pretty. But she had a point.

"We don't have a car that'll get us far." he said.

She nodded. "Yes we do, Puddin'. The Corolla works fine, and that Mustang is just sitting out there."

He shook his head.

"The boss knows those cars, knows the plates. He'd catch us in a minute."

"Don't worry," she said. "If I want to, I can get a car. I can go into any bar in Troy right now and some idiot will let me borrow his car. I know how to get guys to do what I want. Or, better yet, bring him back here and tie him up—then it would take longer before the guy reports it. And he'd take the fall for the girls."

"I dunno, Chas. That seems awfully risky," George said, not even wanting to start that conversation about what she'd need to do, or show, to get a car. He didn't like to think about what she did when she went into town. She would always come home late, or some random car would drop her off a mile or two up the road. And she always had money and sometimes a little bag of coke or weed. George shook his head. "I'm not ready to go yet, but I'll call the boss and see what's going on. I'll tell him the Mustang is ready, and we're ready. But what about the girls?"

Her face went red, and for a second George thought she might punch him. She got exasperated a lot.

"George! Jesus," she shouted. "I don't give a shit about the girls. I'm worried about us." She stepped closer and putting her hands on his shoulders, pressing her breasts against his crossed arms. He looked down at them. She kept talking, but he didn't look up. "We gotta get ready to go, if we have to," she purred. "Get packed, so we can leave in a second. Right?"

He nodded. He always found it difficult, at times like these, to contradict her.

15

Long shadows stretched between the buildings downtown as Chief King and the rest of the CMPD stationed themselves at various locations around the historic downtown shopping district. To the west, a train rumbled through town at exactly 5:58 pm, eight minutes ahead of the time for the ransom drop.

The money was ready and in a black leather satchel, as requested. Nick Martin was standing next to King on the steps of the Cooper's Mill Public Library, nervously adjusting the bag on his shoulder. King waited, looking east up Main Street. On the steps around them, and around the entrance to the library, a dozen carved and decorated pumpkins littered the stoop. Other Halloween decorations hung throughout the downtown, decorating every shop window. Eight-foot-tall corn shocks adorned each light pole, a simple but effective project by a downtown booster organization that really gave the downtown a "harvest time" feel.

"$1,000,000 is a lot of money," King said, making conversation. Nick Martin was fidgeting, and King needed him calm and collected. Even with cops stationed all over town, and roadblocks to the east and west and south, by the tomato cannery, things could go wrong in a hurry.

"It's worth it," Nick responded.

Chief King was still trying to gauge whether or not the father was in on it. He looked sufficiently nervous, but King had heard about things like this going down before—not in Cooper's Mill, of course, but in larger towns. Kidnappings for ransom were rare and complicated, and Chief King knew they almost always turned out to involve someone in the family or close to the family.

Nick Martin was a local celebrity, though, so that made the demand for a huge ransom a little more believable. King knew that everyone in town thought that Martin was wealthy, mostly because of where he lived and what he did for a living. But King had learned over the last week the truth: the Martins weren't as well off as everyone thought. Much of their "Martin Construction" company money had gone away with the housing and construction downturn in 2008 and 2009. The rest went to keeping the lights on in their offices and the Martin's palatial home on Hyatt Street, one of the largest in town.

In fact, some of the money in the black leather satchel hanging from Nick Martin's shoulder was borrowed. There had been no way the man could gather the needed funds that quickly. Nick had already sold off two large investments, including his share in a Dayton condominium project near the Dayton Dragon's stadium. After all that, he'd still ended up borrowing money from the FBI.

It had been an interesting discussion, helping Nick decide what to sell off. Nick Martin had wanted to keep the projects that might be the most lucrative in the future, but his focus was clearly his daughter and raising the money. He'd also been partial to some of the smaller projects. King and Nick Martin and the other senior officers had been sitting around the big conference room table in the police station, going over the finances. That was yesterday afternoon, after the call from the kidnappers.

The FBI guy had kept his mouth shut—he evidently didn't have any experience in the area. Sergeant Graves, one of them at the table, suggested Nick Martin sell off the Holly Toys Lofts project. Nick said he had a lot of dead money tied up in that project. Weeks before, his business partner, Matt Lassiter, had offered to buy him out. The building was a former toy factory and a local landmark of sorts. When the property had come onto the market, Nick and Matt had bought it, planning to turn the massive brick building into block of luxury condos. It would have been a smart play, as well—there were no apartments or condos that close to the historical downtown, and the units would have been beautiful, fully-appointed homes. And they would have cost a pretty penny. But then the market tanked. The building was still sitting empty, with only one condominium completed as a model unit.

But Nick evidently had a soft spot for the property. "I think that could be very lucrative," Nick had said, frowning. "I used to play on the tracks right there."

After a long discussion, they had finally helped him figure out two deals to close, including selling the Holly Toys building. In a matter of two hours, he'd raised almost $850,000.

King wished he could pick up the phone and make that kind of money appear from thin air.

The FBI Liaison, Ted Shale, arranged for the rest, and now they were here on the stone steps of the Library, waiting. The clock on the Monroe Township Building began to chime, ringing loudly, six times.

"Okay, six minutes. Everyone ready?" King asked into his radio. He had cops stationed on both ends of Main Street in squad cars, along with several more in discrete locations. There were two in plain clothes, Detective Barnes and Deputy Peters, sitting on the wooden benches in front of O'Shaughnessy's Restaurant. King also had police in from

Dayton and Troy to help man the roadblocks downtown. There was even a roadblock uptown near the Taco Bell, blocking access to the highway.

"Yup, we're good," the voice came back. It was Sergeant Burwell, stationed on the east end of Main, near Ricky's. That was the only way in and out of town to the east, unless you jogged several blocks north or south—and both directions were covered.

"Yeah, me, too," answered Sergeant Graves over the radio. He was up at the corner of Fifth and Main, next to the railroad tracks.

Burwell and Graves were good cops. Along with Detective Barnes, they were his three top guys, and King would feel comfortable with any of them taking over after he was gone. With Burwell blocking access to the east, and Graves making sure no one got over the tracks and uptown, the place was bottled up tight.

There was no way these kidnappers were getting away. And even if the real kidnappers sent a go-between to retrieve the money, capturing them would put the investigation on the fast track to recovering the girls.

King nodded to Nick Martin, who started down the steps and started walking slowly up the sidewalk east, up Main Street.

Nick passed the alley and the Harvest Moon Cafe, another popular downtown restaurant that featured a rooftop lounge. As Chief King watched, Martin passed the toy store, passing in front of the oversized Lego people in front, and stopped in front of the Italian restaurant on the corner, waiting for the light.

King scanned the pedestrians and traffic. It was a Tuesday evening, so there were quite a few people out window shopping. King had chosen to not shut down all vehicular traffic in and out of downtown to make the place look busy. He thought it might spook the kidnappers if the place was a ghost town. But now, with several cars cruising up and down Main, he was regretting that decision.

When the light changed, Nick Martin crossed the street and stopped in front of the Old Hotel, a collection of shops built into an old hotel on the corner of Second and Main. The intersection constituted the center of Cooper's Mill. Although all the streets downtown were numbered westward from the canal, this was the busiest intersection in town.

Nick Martin took the black leather bag off his shoulder and set it on the lip of a large, decorative trash can, attached to the sidewalk in front of the Old Hotel. King watched as Nick Martin tipped the zipped black bag over—it fell through the round opening and into the trash can. Martin glanced around and, unsure what to do next, retraced his steps, crossing Second Street and heading back toward the Library and Chief King. After a long minute, Martin walked up and stood next to the Chief.

"Now what?"

King nodded at the bag. "We wait."

Ten minutes passed with nothing happening. Three small groups of pedestrians walked in front of the trash bin, but no one reached inside. Another group of shoppers admired the Halloween displays in the front windows of A World Apart, a home decorating shop across the street from the toy store.

Chief King stood next to Nick Martin, as they watched impatiently up the street, but nothing was happening. A breeze stirred the fallen leaves and blew them down the street, skittering against the sidewalk and gutter.

16

On the benches in front of O'Shaughnessy's, directly across the street from the trash bin, the two plainclothes cops watched while carrying on a fake conversation.

"This is bullshit," Detective Barnes said under his breath. "They should have been here by now, if they were coming."

Deputy Peters kept his eyes on the trash can across the street. Even though he was the youngest man on the CMPD, he knew as well as anyone that these next few minutes could be the most important moments of the investigation. "Yup. Though I'm not sure how cursing is going to help."

Barnes looked him. "What?"

"Cursing," Deputy Peters said. "You know it's just a crutch, right? My mom used to say that smart people can figure out other words to say."

Barnes shook his head and looked back at the drop location. "Well, I'm your superior, and I sure as shit don't agree," he said, smiling.

A young blonde woman in a short skirt exited the doors from O'Shaughnessy's, her long hair blowing in the breeze. She turned and started up the sidewalk in front of the two policemen, and Peters noticed her out of the corner of his eyes. She was under dressed, to say the least, for the crisp weather. She was wearing a very short skirt, long brown boots, and one of those tight push-up tops that made her breasts look like dogs sitting up for a treat.

As she passed in front of the men, they both turned to look at her. She smiled at them and then stumbled awkwardly, falling to the sidewalk and cursing loudly. Her purse fell to the ground, and the contents scattered on the sidewalk—wallet, keys, money, even a deck of playing cards. Dollar bills fluttered in the air and blew away.

"Oh, come on!" she yelled, pulling at her top.

Both of the police officers stood to help her. Deputy Peters couldn't help but notice that her small skirt had ripped in the fall. A hint of purple panties showed from underneath.

"Are you okay?" Detective Barnes asked, leaning over her. He was hurriedly helping the young woman. Peters thought he was trying to get the woman out of an active police scene.

She smiled up at him, a hand over her breasts. "I think I'm okay, but I popped out of my top!"

Barnes smiled at Peters, his eyebrows going up.

The woman fumbled at her top, her breast flattened with one hand as she worked it back into the tight shirt. Barnes and Peters gathered up her purse and the items that had spilled out. Cigarettes, the wallet, money, and a deck of playing cards, which had gone everywhere. Coins littered the sidewalk. Peters fumbled with the cards and dropped some of them as he tried to hurry, gathering them up while trying to keep one eye on the trash can across the street. It took them a minute to gather the items.

From up the street, someone was shouting.

Barnes looked up and saw Chief King and the father of the kidnapping victim. They were both running down the sidewalk in front of the toy shop, pointing.

"He's got the bag!" Chief King was yelling. "He's got the bag!"

Peters and Barnes turned. They saw a young man running up Main Street away from them, away from the trash bin.

He had the bag.

The young man was in his twenties, scraggly hair, and wearing a camouflage jacket. He sprinted across the street, catty-corner away from the cops and the woman on the ground, and ran up onto the sidewalk on the O'Shaughnessy's side of the street, heading east. He ran past the Clean Soap store and ducked into the new antique store just past it.

The cops bolted after him. Deputy Peters could hear King shouting into his radio for Sergeant Burwell and the other police at the eastern roadblock to leave their positions to assist.

In moments, Barnes and Peters chased the young man into the new antique store, though the young man had gotten a good head-start. Two years ago, this had been a small video game store known as the Big Robot Game Café. Deputy Peters had been in here on a few occasions. It had been a unique, play-by-the-hour video game store where kids paid to play video games on big screen TVs. They had occasionally held overnight events and costume parties for the youth that showed up to play, but it hadn't taken off. Peters had dropped in once in a while to chat with the owner, who had gone on to be a writer for the local paper. The business had closed in 2010, and the space was now occupied by a new store, Elise's Antiques.

He and Barnes burst in the door, looking around. There was no one there.

"A kid just come in here?" Barnes shouted into the store, his gun out. "Hello?"

Peters looked around. He could see the large sales floor in front of them, covered with antiques. To the left was a hallway that ran back to other rooms, and a staircase that ran upward. To the right a storeroom. Two displays of merchandise were knocked over, and a table that had been upended, its contents strewn across the carpet.

"Up the stairs!" Barnes said to Peters, pointing. Peters turned and sprinted up the wooden stairs that led to a loft area, piled high with old furniture. In one corner stood an old jukebox, and an older gentlemen stooped over it, repairing the front.

"Excuse me—did anyone come up here?" Peters asked.

The old man turned and shook his head, surprised by the interruption. "Nope, been slow all day. Why?"

"We're pursuing a suspect," Peters said quickly. "He came in here and disappeared."

The old man nodded. "I heard something downstairs, but I thought it was the wind. You might check out back."

Peters was confused. "There's a back door?"

"Off the storeroom," the old man said slowly. "There's a curtain."

Peters shook his head and ran back downstairs. He saw Barnes coming back up a short hallway that led to two rooms and a bathroom in the back.

"Nothing," Barnes said. "Storeroom and three other rooms that branch off the hallway but nothing else. You?"

Peters shook his head and pointed. "The owner says there's a back door, off the storeroom."

Barnes shook his head. "No, I looked in there."

Together, they bolted behind the sales counter and into a small storeroom. The room was piled high with boxes and furniture. One corner was free of boxes. The wall was draped by a floor-to-ceiling curtain.

Barnes walked over and pulled it aside. Behind the curtain was a door to the outside. Peters could see light coming in through a security peephole in the door.

"Oh, Jesus. I didn't see it there."

Barnes yanked the door open.

Behind the antique store was a large, unkempt lot. The last time Peters had seen it, the lot had been filled with scrub brush and gravel, but the new occupants of the shop had converted half of it to an outdoor shopping area. Old doors leaned up against the adjoining buildings, and vintage bathtubs and shutters, marked for sale, hunkered in the short grass. A low fence ringed the merchandise. It was broken only by a hinged gate that stood open, leading to the other half of the back lot, nearest the alley, used for employee parking.

Across the alley, which ran east to west, was the large parking lot for the new A Cut Above Hair Studios. He remembered the parking lot, which had caused quite a bit of controversy related to its previous owner, a small grocery store. Across Dow Street from the parking lot, another alley ran south away from downtown.

In the alley, Peters saw a car, racing away. It looked like an old Mustang.

"Barnes, look," Peters said, pointing.

Detective Barnes cursed under this breath and tabbed the radio at his shoulder. "Dispatch, suspect escaped—he ran out the back of the old Big Robot. He must've had a car waiting here by the alley. He's in an orange Mustang, '70s or '80s, headed south in the alley between First and Second streets."

Chief King came on the radio.

"Roger that, Barnes. Burwell, other units head south to Broadway to intercept. He's probably heading for Canal Road and points south and east."

Peters nodded. It was just about the only way out of town heading south on that side of the tracks.

"Meet you out front," Barnes answered into the radio, shaking his head.

They walked back inside, thanking the proprietor, who was picking up merchandise that had been knocked over. They apologized for the excitement, then walked out to the front steps and saw Chief King, who looked at them.

"How did you lose him?"

"There was a back door I didn't know was there," Barnes said. "The space has several small rooms, which we cleared first. He must've had a car waiting in the lot behind the store."

Peters spoke up. "When it was the Big Robot place, I used to come in here all the time. Never knew there was a back door. I always thought it was just storage."

King nodded.

"Let's see," Chief King said, starting into the store.

"I'm gonna help the girl," Peters said.

King stopped and looked.

"What girl?"

Deputy Peters turned and looked. The sidewalk in front of O'Shaughnessy's was empty.

"There was the girl that fell," Barnes said, looking up the street in both directions. "She tripped and tore her skirt, and...oh crap."

King shook his head.

"I saw her, too. She was attractive, I'll give you that. But I can't write this off as coincidence. She was gone when we got here, so either she recovered remarkably quickly—"

"Or she was in on it," Barnes said.

King nodded. At their feet, several of the young woman's playing cards skittered through the gutter to join the carpet of fallen leaves.

17

The car raced away from downtown Cooper's Mill, heading south, weaving through the tight alleyway before coming out in a parking lot that fronted Broadway. George knew the town of Cooper's Mill very well. He took Broadway to Second, turned left, then right on German and came out on Third. He turned left again, following Third until the road abruptly swerved to the right, turning up and over the train tracks behind Maple Hill Nurseries.

This had been one iffy part of the plan—if a train had been passing through town, George might have been trapped on this side of the tracks until the train was gone. Bad idea, with a big bag of money sitting next to you and the cops behind you. Fortunately, the boss had double-checked the train schedule. It had accounted for the odd time required from the ransom drop. They needed to time it so there were no trains.

Across the tracks, the road became Maple Hill and wound between several large greenhouses and warehouses behind the retail Maple Hill Nurseries operations. Maple Hill Nurseries took up dozens of acres of land on the south side of town, but nobody ever came back here, unless they worked at Maple Hill. The whole area was taken up with greenhouses and loading docks and employee parking lots. The rarely-used road continued south, away from the greenhouses, and crossed a tiny, one-lane bridge, screened by an overgrowth of trees. Half of the people in town probably didn't even know this bridge was there. Passing through a large stand of trees and over a thin, dark creek, the road emerged back into the sunlight, coming out on the northern edge of Maple Hill Cemetery.

The car snaked through the headstones and stopped near the exit to Hyatt Street, well south of the downtown area and the roadblocks the police officers had set up. George stopped under a large tree and idled quietly.

While he waited, he glanced over at the leather satchel. He'd been told what to do with the contents.

First, he carefully opened the bag. Even though he'd been assured against it, there was a chance there would be an explosive dye pack inside. George had been told about dye packs, which are used in nearly 75% of bank robberies in the U.S. and usually consisted of a hollowed-out stack of real bills that would explode on a timer, staining nearby money and the thief with a red dye.

George opened the bag carefully, but nothing happened. He took out one pack of money at a time, flipping slowly through it, looking for anything odd. He found a thin, metal device hidden inside one stack of money and pulled it out—it was a tiny GPS device—and tossed the money into the back. He continued through the stacks, finding several more metal devices while he waited.

After a minute, he heard the low buzzing rumble of a small, gasoline-powered scooter coming down Hyatt Street toward the cemetery. He looked up and saw the scooter with a young woman driving. The vehicle was nothing more than a push scooter but, with the attached engine, it puttered along Hyatt, moving quickly in front of St. Jude's Catholic Church. George got out and opened the trunk. When the scooter reached the entrance to the cemetery, the woman directed it off the pavement and over to the car. She climbed off.

"Everything go OK?"

"Yup," Chastity nodded. "But I tore my skirt."

Indeed, her tiny white skirt was torn, showing off a stripe of purple beneath. He folded the scooter in half, lifting it up into the trunk. She straightened her skirt and climbed into the passenger seat.

The young man in the camouflage coat slammed the trunk lid and got back into the car. He put the Mustang in gear and smiled at her, then pulled the car out onto Hyatt and turned south, driving out of town.

He took Evanston and then a series of back roads, heading in the general direction of the airport.

"Don't worry," George said, handing her a bottle of water and nodding at the large leather bag between them. "When we get to San Francisco, I'll buy you another one. Heck, I'll buy you twenty. Really excellent ones. Here, I got about half of the money checked."

She smiled and opened the bag, searching for more trackers. As she found them, she tossed the packets of money into the back. She finished searching all the money and put the trackers—they had found almost a dozen of them—back into the black satchel. She twisted the lid off of the bottle of water and dumped the contents into the bag, keeping the bottle. He drove on for another quarter mile and then, at the next corner, he slowed. She tossed the bag into the ditch next to the road.

"That will work?" she asked.

George nodded and turned the car, heading to the airport. "The boss said the GPS trackers will lead to here, water will kill the bugs and anything sewn into the lining of the bag. By the time they find the bag, we'll be long gone."

She smiled and climbed over the back. He couldn't help but steal another peek at her panties as she wiggled over the seat. Chastity grabbed another bag, a green duffel, and started stuffing the money inside, checking each stack carefully, again, for trackers they might have missed.

They were to leave the money inside the Mustang in the long-term parking at Dayton International Airport, taking the waiting Corolla home. Someone else would retrieve the cash and probably just leave the car at the airport. It was great place to ditch a car. So many people came and went. And the boss had said that any surveillance footage of the parking lots would take weeks or months to process.

"You know," she said from the backseat. "Once we know this money is clean, we should just keep driving, Puddin'. We've got the money, and this car, and..."

George shook his head.

"Nah, the boss would find us," George said. "Even out in California. And this car is stolen anyway. No, let's do the deal and wait for our cut, then we can leave together."

He glanced in the mirror at her, but she wasn't looking at him. Chastity was staring out the window, deep in thought.

18

"What a god-awful mess."

Chief King was not happy. A million dollars, and their best leads, gone.

He and the other police officers and investigators sat around the police station conference room table. The disaster known as the ransom drop was hours ago, and they had met to try and figure out what had gone wrong.

"I don't even know where to start," King said, looking at the others around the table. "I can't believe we've got nothing. Even after they got away, I assumed we'd pick up the trackers, or get a sighting, or something. How did they get away?"

No one answered him.

"First of all, we didn't cordon off the right streets," King said. "Agent Shale? Graves? You guys set up the roadblocks."

Everyone turned to look at FBI Agent Shale and Sergeant Graves, waiting for an answer. Graves glanced at Shale, who didn't answer.

"We blocked the major roads in all directions, as you know," Graves finally said, looking at notes on a piece of paper in front of him. "But the driver used the narrow alleys. He had a car hidden behind one of the downtown shops. The young man, described as early 20s with a camouflage jacket and short brown hair, grabbed the money from the trash receptacle outside of the Old Hotel and crossed the street while our plainclothes were distracted by the female. Presumably, she was working with him. He ducked inside the shop, as everyone saw, and went through to the waiting car."

"Had to be a local," Deputy Peters said. "And those alleys are hard to navigate. How fast were they going?"

"Not sure," Graves answered. "Pretty fast. By the time we figured out, they were at least two miles south of town."

The Chief shook his head. "Sixty miles an hour down those narrow alleys? That's impossible."

"That's what happened, as far as we can tell," Graves said. "I thought we had them boxed in, between the river and the tracks, but they went south out of town, crossing near Maple Hill Nurseries and coming out by the cemetery.

The Chief nodded. He knew that back road well; it was popular with teenagers trying to get a little privacy. He'd shooed plenty of cars off that little stretch of road. He turned and looked at Agent Shale.

"No one was stationed on Canal Road?"

Shale looked at the Chief but didn't answer. Chief King was starting to get the feeling he was lecturing a surly teenager for not doing their homework.

Finally, Graves spoke up again. "Yes, but further south. We couldn't know they would take the alleys and skirt the roadblock. It was a lucky guess, on their part, to go west. If they had gone east, we would have caught them at Kyle Park, at the roadblock on Canal road. They just got lucky, sir."

The room went quiet.

Chief King didn't know what else to say. They were back to square one. He shook his head, livid, and looked around.

"Where did Nick go?" he asked.

"I took Mr. Martin home, sir," Deputy Peters said. "He was pretty shaken up when they got away."

King was so agitated, he couldn't sit still. He stood and started pacing in a circle around the table.

"Well, that's it," King barked, furious. "Our best, and really only lead, gone.

Deputy Peters leaned forward. "Well, we do have good descriptions on both of them. If they're local, someone will recognize them, especially the girl."

King nodded. It was something, at least.

"Okay," he said. "We need to get sketches made. Get the artist in here tonight and get the sketches out to all local precincts, especially those to the south, where the car went," King said. "And let's do another round of interviews—see if anyone knows these two."

"We should polygraph everyone again," Agent Shale volunteered. "See if anyone—"

Chief King put his hand up.

"I think we've done enough of that," King said, shutting him down. "And putting you on point on this isn't working. You had the 'blocks in all the wrong places."

The young agent looked up at the Chief, and King could tell the kid was trying to decide whether to argue or not.

"I was going by the book—"

"Field experience," the Chief said, sitting back down. It came out louder than he thought it would, but he didn't care. "You should get some. Especially before coming in here and telling people what to do.

Experience tells you when to follow the book and when to ignore it."

Agent Shale looked down at the table. King looked around at the rest. "Anyone else?"

There were no takers.

"Okay, then get to work."

The rest of the police department stood and filed away, talking quietly among themselves. No one approached King or tried to talk to him. He knew that meant they were all out of ideas.

Agent Shale looked at King for a long time, like he was trying to decide what to say. King thought he might be trying to apologize but wasn't sure how. After a time, Shale simply stood up, nodded at King, and walked away.

The Chief stared down at his notes, flipping through all the sheets of his current pad, #4 for this investigation. For the first time during this investigation, he had nothing. No searches, no files, no information that needed to be gathered. He had all the information already, but it simply didn't line up.

He sat back and looked around at the others. Some were hunched over their phones or flipping through computer screens. Others had simply left. King didn't see Agent Shale anywhere.

King's cousin, Deputy Peters, was sitting across the room, looking at King and shaking his head. After a second, he got up and walked over.

"You okay?" Peters asked.

"This case doesn't add up," King said.

Peters nodded, sitting. "You've been doing this a lot longer than I have, Jeff. What do you do when you have to start over, and redo it all from scratch?"

King shook his head.

His cousin looked at him, and King could tell the young man was worried. "What do you do when you're stuck?"

"I don't know," he said, but he had one more idea. "Will you get me some coffee? Have Lola make a couple pots, if she's still here. It's going to be a long night."

Deputy Peters stood and left, and King gathered up all of his files. He went back to the beginning, grabbing the other notepads from his desk and spreading them out on the conference room table. He scanned each, flipping through them slowly. He looked at pages and pages of notes: his first walk-through of the crime scene, interviews with everyone involved, thoughts about the ransom call and the Martins. Notes on some of the anonymous phone calls that had come in to the tip line. And, near the end, details he didn't want to forget about the botched ransom drop.

Peters returned with two cups of coffee and sat, not interrupting the Chief's process.

King reviewed all the other details he'd jotted down—unimportant at the time but still captured in the lined yellow pages. Which volunteers had signed up to help with the park searches. The weather each day of the investigation. Recorded times of phone calls with other agencies. Notes from his phone conversation with the Bureau office in Cincinnati, before they sent Agent Shale. Calls from concerned citizens. Pages and pages of notes and drawings and reminders—

He spotted something he'd forgotten, a loose end he'd never followed up on. King looked up at Peters, then held up the pad and pointed to a scribbled note in one corner of a lined yellow page. In King's blocky script, it read WHO IS FRANK HARPER?

"That's what you do, Deputy," King said. "You bring in fresh eyes."

19

A few minutes later, Chief King walked out of the police station. It was raining.

He was immediately assaulted by flashing lights and shouting voices. The press, who had been following every development in the case with their usual morbid excitement, were positively foaming at the mouth after this afternoon's botched ransom drop. Word had gotten out almost immediately, somehow, and he and Agent Shale had held a press conference at eight p.m., only minutes after they returned from searching for, and finding, the black bag that had once contained the ransom. They had found only the ruined trackers.

All the print and local TV stations were still there. The TV reporters were waiting to do live shots on the evening news at 10 or 11, depending on the station.

"Chief! Any news?" one of them shouted out. The others gathered around King.

"Have you made any progress on identifying the driver?" another one yelled.

Chief King shook his head. "We may know more by morning," he said and pushed his way through the ring of reporters and cameramen.

"What about the Martin family? How are they holding up?" King recognized the voice. It was Ken Meredith from CM-TV, their local public access channel. In a normal situation, he would have stopped and answered his question, but King knew he had to ignore the man. Rule number one with the press: "just keep walking."

He got to his police cruiser and drove away. Photographers braved the falling rain and chased him to his car, flashes of light breaking the night, as he was photographed leaving the station. Didn't those photographers have anything better to take pictures of? As excited as the reporters were, King was surprised none of them followed him away from the station.

Deputy Peters had called around and found out where the guy was tonight. He didn't live in the area but was just visiting, staying at the Vacation Inn. The night manager had told Peters where to find him.

King drove downtown and found a parking space near Ricky's. He almost never went in there while he was on duty, but tonight it couldn't be helped.

He headed inside. Even with the cold rain falling outside, it was stuffy and warm in the bar. King saw a dozen furtive glances meet his as he walked in and looked around. Having a cop in here would make a few people nervous.

King nodded at Rosie, the bartender and owner.

"Hey, Chief," she said, smiling. "Get you something?" she asked good-naturedly. She knew, as well as anyone in town, that he didn't drink.

"Thanks, Rosie. Just in for a minute."

King looked around and spotted the guy instantly. He was one of the few people sitting alone. King walked up to his table.

"Mind if I join you?"

The man looked up. King was struck by his eyes, how deep and penetrating they appeared. He looked like a thinker, but a pissed-off one. And half in the bag.

Maybe this was a bad idea.

Mr. Harper sat back and looked at King, then waved at the seat across from him.

"It's a free country."

The Chief sat down. The guy looked like he was past help—either past anyone helping him or him helping King with the case. This Frank Harper person epitomized "rough around the edges."

Chief King set his latest yellow pad and a folder down on the table between them. The tab on the edge read "Frank Harper," in Deputy Peter's precise handwriting. For someone who was such a klutz, he sure had perfect handwriting.

"I know why you're here," Harper said, nodding at Chief King. "And I'm sorry. I can't help. Believe me, I thought about it," he said, raising the beer he was working on—there were four other empties already on the table—and waved it at King. "But I do wish you luck."

"Is that why you decided not to help when Sergeant Burwell asked for assistance?" the Chief asked, nodding at the beer in Harper's hand. "Cutting in to your 'me' time?"

The man looked up, and King could see he'd struck a nerve.

"I figured you'd be talking to me soon," Harper said, glancing around the bar. "Maybe about your Stan situation, but more likely about your case. That ransom drop was a fiasco." Harper glanced around, and King wondered what he was thinking. "I couldn't care less," Harper continued. "But the news is all over it—ransom paid, kidnappers sighted, kidnappers escape. Sounds like Mayberry."

King looked at Harper sharply.

"Yes, we had a couple of missteps," King admitted. "But Stan is suspended. We didn't realize the extent...anyway, I don't appreciate being lectured by—"

"Screwed the pooch, I'd say," the man said. "A wife beater working in your office is bad enough. How many of your guys looked the other way on that one? But honestly, you looked like a cornered animal at that press conference. That FBI kid behind you was just staring at the floor." Harper laughed, sharp and cold. "He looked like he'd just been grounded."

Chief King didn't know what to say. The assessment was harsh and painfully accurate, but King was most surprised by the man's sudden sobriety.

King tapped on the yellow pad on the table. The page was covered with notes and scribbles. In one corner, it read "Birmingham Office" and "N.O.P.D.—Retired" and "St. Bartholomew's Parish Hospital."

"We need a hand," the Chief said, shaking his head. "This is something we don't have a lot of experience with. You do, or so your case file says."

The man didn't respond.

"Why won't you help? It's standard, helping out other offices. Your file said you worked as a liaison with the FBI on several cases. Surely you worked with other jurisdictions before you retired. And you've got experience with kidnappings, more than anyone around here—"

"You don't need my help," Harper said quietly, almost too low from Chief King to hear it. Harper was staring at his bottle, then looked up at King. "I think you're just looking to spread the blame around a little. Today was a mess; you should get the Bureau to send you a more experienced agent. I'm assuming that was his horror show?"

King nodded as Rosie walked up to the table.

"One of my customers misbehaving?" she asked, picking up the empties.

King shook his head. "No, everything's fine."

"Fine?" she said, looking around and lowering her voice. "Really? My sales are off by half since you breezed in here, Chief."

The Chief glanced around and noticed how many people were nursing nearly-empty bottles. They probably thought he was here on a drunk-driving sting.

"Don't worry," he said to Rosie, then raised his voice a little so others could hear him. "I'll be leaving soon."

She nodded and walked away. When King looked back at the man across the table, Harper was grinning.

"Not even welcome in your own town?"

"Things are tense," King answered, sitting straighter. "And I don't need a drunk drifter to tell me that."

He expected the man to say something sharp, but Harper only nodded, looking at the table.

"Look, trust me. You don't want me involved," the man said quietly. King had expected the man to be defiant and surly, based on the file, but this man sitting across from him just seemed sad. Sad and lost. And alone.

"Why not?" King asked.

Harper looked up at him.

"I haven't done an active investigation in years," the man replied. "I'm retired, riding the cold case desk in Birmingham. Running out the clock, so to speak. You know that already. You pulled my file," he said, nodding at the table.

King nodded and flipped open the file. It was impressive, for the most part. He'd been on the job 21 years, taking retirement in 2010 with a half pension. There was no mention in the file as to why he didn't get the full pension. But the last few years had been rough, after Katrina. Evidently something had happened, something bad enough to break up the man's marriage and send his career into a tailspin. Harper and the NOPD had not parted on good terms.

"Look, is this about what happened after Katrina?" Chief King began. "Because if it is—"

The man's face turned red with sudden fury. "I don't want to talk about that," he said, his eyes boring into King. Harper's fists were clenched.

The Chief sat back. "Okay. Look, I know you're retired," King said, trying a different tack. "I know about some of the things that happened to you. But I don't care. We need a fresh perspective."

"I can't. I hope you understand," Harper said, shaking his head again.

King pressed on. "We just need someone to look over the files, to see what we missed—"

"No," Mr. Harper said quietly and stood suddenly. Before the Chief knew what was happening, the man had paid and walked toward the door. It all happened so fast, King didn't have time to react. Thank God the man hadn't drawn on him.

The Chief sat back and flipped his file closed, flummoxed. This Frank Harper could have been a valuable asset, with his background, but clearly the man was unstable. And unpredictable. It probably wasn't worth it, bringing in yet another wrinkle into a case that was exhausting everyone, pushing them to the breaking point. King didn't need to be trying to solve an impossible case and managing an unstable drunk at the same time.

But King also knew the case needed fresh eyes. It wasn't going any-where but downhill, and fast.

Hurrying, Chief King gathered up his things and followed Harper out the door into the rain, nodding at a relieved-looking Rosie as he left.

Outside, the Chief saw, Harper walking up the sidewalk along the south side of Main Street, just passing the book store. The rain was fall-ing in sheets, and the gutters were small rivers, carrying along leaves of many colors. One of the playing cards from the ransom drop fiasco washed down the gutter and disappeared into a grate.

Chief King shook his head and followed Harper. King caught up with him as they passed under the green awning at O'Shaughnessy's, the restaurant on the corner of Second and Main. The awning was decorated with shamrocks and a leprechaun, the mascot for the restaurant.

"Wait up," King said.

Harper stopped and turned, shaking his head. "Look, I've thought about it, okay? I appreciate the offer. And it would probably do me some good, getting back to work. At least, that's what people have told me. But I had too many of these kinds of cases go bad."

The Chief nodded. Finally, some honesty.

"I understand," King said. "And this one might go bad as well—that's just the nature of our job, right? You do what you can, chase the leads. But we've got nothing. On this case, nothing adds up. And now, with this ransom drop fiasco, we're back to square one."

Harper glanced out into the rain.

"Well, even so, you're better off without me." He started to turn, but King grabbed his shoulder. Harper looked down at King's hand, and the Chief suddenly realized the man was trying to decide whether or not to retaliate.

Chief King let go.

"Look, I didn't want to do this," Chief King said. "But I need your help."

"Didn't want to do what?" Harper said, staring at him, those eyes bor-ing into the Chief. "You gonna arrest me? Over that horseshit with Stan? No way he presses charges."

Chief King shook his head.

"No, no, nothing like that," King said. "But I read your files. Your last few years at the NOPD were rocky, and times have been lean for you. Even with that cold case job, you're flat broke."

Harper didn't say a word. The Chief could tell what he was thinking. It was the same thing King would be thinking, put in the same situa-tion. He'd be calculating, figuring the angles. After a moment, the man looked at King.

"You ran my credit?"

King ignored the question.

"What I'm saying is there's a substantial reward. $50,000," King said. "Or I can pay you for your time. As a consultant, or investigator, or whatever. Either way." King looked at Harper for a long moment. "But I need your help if we're going to catch these guys. There are a bunch of things that just don't add up."

Harper looked at him. The moment hung in the air between them. King had laid out the bait, and, after a long moment, the man finally took it.

"Like what?"

King pointed off into the rain, in the general direction of the crime scene, several blocks away.

"The abduction scene, for one thing," King said. He stepped closer to Harper, leaning in. "Middle of the morning, lots of visibility, lots of houses around there. Right by the school, and no one saw anything."

"That doesn't mean anything—" Harper began.

"It's one of the busiest parts of town on a school day. Someone saw something, and isn't talking. Why? And the girls were gone for almost a whole week before the first contact came in. Why wait so long?" King said.

Rain pounded the green awning above them, rivulets of water making tiny rivers that ran down the fabric and fell to the ground. King watched the man, watching for a decision. Biding his time. They were the only ones out in the downpour, alone except for the rain around them.

The man looked up.

"I'd say the week was for the kidnappers to get the victims situated wherever they are being kept. As for witnesses, people tend to forget. An eyewitness might know what happened, if they were asked right away, or the right way. A week's gap, and folks will not remember any of the details. But none of that matters. It's probably someone close to the family. Or a close family friend."

Chief King nodded, pulling the brim of his hat down. The rain was blowing under the awning. King tucked the files and his yellow pad inside his coat.

"That's what I need—an outsider's perspective. Look, I don't care about all the other stuff. My guys are stretched thin. I need your help." Chief King looked at the wet pavement around them, then up at Harper.

The man was thinking.

"I promise you, it's just a day or two," King said. "Look over my files; tell me what I missed. Interview witnesses, if you want. And you'll get paid. Or claim the reward, better still. You'll at least need gas money to get back to Birmingham."

King looked at Harper. King wanted the man to know that the Chief was smart, and that'd he'd done the homework and still couldn't crack the case. That he really did need help. But the man was just staring at the wet pavement around their feet.

"Can you just consult?" the Chief asked.

Harper stared at the ground, then glanced over at a beat-up Taurus parked across the street. Ironically, it was parked in front of the Old Hotel and the trash can where, earlier, the ransom had been left. Had Harper done that by accident, or was he already curious about the case? Had he looked over the scene for clues?

"You need a new car, too, by the looks of it," King said, hoping the humor came across. "That thing is a real piece of junk."

Harper looked at him sharply, then smiled, getting it.

"Yeah, it's an old Bureau car," the man said. "Shitty gas mileage and a blown radio."

King nodded. "Well, do it for a new car then. So, can you help out?"

After a moment, Harper looked up at the Chief. In the falling rain, his subtle nod would have been easy to miss.

20

Wednesday morning, bright and early.

Frank was sitting in the Perks Coffeehouse, already half-way through his third cup. Frank liked his coffee black and very strong. Sometimes with a little cream to take the edge off. And he'd tipped a little bourbon into it, just to be safe. He didn't need to be getting the shakes this morning.

He appreciated the flavor and sweetness of the bourbon after days of nothing but vodka and beer. Chief King had fronted Frank a little cash to get the investigation rolling, and the liquor store near Dominoes had been his first stop. Now, Frank was settled and happy, ready to get started on the new case. And maybe, if he could help them out and wrap the case up quickly, he'd look a little better in his daughter's eyes.

A young deputy named Peters was supposed to be here soon, but Frank had gotten here early and was jotting down ideas—and getting the lay of the land. Frank was anxious to get started. It felt good, cracking the books again. He'd been pushing papers in Birmingham for two years, and the cold cases never went anywhere.

But the new case was exciting. And to get rolling, Frank knew that you started with the basics. Good old-fashioned police work was as boring as shit, but you had to do the things you had to do. There were no short cuts or easy ways. Of course, computers were making it a lot easier to do some of the grunt work, like cross-checking files for patterns or accessing records from other municipalities.

He remembered years ago, at the FBI Academy, another guest instructor had visited at the same time he was there—they'd flown him in to teach Krav Maga.

Her name was Julie Noble, and she spoke about the power of computers and the interconnections between investigating agencies that could produce amazing results. She was famous in the Bureau for breaking one of the largest cases in the last twenty years. She'd used an advanced computing system–advanced for the time, that is—to catch Jack Terrington, a notorious serial killer. For nearly twenty years, he had stalked the country in his creepy, trophy-filled white van, killing scores of victims. She'd done the work, tracked Terrington, and finally caught him.

Agent Noble had been on the cutting edge of computers and pattern recognition, but she'd still investigated the case by starting with the basics: gather evidence, interview the witnesses, review every scrap of information gathered by other investigators, examine the crime scene, and establish a basic timeline of the events in question. This led to a hypothesis about how the crimes may have occurred. It was always the same, always a lot of work.

But that was the job.

Questioning the suspect, if there was one, came much later. Questioning the suspect was pointless unless you knew which questions to ask. And often there was not just one suspect.

The investigator also had to establish that a crime had been committed in the first place. In many cases, deaths or disappearances turned out to be simple bad luck or accidental or just horrible timing. But you had to nail the crime down. Then, and only then, did you start making your list of suspects.

The list usually started with witnesses and family. It sounded cruel, but people near a crime were likely to be involved. In a completely unsurprising twist, the perpetrator of the crime was often the same person who called it in. Or they were standing around at the crime scene, watching. Sometimes, they even offered to help the investigators with the case. Some criminals seemed to enjoy being involved and often tried, consciously or subconsciously, to draw attention to themselves. Cops routinely photographed crime scenes—and the gathered onlookers—for just this reason.

Coming up with suspect list usually started with the family members. Sadly, most of the crimes committed in America were carried out by someone close to the victim—a spouse or a parent or a sibling. It was just human nature to covet what other people had. Or to be jealous when a spouse moved on to new relationships. Investigating family and close friends, in 80% of cases, nabbed you the perpetrator.

Frank sat back from his notes and looked around. He liked the coffee shop. Chief King had suggested it for its proximity to downtown and the central location. And keeping Frank out of the Police Department meant that Frank could feel free to get up to speed on his own, far from prying eyes. The Chief wasn't interested in putting all of his eggs in the same basket, Frank figured. If things worked as they should, the Chief would essentially have parallel investigations going at the same time on the same crime.

The coffee shop was decorated for Halloween and was far nicer than he'd expected for a little town in rural Ohio. There were the soft couches and ample seating and relaxed lighting that invited people to stay as long as they liked. People came and went, greeting each other and sitting for

a while to catch up over coffee. And the place was sumptuously decorated: there was a beautiful brass sculpture hanging on one wall, along
with large, framed paintings lit with small spotlights. It looked more like
an art gallery than a coffee shop.

And it had been decorated for the season; every surface sported
Halloween props, pumpkins and paper mache spiders. Fake cobwebs
stretched over the front windows. In one corner stood a creepy, full-size
zombie which would move when people passed it. Near the door stood
a large babbling fountain, but, in a demented twist, the water had been
dyed red. It looked like a cauldron of flowing, bubbling blood, with
more "blood" falling into the cauldron from above.

He tore his eyes away from the decorations and went back to his list.

Kidnapping cases were easy to classify, falling into two distinct cat-
egories—a friend or family member, or a complete stranger. The cases were investigated in exactly the same fashion: assume it's a close
acquaintance and work outward.

It could be the parent who didn't get the kid in the divorce, or a
pissed-off grandparent, or the ex-boyfriend. Many times, the estranged
parent or a close friend of the parent was the actual abductor, taking the
child or arranging for the child to be taken, then fleeing over state lines.
At that point, the case became an effort in location. These cases were
often resolved quickly and without incident, especially since the Amber
Alert system was established in 1996 to alert the public to be on the
lookout for individuals fitting the description of an abductor or kidnapping victim.

He remembered that case in Texas in 1996—a 9-year-old girl named
Amber was abducted and murdered in Arlington, Texas, only five hundred and fifty miles from New Orleans. The case had garnered national
attention, sadly, and been the impetus for creating the Amber system,
which had saved countless kids in the last 15 years.

Less often, a child is abducted for ransom. Those cases fell into two
classes: someone close to the family, looking for leverage or a payday.
Or, if the family is rich or famous, an anonymous and opportunistic
criminal looking for money. The child is usually exchanged for money.
Thankfully, it was in the best interests of the abductors to keep the child
alive, at least until the ransom exchange. In Frank's experience, the victim was recovered about half of the time.

But kidnappings by strangers were much more rare, but far more
insidious. In those cases, there was no ransom demand. These were
the cases that always made the news—a kid gets snatched at a county
fair or from the mall and is never seen again. The most famous case
was probably the kidnapping and murder of Adam Walsh in 1981 from

a Sears department store in Hollywood, Florida. The tragedy led his father, John Walsh, to establish the Adam Walsh Child Resource Center, which eventually grew into the National Center of Missing and Exploited Children (NCMEC), a national nonprofit dedicated to finding missing or kidnapped children. Frank had worked with that group on several occasions on local and regional abductions. They had served as a valuable clearinghouse of case histories and an invaluable media partner in getting the word out about abduction. He'd been surprised to hear that the CMPD were not involving the national organization and its vast resources in looking for Charlie Martin and Maya Gutierrez.

Frank looked down at his notepad. Without even noticing, he'd filled up two pages of notes on the case already, and he hadn't seen a single case file.

The bell on the door jingled, and Frank looked up. He was back in situational awareness mode and not resisting it. He loved how all the doors in this town seemed to come with a little bell—maybe it was a town ordinance or something. Could a town legislate quaintness?

It was a police deputy, carrying two file boxes. As he entered, he tripped over the step and nearly fell. He juggled the boxes, nearly dropping them, and folders and papers from the top box slid out, falling to the floor all around the door. Two of the files fell into the red "blood" of the bubbling cauldron, splashing the red water out onto the walls and door.

The deputy let out a yell and set the boxes down, completely blocking the entrance, his backside still sticking out the open door. The deputy hurried to gather up files and papers, mumbling apologies to those around him. A couple waited outside to get in.

Frank stood and walked over and held the door open for the couple, then stooped to help the young cop gather up all of the files. Frank also fished the two folders out of the water and held them over the cauldron to let the "blood" run off. Frank wondered if anyone would be concerned that these two files in particular looked like they'd been dipped in blood.

"Hi, are you Mr. Harper?" the young cop said as he stuffed files and folders back into one box. Neither box was full. "I'm Deputy Peters. I work for the Cooper's Mill PD. I'm supposed to help you out."

Frank nodded.

"I got that, son," he said gruffly. "It's not hard to figure out. The uniform gave it away—that and the big boxes marked 'Police Files' in your hands." Chief King had mentioned his cousin was on the force. Frank wondered if King had assigned him the rookie cop because King could trust him, or because the Deputy was too inexperienced in the field to be helpful in the "real" investigation.

The deputy stood and looked down at the boxes in his hands and smiled, nervous. Frank, carrying the two red files, directed the young cop over to his table.

"Yes, these are the files," Deputy Peters said, dropping the boxes down heavily on the table. Frank snatched up his coffee mug to keep it from being knocked over. "Sorry about dropping them."

Frank shook his head and sat down. The young cop pulled out a chair for himself and almost tipped it over before sitting down. The kid was like a bull in a china shop, full of energy.

"What files did you bring?" Frank asked.

Peters pulled files out of the top box. "Copies—mostly jackets on each person in the family or close to it. Interviews, backgrounds, stuff like that. On top is the scene investigation. Well, it was on top – now it's all red," Peters said, pointing at the two red files Frank had carried over. "Sorry."

"Don't worry about it," Frank said. He flipped open the files to let them dry out.

"Under that is the FBI file," Peters said. "It's pretty small. The Bureau guy, he's a little green."

Frank looked up at him.

"How long you been a cop?"

Peters' eyes went wide, and he shook his head.

"Don't get me wrong—I'm green, too, and I know it," Peters said. "But I've been hanging around with Cousin Jeff since I was eleven. I haven't been a cop long, but even I can tell when someone's out of their depth."

Frank nodded and grabbed the boxes, sliding them around. He started taking the files out and making stacks—incident reports, family, friends.

"So, you on the case?" the Deputy asked, watching Frank get organized.

Frank looked at him.

"I'm just helping out the Chief," Frank said. "Going through the files, seeing if he missed anything. Though I don't know what help I'll be."

Peters looked at the box.

"At this point, any help is needed—and appreciated," he said, smiling at Frank. "Hey, do you mind, if I stay and help you?"

Frank shrugged.

"I don't really care. If you want, stick around and get yourself some coffee. Or, better yet, come back in an hour. That'll give me a chance to get through some of the files first, and then I'll be ready with questions."

The kid nodded and thought about it, then smiled.

"I'll be back in a bit."

Frank nodded as the kid left. Normally, he would have preferred being left alone to go through the files but here, in a new town where he didn't know anyone, he'd have lots of questions. Names, locations, relationships. It made sense to be able to ask questions of someone involved in the area.

Frank went to the counter and had the woman top off his cup of coffee, then sat back down and finished setting up his stacks.

He began with the incident report, peeling the wet pages apart carefully. Thankfully, most of the red paint was on the outside of the file folder, and the report inside was mostly undamaged. The case files on the family, especially the parents, were usually the most germane, but he wanted to get the scene established in his head first.

First call came in on Monday, October 3, from the mother. She'd sent her girl off to school, waving at the girls as they walked up Hyatt Avenue. After about an hour, the school had called to check in.

Nick Martin, the father, said the school had called home about the unscheduled absence, and Glenda had called him at his job. He was in construction and owned a very successful construction firm. He'd driven home and, together, they'd walked up to the school, looking for Charlie and Maya. When they found nothing, they called the police from the school and returned home to meet the police.

The first cop on the scene was Sergeant Graves, a cop Frank hadn't yet met. King mentioned him during their conversation in the rain last night. Graves was #3 on the Cooper's Mill police force, behind Chief King and Detective Barnes, who was lead on the case.

Graves had interviewed the parents and housekeeper, taken photos, done a sweep of the area. He established that the girls usually walked up Hyatt to Broadway and turned. Frank quickly shuffled through the file but couldn't find a map or anything. These guys probably all knew the town so well they didn't need a map. He'd need to get one.

The Martin's girl, Charlie, was eight and in the third grade at Broadway Elementary, located on Broadway between Fifth and Seventh Streets. The other girl, Maya, was seven. As far as Frank could tell without looking at a map, it was a straight shot up Hyatt to Broadway, and the mother usually watched the girls walk up to the turn. On this morning, she did not.

Graves had also noted in the report that Nick had asked Graves to accompany him into the kitchen, away from Glenda and the housekeeper, who were very upset. Mr. Martin had wanted to chat privately about how to proceed on the case and also offered Graves a beer, something that struck Frank as out of place. Maybe they knew each other—either way, it seemed strange timing.

Sergeant Graves had then taken his own walk to figure out where the girls had disappeared. He'd found a water bottle with Charlie's name on it in the gutter at the corner of Seventh and Broadway, within sight of the school. Evidently, all the kids in that school carried water bottles with their names on them. It wasn't explained why in the file. Graves had spotted the bottle in the gutter behind the tire of a car. It wasn't on the Broadway side but instead on the northwest corner of Broadway and Seventh, a short road that intersected Broadway and delineated the western edge of the school property. On this side of the school it was all playgrounds and fences. The road was screened from the front entrance of the school, where most of the teachers and students would have been in the minutes before school started.

King was right. It looked like the girls were taken in broad daylight and within sight of the school. Finding this bottle meant the kidnappers or abductors would have walked the girl down the street to a waiting vehicle. It had to be the case—any closer to Broadway Elementary and even the smoothest, most practiced snatch-and-grab would have been compromised.

It was almost impossible to believe that no one had seen anything, yet no witnesses had come forward. There were several residences on that corner, according to Graves' report. But interviews with each of the residents who were home at the time, and later interviews with those residents who returned home later in the day, turned up nothing.

Graves had continued to the school and talked with several people there—teachers and the principal and a custodian who had been cleaning the grounds within sight of the corner where the water bottle was found—but no one saw anything out of the ordinary other than police cars and patrolmen in the area.

Frank flipped the page and found the file ended—not much to go on, but it summed up the scene that morning. The back page stuck to the file folder.

He set the file aside to dry and finished his coffee. Frank noticed it had begun to rain outside. People were coming in and shaking their umbrellas before leaning them up against the door jamb. Frank stretched and grabbed the stack of case files on each person in the case, ignoring the other wet file for now.

He started with Nick Martin, father of Charlie Martin.

Nick Martin's file was thicker than any of the other case files, but it didn't take long to figure out why. The guy was a veritable pillar of society in this tiny town—successful business owner, local celebrity, City Council, sports hero in his youth. He was a Golden Boy—a phrase Ben Stone had always used—a person who'd always gotten everything they wanted or needed, just when they needed it.

This "Golden Boy" had been the star of his Cooper's Mill High School football team, quarterback and everything. Played all of his games at the downtown stadium, broke records, led his team to the championship, et cetera, et cetera. It was too much like a movie. Frank was tempted to peek at the wife's file to see if she had been the head of the cheerleading squad.

But Nick Martin had done well in school and parlayed that into a scholarship to Ohio State, where he'd also played ball until an injury to his shoulder, during a game in his sophomore year, ended his football career.

Martin had finished out his schooling, getting a degree in architecture and then joined the Army, doing a short stint in Iraq before returning to Cooper's Mill. He'd worked at several local design and construction firms and then struck out on his own, pooling his resources and starting Martin Construction. The firm grew quickly. It looked like Nick Martin wasn't shy about using his local connections to win projects and close deals. And between his persona as a local sports hero and his business acumen, the firm soon grew to be one of the most successful, and profitable, in the area.

Nick had branched out, making investments and buying small businesses and rolling them into the larger construction firm. He'd taken on two partners, both of whom were heavily involved in the day-to-day activities of Martin Construction, and three other "silent partners" who had paid into the company to take share of future profits.

From the financials Frank was reviewing, it looked like the kidnappers had failed to do their homework. From the outside, the Martins and Martin Construction looked to be flush—owning possibly the largest house in town made that much clear—but the economic downturn had gutted the construction company.

First, Martin Construction had been heavily invested in a large housing development south of town, someplace called Sunset Ridge. It was planned as a subdivision of about 20 homes near the cemetery, but only 4 were completed and sold by the time the housing crisis began to impact the market in Ohio. Another three houses were in various stages of completion, with the rest of the lots sitting empty.

Martin Construction had taken a bath on that development—they hadn't even been able to sell the empty lots. The estimated sales prices for the homes under construction fell so precipitously that all work simply halted. According to the paperwork, the subdivision was still sitting unfinished, waiting for the economy to turn around.

Most of the other local construction work in the area had also dried up in 2009. 2010 and 2011 had been very lean years for the company. People were let go, and Frank jotted down a note on his pad to ask King if all the ex-employees had been interviewed. Few things made people angrier than being fired. And other large projects had been put on hold—a large investment in a strip of commercial properties west of town and the Holly Toys Lofts project, a warehouse/condo conversion project.

The commercial strip was a planned development located near the highway, a small group of six retail and commercial spaces near the Bob Evans. The commercial strip had been under construction and fully rented out in late 2009, but as the building was nearing completion, two tenants backed out. Two of Martin's silent partners had been hurt badly in that deal, losing a chunk of change. The exact numbers weren't listed in the financials, but one of the "silent" partners was pissed off enough to take Nick Martin to court over ownership of the property. The case had been settled and the partner, a Jimmy Weil, had sold his shares and left Martin Construction. Frank made another note to look up the interview, if there was one.

The other outstanding property concerned one of several properties that Martin and his primary business partner had purchased together. The Holly Toys building was a massive brick building, from the picture in the file. Located near the downtown, next to the train tracks, Martin Construction had picked up the building at auction in 2007 for a song.

Nick and his main business partner, Matthew Lassiter, had moved forward with plans to remove all the rusting equipment from the old toy factory and gut the interior to create retail and commercial space on the bottom two floors and condos on the top two floors. Again, this project was on hold. The money ran out. The only current expenses on the project were to pay a full-time security guard to keep the curious away.

The last project of note was partial ownership of a building in downtown Dayton. Martin Construction and the Martins personally were members of a consortium of investors putting money into a large industrial building that overlooked the baseball field of the local AA baseball team, the Dayton Dragons. The property was undergoing a six-year renovation and conversion to apartments, condos, and retail and office space. It appeared that the Martins were enthusiastic backers of the project, but it, too, had fallen before the economic tide and was on hold, awaiting more funding and support from the local community.

The last page of the financial report disclosed three other properties that had been sold off by Martin Construction over the past six months to help keep the company afloat. A few construction projects had trickled over the summer, but it looked like the company would be finishing out 2011 in the red, with a bunch of unsellable properties and partially-completed projects on the books.

There was a page at the end about Martin's city council seat. He'd run for the position and won it in November of 2010, so he'd been on the Council a little less than a year. He'd been a fiscal conservative, refusing to vote for any expenditure of funds on anything but the essentials. He'd voted against a few borderline "amenities," and been the only "no" vote to fund the city's annual downtown Christmas lights. He'd gotten a reputation as stingy with the city's money. Some people liked it, and some most sincerely did not.

In fact, he'd developed quite a following of people who were not at all happy with his Council decisions. A handwritten note on the page noted that 17 locals had been interviewed in the last five days about angry emails, letters, and phone calls sent in or made to Martin, voicing their displeasure with some of his votes. In all cases, Martin's "fans" had turned out to be harmlessly expressing their displeasure with his voting record. At the very least, it sounded like Nick Martin would have some work to do if he wanted to be reelected when his next campaign rolled around in 2014.

Frank closed the folder on Martin and sat back, thinking.

Either the kidnappers were badly informed, or they knew what they were doing. If they thought Nick Martin was rich, they'd ask for a bigger ransom, assuming he could get it. If they knew he was on the ropes financially, why ask for so much, and only give him a day to get the money together? Did the kidnappers assume the Bureau was involved? The FBI routinely "assisted" with pulling together the ransom money in a timely fashion. It was almost always the victim's "money," but the Bureau would facilitate getting the bills in from a local large bank, acquiring consecutive bills, recording all the serials and, often, marking the bills with a UV-reactive dye or some other tracking/identification method.

It was still pouring outside. Frank watched the rain spattering against the windows and drenching the metal table and chairs just outside his window. People outside ran comically from awning to awning, trying to stay dry.

He wondered where the little girls were, if they were out in this downpour. Dead or alive, they had to be somewhere. Chief King had said that half of the town had turned out for organized searches of every park, common area, ditch, and culvert in the city limits. Groups of volunteers had scoured the Great Miami River, which wound along the eastern edge of town. They had walked the riverbanks and thick tangles of trees on either side of the river for two miles up and down stream.

Another group had meticulously worked their way down Canal Road and the under-construction bike path. King had said that the twisty road wound south along the route of the old canal. Bicyclists were apparently struck on a regular basis on the narrow road by passing cars, so a new bike path twenty feet off the road was being put in. One early theory had been that the girls had somehow gotten far south of town without any-one seeing them. Perhaps been struck by a motorist, their bodies thrown into the thick brush or corn fields that line both sides of the road. Then the ransom call had come in, and the police had altered their thinking. They were still continuing with the searches, just in case, their primary focus being the ransom demands and the kidnappers.

Frank shook his head and grabbed the next file—Glenda Martin.

21

It was all there.

$1,000,000 in cash.

No trackers, non-sequential bills. The man had never seen so much cash in one place before. Certainly not laid out on his bed, stacked up in beautiful piles of green.

He'd retrieved the money from the airport parking lot this morning. He thought it would be prudent to let the money sit overnight, in case it was still being tracked. The two kids hired by his partner were supposed to clean the money, but you could never be too careful. He'd arrived at the airport and sat in his car, watching the old Mustang for another two hours before gingerly walking over to it, unlocking the car, and retrieving the green duffle bag from the back seat.

He'd then taken a long circuitous route home, passing through Dayton and another suburb before driving back to Cooper's Mill, stopping several times along the way to see if he was being followed.

At one point, a helicopter flew over, and it put him into a panic, like the Ray Liotta character in "Goodfellas."

But now, as he was standing in his bedroom, looking down at the money, and the much smaller stack of paperwork on the bed next to the money, he realized that he'd never actually thought this would happen. Together, these two things represented six months of planning, laying the groundwork, associating with people out of his circle. He also hadn't thought the girl's father, Nick Martin, would be able to come up with all of it that quickly.

But there it was, all laid out on the bed. His part of the ransom would be a big help. The rest of the cash would go to his silent partner.

The man walked over to the window and looked out. His apartment overlooked the quaint shopping district in downtown Cooper's Mill. He leased one of the few second-story apartments downtown. He'd been lucky to find it and even luckier to buy the building for cheap. Of course, he'd sold it later at a profit and kept back the apartment for himself.

Profits—that's what he needed now. Clearing out all of his investments was the only way to get enough money to get square. It wasn't really his fault—he'd just gotten in over his head.

You knew it was bad when a thick guy from Vegas with no neck showed up in the little town of Cooper's Mill, Ohio, reminding you of your "payment plan." It wasn't a very flexible payment plan, certainly. And if you didn't stay on the plan, the balloon payment at the end would kill you. Literally.

Or, at least they'd wait on killing him until they'd squeezed every penny they could out of him. Obviously, Vegas was not happy with him. But now, things were looking up. He had a plan, and skills, and assets that could be cashed in.

The man walked back over to the bed. The apartment was small, but it had always been enough for him. He liked intimate settings and opulence and style, and he took pride in knowing that his apartment was probably the nicest bedroom in town. Not that that was saying much.

The people here were nice and had accepted him with aplomb. And he'd brought them a little style. But his time here was nearly over.

The man opened the FedEx box and slipped the paperwork inside, stopping for a second to triple-check that he'd signed the deed over. Wouldn't that have been a fun phone call? "Hi, we got the money and the paperwork on the building, but the deed isn't signed. What are you trying to pull?" It would have been followed by the usual threats, which invariably involved breaking something on his body, usually a leg. Sometimes the guys from Vegas also threatened to cut things off, or out, but mostly they stuck with breaking things. Probably because breaking a leg would hurt like hell but not be a permanent condition. Unless you counted the limp. He guessed clichés got to be clichés for a reason.

The man slid the deed and the rest of the paperwork into the box, along with the $363,000 he had counted out. Seemed crazy to trust that kind of cash to a flimsy cardboard box, but Vegas had assured him it was fine. "Just remember to get the insurance," the guy had said with a laugh.

Between the property and the cash, it was everything he owed. Now, he was square, and Vegas would back off. Just knowing the end was coming was a big relief. All the planning was paying off, and no one had gotten hurt.

The man took another $400,000 and put it back into the green duffle bag—that was for his "partner," a man he'd grown to thoroughly despise over the past six weeks. But doing business like this required working with less savory elements. His partner had handled the whole kidnapping side, including arranging for people to watch what had turned out to be two girls instead of just Charlie Martin. But the partner was being handsomely compensated, even after paying the others out of his share.

With the duffle bag and FedEx boxes ready, the man looked around the room again. He had nearly a quarter of a million left for himself. But it would have to last. He would be leaving this life behind and needed money to get set up somewhere else, somewhere where absolutely no one knew who he was.

22

Frank continued through the files, making notes as he went.

Glenda Martin was the wife—heavily into art and the local art scene. She worked with a small art gallery in one of the downtown buildings, using the space to support local artists. Glenda wanted to turn Cooper's Mill into "another Yellow Springs;" evidently, Yellow Springs was a nearby town with a bustling art scene. Glenda Martin had been involved in establishing the local arts group and was an active volunteer with the local farmers market.

The Martins had met at Ohio State, and Frank was mildly disappointed to find out that Glenda was not a cheerleader. In fact, she had majored in Economics. They had been friends in college and stayed in touch while Nick was in the military, reconnecting when he returned to their shared home town. A year later, they were married. She'd been an early employee of the construction company, helping Nick to keep his finances in order, until he could hire a full-time CFO. She still taught occasional semesters at Wright Brothers Community College, "when her schedule allowed it," the notes said. Frank wasn't sure what that meant.

Sergeant Graves, the first policeman on the scene, had noted in her file that "the mother had been the most upset, visibly distraught" that first morning of the case after learning that her daughter and the daughter of her housekeeper had gone missing. In Frank's experience, people either reacted genuinely or grossly overreacted, playing it up and making sure that everyone around them knew how they felt. The over-actors gave all the classic, outward signs of being genuinely upset, but they piled it on too much, giving themselves away. According to Graves, she'd been holding it together, but on the verge of excusing herself, breaking into tears several times during the discussion.

In these types of situations, women often reacted with tears and desperate sadness, whereas men reacted angrily or insisted that they wanted to help. Sometimes the men seemed like they just wanted something at which to direct their anger. In more cases than Frank wanted to remember, he had taken the brunt of their anger. The woman crying on his shoulder and the man yelling at him. Both unsure of what to do next, both unable to direct their emotion into anything helpful.

Both feeling helpless, frustrated, angry.

There was little else on Glenda.

Frank read carefully several more files, flipping through them and quickly scanning for anything out of the ordinary. He finished the first box, reading various reports on people connected to the case.

The first file in the second box was on Ms. Nora Gutierrez. She had been hired by the Martins in 2004 and had been with them since. When the Martins bought their current home two years later, they had purposefully chosen a home with a live-in suite above the garage for Ms. Gutierrez and her young daughter, Maya, who was one year younger than the Martins' own daughter. Ms. Gutierrez' employment records and immigration status were in order, and her financial report was short and completely unremarkable. She was well-paid by the Martins and apparently happy.

Frank scanned several more folders and was grabbing for another file when Deputy Peters came back into the coffee shop, stepping inside and shaking off the rain like a dog.

"Hi, Mr. Harper," Peters said, setting his wet hat down on the table. "How's it going?"

"Good," Frank nodded. "Grab a drink and join me."

Peters left, and Frank moved the files away from the damp hat. Drops of rain ran down the blue fabric and created tiny pools of water on the metallic table. Each drop formed a perfect circle.

After a minute, Peters returned and sat, sipping his coffee. "That's one good cup of coffee."

Frank nodded.

"But the other place is good, too," Peters said in a conspiratorial tone, his voice lowering. "There are two coffee shops downtown. This one is the 'new' one, and some folks don't even seem to know the name of the place. They just call it the 'new' coffee shop."

Peters sat back and looked around the interior of the place. Frank, unsure if there was more story to come or not, waited, one hand inside the next folder, ready to flip it open on the table in front of him. When Peters didn't say anything for a while, Frank sighed and spoke up.

"I didn't see another coffee shop. What do they call the old place?"

Peters seemed genuinely confused for a moment, then smiled. "Most people just call it the 'old' coffee shop."

Frank smiled down at the next folder. Why did he even ask?

"So," Frank began, "what do you think of the Martins?"

"Oh, they're salt of the earth," Peters said, setting down the mug of coffee. "Everyone in town knows them, mostly because of Nick's school records in high school. Most people like them, as far as I know.

I've known a few people that worked for Martin Construction, short jobs and such, and all of them said he was good to work for. And Mrs. Martin, she's on a bunch of boards down here downtown and is always coming up with some wacky art event."

"Anything suspicious?" Frank asked. "What about enemies?"

Peters shook his head.

"No, nothing like that. Nick Martin has made a few enemies since getting on the Council. He voted down a couple of pay increases for the city employees, folks he works with. There could be some hurt feelings there, but nothing that could...I don't see anybody getting that angry about it. Plus, all of those people have been checked out."

Frank nodded.

"That's assuming that you and Chief King and Nick know all the disgruntled citizens who might hold a grudge and need to be checked out. Anyone let go as a result of the budget issues? Anyone quit?"

Peters shook his head.

"We're looking for someone who hates Nick Martin enough to risk going to jail for the opportunity to make Nick's life miserable," Frank said, mostly to himself. "Or someone who needs money and is under the erroneous impression that the Martin's have it."

Peters nodded. "Sounds like you've been through the financials."

"Yeah," Frank agreed. "And they're not pretty."

"Nope," Peters agreed. "The economy has been tough on folks around here. A bunch of downtown and local businesses closed in 2010 and earlier this year. We're just hoping more can stick it out. It would be a shame to see these downtown buildings boarded up and empty."

Frank looked down at his scribbled notes. "Did the girls have a reputation for running off? It's still possible they skipped town."

"Nah, too young," Peters said. "They are seven and eight. They couldn't have gotten to Troy or Vandalia without someone calling it in."

Frank looked up. "Where?"

"Troy, five miles north of here, on the highway. Vandalia is south. Now, if they had been teenagers..."

"This would be an entirely different case," Frank agreed. "Any extended family for either girl who might have taken them on vacation or somewhere harmless? Just forgot to mention it to anyone?"

Peters shook his head again.

Frank nodded. "It would have been extremely unlikely, but it's best to check off every possibility."

Peters nodded and sipped his coffee. He reached and took out a small notepad and pen from his pocket and flipped it open, jotting down some words.

"I like that," Deputy Peters said. 'Check off the possibilities.'"

Frank looked at the notepad and saw those words written down. "You taking notes?"

Peters looked up. "Chief King does it all the time. And you're miles ahead of that other guy. He hasn't said anything that I thought was worth writing down."

Frank nodded. "Cut him some slack."

"You haven't met him," Peters answered.

"That's true."

Frank flipped open the next file and began reading about the business associate, Matt Lassiter. He'd come to the area a few years ago from out west. He was originally from California, Modesto, but had settled into the Midwest and become a critical partner in much of Martin Construction's success. Lassiter had been hit hard by the economic downturn as well, seeing his net worth fall steeply over the past two years. He had been part owner in a strip mall in some town named Piqua but had recently sold the property. And he and Nick Martin were the sole owners of the Holly Toys building project, splitting the finances 50/50.

Frank looked up at Peters.

"What do you know about Lassiter?"

"Oh, not much," Peters said. "He was at one of the first interviews with the Martins. He's a family friend, and they're close, as far as I can tell. He's from California, you know," Peters said conspiratorially.

Frank looked up.

"Yes?"

Peters was making a face. "Yup, he's from California," he said, stressing and stretching the name of the state.

"What are you saying?"

"You know what I mean," Peters said.

Frank shook his head. "Actually, I don't."

Peters leaned forward. "He's...a little light," he shared quietly. "In the loafers."

Frank got it.

"Oh, you think he's gay."

Peters' eyes went wide, and he looked around.

"Okay, okay, don't shout it!"

Frank shook his head.

"There's a whole big world out there, Deputy," Frank said wearily. "You should embrace it. First, being from California doesn't make him gay. You might want to get a new euphemism for that. And second, gay doesn't make him a kidnapper."

"But he's different," Peters argued. "He has a different lifestyle, and that means—"

"It means exactly nothing," Frank cut him off. "Shit, lots of people have different lives and lifestyles. You and I are different, based on our interests, or background, or upbringing. I like jazz music. Coltrane, Ellington, Benny Golson, Booker Ervin. Have you heard of those guys?"

Peters only stared at Frank, then looked down at the table, as if the case files and folders were suddenly fascinating.

"You would do well to look at the facts in the case," Frank chided loudly. Other patrons looked up at them. "And the facts only. Some things are pertinent, and some things don't matter. It's easy to get caught up in the details, and even easier to get distracted by them. Now, again, what do you know about Matthew Lassiter?"

Peters squirmed in his seat for a moment, and Frank suddenly felt like a teacher chastising a student. After a long second, Peters looked up.

"There's no need to cuss."

Frank stared at him. "What?"

"My mom said that people only cuss when they run out of things to say."

"Deputy, I don't give a shit about what your mom used to say," Frank said good-naturedly. "The only thing I'm worried about right now is finding these girls. Now, stay on task. Matthew Lassiter."

Peters looked at him for a long moment and then began talking.

"Matthew Lassiter seems like a close personal friend of the family," Deputy Peters said slowly. "I'd originally thought something was going on between him and Mrs. Martin, but then after I figured out—well, I ruled that out," Peters said, eyeing Frank. "She didn't seem—well, they were close, but then I got the impression that they were just friends. But he was there for them, sitting in on the interviews when we allowed it. I've always gotten a good vibe off of him," Peters said.

"Even though he's gay?" Frank said, not bothering to take the edge off his mocking tone.

Deputy Peters nodded, sheepish.

"Good," Frank said. "You need to remember to be objective. It can be difficult, but try not to project your bias into the mix too much. His being gay or black or Jewish or bald doesn't matter, unless you come up with something else, some other piece of evidence that MAKES it matter."

Peters nodded as he took notes. It felt strange to Frank, having some-one treat him like a source of actual information. It had been so long.

"Maybe he's involved in a group that makes you curious about his associates," Frank continued. "Or maybe it's harmless and unconnected. Check it out, then dismiss it if you can. Eyes open, that's what my old partner used to say."

Frank set the file down and smiled, as Peters jotted down "Eyes open" on his little pad. Ben Stone would've been happy, knowing one of his sayings was getting passed down to the next generation. Stone was always coming up with shit like that. He should've been a motivational speaker. And he should have avoided dark alleys in Coral Gables.

Frank flipped through the last two—one was on the other major business partner, Jimmy Weil. The file was short, mostly concerning the lawsuit between him and the Martin Construction company over that failed strip mall. Frank read though it quickly, making a note to ask Chief King about it for more detailed financial records on Weil and Lassiter and the other partners.

The last file was on the three "silent" partners. It all seemed very straightforward—they invested in the company, taking varying degrees of involvement in the company's direction or focus. One of the silent partners wasn't even in the state. He was an architect in St. Louis.

"What about these other partners?" Frank asked.

"Nothing much. They're all losing money in the real estate market, hand over fist. All in the same boat. But it all seems legitimate," Peters said and then grew silent. It looked like he had something he wanted to say.

Frank knew better than to interrupt. Often, people used silence to get their nerve up. Frank waited.

Around them, the coffee shop buzzed. The woman behind the counter took orders and made drinks, the brass espresso machine hissing as she steamed milk. Near the window, two teenagers played chess at a large alabaster board. Above them hung a giant fake spider in a thick web. A woman came back from the bathroom and joined her friend, who was flipping through the magazines arrayed on the low tables. The zombie stood by the fountain, the "blood" gurgling like a bubbling wound.

The silence drew on, but Peters finally broke it.

"I don't think it's any of the partners," Deputy Peters said quietly. "No one close to the family seems to be that needy. Of course, I could be wrong, but we did exactly what you're doing. Chief King interviewed everyone, pulled all their credit reports and backgrounds. No red flags, nothing strange—but the case itself. It's like everything doesn't add up."

"Yup, my feelings exactly," Frank said, nodding.

Peters looked up.

"You should speak your mind more often," Frank continued, gathering up the files and putting the two red folders on top. "Use your instinct, but only after you've been through all the hard data. And as you do more investigations, you'll get the hang of what to look for. But we need to keep digging—this information is fine," he said, tapping the files. "But we need more."

Peters nodded, and then smiled.

23

Frank pointed out the car to Deputy Peters as they left the coffee shop, each carrying a box of reports and files. Peters stumbled over the sidewalk coming down the stairs of the coffee shop and almost dropped his box again. Frank smiled and popped the trunk on the Taurus, dropping his box in and holding it open for Peters.

The electronic locks didn't work anymore, so Frank climbed in and reached over to unlock the passenger door. Peters nodded at a group of three women passing on the sidewalk. Frank had parked across the street from Perks, and the three women waved at Deputy Peters before heading inside a small bookstore, The Haunted Bookshop.

Peters sat down in the car and looked around.

"Don't say anything," Frank said.

The interior of the car was a mess, and Frank knew it. There was trash in the floorboards and a crack in the windshield and part of the ceiling fabric had come loose in the backseat, sagging down like a tattered brown curtain. The jury-rigged, battery-powered CD player sat on the floorboard between them, tied into the car speakers with exposed wiring.

"It's…nice," Peters said.

Frank started the car, pulling away from the curb. The music came on, "Beggar Man Blues" by Willie B. Huff. Old blues, from back in the day. Bayou music, they called it.

"Don't lie—you're horrible at it," Frank said, glancing at Peters. "It's an old Alabama Bureau of Investigation vehicle, and I got it on the cheap. It was used in sting operations but got in a crash. The IT guys in Birmingham said the electronics got screwed up—the locks don't work, or radio, but the GPS tracker and speakers are OK."

"GPS tracker?"

Frank nodded. "Yeah, all the Bureau cars had them, especially sting cars, so they could be remotely tracked during operations. Too bad it doesn't work anymore. I should see if it can be fixed. Along with the radio and door locks."

Peters shook his head. "What's the point? No one is going to steal this—"

"Careful," Frank interrupted. "Don't say anything you'll regret."

Peters smiled. "The CD connections look loose—you want me to fix them? I've got some of those plastic zip ties. I take them with me, everywhere I go. Handy."

Frank looked at the wires that led from the dashboard to the CD player on the floor between them, but shook his head. "Nah, I'm good."

Peters nodded and pointed up the road.

"Okay, head back west on Main," Peters said, taking another long, curious look around the interior of the car.

Frank took two rights, passing and recognizing the hair studio where Laura worked. He made a left at the barber shop to get back on the main drag through downtown.

He stopped at the train tracks behind a line of cars, all stopped and waiting for a train that was passing through town. As the train crossed Main, it blew its whistle loudly.

"Doesn't that get annoying?" Frank said, pointing at the train.

Peters shook his head.

"I honestly didn't notice it. You get used to it. I know people who live downtown that can't even hear the train whistle blowing—I guess they just filter it out."

Frank nodded, thinking about it. "Seems like a bad idea, having a slow-moving train come through town multiple times a day. Do they ever block the fire or police calls?"

"Doesn't happen that often that the tracks are blocked," Peters said, looking at the train roaring past them, moving from right to left, heading south to Dayton and points beyond. Graffiti raced past them, painted on the sides of the train cars. "Once in a while, the train stops in town. But you can always get around it. There are crossings north and south, if you know where to look."

The train finally ended, and Frank and the other cars moved in a procession past the signal gates, over the tracks and up Main Street. Frank admired the beautiful old Victorian homes that lined both sides of the street. One of them was for sale, and a crazy idea drifted through Frank's brain that he should buy the house and have Laura and Jackson move in. Any place would have been better than that apartment she was in now.

They passed through a green light and Frank realized that Peters was talking to him.

"What?"

Peters was pointing. "That was Hyatt," he said, as they passed through the intersection. "The Martins live down there," he said, pointing to the left. "I asked if you wanted to drive past the house."

Frank shook his head. "No, let's check in with King. I'll check it out when we do the re-interview."

"Re-interview?" Peters was looking at him.

"Yeah, it never hurts," Frank said, nodding. "And bringing in new investigators is a perfect excuse to conduct new interviews—if only to get the new guy up to speed."

Peters pointed ahead.

"A left up here, at the hardware store, and then the station is on the right."

The building that housed the Cooper's Mill Police Department was smaller than Frank would have guessed. Peters explained that they actually took up half of the larger Government Building, as it was known— the CMPD offices, conference and interrogation rooms and one temporary holding cell. The other half of the building held the offices of the city government—City Manager, tax department, utilities, planning department, and the Council chambers, where the City Council met every other Monday evening.

Frank parked in front and they went inside, avoiding the small group of reporters gathered outside.

"Can I help you?"

Frank turned to see an attractive young woman behind a window. She was doing her nails, an emery board pausing in the air, as she waited for an answer.

Peters walked in behind Frank.

"It's okay, Lola. Thanks, anyway," he said and smiled. She nodded and went back to painting her nails. Peters took out his security card and waved it at the reader, then led Frank through a set of double doors.

Inside was the police station, made up of a large central room and two smaller offices for Chief King and Detective Barnes. A warren of cubicles for the other police officers and deputies took up most of the room. White boards lined the walls, along with corkboards and bulletin boards covered with tacked-up mug shots, faxed police reports, and alerts from other localities. One window looked out onto a weed-grown parking lot and the back of a supermarket.

In the middle of the room was a grouping of conference room tables and freestanding whiteboards. Several officers were seated at the long table, reading from stacks and piles of papers in the middle.

Chief King was talking to a small group of policemen and, following their eyes, turned to see Frank. King said something to the other officers and came over.

"Hi, Frank," he said loudly, shaking Frank's hand. Frank knew immediately that this wasn't for him. King was making a show of welcoming Frank to the office and, by inference, to the case.

Frank nodded and murmured his thanks. King turned and led them over to the group of officers and made the introductions.

"Guys, this is Frank Harper," Chief King said to the others. "He's retired from the New Orleans PD, over twenty years on the force. He's had extensive experience in kidnappings and has agreed to look over our files and lend a hand."

The reaction was decidedly mixed, but one of the men put out his hand.

"Welcome, Frank. I'm Barnes." They shook hands. "Lead Detective. We're working all the leads, but information is thin. And with the ransom drop going south, we could use the help. I really dropped the ball on that, getting distracted like I did."

At the mention of the ransom drop, several of them looked at a young man to Frank's right. He was dressed more formally than the others. He wore a lanyard that read "Ted Shale, Federal Bureau of Investigation." Frank stuck out his hand.

"Ted, nice to meet you. I liaised with the Cincinnati office one time," Frank said. "They still downtown?"

"Good to meet you, Frank," Agent Shale said, shaking Frank's hand. "No, they moved offices—now we're out by the Kenwood Mall. Yeah, that ransom drop thing—that was me. All me. We should've had better roadblocks, and then the car—"

Frank put up his hand.

"Don't blame yourself," he said to Ted. King was right—the kid was young, a sure sign that the Bureau office in Cincinnati didn't think this case was important. Or solvable. "It happens to all of us."

King finished the introductions: Deputy Simon, another young member of the squad, and Sergeant Graves, third in command and next in line for Detective.

"Okay, Frank is getting up to speed," King said. "He's going through all the files first, and then we'll take it from there. Show him all the courtesy you would a fellow officer. Frank, let me know when you're ready, and we'll get you out in the field."

Frank looked at King.

"I'm ready now."

It wasn't what the Chief and others were expecting. Chief King looked at him, suddenly curious.

"I've been through all the personal files this morning," Frank said. "I'd like to see a final report on the ransom drop, and photos, if you have any, and I need to read through Shale's report. But first, I'd like to re-interview the Martins."

Chief King nodded, rolling with it.

"No problem. When?"

Frank glanced at the clock on the wall. "Now, if that's convenient."

Deputy Peters and the others smiled at Chief King, who was looking at Frank. After a moment, King slowly nodded.

"Okay," Chief King said, slightly flustered. "Graves, can you call over there and set it up? Let me get my keys."

24

Frank looked out the car window. The Chief was taking them on a different route, taking the back way through a residential neighborhood.

"So, you've been through all the files already?" the Chief asked. "Really?"

"I'm a fast reader," Frank said, looking at the houses around them. "You guys covered everything pretty good, but I have a few questions for the Martins."

He heard the Chief grunt. "Okay, but I think it's too soon—you could review—"

"Nope," Frank said. "Done enough reviewing. I need to get started bringing in new information, not rehashing stuff you and the others have been through a dozen times already."

They drove in silence until the car turned onto Hyatt, then into a long driveway, and the Chief stopped the car. They climbed out. Frank recognized the house from the police report from Sergeant Graves, the first officer on the scene—a long driveway lined with bushes. He turned and stared up the street for a long moment, thinking. This driveway had an unblocked view up the street to the corner where the girls would have turned—he imagined standing here that morning, watching the girls walk up the street.

King walked up and joined him.

"Straight shot, all the way up to where they turned," King said. "What you thinking?"

Frank shrugged. "Not sure, yet." He pointed up the street. "It's a clear line of sight to Broadway, right?"

King nodded.

"Yup. The water bottle was found just thirty feet down on the right," he said. "Like I said, I can't believe no one saw anything—Hyatt is one of the busiest streets in town, after Main. And the drop-off area at Broadway is always packed. Parents, teachers, an officer, even crossing guards. No one saw anything out of the ordinary."

Frank nodded, thinking, and followed the Chief inside.

Mrs. Gutierrez, the housekeeper, opened the door and greeted them, and Frank could tell she'd been doing a lot of crying over the past week. That kind of emotional attachment was hard to hide and impossible to fake—her daughter was missing, and she was dealing with it.

The Chief introduced them, and Frank shook her hand. Her hands were as rough as Frank's. She knew about hard work. The Chief told her they were doing all they could to find her daughter, and she thanked him in broken English before leading them through the house.

And the house was huge, impressive.

Frank wondered what it would be like to be this well off. He was driving a hand-me-down car from the Bureau, filled with broken electronics. His tiny apartment in downtown Birmingham was a dump. His NOPD pension wasn't impressive, but he could have lived a better life, if he took more side work. Just being surrounded by all of this wealth made him want to revisit the idea of getting out of Birmingham proper, maybe get a nicer apartment, in a nicer part of town. He had very little scratch, but he could make more if he wanted to. And he just needed to be smarter about spending it. Way too much of it ended up at Tammy's Liquor down on Park. Tammy knew how much he liked his bourbon, maybe better than anyone else.

Of course, some of the wealth surrounding the Martins was an illusion. Frank had been through the finances. The Martins were very good at projecting a mirage of stability and success. Frank guessed that rich people had the same problems as anyone else—keeping up appearances, people relying on you too much. Frank's eyes took in the foyer as they walked through. The place was posh, like a hotel lobby. They passed a huge, sweeping staircase and through into what had to be the largest living room he had ever seen.

"Who's this? Another consultant?" A man stood, his arms on his hips. Nick Martin—Frank knew from the photos and the barking attitude. Confrontational and short-tempered when surprised. Frank knew the type.

"I'm Frank. Frank Harper," he said. He didn't bother to offer his hand. He knew that Martin either wouldn't take it, or he'd squeeze too hard just to prove his anger. Instead, Frank turned and started walking around the room, taking everything in. It was a typical suburban living room—couch, chairs, TV the size of an aircraft carrier, and a bunch of low tables with crap on them. Lots of beautiful landscape photos, blown up and mounted on expensive canvas. And magazines, piles of them, everywhere.

"More questions, right?" Nick said, shaking his head and looking at Frank. "Instead of asking us more questions, shouldn't you be out there, looking for Charlie?"

"Well, thanks for seeing us," Chief King said, holding his tongue. Frank would have done the same thing, had he been in King's position. No need to engage the man in a useless debate. "We've brought in a consultant on the case, and that—"

Nick Martin shook his head and turned to look at the Chief. "We don't need another goddamned consultant," the man barked. Nick's voice was getting louder. "YOU need to be out looking. You and everyone on that police force. Why are we paying you people?"

"We are searching, Nick," the Chief said, shaking his head. "We are combing every location we can think of and interviewing anyone that might have a problem with you, or anyone who might know the kidnappers."

Martin looked at him sideways. "That's bullshit. Just about everyone in town has a problem with me. You interviewing everyone?"

"We've talked to everyone on the list, Nick," Chief King began. "And we've got people out there—"

"Mr. Martin," Frank interrupted. "Why does everyone in town hate you?"

The father and the Chief both turned to look at him but with opposite reactions. The Chief seemed mortified, but the City Councilman's face went through four versions of red before settling on a particular rosy shade.

"What? How dare you come into my house—someone I've never met, by the way"—he shouted at the Chief—"and insult me!"

Frank shook his head.

"I'm not insulting you. I'm repeating back what you just said—everyone in town hates you. Why?"

"Are you from Cooper's Mill?" the man challenged Frank.

Frank shook his head.

"I'm on the City Council," Nick said forcefully. "I have a record of fiscal conservancy. I've ended some programs and cut some funding that I didn't think was necessary. We scaled back the police department, for one thing." Frank glanced at the Chief, who gave no outward reaction. "Anyway," Nick continued, "I've led the charge to get the city's books in order. I'm used to running a business, living within my means. We cut some stuff, killed a few projects, and people are mad. I've had threats before, and I can take it. I was in the Army."

Frank nodded at Martin. "I was in the Corps, 7th Brigade."

It was so easy to get ex-military talking. Let them know you were in—it always got them to relax. Martin nodded at him in that brotherly "we served together" kind of way that Frank hated, but Mr. Martin seemed to calm down a few notches. He sat heavily on the couch, letting out a sigh.

"Chief, I don't care who you bring in," Nick said. "I just want our daughter back."

The Chief nodded and sat down on the flowery couch opposite Nick. Frank sat down next to the Chief. He glanced at two thick coffee table books in front of him: "Photography and Darkrooms" and "Ansel Adams—A Retrospective."

"Mr. Martin," Frank began. "Are you a photographer?"

"No, my wife is. She dabbles," he said, clearly not impressed with his wife or her level of talent. "That means she spends lots of money on it, but it never amounts to anything."

Frank took in the coffee table and the stack of magazines—Oprah and Martha Stewart and House Beautiful were on top, but underneath were four about photography. He flipped through one. Beneath it were four large albums of pictures, and Frank picked them up, flipping through each one. Vacation pictures of the Martins, good quality. Later pictures with Charlie, again very professional for an amateur. He knew next to nothing about photography, but the shots seemed well-composed.

"So, Mr. Martin," Frank said, not looking up from the photos or making any eye contact. "Who do you think took Charlie?"

Frank could see Nick shaking his head.

"I don't know—anyone with a grudge, I guess. Isn't that what I've just been saying?" The man was clearly running on fumes. "I just hope that's what it is. If they're mad at me, they might not hurt Charlie. But now they've got my money, lots of it. Maybe the satchel will make us square, in their minds."

Frank looked at Nick. "Okay, so you're unpopular around town. Anything recently piss people off more than usual?" Frank asked.

"Funding," Nick said. "It's always about money. Last month, we cut the Parks Department by four positions, so those guys are gone now. They were let go this week. And the police force"—he glanced uncomfortably at Chief King—"was cut two months ago by three positions. Plus, we had one person retire and one begin a long-term deployment with the military. Those positions will not be filled."

Frank glanced at the Chief.

"Anyone on your payroll pissed enough at Scrooge here to hold back on the investigation? Maybe miss something on purpose?"

The Chief sat up a little straighter. "No."

Frank nodded soberly. "Had to ask," Frank said, and turned back to Martin. "Any other issues? Family problems, bad blood with the neighbors, business deals?"

"Nope, nothing. Glenda will be home soon. She's with a group walking the Freeman Prairie."

Frank turned to the Chief.

"I thought they already checked there?"

The Chief shook his head. "Yes, but the group is checking the prairie again ahead of the burn, and the kidnappers would have known about it as well. It's been in the paper. The fire department burns it regularly this time of year."

"Why?" Frank asked the Chief.

"Standard procedure," the Chief answered. "It borders the town and Canal Lock Park and the bike trail, and kids wander out there sometimes. The grass is tall, and they get lost, and it's far enough away from downtown that no one hears them yelling. There's an off chance the girls could be out there," he said, glancing at Nick Martin. "But it's been checked once before by our group of about 100 volunteers—they did Kyle Park, too, and others," the Chief said.

Frank shook his head.

"So, you're still actively searching for the girls, even though you have a ransom demand and identified possible kidnappers?"

The Chief shrugged. "Still working all assumptions, including the possibility that the kidnapping part of this is a hoax for money."

Frank nodded, thinking. He turned to Nick.

"Is everything fine with your wife? The relationship solid?" Frank asked.

"Yup," Nick said quietly. He looked like he wanted to get offended at the question but just didn't have the energy. "Mostly just money problems, which you probably know about if you've been through the files." Nick turned to Chief King. "Glenda's bringing in a psychic."

"You're joking me," Chief King said.

"No, it's all set up, Nick Martin said, shaking his head. "They'll be here in the morning. She's supposedly good, having closed a few cases."

King nodded slowly. "Okay. The press will love that—but seriously, Nick, we don't need more people poking around here."

Frank leaned in. "Mr. Martin, did Charlie always walk to school alone?"

The man shook his head. "No. Her two friends that she normally walks with were on field trips."

"Who would know that?"

"Anyone with access to the online school calendar," Chief King said. "Though, to figure out she would be walking alone, they'd have to know the girls' names. The teachers' names were posted, but not the students'."

Frank nodded and stood up.

"Well, thank you for your time, Mr. Martin," he said curtly. Frank shook Nick Martin's hand—the man was taken aback by the suddenness of his dismissal—and walked away. Frank heard the Chief apologize and chase Frank out onto the lawn. Frank was standing in the middle of the lawn, staring down at the ground, thinking.

"Okay," the Chief said. "What was all that about?"

"He didn't do it," Frank nodded back at the house. "He doesn't know who did, either, so I decided to not burn any more daylight. The school is that way?"

The Chief pointed. "Five blocks up. Straight shot."

Frank nodded.

"Meet me there. I'm going to walk it," Frank said. He turned and started walking across the luxurious front lawn, leaving the Chief standing there in the driveway alone.

25

Chastity was sitting at the table in the kitchen, working on the white skirt she'd torn. It was her favorite skirt. It made her butt look great but falling down on the pavement in front of those cops had torn it.

She had her mother's sewing small kit spread out on the table in front of her. It was the only thing she had from her mother—a small, ornate, golden orb about the size of an apple. It unfolded on the sides, and the small compartments held tiny spools of thread and a few needles, patches, and a thimble.

The rip in her skirt was a simple tear. She wouldn't need a patch—the heavy white thread, doubled-up, would work fine.

Chastity stabbed the needle through the white fabric, trying to ignore the crying sounds from upstairs. This whole thing was taking longer than it should have, and George's complete lack of balls wasn't helping. Chastity knew what she would have done in his situation—kicked some ass until she got her money—but George was simple and apt to get along.

She didn't care—at least he was taking care of the girls. Chastity didn't want anything to do with them. She'd told George she didn't like kids—the look on his face had been precious, like a wounded kitten—but, in truth, she didn't want the girls to see her face. Chastity was smart enough to know that this "plan" had little chance of coming off without a hitch, and she didn't want it blowing up in her face.

She looped the thread around, tying it off and cutting it, then rethreaded the needle and started again. Her mom had taught her to double-stitch everything.

That, and how to turn her body into a steady flow of cash.

Chastity's mom had checked out doing what she loved best—staring at a ceiling in a dingy hotel, ignoring the john on top of her. Probably counting the money in her head, over and over, as a lethal dose of coke ran through her system.

Of course, Chastity hadn't been old enough at the time to turn tricks, but that hadn't kept her mom from teaching her every detail of the trade. And now, when things were tight, Chastity fell back on her God-given, built-in skill set.

Things had been better, lately, with George. Although he was simple, and sometimes impossible to hold a conversation with, he knew where to score and had money and sometimes a car. And he never hit her.

And this setup here at the farmhouse with George's boss was killer. George grew the pot and prepped it for sale, and she could usually sneak some with no effort. And his boss kept prying eyes away. And Chastity? Well, she got to sit on her ass all day, watching TV, smoking and shooting up. It was the life.

But George had talked so much about California, about heading out west, that Chastity had caught the fever as well. He'd never been, of course. But he'd told her stories about the ocean. He said that the water hissed like snakes as the waves crashed on the sand and went back out to sea. He said that you could look out at the water and know there was nothing for a thousand miles but water and wind and endless waves.

George was an idiot, of course, but sometimes he sounded like a goddamned poet. He was nothing to look at, but when he was in his telling-stories mood, she could listen for days.

Chastity finished up the skirt and held it up to the light. You almost couldn't tell there had been a tear at all. Money was tight—even with George handing it over all the time—and she didn't feel like wasting it on a new skirt, so fixing the old one was good. She never could handle money. It seemed to evaporate from her hands, especially when she was high. Or drunk.

She slowly gathered up the items from the table and carefully folded them back into her mother's ornate sewing kit. It really was beautiful. When closed, it looked like a large golden apple. Chastity had no clue where her mother had gotten it, or how she had managed to hang onto something so beautiful for so long, living the life she had. But Chastity was happy to have it.

Chastity walked to the stairs and went up. The girls were finally sleeping, by the sound of it. The little Mexican one almost never shut up, whining on and on in Spanish, and Chastity had gotten tired of yelling at her. At the top of the stairs, she stopped and listened but didn't hear anything.

She and George shared one of the four bedrooms, and Chastity went into their room and locked the door behind her. She pulled the drawer open on the tall bureau—all of the furniture was old and had come with the house in the foreclosure—and put the skirt and sewing kit away.

Someone started crying quietly in the next room, but she shook her head and ignored it.

Chastity caught sight of herself in the floor-length mirror on the back of the door. She'd insisted George put one in when she'd moved in. Slowly, she stripped off her clothes, letting them drop away to the old brown hardwood floors. She watched in the mirror as she ran a hand down her body, admiring the curves and the flat stomach. The rise of her breasts as she breathed slowly in and out.

She knew she was beautiful.

The looks she got whenever men were around only confirmed what she already knew—and what her mom had said, over and over. It had started at fourteen—her mom had still been alive and had clucked appreciatively at the catcalls that started to come whenever Chastity was out in public.

"That's your ticket, honey," she'd said, one of the last things Chastity remembered her mom saying. "Them boys are gonna pay your way, if you let 'em."

Chastity smiled at the memory and dug back into the top drawer, getting out her other kit. She rolled it out on the bed and sat down next to it. Needle, spoon, lighter. A vial of white chunks of crack cocaine. She didn't know where George got the stuff, and didn't care. But he could touch her all he wanted, day and night, as long as the stuff kept coming.

She spooned out a chunk and crushed it in the spoon and melted it into a liquid with the lighter, then shot up. The warmth flowed into her, a sharp fire that burned through her veins and skin and hair and right into her soul. Chastity lay back on the bed, enjoying the ride, letting it burn through her. She loved the feel of sheets against her when she was high. No clothes. They were too rough against her warm, tingling skin.

The sounds of crying coming from the next room faded away into the silent inferno that engulfed her.

26

Frank slowly walked the five blocks to the school, scouring the bushes, sidewalks, and gutters as he went, but he found nothing out of the ordinary.

This case was getting odder by the moment.

First, no one saw the actual snatch. In a town this small, someone had to see something or know something. People talked, and in a town like this, everyone was somebody's cousin or ex-wife or boss.

And Frank knew that half the town could logically be suspects in the kidnapping case. Nick Martin's cost-cutting zeal had apparently pissed off a lot of people. But how many of them were angry enough to take a kid and hold them for money? Planning a kidnapping took months of work and a whole other level of zeal. It seemed like a stretch for someone pissed off about getting let go from a job.

And then there was the whole mess with the ransom drop and ensuing getaway. Bad planning and setup of the scene. Horrible perimeter control, allowing the kidnappers to take back streets and alleys to get away. And the electronic trackers, easily found and removed.

Added together, it gave Frank half a mind to suspect Chief King or one of his cops of involvement. But if the Chief were somehow in on it, he'd be an idiot to bring in outside help.

As Frank walked the five blocks up Hyatt, he tried to organize all of the facts in the case in his head. There were a lot of details to track.

Hyatt was a nice street, one of the nicer he'd seen in town. The houses were large and spread out on the west side, closer together on the east. Plenty of houses and doorways and windows.

He got to Broadway and turned. The location where they found the water bottle was thirty feet up on the right. Frank turned to look back at the Martin house. He could clearly see the long driveway, and, from this corner, he could see the crime scene as well. The Chief was right. It was hard to believe no one saw anything.

He wished he had an iPod or some way to listen to music. It helped him think.

Frank started off again, walking slowly up Broadway, looking at the bushes and trees and driveway and houses that lined both sides of the wide street.

He saw Chief King up ahead, waiting for him in front of the school, but Frank did not hurry. After a minute of careful searching, he came to the location of the water bottle, marked with a fading chalk circle in one gutter. Other than the chalk circle, there was nothing to indicate anything had happened here.

"Anything?" the Chief asked, walking over.

Frank shook his head. "There's a clear line of sight from the corner to the Martin house, and a clear line of sight from here to the school," he said, pointing at the massive elementary school, just a hundred yards away.

The Chief nodded.

"Like I said. This case is weird."

27

"What?" George asked.

Chastity, bleary eyed and angry, was standing too close behind him, trying to listen in on the call.

The boss was on the other end.

"Look, the other guy is wrapping things up," the boss was saying. "He's getting me the money tomorrow, but you have to stay until Saturday, before HarvestFest. Everyone in town will be busy until then. After that, we can wrap this up. I just need another three days. Let things quiet down. Just keep the girls quiet—"

Chastity, behind him, cursed loudly and stormed off.

George nodded, although no one could see him.

"Sure, boss," George said. "I'll make sure they're good, but...um... what about our money? We're taking the biggest risk, being here with the girls all the time. If the cops come—"

"The cops won't come," George's boss said on the other end of the line, cutting him off. "When was the last time they came, took you to jail, and burned down the crop?"

George thought about it for a second.

"Never?"

"Right," the man on the other end of the phone answered. There was a loud rumbling in the background. It sounded like he was driving. "Stay put, and your share will go up for the extra days. But you gotta keep that woman on a leash. She sounds ready to bust."

George agreed and hung up.

Chastity was standing there, exasperated.

"Well?"

"That was the boss," George said. He thought she knew that.

"No shit. I know it was the boss," she screeched at him. "Tell me what he said, Puddin', or I swear to GOD I'm gonna get dressed and leave. I'll just start walking," she said, her arms crossed. "It's not that far into Troy. I've walked it, plenty of times, when I ran out of smokes. Someone there will give me a ride to anywhere I want to go, believe me. I just want this whole thing to be over."

"It almost is over," he said, smiling at her. "We're going to get our money, plus extra. The boss said we're getting paid Saturday. So we just need to watch them a couple more days—"

"What?"

George put his hands up.

"But I liked your idea," he said, trying to get her to calm down. "The excellent one where we pack and get ready? I'll take care of the girls, and Sunday, Sunday we'll leave. Even if they haven't come up with the money, we'll leave."

Chastity did the math in her head and slowly agreed.

"OK," Chastity said. "But we should get paid more—"

"We're gonna, for the extra days. The boss said."

Chastity nodded and then turned and left the kitchen, heading upstairs. She was completely naked again. George thought she looked tired and out of it. George knew she was high again; she always got high when she was stressed.

28

The Chief drove them back to the police station.

Frank wasn't in the mood to talk. The conversation with Nick Martin had not helped, and the wife hadn't even been there. He really needed to talk to her and asked the Chief to set something up.

"Now what?" King asked, as they walked inside, avoiding the throng of reporters and their questions.

Frank shook his head.

"I'm not sure," Frank said. "Frankly, I thought I'd go through the files quickly and pick out something you missed. Now, I'm not sure."

Inside, they went back into the meeting area in the middle of the large central room and joined the others who were waiting for the Chief to return to hold a status update. Frank listened to the other cops go through their reports—Chief King literally went around the table, letting each Sergeant and Detective and beat cop talk about the various aspects of the case they were handling. Frank listened and took notes, but half of his mind was trying to come up with options and angles.

At the end of the meeting, King covered a few more procedural things and assigned a few promising leads to those involved in the case. Detective Barnes also reviewed a few new items that had come up in the investigation, but Frank didn't think any of them sounded relevant. As the meeting broke up, Chief King invited Frank into his small office.

"So, what do you think?" Chief King said, checking his email while they talked.

Frank sat down heavily. "I don't know. You guys are working it, covering all the bases and dotting all the 'i's. There wasn't anything wonky mentioned by anyone at the meeting, and I can't think of anything you've missed."

Chief King looked at him.

"You sound frustrated."

"Yeah," Frank said, nodding. "I guess I was hoping to come in here and wrap things up quickly. Maybe find a clue that you all had missed or something."

Chief King smiled. "Wanted to school us?"

Frank smiled, looking up at King. "Maybe a little."

King steepled his hands together, looking like he was almost praying.

Ben Stone used to do that, and said once that he liked to do it because he thought it made him look smarter, more studious. Frank wasn't too sure.

King looked directly at Frank.

"It's like I said. I've been here a long time, and we've had strange cases. A few cases we lost because we couldn't get the evidence cleanly or in time. We mostly get OVIs and domestic violence, but we like to think we can handle these big cases, when they come along. But I'm stumped."

They sat in silence for a long time—Frank tried to not interrupt silence. It was often a forge for new ideas. People could be tentative with their opinions, and he'd learned to not talk over them.

When it was clear that King was done talking, Frank spoke up.

"I don't know," Frank said. He thought about the two boxes of files, a couple of them stained red. "But I am going to go through all the files again tonight. Hopefully, I'll find something."

Frank left, avoiding the reporters. They didn't know who he was, and Frank wanted to keep it that way.

He drove back to the hotel and carried the file boxes into the hotel. He was sweating up the stairs and set the boxes down on the bed. But he didn't open them; he'd lied to King. He had no intention of going through the files again.

He wanted a drink so badly his face was starting to hurt.

Sitting through that interminable meeting, all he could think about was the bottle back in his hotel room.

Once the TV was on and Frank had gotten three good sips of bourbon in him, things started to calm down. He relaxed into it, feeling the alcohol warm him from the inside out, letting his troubles drift away like smoke.

29

Thursday morning, Chief King was waiting for him in the Vacation Inn parking lot. Frank's head was killing him.

"Morning," King said.

Frank nodded, grumbling. "Am I gonna get this kind of treatment every day?"

He didn't remember going to sleep at all. The bourbon had washed his night away. The last thing he remembered was watching Craig Ferguson. All he knew for sure this morning was that every drop of alcohol in his place was gone, even all the little mini-bottles from the mini bar.

Frank had awakened in the same clothes he'd been wearing Wednesday night. He'd barely gotten changed and cleaned up after the call had come in that King was picking him up.

"Nah, I just wanted to chat with you before we meet with the others," King said as Frank got into the police cruiser. Frank was jealous—King's car was spotless, with exactly zero pieces of ceiling fabric hanging down like tattered curtains. Frank glanced over, but the Taurus was still there—he guessed they didn't have a lot of cars getting stolen around here.

"Plus," King continued, "there are more reporters at the station, and I need to make a press statement this morning. Find anything?" King asked, as he drove out of the hotel parking lot.

Frank shook his head and then stopped immediately—it made his headache that much worse. He reached up and steadied himself with the dashboard.

"I didn't go through the files," Frank said, barely shaking his head. "I was—after reading them all yesterday morning, I needed to just absorb for a while. I'll sit down and go through them again this evening—can I borrow Peters? He's handy."

King nodded, unhappy. "Sure."

They drove on in silence for a minute until King spoke up.

"Look, Frank? Can I call you Frank?"

Frank nodded.

"Sure."

"I need you sober on this," King said, staring at the road. A light rain fell, and leaves blew across the lanes and swirled around the wet gutters.

Frank looked at him. "Look, I'm fine—I had a couple last night—"

"I know what a drunk looks like," King said quietly, pulling the car out onto Main. "My career has been full of high-functioning drunks—bosses, friends, coworkers. I don't really give a shit what you do to yourself," he said. "But for the duration of this case, no alcohol. None. Got it?"

Frank didn't know what to say. He wasn't a fan of ultimatums, but the guy was taking a chance on him.

"Okay," Frank said quietly. The bumping of the car threatened to make him vomit. "I can do that. It won't be easy—"

King looked at him. "I'm serious. We're already screwed on this case. But I can't have you making it worse."

Frank nodded, already wondering how he would get through the next few days—assuming they closed the case soon. He could already feel his insides craving a drink. Now that he was thinking about it, he wanted one, even with the headache still pounding.

"Okay, got it," Frank said, unsure of what else to say. He felt like a kid in class, getting reprimanded. No one had spoken to Frank like that in a long time, maybe not since Trudy left. She'd ripped into him time and time again over the drinking, and his career, or what was left of it. But at the end, when they'd spoken that last time, all the anger was gone from her voice. There was only disappointment and regret.

Somewhere along the line, she'd given up caring.

"And I'll go through the files again," Frank said. "Today."

King nodded, as they crossed the highway into Cooper's Mill. Frank saw banners on the lampposts advertising "HarvestFest 2011," an event coming up downtown Saturday night. The banners whipped in the wind and rain. Fall was coming in earnest, Frank could see. They didn't get a lot of "fall" down in Louisiana, but he'd seen more of it after moving to Alabama. But growing up, they'd never had falling leaves, or this cold rain that never seemed to let up. It had snowed a few times in his youthful winters, but only during the rare cold blast. But here, the rain was cold, and the raw wind didn't help. He didn't even want to imagine winter.

"Does it ever stop raining?" Frank asked, rubbing his head. He was trying to use sheer willpower to make his headache go away. But at least getting called on the carpet by Chief King had sobered him up a little, helped him focus.

King looked over at him and smiled.

"Yeah, it's been wet lately. Played hell with the searches last week. Oh, and to your earlier question, 'yes,' Peters can help you out. He knows all the players and sat in on a bunch of the interviews."

"He's a good kid," Frank smiled. "And he knows where all the coffee is in town."

As they pulled up in front of the police station, Frank saw the group of reporters.

"You do a lot of these?" Frank asked.

"Not if I can avoid it," King said, frowning. "They used to show up only when we called a press conference, but after that first ransom call came in, they're here every day."

"Really?" Frank said, looking at King. "They can be a hassle, that's for sure, but you can also turn them into a tool."

"What?" the Chief said, glancing at his watch as they crossed the wet parking lot. "I don't have anything new to report anyway, so why bother? They just want to see us sweat."

Frank smiled. He had an idea, a sudden and glorious idea that cut through his brain fog like a knife.

"Introduce me," Frank said.

The Chief stopped walking and looked at him.

"What? Why? I thought you wanted a low profile."

"Normally, yeah," Frank agreed. "But this is good—fan the flames. We've got nothing new to go on, and we could use a break," he said, looking at the gathered crowd waiting for them in the lobby of the station. "Just say you've brought in an outside expert on kidnappings, and I'll take a few questions."

Chief King looked skeptical, pulling his hat down to keep the rain out of his eyes. "You sure?"

"Trust me."

A high-pitched voice shouted out to them as they approached the station. One of the reporters ventured out into the rain.

"Any word yet, Chief?"

Frank turned to see a young woman talking to King as he approached the open doors of the police station. She was holding a tape recorder up to the Chief, trying to get him to comment. Oddly, even in the falling rain, she was wearing a large pair of sunglasses that completely covered her eyes.

"A couple of developments, Tina," King said, not slowing down. "We'll cover it inside."

As they walked inside the police station, Frank asked about the young woman reporter.

"Tina Armstrong. Runs the local paper," the Chief said under his breath. "She's loving all the press. They're all following her around, asking about behind-the-scenes stuff here in town."

"What's with the shades?" Frank asked.

King shook his head. "Photophobia—she's very sensitive to light, I heard."

Minutes later, Frank found himself before the cameras, listening to Chief King. There were five TV reporters and camera operators and lights, along with another half-dozen print folks, all crowded into the small lobby of the police station. Around the walls were wooden cases and display shelves filled with memorabilia from the department's history; one display case contained a small metal car that was shaped like a miniature soapbox derby vehicle.

The Chief was talking.

"...and we're making progress. Our latest searches have not turned up any additional evidence, but we're confident that we will find the kidnappers and recover the two girls safe and sound. To that end," the Chief said, glancing at Frank, "we've brought in an outside expert. Frank Harper is a retired police officer with over twenty years' experience, including a background in child abduction and kidnapping cases."

Frank nodded to the Chief and stepped up to the microphone.

"Hi, thank you for coming. I'm Frank Harper, and I was with the New Orleans Police Department for twenty-one years, retiring in 2010." He paused, giving them time to write it all down. Frank glanced over at Chief King, who had been joined by Sergeant Graves and Detective Barnes. He also saw Officer Stan Garber, cradling a cast. Evidently, the suspension was over. The guy glared at Frank, who ignored it. Served him right.

Frank turned back to the press.

"First, just let me say that I'm happy to be assisting the Cooper's Mill Police Department with this investigation," Frank said. "I'm getting up to speed and going over the facts in the case. We are starting to re-interview people involved, and, as soon as we have anything, we'll get it out to you. There have been a few developments, which we are aggressively pursuing. Questions?"

All of their hands went up. He recognized one of them, the fat guy from Channel 4, and nodded to him.

"Scott Bumpers, Channel 4. How do you spell your name? And what is your background with cases like this one?"

Frank spelled his name. He'd forgotten how that was always the first question, or the last. Or maybe the reporter just hadn't been paying attention.

"As Chief King said, I've got extensive experience in abduction cases, both child and adult," Frank said. "I worked many abduction cases in Louisiana and Mississippi and liaised with the FBI and NCMEC on many occasions."

Frank nodded to the young woman in the front. He recognized her sunglasses, which she was still wearing even though they were inside.

"Tina Armstrong, *Cooper's Mill Times*," the woman said. He couldn't tell if she was looking at him or not. "What is NCMEC? And have you had any more contact with the kidnappers since the ransom was paid?"

Frank shook his head.

"NCMEC is the National Center for Missing & Exploited Children, based in Virginia," he said. "I've worked with them in the past to publicize information nationally on missing children and young adults. I can tell you that we plan to reach out to them for assistance on this case," he said, pausing to let that sink in. All the print reporters were scribbling to write it all down. "And no, nothing yet, other than the fact that the kidnappers exited Cooper's Mill to the east and then headed south, in the direction of Huber Heights."

He paused a moment, and then pushed forward.

"And we've identified the two suspects who picked up the ransom," Frank said, smiling.

The gaggle went silent for a second, and then they all shouted at once. He put up his hands and continued.

"I can't give you their names, obviously, because it's an active investigation," Frank said. "But I can say that one is a 25-year old male, and the other is a 22-year old female, both from the area. We'll get the names to you later today, if we can. But we're petitioning for search warrants now. As soon as we have pictures, we'll get those out to our friends in the press."

The print reporters were scribbling it all down, but the TV folks didn't bother. Frank remembered why the TV folks were looking up and around when the print folks were writing: the TV reporters always taped everything in the field, then replayed the video back in the studio, taking their notes from the recordings.

Frank nodded at another reporter.

"You say you have their names?"

"Yes, they've been ID'ed," Frank said, nodding. "We got lucky and found footage from a security cam at a nearby restaurant. The FBI office in Cincinnati has positively identified them through facial recognition software."

More scribbling, more hands in the air.

Frank glanced at Chief King, who was staring at Frank, his eyes wide. Graves was next to King, looking at the ground and shaking his head. Bumpers put his hand back up.

"Any more news on the family? There are reports that they have brought in a psychic."

Frank shook his head.

"That's the first I'm hearing about that," Frank said, lying again. "The family is holding up as best as can be expected. And for the record, the family and their circle of immediate friends have been eliminated as potential suspects. This is clearly the work of an outside party attempting to extort money from the Martins. OK, last question."

Tina Armstrong didn't wait to be called on. She leaned forward and shouted out her question.

"Have you lost any kids?"

The room grew quiet.

Frank looked at her. "What do you mean?"

She looked around at the other reporters and soldiered on, her glasses reflecting Frank's image back at him.

"In your time on the job, how successful were you?" she asked loudly, holding up her tape recorder. "What was your track record, and how many cases did you fail to solve?"

Chief King started to step up to the podium, but Frank waved him back and smiled.

"I understand your curiosity, Ms. Armstrong," Frank said. "I obviously can't get into operational details, but I've solved many cases, and I have recovered many kidnapping victims. But yes, I've lost a few, too. And those stick with you. Each one is an eye-opening and painful learning experience."

Frank stood at the podium for a long moment, trying to forget about that empty patch of land in Atlanta and that buried cardboard box. After a moment, he looked back up at the woman in the sunglasses and the other reporters and cameras around her.

"Thank you," he said.

He turned and stepped down, ignoring the shouts from the reporters. Frank followed the Chief past Lola, the receptionist, who looked like she was on the verge of tears. King pushed through the double doors and led the officers and Frank back into the station offices.

As the doors closed, Frank heard Deputy Peters talking to the reporters who had gathered around the doors, answering a few remaining logistical and administrative questions. There were always those kinds of questions, before and after news conferences, where no information of substance was shared. Names were spelled, agendas and paperwork distributed, and future news conferences announced.

The other police thankfully held their outrage at Frank until the doors closed behind them.

"What the hell?" Detective Barnes said loudly to Frank. "What was that bullshit?"

"Wow," the Chief began, agreeing. "OK, hold up, Barnes. Frank, you've put some information out there, that's for sure. I don't see how that gets us anything." They walked over and sat back down at the conference room table. In moments, the entire investigation team was arrayed around the table, shooting daggers at him.

"That was impressive," Agent Shale said caustically. "I didn't realize we'd identified the kidnappers. Or asked my office in Cincinnati to help."

Frank smiled, sitting down.

"The press can be a powerful ally," Frank said to Shale and the others. "We don't have much, but making them—and the kidnappers—think we have more than we do can always be helpful. We can always back off of it later, but beating the bushes never hurts."

"I disagree," Sergeant Graves said. "You put that kind of information out there, and people start to think things. Or they get scared, or start looking at their neighbors differently." He looked around at the other police.

Barnes agreed. "I can't believe you said we had identified the kidnappers. So exactly what do you want to release to the press?"

"I understand that you are angry," Frank said. "And I apologize for springing that on you guys, especially Barnes. It's your case, so you should be setting the pace. But we need breaks in this case, and letting those kids from the ransom drop think we've identified them won't hurt."

"What if they kill the girls?" Graves asked. "You freaking them out—"

"The girls are already dead," Frank cut in.

The room fell silent. Every eye in the room turned to him.

"Or they're not," Frank continued quietly. "Either way, every day past the delivery of the ransom is a day they don't have to waste. We need to set a fire under those involved. If they were going to kill the girls, they would have already done it, as soon as they got the ransom. No phone calls means that they're not going to ask for anything else. So what's keeping the girls alive, if they are? The kidnappers have a plan. We have to figure out what that plan is and get ahead of it. Or compress the timetable."

Chief King nodded. Sergeant Graves seemed unimpressed and excused himself, saying he needed some fresh coffee and time to think. The others didn't seem any happier about what Frank had done, but they accepted it. They had to—there was nothing any of them could have done anyway. After a minute, Chief King put up his hands to stop the debate, which threatened to go on for hours.

"OK, we'll roll with it," Chief King. "But Frank, no more surprises.

Check with me first. OK, reports, please."

"I'll go first," Sergeant Burwell said, leaning forward. "Nothing yet from forensics on the water bottle. There was a fast food bag found nearby. It went in to the lab with the water bottle, but they didn't find anything," Burwell said, glancing at Frank. "It's from the Sonic drive-through restaurant up in Troy, probably—there aren't any nearer. There's one up in Piqua as well. It might have been dropped by whoever took the girls, but the wrappers and trash yielded nothing, and all the franchises use the same distributor, so we can't track it back to a particular location. Same goes for two other items found in the gutter that morning—a gum wrapper and several pistachio hulls."

King nodded. "OK."

"Unless the kidnappers had breakfast while they were waiting to kidnap the girl, you're just chasing trash," Ted Shale said, but no one else nodded or agreed with him.

Peters came into the room and sat down.

"Deputy," the Chief said. "Get us up to speed on the searches."

Peters nodded. "We did Freeman Prairie again this morning—that's the second pass. They're doing that field burn Sunday morning, so we wanted to check that whole area again ahead of the burn. We've done Kyle three times, the bike path twice, and every other field in and around Cooper's Mill at least once." Peters nodded at the map on the wall behind them. "We also went along the riverbanks, a mile up and downstream from the bridge. Nothing. Huber Heights is handling the river south of town."

"Isn't the water level too low?" Frank asked.

Peters nodded. "Too low to wash a body downstream far, without it being caught on something, but we did have a body lost for a while in the river near Dayton two years ago. They're checking everything again."

The men continued with their reports, going around the table, but everything was coming up zeroes. Graves came back in with a half-finished coffee and reported on the tip line—so far, nothing had come in as a result of Frank's fictitious "news."

Detective Barnes went next, and his report was the longest. As lead on the case, he was theoretically pursuing the best leads, but there had been no real breaks since the ransom drop. No one had spotted the car, or the people involved. Another full work-up of the Martin's finances had been completed yesterday, along with new work-ups of close family and friends, but they'd found nothing. Those had been requested by Frank, although Chief King didn't let on.

Today, Barnes was concentrating on having witnesses on Main Street during the ransom drop go through books of mug shot photos, trying to find the two young people involved. Barnes was also working an angle with the Dayton police that the kidnappers might be using an abandoned property in Dayton to keep the kidnapped girls.

Agent Shale reported on the money. He talked and talked and said nothing. No sign of the ransom money. The Bureau was tracking the serial numbers on the bills. But Frank knew that, if they were smart, the kidnappers would be sure to launder the money before spending it, or at least sit on it for a bit. Buying drugs with the money was one sure way to keep the cash out of regular circulation, at least for a while.

Frank listened to them talk, and it sounded exactly like all the other cases he'd ever worked—good men, doing the work, chasing down leads. But none of these leads were panning out.

Lola, the receptionist, came into the conference room.

"Chief King?"

"Yes?"

Frank saw that her nails were painted a different color today, a bright green. She pointed at the Chief's office.

"It's Nick Martin on the line. They got another call from the kidnappers."

30

Frank leaned in.

"Play it again," he said.

They were all in the Martin's kitchen, gathered around the largest kitchen island Frank had ever seen: Nick Martin, Frank, Chief King, Detective Barnes, Sergeant Graves, Agent Shale, and Deputy Peters. Glenda was in the living room, working on what looked like a scotch and rocks. Evidently she'd heard it enough times.

King pushed the button on the iPhone on the island. A voice came out over the tiny speaker, repeating the message again.

"Mr. Martin," the voice said. "The payment we received was insufficient. We now require another $500,000. Deposit the money in a similar bag and leave it in the middle of the high school football field at noon on Saturday. You have 48 hours. If you do not comply, the girls will be killed."

The call ended.

"Came in a few minutes ago," Nick said. "They called my wife's phone again, and the number was blocked. I told her to let it go to voicemail. We've been getting a lot of calls, and even the sympathetic ones make her upset. I listened to it and called you."

"It's not the same voice as before," King said, glancing down at his yellow pad of paper. Frank had figured out the man never went anywhere without one of those pads. "Or at least it sounds different, or they changed the setting on their voice changer, or whatever they're using to mask the speaker's voice."

Frank nodded.

"Male, late-thirties," Detective Barnes said. "Probably not the getaway driver—doesn't fit the age range."

Chief King nodded.

"Spoke slower, too," Frank added. "More deliberate."

"Do you think they're panicking?" Deputy Peters asked. "Because of what you said at the press conference?"

Frank shook his head.

Detective Barnes pointed at the phone. "Nick, can you get that kind of money together that fast, after what you just did to get the million?"

Nick shrugged. "I'll have to."

"I can't believe how greedy they're being," Sergeant Graves said. "Isn't a million dollars enough?" He looked around at the other nodding cops.

"No, I think it's a 'goose'," Frank said.

"What's a 'goose'?" Deputy Peters asked.

"A wild goose chase," Frank said. "We'd get these once in a while, when the kidnappers were stalling for time. Remember what I said earlier about figuring out their plan? They always have a plan. This sounds like busywork, a distraction. No idiot would ask for more money from you right now, or pick a central location like that—I'm assuming that's central, right?"

The others nodded. "It's near City Park," Graves volunteered. "Right in the middle of town."

"They know we'd go all out to not mess up another ransom drop," Frank said, looking at the phone. "No, this is something else."

Chief King nodded, but Nick Martin was shaking his head.

"I don't care," Nick said. "I still have to assume that it's for real. I'll get started on the money."

Sergeant Graves nodded, agreeing. "It only makes sense. Maybe the kidnappers realized they could get more money out of Mr. Martin."

"Yes, get the money," Glenda said. "And Meredith will be here tomorrow," Glenda spoke up from behind them. Everyone turned to see her standing in the doorway. Frank could smell the scotch from six feet away, but he could also see why Nick had married her. She was beautiful, even standing there sloshing her drink around in the glass in her hand. But her face was lined, drawn. She looked like she hadn't slept in a week.

"Meredith's the psychic?" King asked, and both Nick and Glenda nodded. "We'll show her every courtesy," King said, "but we can't let it distract from the case."

Graves and Shale shot the Chief a funny look.

"Nick, work with Agent Shale, get the money ready." King continued. "Graves, come up with a duty roster and get eyes on that field tonight. I want surveillance through Saturday morning."

The others filed out, but Frank hung back. When he was alone with King, he leaned in.

"This doesn't feel right."

King nodded. "I agree."

31

Frank Harper sat in a booth at the restaurant, waiting, his head pounding. He had never wanted a drink so badly in his life.

He was someplace called The Drunken Noodle, near the highway. Across the expanse of concrete, on the other side of the highway, he could see the sign for his hotel.

The town was small enough. He was starting to get a feel for where most of the landmarks were located. And, as he'd crossed the parking lot and entered the Asian restaurant, he started to understand why so many people preferred to live in small towns, much like the town he'd grown up in outside of Baton Rouge. Small towns were just more comfortable. This place was nice, except that everyone in town seemed on edge. Or maybe it was just because he wasn't from around here and not a familiar face.

He stared at the frosty glass of water in front of him, wishing it was a beer or a shot of anything. Instead, he picked it up and took a long, slow sip. He needed to be steady. Frank was waiting on Laura, who had agreed to meet him for a quick lunch and suggested this place.

Shaking his head, he tried to think about the case. Thinking about beer or bourbon would only lead to another backslide. And he didn't need that, or another dressing down by the Chief, especially after the man had brought him in on the case.

The case. It had absorbed every waking minute of his last 48 hours, ever since he'd been standing in the rain with Chief King and nodded. Now, he was starting to wonder if that had been a good idea.

Going through all the case files over and over hadn't really helped, but it had steeped him in the facts and figures and people of the community. Looking around the busy restaurant, he wondered idly if any of those case files represented people he was looking at. But things were just not adding up. He'd worked enough cases to know when he was making progress and when he was just spinning his wheels. Usually, he had a running tally of suspects and leads in his head to work on at any one time—but with this case, everything checked out. The whole thing was too neat.

And this second ransom call didn't make any sense at all. It was like getting blood from a stone—the kidnappers must think the Martins were swimming in cash.

Or the kidnappers knew something that Frank didn't.

Frank heard her voice and looked up as she came in. Laura was carrying a little boy—Jackson.

Frank stood and smiled.

"You been waiting long?" she asked, walking over to the table and setting down a large purse. He couldn't take his eyes off Jackson, who squirmed in his mother's arms. He looked so much like her when she had been a toddler, but the shock of hair was not from the Harper side of the family.

"Dad?" she said, and he glanced at her as they sat down. "You been here long?" she asked again, smiling.

"What?" he asked, looking back at Jackson. "Oh, no, just got here," he said, pointing at the water.

Laura slid into the seat and let Jackson go. The little boy turned around and sat at the table expectantly, like someone was going to pass him a scotch and soda.

Frank smiled.

"He looks big, bigger than I thought he'd be."

She smiled and tousled Jackson's hair.

"Yeah, he's getting heavy," she said, her eyes sparkling. "You're gonna have to walk more, monkey!" she said to the boy, who was looking across the table at Frank.

Frank smiled. "Hi, Jackson."

The boy looked a little wary. He glanced up at his mom for direction. Frank remembered when Laura used to do that, glancing at him or Trudy for guidance. She would always do that when something funny happened to see if it was okay to laugh.

Laura nodded. "It's okay, Jackson," Laura said. "This is who I was telling you about. This is my Dad, and your granddad. His name is Frank."

Jackson looked back at Frank and, after a moment to think about it, nodded as well.

"Hi."

"Hi, Jackson," Frank said, smiling. "I'm Frank. Do you like to be called Jackson, or do you prefer 'monkey'?"

"I like 'Jackson,'" the little boy said brightly. "Monkey sounds funny to me. But Katie calls me 'monkey' sometimes. Katie's my friend at school," Jackson said matter-of-factly.

"Great, that's great," Frank said. "I like Jackson," he said. Frank turned and picked up the item on the seat next to him and slid it across the table. It was a small box, wrapped in green striped paper. The woman at the toy store had done it for Frank, or the wrapping job would have looked a lot rougher around the edges.

"I got you something."

Laura smiled in a way that Frank had not seen before. It made Frank suddenly understand that he was doing the right thing, being here in Cooper's Mill, trying to make that connection again, or any connection. Maybe it wasn't the old connection they'd had before, but something completely new. Her eyes teared up a little, and Frank looked away, staring at the present, as Jackson pawed the paper off. Inside was a package of plastic dinosaurs.

"Awesome!"

Frank smiled—he was smiling a lot more than he was used to.

"I wasn't sure what to get you, but I figured you liked dinosaurs," Frank said. "Everyone likes dinosaurs, right?"

Jackson nodded, smiling at the package.

"What do you say?" Laura asked the boy, dabbing at the corner of her eye with a cloth napkin.

Jackson looked away from the dinosaurs and up at Frank.

"Thank you," he said in a sing-songy, genuine way, and then tore into the packaging, using his fork to pry at the plastic. In moments, Jackson had liberated the dinosaurs, and they were growling at each other and teaming up to attack the grouping of condiments situated in the center of the table.

"Thank you," Laura said to Frank, who was enjoying watching the dinosaurs gang up on a helpless bottle of soy sauce.

"It was no big deal," Frank said. "I just went by the toy store downtown…"

"It is a big deal," she said, interrupting him. "For me, and for him," she said, nodding at the boy.

Frank nodded, and picked up the menu.

"So, what's good?"

Laura made a couple of recommendations and helped Jackson pick out something from the kid's menu. Frank needed something light—his stomach was doing flips after being cut off so abruptly from Frank's dietary staple, alcohol.

When the waiter came around, Frank let Laura go first, and he suddenly realized how pleasant it was, just sitting here with her and Jackson and listening to her order. It was no big deal, and, at the same time, a huge deal.

After their food was ordered, he and Laura chatted for a few minutes about his hotel and what he thought of Cooper's Mill. Then the conversation turned to the case.

"Oh, it's coming along," he said, setting down his water. "I'm reviewing the case, up to this point, and trying to find anything they might have missed." Frank hesitated, not wanting to get into the details. He didn't need her worrying about him. And even though Jackson was busy playing with the toys, Frank didn't want to scare him.

That was how the trouble had started with her mother—first, Trudy had been worried about him in the job, and then, after Katrina, when he was in a very dark place, she had worried about him. And what he might do to himself.

"Good," Laura said. "They could use you, I'll bet. They're just a small-town police department. They are amazing at what they do, but I think kidnapping is a little bit out of their comfort zone. I doubt if anyone over there has actually investigated one before."

"No, they're good guys," Frank said. "One of them went to Quantico for basic FBI training, including kidnappings, hostage taking and negotiation. Plus, we have an agent up from Cincinnati, and he's well-versed in all the techniques."

Frank didn't elaborate. His daughter didn't need to know the guy was an idiot.

They watched Jackson play for a few minutes, chatting about other things unrelated to the case. It was nice to talk about, and think about, other things. Frank had been so immersed in the case for two full days, the conversation was a welcome respite.

And, as they talked more and more, and slowly seemed to become more comfortable around each other, Frank wondered at the future of their relationship, him and his daughter. He liked this—just sitting here, together, talking. They were talking about their lives, what things were like at her salon, how Jackson was doing in school. She cracked a couple of jokes, and they laughed together. He made a wry comment about something she had done when she was young, and for a moment worried that he had gone too far too fast, but she laughed heartily, a laugh he hadn't heard in probably ten years.

This was what life should be about, these types of moments. Not dusty fields or flooded hospitals, or obsessing about things that had already happened and could not be changed. Not running from one case to the next, worrying about completion percentages and bosses that didn't understand that, sometimes, the case simply could not be solved.

No, Frank liked this feeling a lot. It was like he was needed.

He didn't want to push it and upset the apple cart. When the food came, they made small talk that was, at the same time, completely pointless and heartwarmingly precious.

An hour later, Frank still didn't want lunch to end. They had covered a far range of topics, everything from his apartment in Birmingham to her warm feelings about Jackson's school and the staff. But the lunch had to end. Laura needed to get Jackson to school, and Frank needed to get back to the case.

Frank paid, something he was happy to be able to do. The money fronted by Chief King was really coming in handy. Being able to pay for their lunch, and being casual about it, made Frank feel an almost overwhelming sense of pride.

Frank carried her bag out as they left the restaurant and walked to her car, a small red Honda that looked like it had seen better days. Like father, like daughter, he thought, glancing over at the Taurus. She opened the car, and Frank buckled Jackson into his seat, giving him a quick peck on the forehead.

Frank smiled and went around the front of the car and, before she said goodbye and climbed into her car, Laura surprised him with a heartfelt hug, long and pleasant. She smelled vaguely of shampoo and perfume, some scent akin to tangerines. And even as he waved, as she drove away, Frank could still detect the scent in the autumn air.

32

Thursday evening, two cars sat in the dark and expansive grocery store parking lot. The pavement around the cars was shiny. Behind them, the Cooper's Mill Burger King stood next to Main Street.

The rain that had been coming down off and on for three days had let up momentarily. Only a light mist hung in the air over the two cars, which had been positioned so the driver's windows faced each other.

Tyler, the man sitting in the police cruiser, spoke first.

"You sure about this?" he asked.

"Yes," the other man said, his face hidden in the shadows. "I'm sure."

The two drivers spoke quietly, occasionally glancing around to make sure they were not being watched.

The man reached over and passed Tyler the green duffel bag, passing it between the open windows. "There's your money, plus whatever you get from the second ransom on Saturday. Bad idea, by the way."

Tyler nodded, taking the money. The bag was heavier than he expected. He put the money in the floorboard.

"Thanks," Tyler said. "My people are getting itchy. But I don't think it's a bad idea—gotta keep Chief King and the others distracted. And this will all be wrapped up by Saturday night or Sunday. And then it will be 'Buona Sera,' as my mom used to sing."

The other guy nodded.

"What are you doing about the girls? I don't want anyone to get hurt," the man said. "You promised me."

"I know," Tyler said, nodding. "Everything's going to be fine. But that's one reason I asked for the second ransom—I need more cash to cover the extra expenses. The little girls have spent time with my contacts and know what they look like. So my people need to leave the area—and I'm leaving, too. After this, my contacts and I are going away for a long time."

"I just wish you had told me about it first," the other man said, shaking his head. "I didn't like hearing about it on the news."

"Had to be done," Tyler added. "Besides, Nick Martin and his pretty wife are good for it."

"What about that new guy?"

"He's no idiot," Tyler said, glancing around. "He's retired PD.

Digging into the case, talking to everyone again. Re-interviewing the Martins, going over the evidence."

The other man shook his head.

"I don't like it. Do we have to get the second ransom? Why can't we just wrap this up now?"

Tyler looked at the man. "Hey, you got your money, right? So, I'm just supposed to go away and never bother you again? And my contacts are just supposed to disappear?"

The other man shook his head. "No, but there's a lot of money in that bag, more than enough—"

"It's not enough," Tyler said. "Not by a long shot. So drop it about the second ransom. I'll handle it, and then we'll wrap things up. Girls go back to their families, you and I part ways, everyone's happy."

The man nodded slowly.

"That would be fine, except for this new guy. What was that he said at the press conference about identifying the kidnappers? That can't be true, is it?"

Tyler shook his head, but waited a moment before speaking. He loved that look on people's faces when he had information that they wanted, and he held it back.

"He's just fishing," Tyler said. "Looking to stir things up. Getting the press involved was his idea, too—before, Chief King was holding them off."

The other man shrugged. "I don't like the attention. Will he find anything?"

"Don't worry about them," Tyler said curtly. "Things are moving along. And then 'There'll be no next time,'" he said, singing the Louis Prima tune. The song sounded odd and out of place in the dark, but he didn't care. "But this is it. No more meetings, unless you've got more money for me."

The police radio squawked loudly, announcing an EMT run in progress in Cooper's Mill. Tyler reached over and silenced the radio.

The other man was quiet for a moment, and then nodded slowly. "OK, no more meetings. What are you going to do with the girls?"

Tyler shook his head.

"Beep boop—like I always say, it's taken care of. I said don't worry about it, just like I said don't worry about that money from the second ransom. I'll take care of it."

"Good," the other man said sharply. "Good luck with the money."

Tyler nodded.

"Nothing to worry about," Tyler said.

33

It was late on Thursday evening, and Frank was back in his hotel room.

He had spent most of the day at the police station, watching the videotaped interviews with the principals in the case. He'd also talked to each of the police officers and investigators in turn, even holding a short and snippy conversation with Deputy Stan Garber, nursing his broken arm. Frank let each one talk, asking questions and trying to find any information that might have been gathered by the cops but had failed to make it into the written reports.

He was trying to stay busy. Every time he slowed down, even for a moment, his hands started to shake and he started thinking about a bourbon on the rocks. Or five.

A solid two hours of the day, after lunch, had been taken up with a long meeting with Agent Shale, going over the finances for Martin Construction again. Frank had been through the financial reports on Wednesday, back at the coffee shop, but this time, he and Shale went through each and every Martin Construction investment—and there were many—and determined who might gain from bankrupting the company. Between both ransoms, Martin was back on his heels.

Nick Martin and his company had had their fingers in a lot of pies. Frank had heard that saying from Ben Stone, and it had stuck. And Ben and he had investigated enough cases together to know that somehow, it all fit together, if you did the work. More times than he could count, Frank and other investigators had broken a case wide open by finding a seemingly-pointless gas station receipt or other scrap of information. In one case, the identification of the kidnappers had turned on the mention of a limited financial partnership in an obscure legal document, a document that had been sitting in the case file since the day the investigation started.

Frank and Agent Shale had gone through all the construction projects, finished and unfinished, and made a list of all of the "partners," or people, that could benefit. It tied into Frank's newest theory: that, somehow, the entire kidnapping was really a way to put financial pressure on the Martin's and Martin Construction.

Soon they had a nice short list of business partners and other businesses to look into, and Frank had tasked Shale with running down reports again on all of those people. They'd run credit checks/histories on all of them before, but Frank wanted more information, anything the FBI could dig up. All the other files were stacked up on the table next to the hotel room window, ready to be referenced again, if needed.

But first, he was sketching out the connections, as he remembered them. He was drawing a "map" of the members of the community and how they were connected. He was making visual notes on several sheets of paper, drawing circles with names in them and connecting them to other circles with names in them.

Steve Furrows, the ex-partner who had been such a pain in the ass when he was trying to quit smoking, had used this methodology, called "mind mapping," to link together everything in the case and make a map of those involved. Steve had said it helped him see the big picture and to trace all the linkages back to the original crime. Frank had found it worked particularly well in cases like this one, with lots of people involved and all of them seemingly connected in one way or another.

So Frank worked, head down at the small round table by the window, drawing on sheets of white paper and taping each of them up on the window. Back in his field days, he would have done this in his office, posting the map in a central conference room where everyone working on the case could see it. Instead, he was working this one by himself, apart from the other cops, at the request of Chief King.

Frank knew that reviewing all the case files again, after spending six hours today reading them, would be overkill—and it might overtax his weary mind—but there was just something off about this case.

On first blush, the case looked like a slam-dunk, but nothing strange had come up in the profiles of any of those people connected to the family. Everything seemed on the up-and-up.

It was going to be a long night.

Frank sighed and muted the TV—he had it on to watch the news when it came around. He wanted to see the press conference and any other press coverage. Frank really didn't care about how he ended up looking or sounding on the TV—he'd been in enough high-profile cases to get his ugly mug on TV before. But he was interested in how the news stations reported it and what, if anything, would be the reaction in the community to the "news" that the kidnappers had been positively identified.

He tried to ignore the sealed bottle on top of the mini-bar.

Frank had had a nice dinner downtown at "O'Shaughnessy's." He'd sat in the bar, and one entire wall of the place was this beautiful, old, exposed brick. Great food, too. But on the way back to the hotel, he'd found himself at the little liquor store located next to Domino's.

He'd gone inside and grabbed one of those baskets, filling it up with great stuff, but then ended up putting almost all of it back except for one bottle of Maker's Mark. Maybe he'd been embarrassed, looking down at the basket. How sad was it that his first reaction to a windfall of cash, something he'd been deeply worried about only a few nights ago, was to blow it all on bourbon?

Or maybe he was worried about the promise he'd made to Chief King.

Frank knew that he shouldn't, but he needed it to think. His brain just didn't work right without a drink or two. It was the lubrication that made his mind operate, like oil in an engine. He needed to go through all the files again, one by one, making notes and diagrams and staying up as long as it would take. The bourbon would help. His internal debate only lasted a few more minutes before he retrieved the bottle and slowly opened it, taking in the rich aroma. Frank poured himself out a measure in a glass and threw it back.

The warmth spread slowly through him, calming him. Bourbon always made him feel warmer and somehow stretched out, flatter and looser, more mellow. Nothing was out of reach, no puzzle too difficult to solve. He tipped another measure into the glass and drank it quickly, then a third measure went into the glass, and he walked over to the table and sat down, setting the glass next to the stacks of files.

He looked out the window, past the few sheets of his "map." The trucks hummed on the highway, racing into the night. The cars and trucks and their drivers were whizzing past the exit to this little town, oblivious to what was happening just a mile away. The people in those cars probably didn't know about the kidnapping or the botched ransom drop or the bewildering second ransom call from the kidnappers, something exceedingly rare. He'd only heard of it happening a few other times. No one ever went back to the well. It was just too dangerous.

But the people in those cars didn't know. Or care.

He wished he could walk away. Why had he allowed himself to get caught up? He hated himself for being so weak, but, at the same time, the case was helping his mind—even if it was baffling, at least his mind had something to work on for the first time in a long while.

Frank shook his head and looked back at the files. He knew he could just stare out the window for hours, watching the cars whiz by and relaxing into the warmth in his belly. But he needed to be making progress. He needed to find something, anything, that he could add to the map and point him in a new, and fruitful, direction.

He opened the first box of files and set aside the stack of pens, tape, and a pair of scissors resting on top. Peters had thrown in some school supplies when Frank had mentioned he'd be working on the files away from the police station.

The first file was one of the red ones, the incident report. It was the first file he'd ever read on the case, only 36 hours ago at the coffee shop, Wednesday morning, when Deputy Peters had dropped the boxes and two of the files had fallen into the "bloody" water. This would be Frank's fourth time through all the case files, but he figured he'd better start over, right at the beginning. He took the case file, labeled "Incident Report Scene Investigation," flipped it open, and started reading.

34

George drove the Corolla down the long, straight country road that ran north out of Troy and into farmland that stretched off into the night. He loved driving at night, the windows down, especially when the weather was excellent and allowed it. And the Corolla wasn't nearly as nice as the Mustang, which had come and gone from his life. At least it was better than sitting at the farmhouse, listening to Chastity complain.

Finally, he spotted the turn and edged the Corolla off the road and around the bend that marked the small paved road that led up a low hill to the farmhouse. The boss had called and needed George to run a couple of errands, and George had jumped at the chance.

She was still waiting up when he got back to the farmhouse.

He saw her standing on the porch, her arms crossed, when he parked the beat-up Corolla out front. He always wondered why she didn't get colder when she was outside. She never seemed to be wearing much.

"Puddin'—this isn't working!" Her voice was so shrill—it carried out into the night. He hoped the barn-owl shrieking didn't wake the girls upstairs. He walked past her on the porch and headed inside.

"Chas, I'm back, but I'm tired. What's wrong?" he said.

She nodded.

"I don't hear you talking about getting more money. Plus, they just said on the news that they've identified us!" Her arms were crossed, and she looked tired, so tired. He wondered what she'd been doing this whole time. He could hear the TV on in the living room, so she must've stayed up.

George shook his head.

"No, the boss said it was bullshit. They don't have a clue about us, just a vague description. He said the cops were just trying to spook us. You didn't need to wait up," he said. George felt dirty and tired and the only thing he wanted in the world right now was a shower.

Chastity shook her head.

"I waited up because this whole plan is bullshit. We need to get our money and leave. Or just leave," she said, looking up the stairs. "What if the boss and this other guy just take off, and we're stuck with those girls? What happens then?" she yelled, pointing up the stairs. "What?"

He didn't know what to say and only shrugged. "The boss said this was it."

She laughed, that sharp, cold laugh that he hated.

"They are going to screw you over," she said. "You and me. Either they leave us holding the bag, or something bad happens to us," Chastity said.

George shook his head. "Chas, nothing bad is going to happen. The boss has never—"

"You see what I did?" she shouted, pointing at the door. "You need to do the same."

He looked. There was a packed bag by the door and another smaller bag that looked like toiletries next to it. Her curling iron and that little golden sewing kit she loved so much were sticking out of the top.

"We have to get out of here—at this point, I don't even care about the money," she said. Her eyes were wild, panicked. "Puddin', I know, it sounds like crazy talk. And you know I pushed you into this deal. But I just have a bad feeling this is going to go south, and quick."

George looked at the bags. The boss had never screwed him before, but Chas was right—this was different. The boss had been acting weird lately, not dropped by the farmhouse at all to check on the setup beyond that one visit early on. And the boss hadn't been around to get the next shipment of bricks, which were just piling up in the garage, in the empty area where that old Mustang had been parked.

"You might be right," he said, nodding. "I trust the boss, but it's weird that this has gotten delayed and delayed."

Chas nodded. "Right? I saw on TV that someone is demanding more money. Did you see that? Even as close as that ransom pickup was—anything could have gone wrong, and now they're asking for more? Did the boss ask you to pick that money up, too?"

George shook his head, weary. He started for the stairs. "No, he's handling that."

"'Handling it'—more like he's cutting us out completely," she said, laughing again.

George got to the first step and stopped, nodding.

"Look, I'm tired, but you might be right," he said. "I'm going to shower, and then I'll pack a bag."

Chastity nodded, and he could tell she was happy, or at least happier, for having won the argument. It was amazing, and a little sad, at how often he let her win, or have her way, just so he could see that look on Chastity's face.

35

Charlie could hear them downstairs, fighting again. That was good. The young man was telling the woman that he was worried, and the woman was squealing at him, her voice high and angry. It sounded like a screeching bird. Actually, to Charlie, it sounded more like bending steel.

Charlie remembered one time she'd been visiting one of her father's construction sites, walking around the muddy lot and poking her head into pipes and stacks of metal bracers and sheets of plywood. Her father often took her to work, insisting that she wear one of those large hardhats that bounced on her head. She'd asked before for a kid-sized one, and in pink, but, so far, her dad had made her wear the big yellow ones. They always smelled like sweat.

But she remembered one time they had been watching a group of her father's construction workers—they were hoisting up a metal bracer, or at least that's what her Dad had called it. The metal had spun into place, and then suddenly part of it had caught on something else and the massive bar of metal had bent almost in half, accompanied by a hideous shriek that had made Charlie cover her ears. Her father had cursed loudly—he often cursed at work, and then asked Charlie not to tell her mother—and walked off to try to figure out what had gone wrong and how the metal had gotten bent.

The woman downstairs sounded like that metal bar, bending under pressure.

Charlie wiggled and listened for more fighting. She sat up on the bed and turned, inspecting the headboard where her right hand was securely zip tied to the frame—the wood was too thick here for her to work it loose or cut it free. And the tie was on too tight, one around her wrist and then looped through another around the hole in the headboard.

On the bedside table were a stack of books and a lamp. Charlie gingerly pulled open the small drawer and started rummaging through the contents, keeping one ear on the argument below. She found some pens, a few sheets of paper, stamps, and a bunch of other random stuff. She pocketed one of the pens and wiggled down off the bed. She thought about trying to use the pen to pry off the zip tie, but she had no way to reattach it before the kidnappers returned. Instead, she strained at the zip tie, groping under the bed with her left hand, feeling around but finding nothing.

Angry, Charlie sat back down on the edge of the bed. She knew she was on the second floor and that they were in the country. If she could only figure out a way to get her hand free, she could sneak across the hallway and free Maya. If the door was locked, she could escape through the windows, either those in this room or the smaller one in the bathroom that looked out over a rooftop, and go get help.

She could probably use the pen to pry herself loose right now, but then the kidnappers would know. Charlie looked at her wrist, zip tied to the bed, and started to cry.

36

Frank arrived at the police station with a large cup of coffee from the McDonald's up the street—he was feeling good, bright, and clear. And a little bit proud of himself—he'd had those three shots of Maker's Mark last night before getting down to work and managed to not drink anything else. It had to be something of a record, and a minor triumph.

He had another one of his headaches again, but nothing he couldn't handle once he made it past the reporters, using the magical "no comment" phrase to push his way through. The receptionist, Lola, smiled and buzzed him in. She was in the middle of removing yesterday's green polish and replacing it with a deep shade of indigo.

He spread out his papers and the mind map on the conference table and got to work. He went through the files here at the station – he didn't have copies of everything back at the hotel – and finished his map. Frank hadn't really found anything crucial, just a few more linkages between financial accounts and a mention, in one file, of an investigator's suspicion that Nick Martin's wife, Glenda, might have been unfaithful at some point in their marriage.

After, Frank found an empty computer to type up his notes from last night's scouring of the records.

Chief King wandered over to check on Frank.

"I heard you were in early this morning."

Frank nodded as King pulled a chair over and sat down.

"Yeah, I re-interviewed several city employees and ex-employees, all of whom were affected by the budget cuts pushed through by 'Councilman' Martin," Frank said. "There was no love lost between them and Martin, I can tell you, but I didn't get the vibe that any of them meant him any real harm."

"Did you bring anyone over?" The police department shared the same building as the city government, separated by a windowed walkway between the two halves.

"No, I used their conference room over there."

"Good," Chief King said, nodding. "Glad to hear you're going back over some of that, but it could have been embarrassing, walking city employees over here for interrogation. We might've rushed a few of those early leads and interviews, so double-checking them is good.

What's that?" King asked, pointing at the desk.

"Oh, that's a mind map," Frank said, handing it to King. "It's a visual linkage of all the principals and how they're related. An old partner swore by them when he was stuck on a case."

King looked it over.

"Cool. I guess these are all already in my head," the Chief said, "and everyone else that lives here in town, but it's interesting to see them written down. The way they connect."

Frank nodded and took the sheet back. It was a redone, compact version of the four sheets of paper taped to the window of his hotel room.

King lowered his voice. "Any breakthroughs?"

"Nothing yet, but I'm starting to think this is a deliberate campaign to bankrupt the Martins," Frank said, shaking his head. "These kidnappers don't just want money—they want revenge or justice. It changes who we need to be looking at in this case."

"You're right—with the second ransom demand, it feels very personal now," King agreed. "Whoever is doing this wants to see Nick on his knees."

Frank nodded. "And that's exceptionally rare. I think we need to be looking again at all the people Nick put out of a job—city employees, old Martin Construction employees. This person wants payback, and he's getting it, making Nick jump through all of these hoops. Sounds like a serious grudge."

"What about the ransom on Saturday?" King asked.

"I'm not sure," Frank said. "I was assuming it was a trick—sounds like the kind of thing someone would do if they wanted to leave town without being followed. Tie up the entire police department at one location, as we sit on the ransom and wait for someone to show up."

King nodded.

"Saturday's going to be busy," the Chief said. "The ransom thing at noon and then the HarvestFest that night. And then the next morning they're doing that prairie burn, which can generate a lot of smoke and a lot of calls."

"What's the HarvestFest?" Frank asked. "I've seen signs."

King nodded at a poster on the bulletin board. "Downtown fundraiser and Halloween party. The whole downtown will be packed, with lots of people in costumes. Most of us will work the event itself, providing security and cutting down on the 'open container' situations."

Frank nodded. "Sounds like a great time to get up to no good, when every cop in town is busy."

"No kidding," King said, sighing. "So, you ready?" King asked, pointing at the door.

"Ready for what?"

"Lola was supposed to tell you. We're heading over to the Martins," King said. "Their psychic showed up."

Frank shook his head.

"A colossal waste of time, but lead the way."

Again, Chief King drove. Frank was really starting to like the limo treatment, getting driven everywhere. And in nicer cars than his, to boot. On the ride over, King passed over a folder of papers.

"Meredith Black, psychic."

"Sounds like a made-up name, if I've ever heard one," Frank answered, flipping open the file and reading.

"You'd be right," King said. "She's actually Meredith Peterson, originally from Texas. Got a following there doing her shtick—talking to the dead, making predictions on local television about the weather, that kind of thing. She helped locate a missing boy in San Antonio two years ago."

Frank looked at King. "She got lucky?"

The Chief shook his head. "Who knows. At this point, I'm ready to call in the Easter Bunny if it breaks the case. She's probably full of shit, but I've read cases where those type of folks are particularly good at reading body language and teasing out leads from a minimum of information."

"Helps them play their marks, I'd bet," Frank said.

"True," Chief King said, slowing down to stop at the light at Main and Hyatt. Up ahead, Frank saw the small veteran's park with its white gazebo. "Many of these psychics are successful because they give the family hope. If they can pick up on the subtle clues the family is dropping, the psychic can feed off of it and give the family just enough hope to keep the money coming in," King said, turning the police car onto South Hyatt. "But this lady doesn't take any money up front."

"It's a good thing—the Martin's are broke." Frank scanned the rest of the file. The woman had managed to "sense" that the young boy in San Antonio was being kept in an underground location. Not an off-the-wall or particularly brave prediction to make, considering local law enforcement had been searching every structure in the county for three weeks. But the little boy had been recovered, and Meredith had come out of it looking like a star.

Shortly afterward, she'd moved to Los Angeles. For a while, she'd worked for something called the "Psychic Counselors Hotline," doling out Tarot card readings and other predictions by phone. After a year of that, word of her spread, and she grew her following into a small retail shop and a stage show in a local theater. People evidently came from all over to hear her speak. There was even talk of a television show in the works.

They arrived at the Martin house. A large van, markedly different from the TV trucks and news vans parked on Hyatt, sat in the driveway. This new van had California license plates and dark windows. Frank had half-expected it to be purple in color and feature a large, airbrushed drawing of a crystal ball on the side of the van. Instead, it was just black, with no markings of any kind to give it away other than the out-of-state vanity plates. Frank smiled at King, as they headed inside.

Walking through the door, Frank was hit by the smell of incense. He and King walked through to the kitchen and living room, but there was no one there.

"Hello?" King called out.

"We're up here," the voice of Nick Martin came from upstairs.

They climbed the wide, sweeping staircase and followed the sounds of people, coming to what had to be Charlie Martin's room. Frank could see posters of animals and brightly-colored furniture and pink decorations everywhere from where he and King stopped, just outside the room.

Nick Martin rolled his eyes and came out of the room. Sergeant Graves joined them as well.

"Sorry we're late," King said.

"But it's okay," Frank smirked. "She's psychic, so she probably knew we were going to be late."

"This is pointless," Graves whispered, keeping his voice low, but not low enough—a young man with dark mascara inside the bedroom shot him a disapproving look.

Nick agreed. "I understand that Glenda wants to explore—"

King put up his hand.

"It will only take a few minutes, and it's worth it, if it keeps your wife's head in the game. And it can't hurt—"

Nick shook his head. "I don't agree. It's false hope."

The Chief shook his head and stepped into the room, followed by Frank. Nick and Graves stood in the doorway, watching the spectacle.

Inside, Glenda Martin was sitting on the bed and, next to her, a small plate of incense burned on the Dora the Explorer bedspread. Next to the plate, an older woman wearing far too much makeup waved the smoke into her face slowly, using both hands, and mumbled to Glenda.

The two women seemed to be ignoring the other people standing in the room—the four of them by the door, along with Detective Barnes and the young man Frank didn't recognize. The young man must have arrived with the psychic. He was very thin, with jet black hair, dark mascara under his eyes, and too many piercings in his ears and above his eyebrows to count. He reminded Frank of that young girl who'd been in the Tip Top Diner with her angry father and his shit-kicking boots. The young man was holding a notepad, taking notes with a pen with a long fuzzy tail of brightly-colored feathers sticking out of the top.

"I can feel her presence," the psychic said.

"Sorry we're late," Chief King said, directing it to Glenda. Frank could see that she had been crying.

They stood quietly and listened for a few minutes, as Meredith went through the particulars of the case, asking Glenda questions about her daughter, the route to the school, and her daughter's friends. Frank knew it was a waste of time, but if King was going to let it happen, Frank would hold his tongue.

"Was she close to her friends?" the psychic asked Glenda.

"That's why they're called 'friends'," Sergeant Graves commented quietly from the doorway. King shot him a look.

"Yes, they were," Glenda answered, drying her eyes. "They walked together to school, all the time, but not that day. I just wish I had walked with them."

Meredith looked down at the mother.

"You mustn't blame yourself for what happened, Glenda," she said, stroking the mother's hand gently. "I sense that you did everything that you could to keep her safe," she said. Glenda nodded.

Meredith stood and walked around the room, picking up things and touching them. The scented smoke of the incense wafted around them as Meredith interacted with Charlie's possessions, rubbing the young girl's toys between her palms and closing her eyes.

Frank smirked.

"Looks like she's trying to start a fire," Frank said quietly to Graves, who smiled and nodded.

"I'm trying to get a sense of the room, Mr. Harper," Meredith said loudly, not opening her eyes. "Your negative energy isn't helping."

Chief King looked at Frank, but Frank ignored him. It was more difficult to ignore the pained look on Glenda's face, but Frank plowed on. He didn't have time for this shit.

"I'm glad everyone else is enjoying the show," Frank said, loudly. "But this isn't getting us anywhere."

The mousey assistant spoke up. "You should stay silent—Lady Meredith needs to work."

Frank shook his head. "No, I need to work. And it's 'Lady' Meredith now? I thought it was Meredith Black—or is it Peterson? I can't keep track."

The woman opened her eyes and looked at him for a long moment.

She peered at him as one would notice a small animal, unworthy of attention. He held her gaze, staring back.

"Yes, I changed my name," she said quietly, her eyes boring into him. "The cases I solved in Texas were very traumatic and took their toll, so I moved and changed my name. I was looking for a fresh start. But you know all about fresh starts, right, Mr. Harper? And trauma. Still enjoying your bourbon?"

Frank looked at her. He felt his hand go cold.

"That's not relevant," Frank barked.

"Isn't it?" she countered, holding his gaze. "I think the only relevant thing about you is the possibility that you're drunk. Right now," she said, smiling.

Frank shook his head. "You can say whatever you want, but this is a waste of time," Frank said, looking at the psychic. "We, the ACTUAL investigators, need to be out there, looking at leads and interviewing people. Not listening to you blather on about 'auras' and the same hokey bullshit that every pandering 'psychic' has been selling for two hundred years."

She stood quietly, taking in his rant, enjoying it, reveling in it. She looked like she'd heard it all a thousand times before. It washed over her like a gentle rain.

As Frank spoke, she slowly smiled and waited for him to finish.

"Done?" she asked, smiling.

"No," Frank said. "Not by a long shot."

Chief King put his hand on Frank's shoulder. "OK, Frank, let's not get all worked up..."

Meredith ignored Chief King and stepped closer to Frank, looking up into his eyes. She stared at him for a long moment, her eyes playing over his face and hair. She reached up slowly and placed a hand gently on his chest.

"Don't touch me," he said.

She looked into his eyes.

"Do you still think about drowning?"

Frank felt his insides drop. The hairs on the back of his neck stood up. "What?"

Meredith smiled.

"You heard me, Mr. Harper," she said, her voice barely above a whisper, yet everyone in the room could hear it. "I speak with perfect clarity, whether those around me have the capacity to hear me or not. I asked if you still think about what happened. In St. Bartholomew's."

Frank was flabbergasted. She'd been through the files, obviously, but had somehow found the one thing that would cut him to the quick. Of course he thought about it—too much—

"That…that happened a long time ago," he stammered. Frank felt this stomach reeling, twisting up inside of him. He backed away. Last night's bourbon surged in his belly, a wave of dark water, like the splashing, murky water in St. Barts. The room suddenly felt ten degrees warmer.

"The water was rising, wasn't it?" she said quietly, smiling, enjoying her new toy. He was not the cat anymore—he was the ball of yarn. She leaned closer, her voice almost inaudible. "They left you behind, didn't they? And you were hurt, and the water just kept coming. And coming," she said. She reached down and touched the long scar than ran up his arm and disappeared under his shirt. "And there was no help for you."

Frank backed away, bumping into Chief King. "I'm leaving," he said, louder than he had planned. Frank struggled to keep his wits about him, but all he could think about was the rising tide of water, full of floating bandages and syringes. And the bodies.

Some part of his mind spoke up, trying to keep him tethered to reality by informing him that it was all public knowledge. Anyone who wanted to could find out what had happened. Frank glanced at the young man with the greasy black hair—the kid was wearing a wicked grin.

"Good," Meredith said, smiling. "Please go. Your presence isn't required."

Frank started to say something else, but nothing came to mind. His mind was already stuffed full of memories he despised, memories he'd worked for years to push down into the darkest recesses of him.

Frank backed through the door, his eyes still on "Lady" Meredith.

Chief King left with him.

"Don't worry about it," King said. "Let it go."

Frank held his tongue, something he wasn't used to, and turned and stormed off, trailing the others in his wake.

37

George carried both trays back down the stairs again, negotiating the two bags George had gathered for their trip. Why Chastity had piled his things on the stairs, instead of where he'd had it by the door, he had no idea.

Charlie had eaten most of her food—she was in better spirits today, despite the fact that she'd been zip tied to a bed for ten days. George thought that maybe the little girl had decided to stop fighting the situation and just deal with it, much like he'd long ago decided to stop fight Chastity on every single issue. Sometimes it was just better to agree, especially when Chastity was yelling at him or, even worse, when she started in with that barn-owl screeching that put George's nerves on edge.

The other tray was nearly full.

He was worried about Maya, the little Mexican girl. She cried all the time, rarely stopping, and didn't eat much of the peanut butter and jelly sandwich and other food that George had carried upstairs. She had certainly not accepted the situation. Every time he came into the room, she shouted at him in a mixture of English and Spanish and fought his every command. Getting her untied and to the bathroom and back was always a fight, but over the past few days she had gotten even more combative. Kicking, hitting, punching. Today, she'd caught him under the chin with a knee and almost knocked him off the bed. He'd explained, over and over, that they would be released when the ordeal was over, but either the little girl didn't understand him, or she didn't believe him.

Either way, caring for the girls had become an exercise in opposites. And keeping Chastity calm just added to the drama.

But it was nearly over.

The boss had called again last night, explaining about the second ransom and how some of that money was for George and Chastity and their extra time, money for them to start a new life somewhere else. And the boss had said again that everything would be square. Chastity had seemed pleased with the news, but she was still on the fence about just taking off. George would have agreed with her if it weren't for the girls.

George carried the trays into the kitchen and set them on the counter, which was still piled up with dishes and old plates. Chastity was supposed to be in charge of keeping up the house. That had been her "rent," they'd agreed, and George would take care of the house itself and all of the chores and work assigned by the boss—but she was slacking off. George knew she'd been getting high a lot more than usual, and he'd assumed it was stress. He rolled up his sleeves and started washing.

When the dishes were done, he went to look for Chastity. Sometimes she went upstairs to their bedroom to get high and forgot to come back downstairs. Sometimes she went walking out in the marijuana field. One time, he'd found her wandering the field at night, stark naked. Other times, he would find her at the dining room table, playing with the golden sewing kit from her mother that she held so dear. She would take everything out of the sewing kit, lay it out on the table or bedspread or wherever she happened to be, and then slowly put it all away. Sometimes, when she was finished, she would start over, packing and repacking the sewing kit over and over. He felt sad for her, and a little worried. Sometimes he just didn't understand what was running through her mind.

He looked through the house and outside, but didn't find her until he went into the barn.

She was asleep in the rusting Corolla.

She really wanted to leave. He knew it, but he'd been putting her off for days. The boss had said it was almost over, and George was torn. He needed to keep her happy, but he'd also promised the boss he'd see this through to the end.

And he was worried about the girls. He hadn't told anyone yet, but George wanted to wait until the very end, after the money had come in. Once he figured the boss was coming for the girls, George would act.

George planned to put the girls in his car and let them go outside of Cooper's Mill. It would mean defying his boss, but George and Chastity would be leaving the state with their part of the ransom money anyway, heading for California. If George could save the girls, he could afford to piss off his boss one more time.

George looked into the car to check on Chastity. She was sound asleep, her bag on her lap. Her arms were folded on top of her bags, and, in one hand, she clenched her mom's sewing kit. Suddenly, George felt sorry for her.

38

Hours later, Frank was still shook up from the encounter with the psychic.

Chief King hadn't said anything about it on the drive back to the police station. Once there, Frank had gathered up some files and headed out—he needed to drive, alone, to clear his head and follow up on a couple of out-of-town leads.

First, he'd driven down to Dayton and met with a pair of banker types in a very slick conference room. Nick Martin had invested in a condominium development near Dragon's Field, a beautiful ball diamond in the downtown area and home to the local minor league team. The conference room looked out over the grassy infield. As Frank and the others met, he could see a team of groundskeepers far below working on the sandy infield, flattening it and smoothing out the dirt with rakes and brooms.

Frank had been impressed with the plans. The field had been built in a run-down part of town, surrounded by old factories and manufacturing buildings. Investors in the project were buying up the old buildings and converting them to apartments and condos. Frank found the project impressive and completely above board. He thanked the men for meeting with him and left.

Now he was headed north again, passing through Cooper's Mill and heading east out of town to New Stanton, a town a few miles to the east of Cooper's Mill.

Frank was driving to meet with a friend of Glenda's. The woman had been friends with the Martins for years and had agreed to meet Frank to talk about their relationship.

In the past twenty-four hours, Frank had worked up three competing theories about the case.

Theory number one went with the idea that whoever was behind the kidnapping was out to punish the Martin's, either by bankrupting them or "bringing them down" to the level of the normal folks. He'd been working from that assumption yesterday and interviewed everyone he could find that might be negatively affected by Nick Martin's fiscal decisions on the City Council or by layoffs and cutbacks in Martin's construction company.

Nothing.

No one was happy with Nick Martin, that was for sure. But Frank couldn't find anyone that even remotely fit the profile of taking it to the extreme and kidnapping Nick's daughter.

Frank's second theory was a little weak, but it never hurt to investigate the time-honored tradition of marital infidelity. It was stunning how many crimes could be laid at the feet of this go-to problem: cheaters and the cheated-upon. In this case, there had been some rumors that the marriage wasn't stable and that Glenda might be stepping out on Nick. Frank was on his way to meet with Glenda's friend to look into that situation.

The third theory had popped into his head late on Thursday night, after the bourbon and five hours of going through all the files again.

The case might be dirty.

It was never good to leap to that conclusion too early. If a kidnapper or other criminal involved with the case had an inside source, it did answer a lot of the outstanding issues, not the least of which that every single lead that came along seemed to dry up with frightening speed.

But Frank was going to hold off on that theory for a while. Going down that path was a one-way trip. Frank had only been on the case since Wednesday. It was too soon to start burning bridges.

So he was working theory #2 for the moment. Others had mentioned that something else was going on in the Martin's marriage, based on a few clues that he'd gotten over the last few days. King had said something off the cuff after they left the psychic. And Frank had noticed that the Martins almost never stood together when talking to the police, and rarely looked at each other or comforted each other. Frank had never seen them hold hands.

When the second ransom call had come in, Nick had joined the policemen in the kitchen to review the call again, but Glenda had stayed away, content to nurse her drink and listen to the conversation from the next room. She'd not gotten involved until she'd decided to come into the kitchen to let everyone know that the psychic would be arriving.

The woman Frank was meeting owned a small coffee shop and art gallery in downtown New Stanton. Frank found the place with ease. New Stanton was smaller than Cooper's Mill and consisted of nothing but one main street surrounded by a small neighborhood of homes.

From the outside, the gallery wasn't very impressive. The rest of the town also seemed a little worse for wear. But inside, the space opened up into a large room with brick walls that held dozens of large paintings and photographs. The art gallery was light and airy and, in the back, there was a coffee bar and small bakery. The woman found him looking at the art, and they sat at a small table in the main room.

"Hi, I'm Jackie," the woman said. She was in her late fifties and brimming with youthful energy. Her hair was streaked with a playful stripe of blue, and Frank got the distinct impression that the woman had once counted herself among the hippies. He had noticed her bustling around inside the gallery before she'd approached him.

"I'm Frank, Frank Harper," he said, shaking her hand. "I'm working with the police on the Martin kidnapping."

She nodded, her face turning somber. "I saw it on the news. Just terrible. I hope they get those little girls back," she said and suddenly stood and excused herself. Moments later, she returned with two coffees.

"Here we go," she said, putting a mug in front of him and sipping at her own. "I was waiting on a fresh pot to brew."

He nodded and sipped, thanking her. The coffee was hot and very strong, with a hint of cinnamon or something.

"Hmm, that's interesting," Frank said, nodding at the mug.

"Oh, it's chicory," she said. "I'm from Texas, and we usually throw a little in there for spice."

Frank took another sip and nodded, then put the coffee down. "That is good. So, you know Glenda Martin, right?"

Jackie nodded again. "Yes, she's over here about once a week for painting and photography lessons, usually on Thursday afternoons."

Frank looked up from his notes.

"Oh," Frank said, surprised. "I was under the impression that she was coming over here regularly, but there was some talk about her meeting a friend for coffee. A male friend."

"Oh, my," Jackie laughed loudly, loud enough to draw the attention of the other people in the shop. "I have no idea about that—but I doubt it. She's had some trouble with her husband over the years, but as far as I can tell, it has nothing to do with infidelity. He's just not very supportive of her."

"What do you mean?" Frank asked.

Jackie leaned back on the couch. "Oh, you know how it is, sugar. Men can be threatened by a powerful woman, or a woman who doesn't derive her strength through her looks," she said, smiling. "Don't you agree? Glenda is passionate, and beautiful to boot, but Nick has rarely supported her choices. To most people, she's just a pretty face. She gave up photography after several years, after Nick made some comment about one of her shots. It's too bad—she had a great talent for it," Jackie said, pointing at the wall.

Frank turned and looked. There was a three-picture grouping of wheat fields surrounded by fall colors, trees in red and yellow and fallen leaves. The photos were beautiful.

He was surprised again. "Glenda took those?" he asked.

"See how she's framed the field with the trees," Jackie said, nodding and standing to point at the group of photographs. "The leaves along the bottom and in the second photo pull it all together nicely, don't you think? And that branch in the foreground gives the photo a nice depth."

Frank looked at it and nodded, trying to follow what Jackie was saying. It was a beautiful shot, but it was difficult for him to explain why— it just was.

"I've sold a lot of her work," Jackie said. "But Nick thought she was just out 'taking pictures' and didn't bother to notice how good she was. She still has a bunch up in her house, I think."

Frank nodded, remembering the large framed landscape photographs in the Martin's living room. He turned back to Jackie. "So, she's moved on to painting?"

"Yes, and she's working through the different techniques, trying to figure out what she likes," Jackie said. "She's thrown herself into it. I doubt she's got time for a man on the side. Might not have time for the man already in her life. She said she wanted to take courses out of town, mostly for the privacy. Everyone in that town knows her. Of course, she's not been back since the kidnapping."

Frank wrote it all down and remembered how dismissive Nick Martin had been in their first interview when Frank had brought up his wife's photography.

He turned back to look at the photos again, and another painting caught his eye. It was an abstract painting of what looked like a house. Frank knew dick about art, but he knew enough to know that if you liked it, and your eye was drawn back to it, that was the kind of art you bought. Not that he had any money.

She turned and followed his eyes up to the painting. "You like that? Me too. It's a Hochstetter."

"I'm just a cop," Frank said, smiling and turning to her. "I don't know anything about art, but I do like it."

She nodded.

"That's how I got into it—my husband and I were traveling in Mexico, on a vacation," she said, remembering. "I saw a painting of a palm tree hanging in the hotel restaurant, and I was hooked. Before that, I couldn't care less about art. Now, I'm in the business."

Frank looked at the painting again. "How much is it?"

"Well, if you have to ask…" she started to say, then smiled and slapped him on the knee. "Oh, I'm just kidding you, sugar. That's what we always say. It's $150. It's not an original, but a print."

"I don't know what that means," Frank said, looking at the painting.

Jackie smiled. "Oh, Louis lives here in town, but he has quite a following. His original paintings go for upward of $1,000 or even $2,000. That's a print, which is essentially an oversized photograph stretched over canvas," she said, pointing at the painting and others nearby for comparison. "If you touch it, there are no brush strokes, but that's about the only difference."

Frank nodded and then looked at Jackie. "Thank you for meeting me. I think I've taken up enough of your time." He stood and shook her hand.

"Did you want to get the piece?" she asked, smiling.

"No, no," he said. "I'm just in town for a few more days," he said, but his eyes were drawn to it again. After he said goodbye and walked to the door, Frank couldn't help himself and looked again.

Driving back to Cooper's Mill, he thought about the painting again and what Jackie had said. The art "spoke" to him, bringing out an emotional reaction in him that he had not expected. It was much like when the psychic lady had brought up what happened during Katrina—it had spun him off in an entirely new and different direction from what he'd been expecting.

That little smirk on the young man's face hadn't helped Frank's mood at the time, either.

Of course, they had looked up Frank. The psychic and her little helper had done the work, probably pulling together files on everyone involved in the investigation. He would have done the same thing in their position. But to have it just thrown out there like that had taken Frank by surprise. He should have known better, been more prepared. Instead, he'd looked like an idiot, standing there clenching his fists and then storming out like a pissed off little kid.

But making progress on the investigation had turned his mood around. He had poked a few large holes in theory #2 and, at this stage in the investigation, any progress was good. From all the files he'd poured through, it didn't feel like this case would end up centered around infidelity, but it was good to eliminate that as a motivator.

And the painting had cheered Frank up. Maybe that was all it meant, or all it was good for. But it had worked, one way or the other.

The CD ended, and he flipped through the CDs, finding another jazz favorite. This one was "Easy Does It" from Sonny Stitt and Oscar Peterson. Nice relaxing piano with a standing bass. Great for driving in the rain, or late on a summer evening.

As he drove back into Cooper's Mill, he thought about the psychic. It had been stupid, allowing himself to be surprised like that. But the worst part was letting himself get so angry. Clearly, he was frustrated with the case, but he needed to remind himself that he was making progress. Or, at least, he needed others to think he was making progress.

Especially with that third option looking more and more tangible with each passing hour.

He'd essentially eliminated the infidelity theory with his drive to New Stanton. She seemed like an angry wife, distant, but if what Jackie had said was true, it explained the distance and the lack of comfort. Nick didn't support her, something Frank had witnessed directly. And it explained all the pictures and photographs in the Martin house—she was always taking photos.

Photos.

Maybe she had more photos, photos that she took that morning, the morning of the kidnapping. No, if she'd had photos, she would have mentioned it, right? Frank jotted it down on his notepad propped on the Taurus steering wheel.

Frank followed the road, crossing the open expanse of fields that stretched between the river and Cooper's Mill proper, which sat on a rise. Stitt and Peterson played, the piano and soft drums carrying the tune as he drove. Frank pondered about all of the facets of the case, how they wound back and forth, in and out of each other like a complicated song.

He was heading west on 571, the road that entered Cooper's Mill from the east after crossing the river. As he approached the rise that marked Cooper's Mill, Frank drove past a large field on his right. A large sign reading "Freeman Prairie" stood near the road and, beyond, Frank saw a group of volunteers walking through the tall grasses and mud that stretched from the edge of the road to the distant river. Another volunteer search, checking the tall bushes and scrub for any sign of the girls.

He followed the road as it sloped up, passing Canal Lock Park on the way to First Street, going from open fields and farmland into downtown Cooper's Mill in the blink of an eye. Frank slowed and stopped at the light at the corner of First and Main, and then, when the light turned green, he pulled into a parking spot across from Ricky's, the bar he'd visited on his first night in town.

39

Frank grabbed his notepad and walked across the street, heading inside.

Ricky's looked different in the daylight—and when it wasn't packed. Eight or ten customers sat at the tables in the back, and one lone guy sat at the bar. The rough rock music they were playing was a jolt after the calming jazz he'd been enjoying.

Frank recognized the woman behind the bar. It was the same woman who'd been in here the first night he'd arrived, long before he knew anything about the case. She'd chastised him for not helping out with the drunk customers.

"Rosie, right?" he asked her.

She looked up. "Ah, I thought that was you on the phone." He had called earlier from the car to set up an appointment. "Have a seat."

Frank wanted to talk privately, but it looked like she was the only one working, so he sat at the bar and took out his notepad, setting it on the counter.

"Get you something?" she asked.

"Coffee, if you have some," he said. "Just you in today?"

Rosie looked around. "Queen of the castle."

"I'm Frank, Frank Harper," he said, shaking her hand. "I'm working with the police on the Martin kidnapping."

"I know," she said. "Glenda's my sister. I hope you find Charlie, and soon. She's a very special little girl."

Frank should've learned by now to not be surprised. It seemed like everyone in this town was related to someone else.

"Sorry, I didn't know."

"It's fine—her last name is Martin now, but I'm still Hanks. Rosie Hanks. Hang on," she said and went away to help a customer, an old gentleman who had his hand raised at one of the tables.

While she was gone, Frank looked around the bar. He located the shotgun—he'd guessed it was behind the counter and now could see the butt of the gun sticking out next to an ice machine. Along the walls, the paint looked more faded and the TV screens cheaper in the daylight. But the place looked clean, at least. He'd been in enough dirty bars to know the difference.

Rosie came back, setting a coffee in front of him. "Sorry about that."

"No problem," he said. "So, what can you tell me about Nick Martin?"

"First, I've got a question," she said.

Frank looked up and nodded. "Shoot."

"Why didn't you help me out the other night?" Rosie asked, nodding at the table where he'd been sitting. "It doesn't really matter. I'm just curious."

Frank thought about it for a second. He was surprised she'd asked and that she could remember the exact place he'd been sitting. "I didn't want to get involved. I'm really just in town to see my daughter."

"Oh? She lives in town?"

Frank nodded. "She works at the hair place around the corner. I was just here to see her and didn't want any trouble. But now I've gotten pulled into the case." He thought about it for a second and then added, "I'm sorry about that."

Rosie shook her head. "Like I said, no big deal. I was just curious. What was your question?"

Frank looked back at his notes.

"So tell me about Nick."

"Nothing you probably don't already know," she said, picking up a clean towel and drying the counter. "He's a good dad and good to Glenda. Pretty good. She got lucky. Charlie adores him, though I wouldn't say the same about some folks in town. He's let people go before, at Martin Construction, but cutting the budget at the City pissed off a lot of people. A couple of well-known people in town ended up out of work. It was quite the topic of conversation in here for a while."

Frank nodded, jotting it all down.

"'Did it all blow over?'"

"I thought so," she said sadly. "It looked like things were getting better, and then Charlie disappeared. Some people think he's getting his karmic due, but nobody thinks it's payback for the budget cuts or layoffs or whatever. I can't believe anyone would do that."

A young man, one of the ones from the bar fight that first night, came out of the backroom and set a large toolbox on the counter. He was in his late twenties, thin, and covered in sweat. His shirt was streaked with mud.

"Well, Rosie, it's not the breaker."

Rosie nodded. "Jake, this is Frank, Frank Harper. He's an ex-cop, helping the police."

Jake Delancy smiled and wiped his hands on his shirt. "Hi, Mr. Harper," he said, shaking Frank's hand. "Working on the kidnapping?"

Frank nodded. "Just helping out."

Jake turned to Rosie. "I checked in the crawlspace, and you were right. But the jukebox—it's not the breaker."

Rosie made a face. "I just bought that from one of the antique stores—it was working yesterday, after they delivered it. I hope it's sturdy," Rosie said. "It can get a little rough in here, and I can't have it quitting every time it gets bumped."

"That's a good point—maybe it's just a loose connection inside, or something," Jake said, nodding. "Frank, nice to meet you, and good luck with your case."

Frank nodded as Jake gathered up his toolbox and walked over, pulling out the jukebox and getting to work on the back of the machine.

"He seems handy," Frank said.

Rosie smiled. "You have no idea."

Frank nodded, getting it.

"OK, I won't ask. So, nobody you know would have a grudge against the Martins bad enough to do something like this?"

"No, not really," she said.

"Anything you can think of the cops might've missed?"

She started to say something but then shook her head. "No, not really," she said. "Those guys are really good," she said, and then a customer called her over. She excused herself, and Frank sat back, relaxing. He watched the crowd for a few minutes, and then, the jukebox powered up and started playing music that competed with the rock music already playing over the speakers. Rosie gave out a little cheer from across the room.

Jake joined Frank at the bar, setting his bag of tools down on the seat next to Frank.

Rosie came over. "Jake, you're good."

Jake put some tools back into his bag. "Oh, it was nothing. Loose connecting wire. What happened, anyway?"

"I'm not really sure," Rosie said, sliding a beer in front of Jake and a refill of coffee to Frank. "There was a scuffle in here last night, and a guy got thrown against the jukebox. It just stopped working after that."

"Well, something got knocked loose in the back," Jake said. "I tightened up everything. I think the power cord has a bad connection. I'll see if I can dummy up something to replace it."

Rosie thanked him and moved away. The bar was starting to pick up, and a second barkeep had joined her.

When he'd first been in here, Frank had thought that Ricky's had all the ambiance of a beer tent at a state fair, but the place was starting to grow on him. Half of the town drank here, it seemed, and it would be a good place to catch a few more folks to discuss the case.

Deputy Peters had mentioned that Ricky's had also been the site of several of Cooper's Mill's most visible crimes, including the case a few years back when a fugitive up from Dayton had holed up inside the bar with a shotgun and threatened to kill anyone that entered. It had ended peacefully, thankfully, but the incident had only served to increase Ricky's reputation as the roughest watering hole in town.

"So, what do you do?" Frank asked Jake.

Jake turned and looked at him.

"Not a lot, anymore, with the economy," Jake said, wiping his hands on a rag and then stuffing it back into his toolkit. It looked like he had one of everything in there. "I did a lot of work for Nick Martin, when they were flush, but there isn't much call for custom cabinetry right now. Or pocket doors," Jake said.

Frank nodded. "Carpentry?"

"Mostly. I do a little carving, too, mostly working with natural materials. I've done some mantles and fireplaces, too, but now it's primarily furniture."

Rosie walked up. "Don't let him fool you, Frank—Jake can do anything. He has like five businesses—he makes his own beer, fixes and reupholsters chairs. He works on cars, does electrical repairs. Last year, he made his own cheese and sold it at the farmers market," Rosie said proudly.

"You sound like a real renaissance man, Jake," Frank said, tipping his coffee cup at the man. "Here's to staying busy."

Jake nodded, a little embarrassed. "Rosie's got the hots for me, so you can't believe anything she says."

"Hots?" Rosie said, putting her hands on her hips and faking a shocked British tone. "Surely you jest. I have no idea what you mean, good sir!" She turned and walked away, smiling.

Jake smiled, following Rosie as she went to help other customers. "Too much 'Downton Abbey'—the woman is obsessed with it."

Frank followed Jake's eyes and smiled.

Jake turned and started to say something when a loud group of men entered the bar, shouting at each other and at Rosie for beers. Frank recognized one of the men as the loud drunk from Frank's first night in town. It looked like the man had already gotten the evening's festivities kicked off, judging by the loud talk.

Jake shook his head, grimacing. "That's Derek and his boys," he said, finishing up his beer. "Rosie, make sure you kick them out if they get to be trouble. Or call me, and I'll come back."

Rosie came back over and nodded.

"You worry too much, Jake. I can handle them."

Jake was looking at Derek's group. "It's my job to worry," he said, smiling at her, and then he picked up his toolkit, nodded at Frank, and left. Through the open doors, Frank saw it was sprinkling again.

The place was getting busy. Frank talked to a few more people as they came in, just getting casual answers about Nick Martin—what people thought of him and his wife, what they thought of the kidnapping. Most people seemed saddened by the fact it had happened in their little town. It appeared that the folks in Cooper's Mill were a pleasant lot who jealously guarded their "small town" atmosphere and didn't like to see it threatened.

It grew warmer in the bar as the crowd swelled. In less than an hour, patrons were stacked three deep along the rickety wooden bar top. More people came in, talking loudly about the high school football game that had just ended in City Park—it reminded Frank that that was the location for tomorrow morning's ransom drop.

Frank felt out of place with his coffee. He was the only one not drinking, and it wasn't by choice. He was watching for people he might recognize as connected to the case, but he knew so few faces, it was probably pointless.

Frank found an open table and sat. He pushed the several empty beer bottles to the side and grabbed the only hostess who dared to come out from behind the counter. Her nametag read "Denise."

"Hey, whatcha want?" she asked him, and he immediately liked her.

"Coffee," Frank said. "Two, since you're here. And two minutes of your time to chat."

She stopped and really looked at him for the first time.

"Pardon me?"

He smiled. "You heard me fine, Denise. I need to talk to you."

She nodded and smiled, scooting away between two groups of men shouting at the TV. Frank noticed there was a game on—it looked like Ohio State, probably a local favorite, which might explain why the place was packed. Or maybe because the economy was in the shitter and everyone just needed to blow off steam.

The girl came back with two cups of coffee and a little plate of creamer and sugars. She plopped down in the seat across from his.

"Three minutes," Denise said. "Rosie's covering for me."

He nodded.

"Thanks—I know you're busy. Do you know the Martins?"

She smiled. "You a cop? Never seen you in here before."

"No, not anymore," Frank said. "I was a cop. Now, I'm helping out with the case."

She shook her head. "Nah, they're never in here. Too snooty. He's rich, and she's hot. When they drink, I'm sure it's at a dinner party somewhere with their snooty friends."

"They have any friends who come in here?"

"Nah."

"OK, last question. Anybody new hanging around town lately, non-regulars in here?"

She looked around the room and shook her head. She was about to add something, when her eyes grew big. He turned to see a fat patron pushing another man up against the bar.

"Shut up, dipshit!" the larger man yelled.

Frank slowly stood as Denise scurried back behind the counter. The shouting match at the bar was attracting everyone's attention, and it gave him a chance to scan the room. Most of the patrons looked half-drunk and bleary-eyed. The cops must just sit outside this place every night when it closed and pick off the slew of over-the-limit drunk drivers.

There were a few people that looked out of place—three guys dressed in nicer clothes near the back, drinking slowly and watching the spectacle. They looked like visiting journalists, in from out of town for the kidnapping coverage and getting a little "local color." Frank might have to swing by and chat with them before the night was over.

Near the back of the place, several couples were making out in the darker confines of the bar, ignorant of the shouting match and the rest of the world around them. One of them looked familiar.

Frank turned to see that the skinny guy, one of the guys who had entered the place with Derek, had broken loose from being pinned against the bar and shoved the fat guy, who moved only a few inches. His arm went up into the air, and he swung, punching the guy in the face. The skinny guy fell backward against the bar and leaned there. Derek and his friends stepped up to help.

"Come on, Taylor," the fat man shouted. "Say it again!"

Taylor, the skinny one, reached for a beer bottle and swung it crazily. Out of luck—certainly not skill—it connected with the fat guy's head and shattered, sending glass flying in every direction. Other patrons ducked to avoid the glass, or at least those sober enough to understand what was going on ducked.

The fat guy staggered, his hands at his bleeding head. Three other big guys joined him from the crowd, and they stepped toward Taylor. Derek shielded him, and Frank could tell that, while he was drunk, Derek looked sober enough to be primed for a fight.

Frank shook his head and stepped between them.

"That's OK, he's learned his lesson." Frank said loudly, his hands up.

Frank turned and took the broken bottle out of Taylor's hand and set it on the bar. "He's done."

The fat guy looked at Frank.

"We're just getting started, friend. I'd suggest you move along."

Frank nodded, smiling. "I understand. Let me take Taylor and his friends out of here and get them off to home and then—"

The fat guy swung at Frank.

Frank had been waiting for it—the muscle flex in the fat man's right shoulder had telegraphed the swing a full half-second before the beefy arm even started moving.

Frank put up his left arm and blocked the roundhouse punch. At the same instant, he spun and slapped an open, flat palm hard into the bloody wound on the man's temple. Frank felt the glass grinding under his fingers. Then he brought both hands down, keeping them together, and shoved at the fat man's neck, aiming him backward into one of his approaching friends.

Derek and another friend stepped up and started punching one of the fat guy's friends, and Frank knew this would quickly devolve into a nasty bar fight, if he didn't incapacitate some of them quickly.

Another friend of the fat guy's stepped around the pair and kicked at Frank, but Frank spun away and caught the foot in midair. Using the foot's momentum, he pulled upward on the foot and leg, sending the third assailant to the floor. Leaning down, he punched the man on the ground hard across the jaw, knocking him out, hurting his own hand in the process.

The hardest part was keeping track of everyone in his head. Situational awareness.

Okay, it was the fat guy and his three friends versus the skinny guy Taylor, Derek, and two other friends. Four on four, with Frank in the middle.

Derek had gotten one of the fat guy's friends into a bear hold, choking him.

While he was counting, the fourth friend of the fat guy circled around Frank and landed a punch into Frank's back, and it hurt like hell. Frank turned and used an upward strike to hit the man's crotch twice in rapid succession. As the man bent over, Frank turned and grabbed the man's arms, pulling him down to the ground. With a rolling motion, Frank was back up on his feet.

The second guy had climbed out from under the fat guy, and he and the third guy approached together. They were moving together, getting smarter.

Frank moved to the side so that one was closer than the other. Krav

Maga taught several basic tenets, among them never fight more than one person at a time, and get away as soon as possible. Frank slid to the side, so the second guy was closer, and Frank was five feet closer to Derek's group.

By now, the place was silent and an open space had miraculously cleared out in the middle of the bar. No one was jumping in to help Frank, but, then again, no one was coming to the aid of the four fat guys either. And one glance told Frank that the couples making out hadn't yet noticed that anything was happening.

The two friends of the fat guy charged him together.

Frank calculated the possibilities. Derek's group was complicating things, but the four larger men, the friends of the fat guy, were the primary threat. Derek and Taylor and their two friends were smaller and scrawny. But Frank needed to end this quickly, before someone really got hurt.

The two men ran at Frank, and he, again, shifted sideways, so that one would get to him first. Frank ducked the first punch and lowered his head, sliding to the side and pushing the rushing man down and to the side, using his momentum to trip him.

Frank turned and caught the second guy low in the stomach with a pointed elbow—the man had punched at the open air where Frank's head had been a moment before. That was always one of the hardest lessons to teach his students—Frank had always stressed the point. It was not logical, but you didn't punch where your assailant was at the time. Instead, you needed to predict the future location of the assailant and aim there. It took some practice to get good at it.

Frank had had plenty of practice.

The man doubled over just as Frank stood up quickly, head-butting the man under his chin. Blood exploded from the man's mouth as Frank landed another hard punch to the man's stomach. Getting an assailant to bite his tongue could end their fervor in an instant. Frank helped the man into an open chair and turned.

Two of the well-dressed men Frank had seen before snapped photos of the fight in progress from a safe distance, and he knew he'd been right about them being press.

Derek still had one arm tightly around a man's neck, and Rosie was scrabbling at his back, trying to get him to loosen up. Frank stepped quickly over and punched Derek in the kidney, just hard enough to break his stranglehold on the man, who collapsed to the floor.

Taylor and the other three men were fighting—the fat guy, still bleeding from his head, was pounding on Taylor, and one of Derek's friends had the last fat guy on the ground, punching his face into the floor.

This was going to get out of control, and then someone might really get hurt. Frank took out his gun and waved in the air. He gripped the gun tightly, even though his right hand was screaming with pain.

"Stop," Frank said loudly. "Or I will shoot."

The fat guy turned to see the gun pointed at him and backed off— for a moment—one fist hung comically in the air. The guy on the floor stopped punching, and the sounds of shouting and breaking glass were replaced with moaning from Derek on the ground, along with the raspy breathing of the man he'd been strangling.

Christ, Frank thought. What a mess.

40

The man stood by the window of his apartment, looking out over the downtown scene. Lights and sirens and several cop cars parked in front of Ricky's—just another night.

The man had a cell phone propped up on the window sill, talking to someone over the speaker.

"Good, that's really good to hear."

A deep voice came back, made tinny by the phone's small speaker.

"That's a great property. After a certain amount of time has passed, we'll get you back involved, on a consultancy basis," the man with the deep voice said. "No way I'm leaving Vegas and moving to that hick town of yours."

The man smiled, not wanting to answer at all, but he needed to acknowledge what the man was saying, even if he didn't agree. Vegas didn't know he wouldn't be around to manage the location for them.

"Sounds good. Glad the FedEx came through."

"Yup," the man on the other end said. "Anything else?"

The man looking out the window was sweating. This wasn't a conversation he'd been looking forward to having. But the question needed to be asked.

"Yes, one more thing," he said gingerly. "With that delivery, we should be square."

There was no response from the other end. The man looking out the window could hear nothing except for the tall grandfather clock that ticked away in one corner of his apartment.

"Yes," the deep voice finally answered. "You're all paid up."

The man by the window thanked the man with the deep voice and hung up, his hands slick with sweat.

Free and clear.

The man smiled and looked out the floor-to-ceiling windows that overlooked downtown Cooper's Mill. This really was a great apartment—it was one of the few things he would miss about this town.

The streets were dark and shiny from the recent rain—it seemed like it had done nothing but rain for the past two weeks. The only things he saw of interest were the spinning lights of several police cars and an ambulance in front of Ricky's, two blocks down.

41

Saturday morning, the sun shone brightly into Frank's hotel room window. He'd gotten home late and stood by the window for a long time, looking out over the highway. And when he'd finally gone to bed, he'd neglected to close the blinds.

He sat up groggily and looked around. The room was a mess, with papers and files strewn over every flat surface in the half of the room next to the window. The table was covered with six stacks of papers, notes, and files. The two boxes sat leaning up against the wall, empty except for some pens, a roll of clear tape, and a pair of scissors.

Chief King was pissed at him.

The fight hadn't been Frank's fault. In fact, he'd argued with King and Graves that Frank had been the one to keep it from escalating out of control.

They didn't seem to buy it. Frank didn't have a scratch on him, but everyone else on both sides of the fight was hurting, moaning to the EMTs. Rosie had backed his story, and King had carted everyone outside for processing. But, after everything was wrapped up, King had pulled him aside and accused him of drinking again.

Frank shouldn't have been surprised. He was in a bar, after all. But Frank had patiently explained what he'd learned over the afternoon from his trip to New Stanton and his time in Ricky's, and King had finally come around. It hadn't hurt that Frank was stone cold sober.

But Frank wasn't too sure how long he'd be in King's good graces. The man had taken a chance on Frank, risking alienating his entire staff to play a hunch and bring in an outsider. And, so far, Frank had produced nothing, other than a bar fight, a policeman with a broken arm, a pissed-off psychic, and exactly zero new leads.

Frank hadn't shared anything with Chief King yet about theory #3.

To burn off some of his aggression, Frank climbed out of bed and worked out. He flipped on the TV and watched the morning news shows. Different ones ran on Saturday mornings, but they were as equally pointless and insipid as the weekday shows.

Frank rewrapped his right hand again—the bandages were just to keep the swelling down. It wasn't broken, just sore. He needed to be icing it; instead, he worked out and showered, then headed across the parking lot to get breakfast.

The waitresses and greeter were happy to see Frank, and seated him in the usual booth—he'd been in here almost daily since arriving in town—but Frank noticed a change in their treatment of him. Since the incident with Gina's husband, they treated Frank like a rock star, bringing him anything he wanted. Dessert had been on the house every meal since. And, without fail, someone would recount the story for other patrons, making Frank squirm.

Apparently, Gina got first dibs on Frank's table, as she was his waitress now every time she was in. She made faces at his hand and the scrapes on his face from last night's fight.

"Oh, Frank," she said, setting down coffee and water and the day's paper. "What did you do to your hand?"

"Thanks, Gina," he said. "Ah, broke up a bar fight last night in town. How are you?"

She rubbed her arm where Stan had tried to wrench her from behind the counter. Frank could see a large black bruise in the shape of a hand.

"I'm okay," she said. "I'm just glad you were here that day," she said. She always said the same thing, and she meant it, every time.

He said what he always said.

"I was glad to help—actually, I talked to Stan yesterday on something unrelated," Frank said. As part of the investigation, he'd talked to all the on-duty officers, including Stan, who had been returned to duty to assist with the kidnapping investigation. Even though he was still under observation, he was helping out with the tip line. "I think he's calmed down. Have you talked to him?"

She shook her head. "No, just that day in the ambulance, when he apologized. I think…I think he's taking some time."

Frank nodded. "Probably not a bad idea. Just keep an eye on your doors and windows."

The smile faded from her face. Again, he couldn't just give her the comforting words that someone else would have. Even before they were out of his mouth, he heard himself being overly honest with the woman.

She nodded and quietly took his order, then left him alone. They somehow sensed how much he liked his quiet time, and even his new-found celebrity status wasn't an excuse to interrupt him too often. The wrapping on his right hand made it hard to eat, so he unwrapped it before digging into his ham and cheese omelet. He was happy to see the swelling was going down.

An hour later, he drove to the location of the second ransom drop, parking where instructed.

The second ransom drop was taking place at the high school football field. Oddly, the high school itself was located in another part of town, up on North Hyatt, a mile north of town and surrounded by corn fields. But the football team still played at the old downtown field next to City Park. It was located between the tall trees of the park and the new Cooper's Mill Pool to the north. To the east sat the extensive parking lots built for the new pool and, beyond the parking lots, a row of tall pines that lined the banks of the river beyond.

For someone trying to retrieve the ransom money, it would have been difficult to choose a worse location.

There were clear views of all approaches from the park, the pool, and the parking lot. The field was surrounded on all sides by tall bleachers. The center of the field would be impossible to reach without crossing at least thirty yards of open grass. It was a police sharpshooters dream, if the Cooper's Mill Police Department had been able to bring in a sniper to incapacitate whoever showed up to retrieve the ransom.

No one in their right mind would pick this as a ransom drop, and Frank said so to Chief King, Graves, Barnes, and the others when he arrived. To a man, they all agreed.

The group of men waited in the park under a line of trees, watching the field. Nick Martin was walking back from dropping off the satchel of money, which was now sitting in the middle of the sunny, grassy field, right on the 50-yard line. The grass was beat down from last night's football game.

"This is never going to happen," Graves said under his breath. "Why would someone pick this location?"

"I don't know," King said. "But we still have to go through the motions," he said, taking another sip of his coffee. "I didn't put all my eggs in this basket, though—I've got patrols stationed at all the major exits from town, looking for anything suspicious."

Agent Shale stood next to them, watching the money through a set of binoculars. "Whoever this is, we'll catch them."

Frank wasn't so sure, but he didn't say anything. His back was still smarting from the fight last night, where that fat guy had suckerpunched him. Frank thought he might be slowing—the guy had caught him by surprise.

A few more minutes passed.

Frank had another donut from the box that Deputy Peters had passed around earlier. They were excellent. The box lid said "Tim's Donuts, Vandalia" on the top, and Frank made a mental note to check that place out at some point in the future. He sipped at his coffee, holding it in his right hand, rewrapped with the bandage.

A black leather satchel, identical to the first one, sat in the middle of the sunny field, untouched. White stripes marked out the lines on the football field.

Frank wondered why they were being played. Clearly this whole thing was a big distraction, a pointless exercise. But was it to distract them from something going on elsewhere? Frank couldn't see the point. He noticed a stretch of asphalt on the other side of the field.

"What's that?"

King followed his eyes.

"Bike trail. Goes south to Kyle Park and north along the river, all the way to Troy. I had it closed. We've got men on bikes on either side, out of view. I thought maybe that was the play, someone on a motorcycle could swoop in and out of here pretty easily by taking the bike path, but they'd still have to get across the field to get the money. And without a pretty girl in a low-cut top to distract us."

They waited another half hour, but nothing happened. Nick Martin was getting increasingly agitated, but there was nothing that Frank or anyone else could say. Finally, King called them all together and announced they were canceling the drop.

"Now what?" Nick Martin asked.

King shook his head.

"First, we wrap up here," the Chief said. "We'll retrieve the money and lock it up. If they don't call soon, we'll get the money back to you. As for how we proceed from here, we need to regroup. Let's get back to the station and sit down and talk out our options."

King turned to Sergeant Graves. "Can you take Nick and secure that satchel? I want it locked away for now."

Graves nodded, and he and Martin walked off, passing the squat modern building that housed the park's bathroom facilities.

Frank was thinking and shaking his head.

"What?" King asked.

Frank glanced around, and the others were all out of earshot. "This doesn't make any sense," he said quietly. "It's all just been about wasting our time."

King nodded for him to follow. The two of them started across the park to where King's police cruiser and Frank's Taurus sat parked. As they crossed the park, they passed a strange building that appeared to be eight-sided. Beyond were tennis courts and playground equipment.

"Chief, I've got a theory, but you won't like it," Frank said as they walked.

"Go on."

Frank glanced over at him—they were alone, and it was time for him to speak his mind.

"I feel like we're being played," Frank began. "And always two steps behind. Now, with every lead turning up dry, and this wasted morning, I'm starting to think that the kidnappers are getting information ahead of time. It's not good to think about, but they might have a source in your department."

King stopped walking and looked at Frank.

"Look," Frank said, "I know that's not something you want to hear—"

King put up his hand, stopping him.

"Actually, it's been on my mind too," the Chief said. "A lot. It would explain a few things." Chief King turned and kept walking. "The fact that I've been through the case files so many times without coming up with a decent lead might mean something's been left out of the files. If that's the case, it's someone on my staff."

Frank walked along, not sure what to say. No one wanted to think they had been betrayed, but—

"Who do you trust?" Frank asked quietly.

King glanced at him, then back at the others across the park. "Peters, of course. He's my cousin. And Graves—he's the best I've got. And Barnes. And you, when you're not in the bag."

Frank looked at him. "Hey, things were screwed up before I got here."

"True, true," King agreed, smiling.

"Then have Graves look into it," Frank said. "Barnes has his hands full. If it were me, I'd have Peters and Graves dig into the records, see if any files have gone missing, or anything has leaked that shouldn't have."

They got to the cars.

"Where to?" Frank asked.

"Well, we should be going back to the station and get updates," the Chief said. "Then I can talk to Graves and Peters in my office. Then go through the files again? It seems like we're just spinning our wheels," King said.

"I know what you mean," Frank said. "I did that again last night— found a couple new things, but nothing that would break the case open. But if you talk to Graves or Peters, do it out of your office. Take them for a stroll."

"You think my office is bugged?"

Frank shrugged. "Better assume so."

The Chief nodded, thoughtful. "But first, I've got to go check on Glenda Martin and her psychic down at Kyle. Wanna tag along?"

Frank grimaced. "I guess I have to."

42

"Anything yet?"

Deputy Peters turned to see the Chief and Mr. Harper walking across the soccer field toward him. Peters was in Kyle Park, at one of the furthermost soccer fields, to "assist" Glenda Martin and the psychic with anything they needed.

Peters shook his head. "Nope, nothing."

Mr. Harper grumbled. Peters liked the man, but he was hard to interpret. Sometimes it seemed the man was angry at the world, and, at other times, he could be very pleasant. Although Peters could have done without all the cursing, he'd already learned more from Mr. Harper than from any of the other cops at the Department. Except for Cousin Jeff, of course.

"I wonder how long we should give her," Mr. Harper said, looking across the soccer field. The psychic woman, Mrs. Martin and the psychic's assistant were visible just inside the corn field that ringed the patch of grass. "She's not going to find anything out there, right?" Frank asked Peters.

He shook his head.

"No, sir. We've looked at that field four times now, and all the other fields around here, all the way to the river."

Peters wasn't happy with the kidnapping case, obviously, but he'd been happy with the opportunity to expand his usefulness and prove to his cousin that he could be a valuable member of the team.

Initially, Chief King had gently persuaded Peters to not choose a career in law enforcement. After the initial ire had passed, though, Peters took it upon himself to prove his cousin wrong. He'd thrown himself into the books and night classes that led up to an intense ten weeks at the State Police Academy. He'd been the smallest officer-in-training in the class, and the klutziest, but he'd tried to make up for it with study and endurance, and graduated third in his class. After that, his cousin had been unable to refuse him a place on the local force.

And now, Peters was taking advantage of the case and the fact that the department was stretched to the breaking point. Everyone was slammed with background checks and witness interviews and running down the two dozen "leads" that were phoned in each day since the two little girls had gone missing. None of the leads had helped much, but Peters was learning more and more every day.

It might seem cruel, but on some level, the kidnapping was the best thing that had ever happened to Peters and his career.

And now Mr. Harper, ex-cop and current bad ass, was in the picture. Peters had volunteered to be his departmental liaison. Working with Harper on case file reviews had already taught Peters a few things, and he'd enjoyed helping Mr. Harper familiarize himself with the case and the town.

And, as he had been taught by his more successful cousin, Peters had written down almost everything Mr. Harper said, no matter how trivial it might seem. The point was to absorb as much as he could from Harper before the man was gone.

Chief King shook his head.

"I wanted to talk to Glenda," the Chief said. "Maybe dissuade her from putting too much faith in this woman. But now I'm thinking the distraction is good for her. She's focusing on something, at least," he said. "Frank, what do you think?"

Peters turned to see Mr. Harper staring out at the field. "These wheat and corn fields can be quite spectacular," he said, surprising Peters, who had never heard him talk like that. "Did you know that Mrs. Martin had quite a career in photography? She was pretty good, good enough to have her stuff in a gallery."

"I saw the photo albums at her home," King said.

Mr. Harper nodded and turned to look at them.

"And on the walls, I suspect. Those big landscape shots? Those were hers, I think," he said. "I talked to the gallery owner over in New Stanton yesterday. Glenda's work was good enough to sell, before she gave it up. Nick didn't support her, evidently. Now she's painting."

"Here they come," Peters said, indicating the two women coming out of the field, trailed by the young man with the mascara. They walked up to the men—the psychic woman was smiling, bemused, but Glenda Martin just looked sad and drawn.

"Any luck?" Chief King asked.

Glenda shook her head. "No, not yet."

"Lady Meredith was getting some visions," the boy offered. "But your bad energy put a damper on it."

Peters could tell Mr. Harper wanted to say something profoundly snippy, but the ex-cop demurred to the Chief.

"Oh, sorry about that," Chief King said. "We'd be happy to hear anything you've got to say."

Meredith sighed.

"Well, I know the children are alive," the psychic began. She spoke slowly, deliberately. Peters thought that she might enjoy having everyone's attention—she seemed to feed off of the energy.

"And where they are being held—it feels like a cave, or a forest. They are surrounded by wood. It is cold and dark, but not the kind of place a policeman would think to look," she said, looking at Glenda. "Their hands are bound, handcuffs or something. And I hear a scraping sound, like nails on a chalkboard."

King nodded, jotting it down.

"I hope you can understand—we appreciate the help," the Chief said. "But we've searched everywhere several times, so it makes sense that, if the girls are still alive"—he shot a glance at Glenda, who was hanging on Meredith's every word—"they would be in a strange location."

Meredith smiled.

"That's not what I mean, Chief. I'm not saying they're in a strange place, because you've already looked elsewhere. I'm saying they're in a strange place."

"But where should they be looking?" Glenda asked, her eyes wider than Peters had ever seen them. He remembered her demeanor on that first morning he had met with her, when he'd directed the first spate of Kyle Park searches. Now, she seemed relieved, filled with hope. It was nice to see her spirits buoyed. But it would be doubly cruel if her daughter were never found, or turned up dead.

Peters had been surprised when he'd heard that Chief King was allowing the psychic access to the case and to the Martins. He'd assumed the whole thing was a big waste of time. Jeff had explained over beers one night that, sometimes, it was more eyes on the case, even from something as outrageous as a civilian or a self-professed medium, that could break a case open. She might not have any "powers" whatsoever, but she might bring a new perspective to the case. Much like bringing in a washed-up ex-cop, fresh eyes could sometimes tease out a new lead or a new approach.

Lady Meredith smiled.

"I'm not sure," she said. "But I feel like it's a forest or a cave. Somewhere dark. Cold—I got a shiver when I sensed it."

Peters saw Mr. Harper give the Chief another look—clearly, Harper thought this was all a load of crap, but he was holding his tongue.

Chief King nodded. "That's very interesting. We'll expand our search to include those types of locations."

Glenda's eyes got bigger, and Lady Meredith smiled. "We'll continue our search," the psychic announced. "Glenda, can you take me to the exact location where the girls were taken?"

"Certainly," Glenda said, nodding.

"Deputy Peters, can you accompany them?" Chief King asked. "Give them whatever help they need, okay?"

Peters nodded. He knew he was taking one for the team—he'd rather be out in the field, helping the Chief or interviewing friends of the family with Mr. Harper. At this point, Peters would have volunteered to staff the tip line if it had gotten him away from Lady Meredith and her creepy lap dog with the dark mascara. He just walked around, taking pictures and writing things down. He almost never spoke.

Instead, Peters nodded. Maybe something would come of it.

43

After the meeting with Mrs. Martin and the psychic, Chief King and Frank had driven separately back to the police station. Frank ran back to the hotel and grabbed more of the files—he'd made notes on a few things and wanted to look them up at the office.

In the car by himself, Frank had tried to listen to music to calm down, but there was no denying the psychic got under his skin. He had held his tongue this time, but he could tell she was waiting for an opportunity to nail him again on something.

Some low, quiet piano jazz helped, although he was starting to get tired of the same stack of CDs. He wished he had an operating radio in this car, or a ceiling that didn't hang down like the decorations in some Middle Eastern harem. If this case turned out well, and he got paid, or if he could somehow manage to earn at least some portion of the $50,000 reward, one of the first things he would buy was a new car.

He'd always wanted a big, solid El Dorado. Black, spotless interior, with bench seats and a dashboard that went on forever. Ben Stone had had a friend who owned one, and Frank had gotten a chance to ride in it once. It was like floating on a cloud. A black, armored, tank-like cloud, but smooth. A Cadillac from back when they made Cadillacs for businessmen and stock brokers and not gangsters and rap stars.

When Frank arrived at the station, King was already conducting yet another press conference, one filled with absolutely no new information other than the news that the kidnappers hadn't showed up to claim the ransom. More stupid questions were asked. The TV reporters and newspaper guys needed fodder, even if it was nothing more than reassurance from the police that they were "still working around the clock" on the case. Tina Armstrong was there again, still in her sunglasses. Frank watched her but could never tell where she was looking. He wondered about her photophobia, what caused her extreme sensitivity to light, and how it affected her job.

After the press conference, Frank and King and the other senior staff met again, going around the table once more and reviewing all the active leads, of which there were only a handful.

Sergeant Graves covered his investigation of the ransom drop this morning and speculated about why the kidnappers hadn't shown. It still confused Frank. He'd thought it was a ruse, or a distraction, but nothing had come of it, and the money was now sitting in a nondescript cardboard box locked in the evidence room, waiting to go back to the bank and into Nick Martin's accounts.

Ted Shale, the FBI liaison, reiterated that neither he nor the FBI contacts he'd reached out to could get any traction on the case. He seemed as frustrated as Frank.

King covered the psychic involvement and, to his credit, even mentioned the new "information" that the girls might be being held in somewhere dark and cold, surrounded by wood. The others nodded and smiled.

"That helps," Sergeant Burwell said, shaking his head. "Now I can stop searching all those sunny, open fields."

"Maybe you were looking for unicorns," Graves said, smiling.

King looked at Frank. "You got anything?"

"I've spent the last two days interviewing people involved in the case," Frank said, shaking his head. "But couldn't come up with anything new." He kept the information about Glenda and her new career to himself for now. And he looked at each man in turn, trying to see any hint of trouble, but they all looked him back in the eyes. If his hunch was right, and someone was feeding police information to the kidnappers, it couldn't be one of these people seated around the table. They each appeared to be working hard to break the case.

Maybe it was office staff or something like that.

They wrapped up the meeting, and Frank and Chief King headed back to the Chief's office and were starting to talk when Graves knocked on the door.

"You guys got a sec?"

King nodded and waved Graves into his office, but the man shook his head.

"Let's go for a walk."

They walked through the station, taking the glassed-in walkway over to the government side of the building. Graves kept walking, heading right out the front doors, which faced away from the front of the police station and the gaggle of reporters gathered around the entrance. Sergeant Graves turned and pointed at the McDonald's around the corner, then started across the wide field that separated the building from the lot. King and Frank hurried to follow.

"You got something?" King asked.

"Maybe," Graves said, glancing around as they walked. "I looked into it, like you asked before the press conference. And Frank might be right—strange things are turning up. Maybe that's why there have been no breaks in the case. Anyway, I found stuff missing from the case files."

Chief King looked at Frank, then back to Graves. "What kind of stuff?"

"I'm still pulling it together," Graves said. "But it looks like someone on the staff."

"Who?" King demanded.

Graves shook his head, as they reached the parking lot and weaved between the cars, all of which were covered with white plastic. This parking lot apparently was an auxiliary lot of new cars for the Honda dealership across the street.

"I can't say yet," Graves said. "But it does seem to be someone in the department."

"Administration?" Frank asked. "A secretary or janitor?"

"Sadly, I don't think so," Sergeant Graves said, shaking his head. "One thing I did find out for sure was that some of the tip line calls have been deleted."

"Dammit," King said. "That sounds like someone covering his tracks. And those aren't accessible by just anyone."

"Stan is working the tip line, right?" Frank asked.

King and Graves glanced at each other.

Graves nodded. "Yes, he is. I'll look into that. But also, I was thinking about this, Chief. That money this morning, from the ransom—maybe it's not safe in the station."

They walked in silence for another minute, then made it to the sidewalk and crossed Garber Avenue to the McDonald's, heading inside.

"You might be right," King said when they'd gotten coffee and were seated. There was an attached play area, separated from the restaurant by large windows. Seeing the kids inside, playing and sliding on the equipment, Frank thought of Jackson.

"Should we secure it offsite?" King continued. "One of the banks? Or maybe Shale should take it."

"I don't know," Graves said. "I'm not sure who to trust."

King nodded. "You should take it," King said to Sergeant Graves. "For now, until we get it figured out."

Graves shook his head, smiling. "No, thanks," he said. "I don't even like handling that kind of money—too much pressure. I didn't even like being in charge of it between the park and the station. I like the bank idea."

King turned to Frank. "You wanna hold it?"

Frank was quiet for a moment, and then nodded. "I hate to agree, but if it is someone on your staff, the bank idea won't fly—the information about which bank will get out. I can secure the money. There's a safe in my hotel."

Graves nodded, agreeing.

"Offsite is best. And it should be Shale or Mr. Harper to hold the money. We know they both are clean—they came into the case late."

Chief King nodded, making up his mind.

"Good thinking," he said. "Okay, Frank, we'll escort you home today and get the money squared away in the safe at your hotel."

They sat, continuing to discuss the case before returning to the police station. The hours dragged on—Frank was so bored he even pitched in and staffed the tip line for a while, but nothing came of it. Frank did it mostly to observe Stan, but the man wasn't working the same shift and wouldn't be in until later in the day.

Most of the other police officers were either out on routine patrol or getting set up for the big HarvestFest event taking place that night downtown. As the sun slid down the sky and peeked in the western windows of the police station, King came around carrying a cardboard box.

"You ready?" he asked.

Frank nodded. "Yup. Let me grab my stuff."

They walked out to the parking lot together, talking casually as they passed through the station. As far as anyone could tell, they were just carrying files out to their cars. A few reporters leaned against their trucks, but after a few "no comments," they left Frank and King alone.

They got to the Taurus and King set the box in the passenger seat.

"Okay," King said. "Secure that, then come out tonight, if you want—it's four now. We'll all be working the HarvestFest, which starts at seven."

Frank nodded. "See you there."

He drove back to the hotel, glancing over at the box of money several times. It made him nervous to be holding that kind of cash but also a little excited—if someone on the police force was dirty, and they found out he had the money, they might make a play for it. They might come for it, and for him. And, if he managed to not get killed, it could be a huge break in the case.

The first problem occurred when he lugged the heavy box into the hotel and set it down on the front counter.

"No, I'm sorry," the young woman behind the counter said. "We don't have a house safe, just the safes in the individual rooms." Frank didn't want to get into the details, or freak out the young lady by saying he had SO much money it wouldn't fit in the room safe. Instead, he just nodded and carried the box upstairs.

If someone was coming for the money, they'd have to go through him.

44

An hour later, Frank was going through his notes and the mind map again, looking for anything.

He was also keeping a nervous ear out for footsteps in the hallway. If some dirty cop was coming for him and the money, he doubted the front desk would be calling to inform Frank he had a guest.

Frank tried to relax and go through the notes. He allowed himself two glasses of the precious Maker's Mark, trying to ration what he had left.

He'd added some items from the recent day's investigations to the large mind map taped to the windows looking out over the parking lot. Frank had begun circling aspects of the case that might indicate a traitor in their midst. He found the reference to Glenda's photographs and made a note to look into that tomorrow. If she was always taking photos, there was an off-chance she'd been taking pictures the morning of the kidnapping, or in the week before. Perhaps someone had been casing her neighborhood, planning the abduction. Or she might have a big stack of boxes of photos somewhere that Frank could go through. It might not hurt—

There was a knock at the door.

Usually, the front desk called up to let him know he had a guest. Which meant either the front desk wasn't paying attention, or the person had snuck in. Either way, Frank wasn't taking any chances—he pulled the gun from his holster, then went to the door, standing off to one side.

"Who is it?"

"It's Peters," the voice came through the door.

Frank smiled. Deputy Peters was, unfortunately, at the top of his dirty-cop suspect list.

The guy knew everyone and everything about the case. But was he just pretending to be klutzy and a little behind the eight ball? And he'd specifically requested to be the one to help out Frank when he joined the case.

And it made sense that Peters knew about the money—King had probably sent Peters to keep him company. Of course, there had to be someone working from the inside, and the only person Frank could really trust was Chief King. Frank hoped it wasn't Peters, but there was only one way to be sure.

Frank pulled the door open.

"Donuts?" Peters asked, holding up another box from "Tim's." "It's getting later, and I heard you were working on the files again. Plus I need to get to HarvestFest, but I was in the mood for coffee and donuts. You?"

Frank hesitated. His gun was behind the door, pointed through the wood at Peters' head. Or maybe the young cop just came to work.

"Cool," Frank said. "Come on in."

Frank pulled the door open all the way, tucking his gun in his waistband for now. The young deputy entered, smiling.

"Isn't that a little clichéd?" Frank asked. "Donuts for cops?"

Peters smiled and set the box down on the small table by the window next to the stacks of files. "You're not a cop. And you didn't complain today at the ransom drop."

"True."

Frank looked around at the room. It certainly looked different from days before, the first time a local cop showed up at his hotel room and asked for help. It used to be clean, but now it was a mess—pizza boxes, empty coffee drink containers, and stacks of paperwork. He'd asked the housekeeper to just make the bed and leave everything else alone—when he was in an investigation, he needed his stuff just so. Of course, he usually had an office and a desk. The housekeeper had argued with him, insisting she be allowed to at least take out the trash and clean the bathroom.

"Find anything?" Peters asked, setting down a paper bag next to the donuts and pulling out two coffees. "All that stuff with the psychic was a complete waste of time."

"I don't know—maybe she's onto something."

Deputy Peters scoffed and sat down. "Nope, just blowing smoke up…well, you know."

Frank smiled and sat down across from Peters. He slid the gun from his waistband and aimed it under the table at the young cop.

"Peters, why are you really here?"

The young cop stopped in the middle of biting into a powdered donut, his eyes wide. There was powdered sugar on his face. It would have been comical if Frank wasn't prepared to shoot him.

"What?"

Frank nodded. "I won't ask again."

Peters set the donut down slowly. "Oh, I get it," Peters said quietly. "You think I'm here for the money?"

Frank shook his head. "Can Chief King keep anything to himself?"

"I don't know," Peters said. "But he trusts me, and so should you. I'm here to solve the case, or at least try. Take my gun if you want," Peters said, raising his hands.

Frank slid his own hand out from under the table, revealing the gun aimed at Peters. The deputy looked at it, his eyes wide, but made no moves. In fact, he raised his hands even higher. Frank reached around and removed the man's gun from the belt. The loop had still been strapped.

Frank checked Peters off the list. If the young Deputy had been here to kill Frank, the kid wouldn't have had his gun strapped in. It would've been ready to pull. But it never hurt to be careful. If Ben Stone had been more careful before heading off to Coral Gables, he wouldn't have died with his gun still strapped in.

"OK," Frank said, putting his gun down.

Peters shook his head. "Wow, you're scary."

Frank put his gun away. "I'm having a hard time chalking this case up to bad luck," he said. "I've been eliminating theories, one after another."

"You think it's an inside job," Peters said.

Frank nodded.

"Who would you suspect?" Frank asked, watching Peters. This next question could be crucial. "Anyone on the team not trying their hardest?"

Deputy Peters sat back to think about it, nibbling on his donut. "I don't know—maybe Stan Garber, but that's because he's dealing with a situation of his own."

"Hitting your wife isn't a 'situation,' it's a symptom of something else," Frank said. "It's completely under his control."

Peters nodded.

"OK," Frank said and slid Peters' gun back across the table. "But think about it. And keep an eye out for anything odd. Now, do me a favor and review the case for me again. Just hit the high points."

Twenty minutes later, Peters wrapped up with the discussion he'd had with Chief King only an hour ago about the possibility of a leak in the department.

"Do you have any ideas?" Frank asked while working on his second donut. Frank had to trust someone. If Peters was in on it, he was some kind of genius. And they were all screwed.

"No," Peters answered. "It's like the Chief said—things are off but nothing solid yet. I'm glad Graves is looking into those missing files and the 911 calls. Either one of those could prove who is dirty, if Sergeant Graves can trace it back to a badge number."

Frank nodded at the boxes around him.

"There is a pattern emerging in the files, a disturbing line of thought that kept popping up, again and again," Frank said quietly. "The girl was taken by someone she knew, but all of the family members and friends of the family were accounted for. That meant that the girl was taken by a person of authority or someone that she believed was a person of author-ity, like someone dressed like a cop."

Peters nodded. "Or a real cop."

"And the kidnappers waited a long time before calling in the ransom demand," Frank said. "Something that rarely happens. In most cases, the ransom call comes within four to six hours after the initial abduction. Statistically, a ransom call has come in that late in only 3% of cases in the U.S. over the past twenty years. So why did the kidnappers delay the call?"

Deputy Peters nodded his head. "To get the girls situated," Peters said. "And to keep us all searching, assuming it was a missing person's case. Our department, and the volunteers, have combed every square inch of open space in Cooper's Mill, and every public building and uninhabited home has been searched multiple times."

"Which was probably all just a big waste of time to keep you guys distracted," Frank said.

Peters nodded.

"Then there was the ransom drop," Frank continued. "It was a thing of beauty—for the kidnappers. The distracting girl, the car parked behind a shop with a back door, and the easily-located tracking devices on the money. No train passing through town, and it's like they knew where all the roadblocks were located. Once they figured out how to remove the money from sight, the kidnappers were essentially home free. No police were stationed on that side of the southern end of town. Then across the tracks and out of town. There is something else going on here, and it all points to an inside job," Frank said, looking down at the table. "I hate to say it, but someone connected to the police department is involved in the kidnapping."

Peters looked at the files in front of him. "It's a very scary thought."

Frank nodded. "I haven't worked a lot of cases like this, where every-thing seems to go wrong. Let's go back through the files again, but this time, look for holes in the information, or places where it looks like things are missing. I'll add them to the map. And jot down who worked on what pieces of the case. There might be a pattern there, too."

Peters glanced at his watch. "I've got an hour before I have to leave," he said, grabbing a stack of files on the table.

Frank excused himself and went into the bathroom. Turning on the sink, he found the bottle of Maker's Mark he'd hidden in the shower stall and took a long pull on the liquid, not caring anymore to ration it out. The warmth filled his belly, and his leg stopped shaking. It had been quivering for most of the conversation with Peters. Frank had thought it would go away on its own, but there was only one drink that helped – and it wasn't the coffee that had accompanied that box of donuts. After a minute, he left the bathroom and sat, diving into the files on the table, searching for anything that could shed a little insight.

45

Charlie was working on the window when she heard steps on the staircase.

She turned and stuffed the small tin of lip balm back into her pocket and tiptoed back to the bed. She'd found it in the side table next to the bed this morning, and after breakfast had found that by slathering it on her wrist, she could work free of the zip tie if it wasn't too tight.

Charlie had seen someone do that in a movie once. They'd stuck a hair clip into a set of handcuffs and popped it off. But she was tied up with plastic zip ties, a new one each time. They were cut off and replaced every time she was let out. A stack of them sat on the dresser across the room. But with the lip balm, she could get out.

She sat back on the bed and wiped the lip balm off her wrist before slipping her right hand back into the zip tie, which was still attached to the headboard.

The door swung open. It was the young man again. The woman never came unless it was dark. The woman didn't want Charlie to see her face, but it hadn't worked, and Charlie had gotten a good sideways glance at her. She was one of those women who could have been beautiful, with the face of a princess. Yet she'd looked so sad and tired, her face had drooped, like she was half-asleep.

"How are we doing tonight?" the young man asked, setting the tray of food on the bed next to her. He was always nice to her. "Need to go to the bathroom?"

She nodded, and he cut the zip tie to let her out. Charlie walked to the bathroom and closed the door, then relieved herself. It was good to be up, walking around. Her legs were starting to ache from so many days lying in bed.

Every time she came in here, she looked out the window for as long as she could manage. After she was done, she flushed and turned on the water, then climbed up onto the side of the tub and looked out.

There was the edge of a roof right outside the window, and she could see the large tree. It had been the long branches she'd heard scraping the window. It had sounded like fingers to her.

Beyond the roof, it was a straight drop down to the yard, but from this angle, she couldn't see anything to jump down onto, or a ladder, or anything to climb down. And it looked like there was no way to get over to the tree.

Beyond the house was a large backyard with a play set. Past that, a tall fence ran between the house and a field. And on the other side of the field, she saw trees. It looked like a forest. The window was big enough. If she could get free and get out onto the roof—

"You done in there?"

She jumped and climbed down, shutting off the water. Coming out into the bedroom, she nodded.

"Thank you."

She climbed back up onto the bed and started to eat.

"Can you tell me another story? About the ocean?"

He smiled and began another story. He must've had dozens, because each one was new. Charlie hoped she would be long gone before she started to hear the same ones again.

"Well, have you heard of Morro Rock?" he asked. "In California, the beach stretches for a thousand miles along the coastline, and it's dotted with hundreds of coves and inlets. Some of them hold towns and villages, and others no one ever visits, except for the seals and sea lions. But in Morro Bay, sitting right out in the middle of the bay, there's a giant boulder called Morro Rock. No one knows where it came from…"

She sat back and listened to the story, eating her peanut butter and jelly sandwich and nodding in all the right places. He might be a criminal, but he'd never been mean to her, and he knew how to tell stories. She wondered if he'd always been bad. But something told her to be nice to him.

After a while, she was done, and he wrapped up his story and began gathering up the plates and tidying the tray.

"My arm really hurts—it's so stretched," she said, rubbing her left arm. "Can I just sleep normal tonight? I can't get out if you lock the door, right?"

The young man thought about it for a moment but shook his head.

"Sorry, I can't do that," he said, smiling. "Honestly. But I could secure the other arm instead, if that helps."

She made a sad look on her face, hoping to sway him, but the woman downstairs started yelling again and he was distracted. After a few seconds of them listening to the woman yell, he smiled and zip tied her left arm to the headboard—again, two connected loops, one around her wrist and the other around the headboard.

"I'm sorry your arm was hurting." He sat back. "Anything else?"

She shook her head. The man turned and left, and when the door clicked closed, she tried the zip tie, but it was too tight. Even with the lip balm, it would be impossible to get out.

Charlie would have to try again when the woman came. She always let Charlie up to pee one more time before bed. After that, she'd get out the lip balm and wiggle free. Or use the pen and just pry it off. But once she did that, she'd have to escape for good.

46

Two cars sat in the same grocery store parking lot as before, their driver's windows facing each other again. Behind them, Burger King stood next to Main Street. Tonight, there was no rain.

"And that's it?" the man said.

Tyler nodded. "Yup. It's all taken care of."

The other man nodded, looking around at a car that passed by, exiting the Burger King drive thru. "It's not safe, us meeting."

Tyler, the boss, shook his head. "Don't worry. Every cop in Cooper's Mill is downtown, getting ready for the big party. You're not going to give me any grief about that money?"

"You keep it," the other man said. "You earned it. I just want this all wrapped up by tomorrow."

Tyler nodded. "Good. I'm glad you're not pressing the issue."

"Hey, it's your deal," the man said, trying to make his point for the hundredth time. For a criminal mastermind, this guy was pretty thick. "I want it over with. What will you do with the girls? Can they identify your friends?"

Tyler shook his head. "Didn't I say not to worry? You should pay me more respect. This whole thing has gone off without a hitch. Not that you need to know, but it's taken care of. Beep, beep, they're going on a trip. The girls will be transported out of state and then freed, and my contacts will be long gone."

The other man nodded. "Good. Just make sure it doesn't get back to us."

Tyler nodded. "No problem."

The other man nodded, not sure of what to say. The cop was always quoting songs and repeating those weird lyrics and attributing them to his mother. That was the problem with getting in bed with a psychopath: sometimes, all you could do was nod and laugh at their jokes and count the seconds until you could get away.

47

Frank was out driving again, trying to clear his head. Peters had left to help out with the HarvestFest security, and King was expecting Frank to drop by as well, but Frank just wanted to get into his car and drive. It was freeing. Over the last few days, since he'd arrived, he'd slowly gotten to know the narrow country roads surrounding the small town.

Frank did some of his best thinking while driving, and there was nothing waiting for him back at the hotel except for those last two inches of bourbon in the bottle in his shower. Even out here, driving in the darkness, Frank could hear it calling to him. He was trying to be strong, but the headaches and nausea weren't helping.

The windows were down and he was listening to the Benny Golson CD again. He'd never really liked jazz until he lived in New Orleans. He's been around jazz since birth, of course, growing up in Beaufort, just outside of the BR. But blues and jazz music had been an acquired taste. Maybe it was something you grew into, or perhaps only adults could really appreciate the music's subtle ebb and flow.

The CD ended—he was driving east of town, past some place called Dalton Farms—and he reached down and popped open the CD player. Even though the player was jury-rigged and skipped whenever he hit a hard bump, it still worked. He'd had it for a while now. Frank found he could easily swap out and start new CDs without taking his eyes off the wheel.

He felt in the compartment in the dashboard that had once held an operational stereo and took out another CD, swapping it out and hitting PLAY. After a moment, blues filled the car—Earl Hooker.

The car engine purred along as he wandered in search of answers or, at least, direction.

Frank reached the light at the corner of 202 and 571 and turned west, approaching Cooper's Mill. The area east of Cooper's Mill was all open fields and low farmland and pitch black. There were no street lights or anything on this side of town to illuminate the road other than the headlights of Frank's beat-up Taurus.

He crossed the river—a black streak in the darkness below the bridge.

It was strange, if you thought about it—rivers and lakes and streams just went about their business, flowing through the night, never stopping, oblivious to all the goings-on around them. They ebbed and flowed, rose and fell with the rain, continuously washing everything they carried to the sea. Frank didn't like water and didn't spend any more time on the water than he absolutely had to, but you really had to respect the overwhelming power of flowing water. As he crossed over it, the river gurgled below the bridge, loud enough to hear even over the engine noise.

Frank passed Freeman Prairie, then climbed the hill into Cooper's Mill, stopping at the light at First and Main.

Downtown Cooper's Mill was lit up and bustling with shoppers and partygoers. It was a busy Saturday night, and visitors were enjoying the brisk weather and getting out for a meal. There were signs everywhere for the "HarvestFest 2011" tonight. Held by a local volunteer group, they shut down part of Second Street and threw a huge, Halloween-themed, outdoor adult party.

The light turned green, and he drove through town to the next light. Second Street was blocked off next to O'Shaughnessy's, and a huge banner that read "HarvestFest 2011" hung from the yellow barricades. Frank saw Chief King and Deputy Peters and several other familiar faces and decided to pull over, parking down the street in front of the library. From the reports, Chief King and Nick Martin had stood on the stoop of the library, waiting to deliver the first ransom.

The second ransom now sat in a nondescript box in the trunk of Frank's car, along with his boxes of case files. He'd toyed with leaving it all unattended in his hotel room, but it just made more sense to keep it with him wherever he went. It had taken two trips to bring it all out to the car.

Frank climbed out of the Taurus and carefully locked up the car before crossing the street. To the west, the sound of the train horn drifted over the town. The gates lowered and a train appeared, the sound low and reverberating through the streets.

A group of volunteers was setting up tables and tents and checking folks into the party. A trailer festooned with a huge "Bud Light" sign was parked inside a fenced-in area; apparently, someone had put up snow fencing all the way around to keep the beer-drinking attendees confined to a designated space. Everyone was dressed in costumes. Beyond, a stage had been set up in the middle of the road, and Frank could hear instruments being tuned. It sounded like a band was getting ready to play.

"Hey, Deputy," Frank said, as he walked up to the barricade.

Peters smiled, turning to see Frank. "Long time, no see. The Chief wants to see you."

Chief King walked up. "Hey, Frank."

Frank nodded and noticed several of the volunteers setting up tables were in costume. "You need any help?"

King shook his head. "No, everyone is pretty well behaved, though we do step up the DUI stops after the event is over. You out at Ricky's again, questioning patrons and kicking asses?"

"Nope, just driving," Frank said, smiling. "Helps me think."

"Good—we need thinkers," Chief King said, nodding. "Just don't get any bright ideas tonight. We're stretched thin, with most of the staff here working this event or out on patrol. No one gets the night off," he smiled.

"Sure you don't need some help?"

King shook his head. "No, we're good. But stick around if you want – they put on a good show. There's a band and costume contests."

"Nah, I'm OK," Frank said, thinking about all that money in his car. It made him nervous, leaving it there on such a busy street, exposed. "After last night at Ricky's, I could use a break."

"OK, we'll see you in the morning," the Chief said.

Frank gave Peters a friendly wave—he was off, helping get the beer tent set up—and made a loop through the downtown on the way back to his car. He saw locations that were starting to become familiar to him—the coffee shop, the toy store, the barber shop. He saw the bench in front of O'Shaughnessy's where Peters and Barnes had waited, and where the buxom decoy had distracted them. He walked in front of Elise's Antiques, the small shop through which the kid had run with the ransom money.

Frank got back to his car. As he was pulling out, another car slowed and turned on its signal, waiting for his spot. He'd never seen the town busy—of course, he'd only been here a few days, but it was good to see an old-fashioned downtown like this one still had a little life left in it.

He drove the streets, familiar buildings moving past him. Frank reached up and grabbed a piece of paper from the dashboard. Peters had made a printout of the various properties and locations in the area owned by Martin Construction.

Frank was still convinced the whole kidnapping plan was really an effort to bankrupt the company, so he'd been driving around and checking out the properties. Yesterday, he'd driven down to Dayton and walked around the old brick building that was slowly being converted into retail and residential space. The building managers had been extremely helpful, taking him on a tour of the space and saying how sorry they were that Martin had had to drop out of the ownership group. Frank had to agree with at least part of the assessment of the property—from the top floor conference room, there had been stunning views of the baseball stadium and the riverfront developments beyond.

He shook his head in wonder at those types of people who could walk through a dilapidated, waterlogged hovel and see through the dirt and mess to envision a thriving retail shop or a beautifully-appointed home. It took a special kind of focus, he thought, to ignore all the details and just hone in on the possibilities that came at the intersection of careful planning and hard work.

Frank had also dropped in on a few of the other properties that had recently been part of the Martin Construction portfolio—open fields, an apartment building, and one sad strip mall between Cooper's Mill and Troy, the larger town to the north.

There was a train passing through town, and he slowed and stopped, waiting for it to pass. He glanced at the papers and saw, near the top, a listing for "Holly Toys Lofts," one location he'd not visited yet. The building had apparently been near and dear to Nick Martin, who had let it go only after much discussion. Nick had grown up near the place and been particularly fond of it. Nick had been able to come to an agreement with his business partner, Matt Lassiter, and the sale made it possible for Martin to gather the entire ransom.

It had been mentioned several times in the files and reports, but Frank hadn't seen it in any of his treks around town. Following Peter's crude map—he'd drawn one for each property—Frank crossed the tracks after the train was gone and slowed, turning right onto North Sixth. Frank found the massive brick building with no problem.

48

The exterior of the Holly Toys building wasn't anything special to look at, but the building was immense. At four stories high, it was one of the tallest in Cooper's Mill and nearly a block long. The massive, 40,000 square foot brick building ran along the train tracks north of Main Street, surrounded by large parking lots on both sides.

Frank slowed at the curb but did not pull in; he wanted to loop around the property before getting out.

It looked like an abandoned warehouse, except for the large, weathered sign out front, advertising the new loft condos that would be available after the building was gutted and converted. Large, attractive renderings showed what the condos would look like, along with a number to call for inquiries. A large, faded banner across the bottom proclaimed, "Coming Spring 2009," so the project was over two years' past schedule. And, from what Frank could remember about the property, they hadn't sold a single condo.

Nick Martin seemed pretty fastidious about marketing, as did his partner on this project. Frank wondered why they had left up that "Coming Spring 2009" sign. It looked bad and would hamper any future sales. Frank wondered if the phone number was even still active.

He continued on, past the large brick building and tried to make a right on Plum, only to find that it was one-way the other direction. He continued up Sixth, did a U-turn, then passed the warehouse, and turned on Walnut, driving past more houses. As he crossed the tracks, he looked to his left and saw the massive brick building running along the tracks, finally getting a real feel for just how large the building was.

He drove on, taking two more lefts and coming back up Plum. The warehouse stretched the length of the block, but the building had definitely seen better days.

Slowing, he turned into the parking lot and stopped his car, climbing out of the Taurus. He thought about what his car held for a moment, but Frank was just going to walk around the building, maybe take a peek inside. He wouldn't be out of sight of the car for more than a few minutes. Besides, it was an empty parking lot, and no one was around. And no one would suspect a half-a-million dollars in cash would be hiding in the trunk of such a dilapidated vehicle.

According to the reports, the downward economy had stalled the project in mid-2009, making it impossible for Martin Construction to complete the conversion. Neither Nick Martin nor his business partner had been able to buy the other out or front the kind of money required to complete the project or overcome the bad economy, so now it sat here, or at least it had until yesterday, when Nick had sold his half to Lassiter.

He was no architect, obviously, but Frank could see the potential. It was a beautiful brick building, and he could see how condos or apartments could be attractive. The bottom floor was supposed to be set aside for retail spaces, if he remembered correctly, making it an even cooler place to live.

And Peters had said there weren't any other high-end apartments or condos in town, so the building owners could probably charge whatever they wanted to.

Frank started across the empty parking lot. It was cracked from the hundreds of heavy trucks that had once delivered raw materials or picked up completed toys for delivery. Nick Martin had said in the report on the project that the Holly Toys factory had operated for nearly sixty years out of this location before closing down in the late nineties.

Frank crossed the wide parking lot and saw one car parked near the front entrance. Next to the doors stood another sign advertising the condo project. This sign had renderings of what the condos would look like on the inside. Frank walked up and studied the sun-faded pictures in the fading light: large, open rooms, floor-to-ceiling windows, and those exposed brick walls that always somehow looked brand new and vintage at the same time.

The night was quiet. In the distance, Frank could hear the sound of the rock band playing at the HarvestFest concert downtown. It felt like he was a long way from the downtown area, but he was really only four blocks off the main drag. He could also hear the distant wailing of another approaching train.

Frank walked around the building. On the east side, facing the train tracks, was another, smaller parking lot. A fenced-off portion contained several pallets of construction materials, a Bobcat, and two forklifts.

"Can I help you?"

Frank turned to see a security guard walking up to him. The older, black man carried himself with a relaxed air, but one of his hands was resting on a gun in a holster. It looked like a small revolver.

Frank smiled.

"Hi. My name is Frank, Frank Harper," he said. "I'm working with the police department on the kidnapping of those two girls. Have you heard about it?"

The man stopped and nodded. "What a mess. Christ, I hope they find those girls. You here 'cause Mr. Martin used to own the building?"

Frank nodded. "Yup. I was with the New Orleans PD for a long time, and old habits are hard to break. I'm checking on some of his old properties, although what you said is right. He doesn't actually own this anymore."

The black man nodded and walked over to join Frank. "I was on the force up in Detroit, before I retired down here. This is all the construction materials and equipment. They put up the fence last year after some of the copper disappeared."

"Theft or vagrants?"

"Mostly vagrants," the security guard said. "They go around and strip whatever they can from abandoned buildings, rental properties—wherever they can find materials—and then take it into Dayton and sell it for scrap. I'm Monty, by the way. Monty Robinson."

Frank shook his hand.

"Ever notice anything odd around here? I'm looking for where the kidnappers could stash the young girls, but I'm sure you'd notice people coming and going. Is the place watched around the clock?"

Monty nodded. "Yup, after those thefts. Me and two other guys. There's a little office, but there's rarely anyone here. Mr. Lassiter was in here a couple days ago, but that's been it for weeks. You cops have been through at least twice. Wanna see inside?"

"Sure, sounds good."

Monty led him through a back entrance and into a first floor office— a small television, desk, coffee maker, and a stack of magazines—and then out into a dingy wide hallway.

"That'll be the restaurant down there," Monty said, pointing into a big open space in the gloom, "along with a couple other retail spaces. Up here, near the doors, was supposed to be the sales office for the residences, along with a small dry cleaner and a little grocery, like a 7-11 or corner grocery. Then the other three floors are all condos."

Frank looked around—it didn't look like they'd gotten far on the retail spaces, but the walls were all up and strung for power. Plastic sheets hung everywhere. "Too bad this place never got off the ground. It would've been a cool place to live."

The guard nodded. "Back here is the loading dock and freight elevator," he said, leading Frank down the darkened hallway to an open area on the northern end of the building. Boxes and shipping pallets blocked the way to two large loading doors. "Wanna see the condos?"

Frank glanced out a window and checked on the Taurus, which sat undisturbed. He nodded, and Monty led him to a rickety elevator. Monty pulled the metal gate across and hit a button that said "Fourth Floor" in old, blocky print.

"They get very far on the residences? I heard they didn't sell any," Frank asked, trying to ignore the fact that he was in an enclosed space. At least it was a freight elevator, with one of those open doors that let you see the floors sliding past.

"That's not exactly true," Monty said. "They sold several, almost half of the ten on the top floor, but all but two of them fell through. Foreclosed, even before they were built. Mr. Lassiter wanted one of the condos for himself, but he ended up buying a building elsewhere. His condo here was the only one they really came close to finishing, and they used it as the model home to show off to buyers."

The elevator rattled to a sudden stop, and Monty pulled the gate open. The top floor was pitch black, except for the light in the elevator. The guard exited the elevator and faded into the dark. After a long moment of silence, lights began flipping on, and Frank could see the security guard at an electrical panel, switching on banks of florescent lights.

"These up here got the closest to being done," he said, pointing. Most of the floor was taken up with open spaces and temporary walls, but on the southern end, he saw a door. They started down the open space that would have been a hallway.

"There was also going to be a gym for the residents, and a common room for them to throw parties and such, down on the second floor. But these condos up here were the fanciest, with the big floor-to-ceiling windows," Monty said, leading Frank across the huge open space. "Thick glass, too, to block the sound of the train."

The guard pushed the condo door open, and Frank could see what he meant. While the residence wasn't close to being finished, you could get a sense of what it would look like. The huge windows afforded a great view of downtown—from here, four stories up, he could see over the train tracks and houses and easily make out several now-familiar shops and restaurants. He could even pick out the corner where they were holding HarvestFest tonight—all the milling folks on the street gave it away.

"Yeah, too bad they didn't finish," the security guard said. "Seems a shame, letting all this stuff just go to waste. But now that it's changed hands, the project should get going again."

Frank turned.

"Matt Lassiter is going to get the project going again? I thought he didn't have the money to finish."

"He doesn't. That's why he said he sold it," Monty replied.

"Wait," Frank said, shaking his head. "I'm confused—you mean

Nick Martin sold it to Lassiter, right?"

Monty nodded. "Yes, and then Mr. Lassiter sold it to another invest-ment group. That's why he was in here a couple days ago—he was gath-ering up all the paperwork. Said he needed all the schematics and a bunch of up-to-date photos of the interior. The new buyer wanted them. The building had some water damage last year."

Frank nodded and walked over to the windows, looking down. The tracks ran right in front of the building—he hoped they were planning to fence off the tracks or something, with people living here.

"Impressive, huh?" Monty said.

"Yes," Frank answered. He glanced out across the downtown, finding the bookstore and the coffee shop. "It's a great view."

"Yup," Monty grunted. "Wish I could afford it."

Frank turned and smiled. "You mean they aren't giving you a free one?"

Monty smiled. "Nah, but if I'm lucky, they'll let me hold the door open for them," he said sarcastically. "Hey, I have to get back to my rounds."

"Sure, and thanks for the tour," Frank said, following the guard out of Lassiter's one-time condo and back down the hallway to the elevator. The elevator descended loudly, as Monty told Frank about his time on the force in Detroit—even then, the place was going to hell. When they got to the first floor, Monty pulled the door open, and Frank followed him to the office.

"Well, that's pretty much it," Monty said, walking him outside. "Let me know if you need to get back in some time."

Frank nodded. "Thanks again."

"No problem—hope it helped. I'm gonna continue my rounds—I gotta go back in and walk the other floors. Not that I ever find anything other than an occasional pigeon, snuck in through an open grate."

Frank started to walk away, then turned back.

"Sorry, I gotta be clear on something," Frank said. "You're saying Lassiter sold it already? Nick only signed it over Tuesday morning."

The security guard shrugged. "What can I tell you? Rich people. It was Thursday when he was in here, going through the papers."

Frank shook his hand. "Thanks," he said.

Monty Robinson disappeared back inside. Frank wasn't sure what to do next—his mind was racing. For him to sell it that quickly, Lassiter must have already had a buyer lined up for the property. Or just been incredibly lucky, or expecting it to be coming "on the market." There was no other way he could turn it over in less than 24 hours. But why hadn't they seen a report on it, or any mention of the sale in all the

financial records? Surely Agent Shale must have known about it—
Agent Shale.

He had access to all the financial records and could have removed anything he wanted. And why had the Bureau sent such a dunderhead—was he really an idiot, or just playing the part?

Frank walked across the parking lot that fronted the tracks. He could hear the rock music drifting up from downtown.

Lassiter had benefited greatly from Martin having to sell his share. But was that reason enough to kidnap his partner's daughter?

Frank wanted to call Chief King but also wanted to wait until he was in the car. He rounded the corner of the huge building and looked ahead—evidently, no one had broken into his car, or if they had, they'd been kind enough to close the trunk after themselves. There was another car parked next to his, a white car he hadn't seen earlier.

Frank took out his phone and dialed Chief King's number—there was no time to waste. This had to be information no one else had, or they would have been looking more closely at Lassiter. And Agent Shale had to have known about the quick sale. If Lassiter had the sale already lined up—

Frank's call went to voicemail. The Chief was working the concert, and probably couldn't even hear his phone ringing over the music.

"Hi, Chief, it's Frank Harper," Frank said, getting out his keys out, as he approached the cars. "I just found out Lassit—"

A massive pain bloomed in the back of his head, sudden and burning hot.

He stumbled, the phone clattering to the asphalt. Frank's head swam, as if wracked by a sudden and massive hangover. His hands felt suddenly numb, but he reached up and felt the back of his head—it was wet. In the scant light of the parking lot, he saw his hand was covered with blood.

Frank tried to turn, to see his attacker, but only managed to fall to the ground. His mind registered the sensation of cold dampness, his face against the wet pavement.

The last thing he saw was a hand, reaching down to the ground. A gloved finger touched Frank's cell phone, ending the phone call. And then something else hit his head again and everything went black.

49

"Sure, boss."

George was on the phone again and she could tell that he was, yet again, displaying his complete lack of balls. To Chastity, it seemed like George always took the easy way out.

She sat at the kitchen table, listening to George on the phone. It was late Saturday night and the little Mexican girl was crying again upstairs. How much crying could one little brat have in her? Chastity stretched her arms and neck—she'd slept in the Corolla again last night, partly to be away from the constant crying, but also to be ready to leave, when, and if, George decided to nut up and bail.

"I understand," George said.

"I understand," she said, mocking his voice. "'Please and thank you,' 'whatever you want, I'm fine with,' 'Yes sir.'"

George shot her a look and covered up the mouthpiece of the phone. He nodded a couple of times, listening as Chastity rolled her eyes at the absurdity.

Her mom had been right: men were stupid. And easily manipulated—it only took the right kind of bra, or a great pair of legs, or a tight little skirt.

She smiled, remembering the hilarious look on those two cops' faces when she'd popped out of her top in front of O'Shaughnessy's. It's like they had never seen tits before. And while she appreciated the power she had over men, she could never understand why they reacted the way they did. It had gone just like she'd planned—she dropped her purse, fumbled with her boobs, and the cops picked up her stuff and giggled at each other like children.

Men were stupid.

George said goodbye and hung up.

"Well?" she asked.

"It's all over," George said, smiling. "The boss says he has our money and is coming over in the morning with it. He said he was planning on being here last night, but something came up."

"'Something came up'," she said, scoffing. "Isn't that just a peach. Two days ago, he said 'Saturday,' and now it's Saturday and surprise! We have to wait around, taking care of these stupid brats for another day!"

George shook his head. "They're not brats—they're just scared little girls. Weren't you ever a scared little—"

"No, I wasn't," Chastity said, her hands on her hips. "Momma taught me better than that. She taught me how to sew and to not put up with STUPID men. So I'm asking again. When are we leaving?"

George shook his head.

"Tomorrow. We leave tomorrow."

She nodded. "Good. After we get paid, we're gone."

He looked confused. "Yesterday, you said you didn't care about the money and just wanted to go. What do you think now?"

"That was before I knew the money was on its way," she said, biting her lip. "If it's only gonna be a few more hours, we wait. Or you wait, and I'll head into town."

George looked confused. "Why?"

She rolled her eyes and grabbed his shoulders, shaking him. "Seriously, how dumb are you?"

He looked at her, confused.

"OK," Chastity said, speaking slowly. She always felt like she was talking to a child. "Say he doesn't want to pay us at all—he shows up here and kills us. And the girls. No muss, no fuss. That's part of why I wanted to go. Momma said money's great, but not bleeding is better. So if he's paying us, no problem. He'll give you the money. But if he's coming to do us harm, he won't be able to do it, if we're not both here. Right?"

George thought about it for a moment, and it was all she could do to not burst out laughing. He could get her coke or crack or whatever else she wanted, and money, and was OK in the bedroom—but JESUS the guy was thick.

After a minute, he figured it out.

"Cause we wouldn't both be here," he said slowly. "It's dumb to kill one of us when the other can tell the cops, right?"

She nodded. It was all she could do to keep from rolling her eyes.

"Excellent!" he said, so happy with himself, but then his face turned serious. "What about the girls?"

"I don't know! And I don't care, and neither should you," she said, exasperated. She walked away, pacing for a second to calm down. "Look, this is almost over. With us out of town, he could just let them go. I don't know."

She hoped that George would just forget about the girls, but she knew he had a soft spot for them. If the boss came to kill the girls, George would make trouble. Chastity was sure of it. If that happened, she'd need a plan. And worrying about the brats wasn't her deal—she had enough to worry about.

50

"No sign of him?" Chief King asked, concerned.

It was Sunday morning, and the entire group of officers was dragging around the station after a busy night.

Deputy Peters shook his head, then closed the office door behind him and sat down in the empty chair across from King's desk.

"No one has seen him, and he hasn't been in yet," Peters said, glancing up at the clock in King's office, which read just after 7 a.m.

The HarvestFest event had gone well enough—only a few arrests for open containers as people tried to wander off with their plastic cups of beer. Peters had caught one man urinating in someone's front yard, and there had been another minor fight in front of Ricky's. And then, after the downtown party, King's men had been busy making sure everyone got home safe, or at least on to their next destination.

Chief King had gotten a call from Frank but hadn't noticed it for a little over a half-hour. The message was weird, cut off, and no one answered when King called back.

"What did they say at the hotel?" King asked.

"No one has seen him, and his bed wasn't slept in," Peters said. "The manager let me into his room. And his car is missing."

"Can we track him, somehow?" King knew that all of his patrol cars were tracked on GPS, and some of the troops carried phones that could be tracked as well.

"He's got an iPhone," Peters said, shrugging. "So we could try calling that in, but that would take a court order. And he mentioned one time that his Taurus was ex-government and has an inactive GPS in it, though I have no idea how you would activate that, or if you even could."

King nodded, thinking about it.

"Well, I wouldn't get too worried," King said. "Frank has shown time and time again that he can take care of himself," the Chief said. "Just to be safe, go ahead and check with dispatch, see if anyone's seen him. Put out a BOLO on his car. He probably just tied one on and is somewhere, sleeping it off."

51

Frank awoke to a cloudy sky.

He was groggy—his head was killing him. He tried to reach up and feel the back of his head, but his hand wouldn't move.

Black smoke moved across the sky in thick clouds. The sky above looked huge, edged by what looked like tall grass in each direction. Grasses and weeds, so it wasn't a cornfield. A cornfield would run in rows, topped with corn. This was scrub—he was in an empty field or some type of abandoned lot.

Frank realized he was cold and felt woozy, detached from the world. He remembered someone, or something, had hit him in the back of the head, back in the parking lot. Was it the next day? Where was he now?

Frank shook his head to clear it and tried to sit up.

He could not.

His hands were caught on something. Tugging, he realized they were tied together behind his back.

He looked down and saw his ankles were bound as well. Frank could see a thin plastic zip tie around the tops of his boots, two plastic strips tied together to interlock his legs. Those were black zip ties, like the ones cops used to restrain prisoners.

For the first time, he caught a whiff of something burning.

Frank couldn't sit up or stand, so he tried to roll over. After a struggle, he managed to get up onto one side. He couldn't see anything except tall grasses and weeds in every direction. He felt around with his hand and found they were zip tied as well—those plastic cuffs were impossible to break. That was why many police departments around the country used them instead of handcuffs—no amount of picking at the lock or twisting and fraying would get him free.

Frank wasn't sure what to do next.

Smoke, dark and thick, blew over his head. He coughed and realized he wasn't in a clearing—he'd simply been dumped in a field of tall grass. The weight of his body was making a temporary depression by holding down the grasses beneath him.

Smoke, and the smell of the fire, gave it away. And the distant sound of unconcerned voices. He was in a field that was on fire. Frank's mind clicked—it was probably Sunday morning.

Frank had been bound and left in Freeman's Prairie, where they were doing the prescribed yearly burn.

He'd been bound and left for dead.

"Hey!" he yelled, but no one answered. The voices sounded distant. The only people around, besides Frank, were probably the local firefighters setting the fire and monitoring the burn. The people who had jumped him were surely gone by now.

"Hey, can anyone hear me?" he shouted, but his voice didn't carry. He was too low to the ground and surrounded by tall grasses. It didn't stop him, though. Frank continued yelling for a few long minutes, but no one came. The smoke got thicker, white and blowing through the tall grass. For the first time, he felt distant heat. And the sound of the fire was getting louder. It sounded like a huge, approaching campfire. The smell was similar, heavy and metallic.

Frank turned his face in the dirt, blowing the grass away from his mouth and shouting again. It sounded loud—his face was an inch from the ground—but not loud enough for anyone to hear over the crackling fire.

Frank pulled his legs up as high as he could and wiggled to get his hands down to his boots. Straining, he held his hands flat and slid them under the soles of his boots. Working them around the soles of his boots, he finally pulled his hand under and around to the front, letting out a sigh of relief. The new position was much more comfortable, and now he could move.

Frank felt a gust of heat as another large pall of black smoke rolled over the field.

Rolling onto his back, he sat up and tried to get his bearings, but couldn't see over the grasses. Frank turned to climb up onto his knees and saw, through the grasses, white square shapes about ten feet away from him, behind a thick stand of grass.

At first, he didn't recognize them. He hopped toward them and saw more. The smoke parted for a moment, and he suddenly knew what he was looking at—papers, scattered in the field.

He hopped closer. His feet were still bound together. He fell once, and again, but followed the papers, until they led to three cardboard boxes on the ground, papers and file folders spilling out of them. One of the file folders was splashed with red.

The boxes from his trunk.

He saw three boxes, two with files and papers and a third box, empty. That had been the money from the second ransom, now gone. Papers blew around the open boxes, files with his notes written in the margins, driven by the rising heat and the smoke and wind of the burn. He could see "Police Files—Confidential" scrawled on the side of one box in Deputy Peters' handwriting. Whoever had hit him over the head had not only taken him but also the money and case files. They had kept the money, presumably—the box was empty—and dropped him and the files here in the middle of the field to burn.

Frank flopped down and started wiggling toward the boxes, pressing down the sharp grasses with his arm and leg and face. He crawled closer to the boxes and finally reached the first one—it was the money box. He pushed it out of the way. It fell over, and one corner hit him in the face. Cursing loudly, he moved his shoulder and head, butting the box out of the way, and continued struggling toward the other boxes. Smoke stinged his eyes. Frank scrabbled over spilt manila folders and papers, and some part of his mind noticed the labels on the folders—all files about people involved in the case, written in Deputy Peters' handwriting. Filled with Frank's notes.

Peters. Frank remembered his talking about zip ties, and how much he approved of them. Could it have been Peters who jumped him? The man was always around, keeping an eye on Frank. But yesterday, Frank had eliminated him as a suspect. If someone wanted Frank out of the way, you could do worse than volunteer to be a helper on the case, all the while looking for an opportunity.

Or maybe it was Chief King. Maybe he'd assigned Peters to keep tabs on Frank, to monitor whatever Frank discovered in the investigation process.

Frank slowly crawled to the next box. It was on its side, spilling out papers and folders. Black smoke blew through the tall grass. Frank grabbed the top of the box and flipped it over, but only more papers came out. He pushed it away and started pushing with his legs, crawling to the last box.

Black smoke and heat rolled over him. The smoke made it hard to breathe. It smelled angry, unrepentant. The gusting wind carried burnt pieces of plant material and burning embers across his vision, and he looked to see some of the flying ember land on dry stalks nearby and begin to smolder.

A draft of heat picked some of the papers up into the air. Frank felt the temperature rise in his small clearing and knew that the fire was quickly approaching. If Frank didn't get out of here soon, he would be roasted alive. Mud caked his shoes and pants and shoulders and hair, and he wondered if the cool mud and dirt would protect him from the fire, when it overtook him, for an extra moment or two.

He found the last box and pulled it to him. It was still closed up. Frank slapped at it and the top of the box popped open. Out spilled more folders, stacks of papers, pens.

And the scissors.

He grabbed at them, turning them in his hands and sawing against the plastic tie that bound his wrists. After a moment, the metal edge sliced through the plastic, and his hands were free.

Frank sat up and started cutting at the plastic binding around his boots. Whoever had tied him up had used several ties, chained together, to reach around his feet. After a moment, he cut the ties and felt the tension on his feet suddenly let go.

Frank stood up, looking around.

He was in Freeman's Prairie. It looked like the whole field was ablaze. Black smoke and flames surrounded him on all sides. He could see the road to his south, with several fire trucks parked along the edge of the field, and the town beyond, blocked by clouds of black smoke. Much of the fire was between him and the road. The field was burning in this direction, and he saw several firefighters in heavy gear, guiding the fire. They had those fire-starting lamps that dripped burning gasoline.

He waved his arms, shouting, but they were too far away through the black smoke to see him. Even if they could see him, there was nothing they could to do help. They couldn't get to him or stop the fire—it was too late for that.

Frank turned around, frantic, looking for a way out. Behind him, Frank saw he was close to the river. The taller trees that lined the bank were much closer than the road. He turned to run and then stopped.

Zip ties.

Frank dropped back down on the ground, searching the grasses and papers, finally found the ones that had been around his feet and wrists. He grabbed two of the file folders as well—they were smeared with mud—and the scissors, and began making his way to the riverbank.

52

"What?" The fire chief turned, looking.

"Look," one of the firemen called out. "There's someone in the fire."

The fire chief was wearing full gear, even though they were out in the middle of a field. It felt odd to be fully dressed out so far away from any structures, but the field needed to be managed.

"Over there, by the river," the man said again.

The fire chief followed where his man was pointing. The helmet made it hard to see anything farther away than about twenty feet, so he pulled off the mask and scanned the riverbank on the other side of the fire.

There was a dark figure slumped against one of the trees.

"Well, I'll be damned," the fire chief said. "That's too far to go through. Call it in. Send the EMT to circle around where the field isn't burned yet and get them out. I'll call the others to slow the burn," he said. "And get the police out here. Now."

53

"You okay?" Chief King said.

He was looking at Frank Harper, covered with mud and caked with black soot. The man was alive, barely, sitting in the back of an ambulance. It had come over from dispatch that a man had been staggering by the river near the prescribed burn in Freeman Prairie. King had already been on his way over when they had come over the radio with a positive ID on the person.

Harper pulled off the oxygen mask.

"Nope, I'm pretty goddamned far from alright. Someone jumped me, hit me over the head, and left me in that field to burn."

He was pissed and had every right to be. He was huffing on the oxygen provided by the EMT. Frank's clothes were torn and he was bleeding from a dozen shallow cuts on his hands and face. The EMT team was working on his face, cleaning off the soot and applying something to the cuts.

"Did you miss me?" Frank asked.

King nodded. "Thought you took the half million and ran."

"What, and miss out on the $50,000 reward?" Frank asked.

"You suck at math," King said.

Frank leaned forward to talk to King privately.

"By the way," Frank said quietly. "I think it was Lassiter. And Agent Shale."

King looked around at the others and climbed up in the ambulance, shooing the EMT and firemen away.

"What?"

"I was checking on the Holly Toys property last night. The guard walked me through, and he said that the place had already been sold to another investment group. Lassiter sold it already. I was calling you when I got jumped."

"I got that part of the message," King said.

Frank nodded. "To have a buyer lined up that fast, he would have had to know it was coming to him. I'd bet a case of Maker's Mark that he's behind the kidnapping—took the girls, squirreled them away, then waited on Martin to liquidate."

Chief King nodded, thinking about it. If Lassiter was behind this, he was playing the long game, setting everything in motion and then waiting for Nick Martin to come to him, hat in hand, and sell the property. "That doesn't make a lot of sense."

"No, not unless he needed money," Frank said. "It's actually pretty smart—he gives Nick money for the other half, so Lassiter owns the property outright. Then he sells it—if Lassiter already had a buyer lined up, he was free and clear. And he'd get some of his original payment back from the ransom, depending on how many other people are involved." Frank said, and then he went back to sucking on the oxygen mask.

"You think Lassiter knocked you out?"

Harper shrugged. "Not sure. But Shale, how could he have missed the property sale? Seems like a big thing to miss. Somebody hit me, but I don't think it was Lassiter or Shale. Though, how they got the jump on me, I'll never know."

King thought about it. "I'll call it in."

Frank shook his head.

"No. It doesn't explain everything. Unless Nick Martin was passing along pertinent information to Lassiter every step of the way, you've still got a leak. Maybe it's Shale, or maybe not. Here, look at these," Frank said, and began fishing in his pocket. He pulled out a handful of zip ties and put them in King's hand. "I was zip tied," Harper said. "Black zip ties, like those used by everyone on your police force."

"And anyone who's ever shopped at Menards," King answered.

"Maybe. But the boxes of case files, and the empty box that held the ransom money, they were all in my trunk. They all ended there in the field with me, and now they're gone. If I hadn't woken up…"

King nodded.

"Glad you did. OK, let me do some work on Lassiter, and then I'll bring him in, personally. You get cleaned up and come in."

Frank looked at him.

"Should I stay gone? Whoever did this thinks I'm dead—maybe that could be helpful."

"Nah," King said. "It's already been on the police band. Anyone listening would know."

Frank nodded.

"Gotcha. Will you have someone swing by Holly Toys and check to see if my car is still there?"

54

Frank had refused the paramedics' offer to go to the hospital—it was just smoke inhalation and cuts and bruises. His wrists hurt the worst—too much rolling around and crawling on the wet ground, struggling with the restraints. He looked bad and needed a shower, but he had something he needed to do first. The EMTs had been kind enough to drop him at Laura's apartment. He'd knocked for a minute before someone answered the door. It was early Sunday morning.

"Grandpa?"

Frank smiled when he saw Jackson, who let him in, and was hugging the small boy when Laura came in. Her eyes grew wide as she took in his burnt clothes and general appearance.

"What happened?"

Frank hugged Jackson again. "You still got those dinosaurs I got you?"

"I sure do," Jackson said. "They're cool."

"Can you go get them for me?"

Jackson squeaked and ran off into the apartment.

Frank turned to Laura.

"Someone tried to kill me," he said matter-of-factly.

Her face fell. "What?"

"I'm going to be straight with you—that's what you wanted, right?"

She nodded, wary.

"Okay," Frank said. "I was working on the kidnapping case, and figured out who did it, or at least I think he's involved. Anyway, last night I was following up on a lead and got jumped, knocked over the head—"

"Oh my God," she said, shaking her head. "Are you OK?"

Frank looked at his daughter.

"It gets worse," Frank said. "They tied me up and left me in a field, east of town, that was being burned. They were doing a scheduled burn, and whoever put me there knew it was going to happen. They wanted me dead." As he talked, her eyes got bigger. "I woke up and got free."

She hugged him, spontaneously, and then backed away. Dust and soot from his clothes wafted between them, and the room suddenly smelled like smoke.

"But the prairie burn didn't start until this morning," she said. "It was in the paper. Where were you all night?"

"No clue," he said. "Knocked out, sedated, probably. My car and phone are gone, but my wallet was in my pocket." King had called the EMT team to let Frank know his car was no longer parked at the Holly Toys warehouse.

Jackson came back into the room and held up the dinosaurs for Frank to see, then plopped down on the floor at their feet and started playing.

She shook her head and lowered her voice. "Something horrible could have happened to you."

He didn't say anything. There was nothing to say.

"I'm glad you're OK," she said. "I'm just so glad that nothing—"

Frank nodded. "But it's not over—they thought I was dead. Chief King is making an arrest soon, but until the girls are found, I need you on your toes.

She made a face that said he didn't understand.

"Me?"

"Yes," Frank said quietly, glancing at Jackson playing on the floor. "I think a policeman might be involved. The person behind the kidnapping knew everything we were doing. Knew where I was. So don't talk to anyone and don't get in any cars with strangers. Even cops."

Her eyes went wide.

"Seriously?"

"Yes," he said. "If it's a cop, they might try to get to me through you or Jackson. My hands were zip tied," Frank said, holding up his wrists. "Civilians don't do that. And I was dumped in the field, and I don't know how I got out there, unless it was from a vehicle."

She bit her lip, thinking.

"Any idea who's involved?"

"Nothing yet," he said. "It might be the guy that's getting arrested now, but I don't think so. Too many things are off about this case."

He watched Jackson play for a moment, then continued.

"Look, I don't want you to worry about me. I'm helping out with the case because that's what I do," Frank said. "And I'm good at it. Your mother always thought I had some kind of death wish, but that's not it. I'm just good at this, good at catching bad guys. But they don't play nice."

Laura nodded.

"You are good at it," she said. "Mom always said you were, but it was just too hard for her. She told me once that she hated the sound of a phone ringing. She always assumed it was someone calling with news about you. Bad news."

He nodded grimly.

"I can see why that's hard for people to deal with," he said. "And I could have been a lot nicer to your mom. She deserved better."

Frank turned to go, but she hugged him again, holding him for a long moment, despite the fact that he smelled like a campfire.

"Take care," she said. "And good luck."

He stepped out onto the front porch of her apartment. Without a car or a phone, he planned to walk the six or eight blocks to the police station, then catch a ride to his hotel to get cleaned up. He needed a shower and a change of clothes. He could have asked Laura for a ride, but he wanted to keep her out of it as much as possible.

There was a cop car idling down the street.

Frank saw it immediately, but he couldn't make out the driver. Frank walked to the curb, and the patrol car started up and drove slowly toward the apartment building.

Frank reached for his weapon, but it was gone. No car, no gun, no phone. He was cut off from his world.

The car slowed as it approached. It was Deputy Peters.

"You need a ride?" he shouted across the scrubby lawn.

Frank nodded, letting out his breath. He wasn't sure who to trust anymore, but he needed a ride.

"Yup, that would be great," Frank said.

Deputy Peters nodded and waited by the car for Frank to climb in. Peters took one last look at the apartment building and then drove away.

"The Chief said you were visiting your daughter and thought you would need a ride," Peters said. "I hung back—not sure how much you're telling her. Back to the station?"

"Hotel, if you don't mind," Frank said. "I need to get cleaned up."

Peters nodded and turned the car toward Main Street. "They arrested Matt Lassiter," Peters said as they drove.

"Really?" Frank said. "I wonder why."

Peters looked over at Frank.

"You're pretending you don't know about it? Jeff said it was your idea."

Frank gave up the charade. "Look, I know Lassiter sold the building, after having it in his possession for less than twenty-four hours. That takes planning, and that means he probably had someone lined up to buy it before Nick sold it to him. That at least deserves a discussion, right?"

Peters nodded. "Oh, you'll get no argument from me. Chief brought him in, and he and Graves and the FBI guy are talking to him right now."

"Shale? That's interesting," Frank said, looking out the window. "So, why were you waiting to pick me up – did you volunteer?"

Peters looked at him again. "Why else would I be waiting?"

Frank shook his head.

"I was zip tied."

"You're joking," Peters said, looking at Frank.

"Nope," Frank said, and looked over at Peters. "It's a cop, one of King's men. The car next to my Taurus in the parking lot last night— white with stripes. I didn't figure it out in time, but it was a police car. And now I don't know who to trust."

Peters drove on in silence for a while—the car travelled up Main and stopped for a passing train.

"Well, I don't know how to get people to trust me," Peters said, his eyes on the train. "I never have been good at that. Even when I was at the academy in Columbus, trying to get good enough for Jeff to take me seriously, I didn't make friends. Only thing I know how to do is what I'm doing, taking Jeff's lead and trying to learn from him. And you. But I'm still thinking about those girls—they're somewhere, scared."

"In a dark and cold underground location?" Frank asked.

"I seriously doubt it," Peters said, looking at Frank. "That's why we need you on this case, people like you and my cousin. Or else it will never get solved. If that means you and I have to part ways, it would be worth it. To solve the case."

Peters turned to watch the train.

Frank kept looking at him, his new "partner," or as close as he'd had in years. Ben Stone had been a good man, but he'd had trust issues. He'd gotten that lead down in Coral Gables, and even as close as he and Ben had been, the man simply hadn't let Frank in. But he'd also tried to be a friend to Frank, inviting him over for saltimbocca.

In the end, though, it hadn't mattered. When he'd really needed to trust Frank, he hadn't, and he'd died in a pool of his own blood in a dirty alley near the only famous building in Coral Gables, the National Hurricane Center.

Ever since Katrina and St. Bartholomew's, Frank had found himself thinking about Ben a lot.

The train continued past the line of cars, all stopped behind the lowered gate, waiting patiently.

Frank was torn. If Peters had knocked him out, he was a cool customer. Cooler than anyone Frank had ever met. Peters was a good kid, as far as Frank could tell, and he wasn't fooled often. But then, to play both sides of the situation, kidnapper and cop, would require a very level head.

The end of the train appeared. Peters sat up and put the car in gear. "So, what did you decide?"

Frank looked at him.

"Do you trust me, or not?" Peters asked. "I'd like to know, 'cause if you don't, I'm dropping you right here, and you can hoof it."

Frank smiled. "Just drive."

55

Peters and Frank drove to the hotel, and Peters waited in the lobby while Frank went up and showered and changed. Peters had been bummed to learn about all the files burning up in the field, but he'd been glad to learn that the scissors had saved Frank's life.

"I guess we won't have to go through those files again," Peters had said in the car on the way over, and Frank had showed him the two files he'd saved, one of them red in color.

"You had to save that one?" Peters said, smiling. "I still feel dumb, dropping those like that."

As soon as he got to his room, Frank went straight to the shower and turned it on, then drank down all that was left of the bourbon. He felt like he was right on the edge. But maybe, if people were actively trying to kill him, this wasn't the best time to be trying to go cold turkey.

Calmed, Frank showered and changed quickly. In minutes, he felt like a new man—clean clothes, clear head, warm belly. Back down in the lobby, Frank smiled at Peters, who had been waiting in the reception area, chatting with the woman behind the front counter. They walked out to the patrol car.

"Better?" Peters asked.

Frank nodded. "I could use some food, but I'm not sure if it will stay down. Can we run through McDonald's and get some coffee?"

Just as they were pulling out of the drive-thru, dispatch came over the radio, ordering Deputy Peters and Frank back the station ASAP. He toggled the radio and reported he was one minute out. The dispatcher replied that they'd been trying to get in touch with him for at least 20 minutes. All patrolmen were requested to report to the station.

They arrived at the station and navigated the mob of reporters to get inside. The questions, and the questioners, were getting more aggressive as the case dragged on. Clearly the reporters were monitoring the police band and had learned about what had happened to Frank. They surrounded him, shouted questions at him about the fire and waking up in the field, wanting to know how he managed to escape. Several of them called him out by name. He couldn't think of anything clever to say, so he'd only confirmed the basic details and ignored their attempts to draw more information out of him. Another reporter grabbed at Deputy

Peters' arm and asked him about the psychic, but he mumbled a "no comment" and went through the doors.

All in all, Frank was feeling good. He'd survived an attempt on his life, and they had arrested Lassiter. A few questions answered by him could blow the case open, assuming he was involved and decided to be truthful.

Inside, Lola was sitting behind the reception window, crying hard. Her entire body was shaking, and her makeup was smeared, running in black lines down her cheeks. When she saw Frank and Deputy Peters, she buzzed them in and began crying even harder.

Confused, Frank and Peters walked into the main room.

Frank was surprised to see Chief King sitting at the big conference table, his head in his hands.

He looked shaken to the core.

Frank turned and saw several cops standing and talking by the holding cells and interview rooms. They looked upset, angry. Two EMTs emerged from one of the holding cells pushing a stretcher—on it was a body covered with a sheet.

"What happened?" Frank asked.

Chief King looked up.

"Lassiter hung himself."

Frank stopped, stunned.

"You're kidding me," he said.

"I wish," King said, shaking his head. "We were just starting to question him, me and Ted Shale and Sergeant Graves. Brought him in, just for questioning, and we started talking, telling him about what had happened to you. Agent Shale told him what we had learned about the sale—you were right. Shale got on the phone and tracked the deed, and the property changed hands yesterday. Sold to some property management company out in California."

Frank nodded.

The Chief seemed to stop for a moment, then reclaimed his thread. "Agent Shale and Graves went at him pretty hard, asking how he could have sold the property so quickly. Lassiter fumbled for answers and then suddenly lawyered up, so we gave him the room."

Frank and Peters leaned in, listening. Frank's stomach started to ache. He suddenly wanted another drink so badly he could feel his mouth starting to water.

King slapped the table once, hard. The sound was like a gunshot in the quiet room.

"I went to call his attorney," the Chief said, seething. "They'd never printed or processed him or anything. We'd brought him in through the government entrance, so the reporters wouldn't see him. We came back a minute later, and…he'd used his belt."

Frank sat down heavily.

"Jesus," Frank said. "Cameras?"

King shook his head. "Turned off."

Peters looked at Frank. "That means…"

"Stop right there," King said, glancing up the corridor. Frank turned to see the EMTs pushing the stretcher up the glass hallway that connected the police station with the government building.

Sergeant Graves walked up to the table. He looked devastated.

"Chief, I had them take Lassiter out the back way," Sergeant Graves said, his hat in his hand. "We don't need the reporters…" he started to say, but then just trailed off.

Frank sat back and looked up Graves.

"He was our only lead."

Deputy Peters shook his head. "Why? Why would he do that? Why would he hang himself?"

"I don't know," King said. "But without him, the girls are gone."

Frank glanced around the room.

"Assuming he was the mastermind," Frank said quietly to King and Graves and Peters. "He would have known where the girls are. But he must've had people working for him. Maybe…maybe a cop was involved. If Shale intentionally buried that financial report, he might have killed Lassiter. Was he alone when he hung himself—"

"That again?" King barked, looking at Frank. Graves and Peters both looked on but held their tongues. "Anyone can buy zip ties. And you said it yourself—maybe Nick Martin was keeping Lassiter in the loop on what we were doing. It would explain everything."

Frank sat back, thinking.

"I think it's someone here in—"

King leaned in, angry.

"I said drop it," he hissed. "I need all these people working the case. I know where you're coming from, but there's no proof. Shale is an idiot—don't you think I'd know? And, besides, he came on after the case began, just like you, Frank."

King looked around at the three of them: Frank, Deputy Peters, and Sergeant Graves. "No. You guys? You're my team. Graves, Peters, get out in front of this mess. Graves, coordinate with the county on the body. We need a full autopsy immediately. Frank, you can't go running around talking about it. I need more information—go get me some. Talk to Agent Shale, get that financial information, try to figure out how long ago the property sale was arranged."

Frank and the others looked at King for a long moment, and then the small group broke up. Chief King remained at the conference table, thinking.

Frank walked over to the map of connected circles he'd drawn a few days prior, the mind map hanging on the white board next to the conference room table. Shale was all over it, but even him being dirty couldn't account for everything.

After a moment, Frank walked over to one of the empty cubicles and picked up a phone, dialing out. He would have to assume it was not a private conversation, but it couldn't be helped. His personal phone was missing, probably burned up in the field along with his files.

She answered right away.

"Hello?"

"Laura, it's Frank."

"You okay?"

"No, not really," he said quietly. "Things are even more complicated than they were an hour ago. The suspect we brought in, the one I was telling you about—he took his own life."

He heard the gasp on the other end.

"Wasn't he the only lead?"

Frank nodded, then spoke. "That's right. We're all—we're not sure where to go from here. But listen, do me a favor—you need to be really careful over the next few days."

"What do you mean?"

Frank glanced around at the others in the room—most of them looked as stunned as Frank was by the sudden turn of events. But he wasn't sure whom he could trust. There was no way to tell who was listening.

"He died here, in the station," Frank said quietly. "In custody."

She didn't say anything, but he knew she was smart enough to figure it out.

"So," she finally said, "what do I do?"

"Just don't get in a car with any cops," Frank said, cupping his hand over the mouthpiece. "If I send one for you, to move you to another location or just for protection, I'll give him a code word. And if they don't know the word, play along and contact me or Chief King, first chance you get. You can get me through the police switchboard."

He heard her laugh nervously on the other end. "Frank, you're scaring me."

"I know," he said. "I mean—you have to take me seriously on this."

"OK, OK," she said quietly. He could hear the panic starting up in her voice—she sounded like Trudy used to. "What's the code word?"

"'I'm not really free to talk," he said without hesitation. "Just think about that place we were talking about recently, the one we visited when you were young. It's abandoned now. Do you remember?"

"Yes," she said. His daughter had the good sense not to blurt it out.

"Good," he said. "But nothing will happen, probably. It's better to be safe, OK?"

"OK."

"And pack a bag and put it in your car, just in case. Not by the door—someone could see it. Put it in the car. If I call you with the code word, drop everything and get Jackson and yourself out of town. Don't tell me, or anyone, where you go. Stay gone for at least a week. Find me when you get back, or watch the news. You'll know, one way or the other, when it's safe to come back."

"Oh, Frank," she answered quietly, her voice level. "I don't like this." He could tell he was overwhelming her with too much information, but he needed her to be safe.

She and Jackson had to be safe.

"Take care," he said. "And I'll call you when I know more." It came out sounding much more ominous than he intended.

"Okay," she said simply, and hung up.

Frank sat back, staring at the phone in his hand. Her mother had been the same—she'd wanted to know what was going on but, at the same time, she didn't. Too much information made her worry, and that kind of endless worry was bad for any relationship.

Frank walked back over to King and Peters, who were discussing the case. Sergeant Graves had already left.

"But he had to have help," Peters was saying. "There is no way he could do this on his own, no matter how much inside information he was getting from Nick Martin."

"If any," King said.

"Lassiter's apartment was clean—Stan Garber and Sergeant Burwell are there now," Peters said as Frank walked up. "Nothing out of the ordinary, and no indication of who he was working with. They're looking for bank records, deposits, that sort of thing. But the girls have to be somewhere."

Frank nodded.

"You're right," King said, glancing at the holding rooms again. "Look, I gotta go. Lola is already getting calls from the Attorney General. I've never had someone die in my custody before. I need to call the county, and make a statement to the press."

He looked at Peters and Frank.

"See if you guys can do anything to break the case open or find the girls. Dig through Lassiter's stuff, make calls, whatever. It's the only way I see this turning out for the better."

Chief King paused, acting like there was something else he wanted to say, then simply nodded and walked away.

"What do we do now?" Deputy Peters asked, looking at Frank.

Frank, watching Chief King walk back over to the knot of police milling around the holding cell, reviewed the timeline again in his head.

Lassiter is brought in and held for questioning in the most guarded building in town.

Lassiter had been surrounded by cops and was dead in less than an hour.

Lassiter killed himself with a belt, something that should have been taken away as soon as he was put in that room alone.

If he was alone.

The EMTs and stretcher were gone. The body was going to the county for autopsy, but Frank doubted they would learn anything new from the careful study of the corpse.

No, something was going on here. The only solace Frank could take was that Peters had been with him when Lassiter died, so Peters wasn't in on it. Unless, he was working with other cops.

It suddenly dawned on Frank that the whole group could be in on it: Agent Shale, Sergeant Graves, Barnes, Chief King, even Deputy Peters. Maybe they were just keeping Frank around for show, to make it look like they were really working the case. Or maybe they were going to pin it on him. Was that why they'd entrusted him with the money?

He looked around slowly at the others in the room and felt a panic rise, the hairs standing up on the back of his neck. The policemen were all on their phones, still working the case. Several of them looked upset, but they all had black zip ties on their person. It could be any one of them—or all of them.

Frank shook his head. That was paranoia talking. They couldn't all be in on it, could they? What was this, some episode of the Twilight Zone? Would he wake up and be back in that chair at Willie's Barber shop, having nodded off during his haircut?

"So," Peters asked again. "What do we do?"

He looked back up at Peters. The young cop's question hung in the air between them. Frank didn't have any answers for him.

56

Nick Martin slumped back into his seat on the couch, beaten. The fight drained out of him—to Chief King, it looked like Nick aged ten years in the span of ten seconds.

"So, that's it."

Chief King nodded at Nick Martin. They were back in the living room of the Martin house, where they'd sat together days before and listened to the ransom call.

"We're pretty sure he had help," Chief King said quietly. Glenda was upstairs. She'd gotten hysterical when King had told them about Lassiter killing himself and had gone to lie down.

"He had to know where Charlie and Maya were," King continued. "But he also had to have people helping him out, or he might have been listening to you talk about the case and figured out what we were doing. We're still chasing down the leads, but it explains some things."

Martin was shaken—King could tell the rug had been pulled out from under him.

"I just can't believe it was Matt," Nick said. "We were friends…" He was looking up at the mantle, and Chief King followed his eyes. Nick was looking at a framed photo of him and Matt Lassiter on a golf course. In the photo, they had their arms around each other's shoulders. Chums.

"It surprised us all," King said.

"He's…he was my best friend," Nick said, staring at the photo. "We worked together on projects, scouting out properties and having long discussions about the future of our parcels and buildings. We went on trips together. He's been over here for Thanksgiving, for Christ's sake. I can't believe…if he wanted the property that bad, why didn't he just ask? Why go through all this. And Charlie—"

King nodded. "Obviously, we were hoping he would tell us where the girls were."

Nick Martin looked up at the Chief.

"You think they're dead," Nick asked.

The question hung in the air for a moment. King wasn't exactly sure how to answer it. Keeping up hope, at this point, just seemed cruel.

"It's likely…it's likely that they're dead," King said. "I'm sorry, Nick. Once Lassiter got the money, there was no reason to keep them alive. We've discovered he'd racked up some pretty bad debts. As far as we can tell, he was under a lot of pressure to make good on them. He apparently had a buyer lined up for the Holly property even before this started. He couldn't convince you to sell it to him outright—"

"I didn't know!"

"I know, I know," King said. "But he was desperate. And desperate people..."

"What about the second ransom?"

King shook his head.

"It's gone. I had a person guarding it, but he was attacked and left for dead. The money was taken."

Nick shook his head, glancing up the stairs. "That's everything we had. What do I tell Glenda?"

"Tell her we're still looking for Charlie," King said. "And we won't stop until we know something for sure. And we're still looking into Lassiter—we're going through everything from his apartment, and we're still running down leads."

Nick shook his head and looked at the Chief.

"You don't sound optimistic," Nick said wearily.

"I...I just wouldn't get my hopes up," King said. "If Lassiter did have partners, they're fleeing the state by now. In my experience, they're tying up the loose ends."

He realized, as the words came out of his mouth, how insensitive they sounded.

57

They had been fighting all day, off and on.

Charlie could hear it—it was a big old house, as far as she could tell, but at least the shouting voices let her know where the man and woman were in the house.

She'd slipped out of the zip tie an hour ago, after the young man had brought them a late lunch. Charlie was getting pretty good at predicting when the kidnappers would come into her room—three times a day for the three meals and once in the morning and again at night for bathroom breaks. Charlie was sure she'd have a while before they came back with dinner—at least that was how it normally worked.

She had found another thing of lip balm in one of the drawers, and now both were in her pockets, along with the pen. She was wearing the same clothes for over a week, and at no point had the kidnappers offered her other clothes or given her a chance to take a bath or shower.

But now she was out on the roof, walking around outside.

Charlie had climbed out onto the roof from the bathroom window. She had never been scared of heights—maybe she had spent too much time with her father on construction sites. She scampered along the slanted roof like a cat, eyeing the ground three stories down. Charlie circled the entire roof, looking for a way down or a way into Maya's room, but there was none. A large barn stood next to the house, but it was too far away to jump.

Her only option was the tree, with the branches that scraped her window. The tree looked like it would hold her, but she'd have to jump, and there was no getting back over to the roof, once she jumped.

Not knowing what else to do, she sat on the roof, watching the sun. It was a few minutes of freedom, maybe the last she would ever get. It seemed cruel, to be free, yet she couldn't get away. It was almost worse than being tied up.

Charlie stared at the sun, letting it warm her face for a long time, thinking about her parents and how much she missed them. She wondered if she would ever see them.

After a while, she sighed and stood back up. Charlie walked the roof line again, circling all the way around, double checking for any way down, but found none. Hers was the only window out onto the roof.

She made it back to the bathroom window, and climbed back inside the house, making her way back to the bed that had been her prison for what seemed like forever.

58

You knew you were making progress when they tried to kill you.

That's what someone had told Frank once in response to an attempt on a cop's life. But someone had tried to kill Frank. Zip tied him, taken him and the files out into the field. How had they gotten him into the middle of that field? He didn't recall seeing any tire tracks. And Frank was a big guy, not easy to carry.

The zip ties had been a big clue, no matter what Chief King thought.

Frank stood at the white board, adding things to the mind map he had made of all of the people connected to the case. He had struck out "Matt Lassiter" with a big red "X," but the case was, obviously, far from solved.

Frank had been a threat, but the way he'd been tied up, it indicated professional training. Any normal person would probably have trussed his arms in the front. It was much easier to tie someone up when they were on their back. Most people, if asked to tie a prone person, would lay them on their backs, tie their feet together, then tie their hands together in front. Very few people outside of law enforcement would think to lay a person on their stomach and truss up a person like a pig on his way to a luau. But that was standard for cops, who tied up suspects that way to make them easier for two men to carry.

Of course, leaving someone to burn up in a field was something few people would think of. Maybe they'd expected Frank to wake up from smelling the fire or breathing in the smoke. Tying his hands behind his back was enough of a delay to kill him.

It would've worked, too, if they hadn't wanted the files and boxes to burn, too.

Frank sat back down and went through Lassiter's file again. Frank's copy was gone in the fire, along with his notes, so he flipped though the original. He spread the pages out before him on the conference room table, fanning them out and studying them, looking for patterns in his finances or the types of projects he liked to invest in. Travel itineraries, family connections, website searches—Agent Shale had been very thorough in the last two hours, perhaps trying to make up for missing something so obvious. Frank tried to ignore the hubbub around him—King and Graves and the others were preparing for a press conference—so he could concentrate on the case file.

A bunch of stuff had been taken out of Lassiter's downtown apartment. Detective Barnes had been going through it when Lassiter killed himself. Nothing suspicious was found yet and nothing tying Matt back to the girls or to any conspirators.

Lassiter had been in bad with some sharks in Las Vegas. Funny how it always came down to money. The property was technically still in escrow, and the sale halted as a result of the police investigation. But it looked like Lassiter was a dead end. Literally. They had his motive and the money trail and nothing else.

Money.

Frank sat back and thought about the money that had been in the trunk of his car. King had given Frank the box of money for safekeeping. Frank had told the others—King, Peters, and Sergeant Graves—that he'd be keeping it in the safe in the hotel room. That's why he'd been suspicious when Peters showed up to help Friday night.

But who knew it was in the car?

Frank was being watched.

Someone was keeping tabs on him and saw him carry the boxes out to his car. He had made two trips, he remembered—one with the money and one for the two boxes of files. Someone knew he had the money and was probably waiting for him to leave it in the hotel room unguarded—the safes in hotel rooms were notoriously easy to crack. They were cheap, mass-produced, and invariably could be accessed by a master key. Too often, hotel guests would lock something important inside and then need the front desk to retrieve it.

So someone had been watching Frank. Probably following him and jumped him at the Holly Toys warehouse.

Frank couldn't imagine it was Lassiter—the guy was shorter than Frank and a lot lighter. Plus, Lassiter had already gotten his money and settled his debts, sending the deed and some of the first ransom to Vegas via FedEx.

If Lassiter had jumped Frank and taken the second ransom, the cops would've found the $500,000 in the apartment when they searched it. Or they would have found some clue as to where it had gone.

No, someone else was involved.

"Mr. Harper?"

Frank looked up. It was Peters.

"Yes?"

"Can we take a walk?" Peters asked, looking around.

Ah, decision time. Frank knew that Peters hadn't engineered Lassiter's death. Frank had to start trusting someone, and Peters made the most sense. Frank played his hunch.

"Sure, where to?"

Peters led him out the back doors, through the connecting walkway and over to the government side of the building. He turned into a large conference room—the same room where Frank had conducted interviews with some members of the government staff days earlier. The City Council used this room, just off the council chambers, to hold smaller meetings and study sessions. In the center of the room sat a large table with stacks of paper, a box of pens, and two phones for making conference calls.

Peters motioned to the table and closed the door behind them.

"What's with the secrecy?" Frank asked, sitting.

Peters smiled. "Not sure who to trust. But I was thinking about your car."

Frank smiled. "Don't worry. I don't miss it. I hated that thing."

Peters nodded. "Though it would be nice to know who took it, or at least where it is."

"Didn't you guys put out a BOLO on it?" Frank asked, assuming they had told area police to "be on the lookout" for his vehicle.

"Of course, after you went missing Sunday morning," Peters said. "No one has called in, but the BOLO went statewide. But it wasn't at Lassiter's address, or anywhere in Cooper's Mill, as far as we can tell. Everyone on patrol this morning was looking out for it," Peters said. "But your car has to be somewhere. Who took it?"

"The same person who kicked my ass," Frank said angrily.

"What about that tracker you were talking about?" Peters asked.

Frank looked at Peters, and it suddenly dawned on him how stupid he'd been.

"Nice." Frank smiled—he'd forgotten all about it.

Peters reached over and pushed a telephone across the table. "I went back through my notes and saw it. Make the call."

A half-hour later, Frank was on the phone with the right IT person in Birmingham. He had called the office in Birmingham, who had directed him through four other numbers until he reached the right department.

Peters had left and come back, bringing a map and more coffee.

Since the car had been sold and was no longer Alabama Bureau of Investigation property, Frank had had to explain the situation several times before he found someone who could, and would, help him.

"OK, it's coming up now," the technician said on the speakerphone. Frank leaned over the map of the area, familiarizing himself with towns he hadn't heard of before.

"Looks like the tracker is inactive," the technician finally said. "I can't get a current location on it. And it can't be activated remotely."

Frank shook his head at the phone.

"Why not? This is part of an ongoing kidnapping investigation, and it could be our only lead—"

"It's not protocol, I assure you," the technician said, his voice tinny and distant. "You've got my full cooperation on this, believe me. But the tracker isn't active—it's in passive mode. It must still be wired to the battery, or it would have died years ago. It's an old one, one they don't even make it anymore."

Peters leaned forward, talking into the phone. "Are you sure you can't ping it or remotely reactivate it?"

"No."

"But you can tell if it's on or off," Frank asked.

The line was quiet for a moment.

"Right, it's on," the technician said. "It looks like it's in maintenance mode, so it must be damaged. It reports in once a day at midnight."

Frank felt a glimmer of hope.

"Can you tell me where it was last night at midnight?"

"Hang on." The line was quiet. "Yup, here it is. I'll give you the last five locations." The technician read off a series of coordinates, longitude and latitude. "Some are nearly identical. Does that help?"

"Yes, thank you. And thanks for pulling this up. It might help us wrap a case."

"Well, good luck. Oh, I'm Carl. Call me back directly, if you need anything else." The technician gave Frank his direct phone number before ending the call.

Frank hung up the phone, but Peters was already waiting by the door.

"Let's go."

They walked out and headed for the government offices—there was the planning department, utilities, tax department and, on the other side, the offices of the city manager and assistant city manager.

"Not going back to the station?" Frank asked.

Peters shook his head.

"Not sure who to trust at this point."

They walked into the Planning Department and found an open computer station—there were several with Internet access for the public to use to look up properties and zoning regulations. Peters pulled up Google and typed in the first longitude and latitude combination.

"Downtown," Peters said.

Frank nodded at the screen. "Tuesday night—King was talking to me about the case at Ricky's. Didn't realize it was that late, but I guess it was."

"The next three are all nearly the same," Peters said, typing the first one in. The map changed, indicating the Vacation Inn parking lot.

"My hotel, Wednesday, Thursday, and Friday nights," Frank said. "I was back before midnight each night."

"Okay, and last night you were at the Holly Toys warehouse," Peters said, remembering what Frank had told them. "Your car was parked in the parking lot, right? When did you get jumped?"

"Around nine," Frank said. "I remember, because I could hear the band playing downtown."

Peters thought about it, as he typed in the last set of numbers. "The HarvestFest started at 7, with two bands. One played 7 to 8 p.m. and the other 8:30 to 10. You could have heard music as late at 10 or 10:15 p.m."

The map came up.

Frank watched as the map suddenly zoomed out from Cooper's Mill completely. The map tracked northward, zooming into an area miles away, displayed a location far to the north.

"Out in the country," Peters said, using the mouse wheel to zoom into the area. It looked like farmland, mostly broken up with houses and smaller roads. Frank saw a large dairy farm and, running along the eastern side of the screen, the fuzzy brown swath of a river.

Peters nodded, zooming in. "It's north of Troy. A farmhouse."

Frank sat back and looked at the map on the screen. "It looks secluded, out by itself."

The farmhouse was very large, two or three stories, with a big barn next to it. There was a gravel driveway and parking area in front and a long driveway that ran to the road, coming out near the river. Frank leaned closer and pointed at the screen.

"That's a big house," Frank said, studying the computer monitor. "No other houses too close, with good access to roads in all directions. Great place to keep the girls."

Peters studied the screen as well, moving the map around. "What's with that fenced-in back area, like a field?"

Frank shook his head. "Not sure. But the house is out in the country, and one town over from Cooper's Mill. I'm assuming that's not in your jurisdiction, right?"

Peters shook his head. "Nope—Troy has their own police department, backed up by Miami County. We're almost never up there. Fire and EMT sometimes," he said. "We need to call the Chief."

"Not yet," Frank said, standing. He didn't want to put the information out there until he absolutely had to. "Let's call from the road. And I hate to ask this, but do you have an extra firearm? Mine was taken."

Peters nodded and smiled, then started for the exit. "I've got you covered."

59

Chief King was back in his office, getting ready for a joint conference call with the Ohio Attorney General and the Miami County Sheriff. Things had been looking so good this morning, after they had found Frank alive. Now the case had all gone to hell.

Instead of out working the case, he had to answer questions about chains of custody and surveillance cameras. Matt Lassiter's lawyer was already out in the parking lot of the police station, talking to the gaggle of reporters, drumming up outrage at the fact that his client had died in Chief King's custody.

It was turning into one hell of a day.

There was a knock at the door, and King looked up. It was Sergeant Graves. Relieved, Chief King waved him in. Sergeant Graves came in and sat, closing the door behind him.

"You okay, Chief?"

King nodded. "Nothing I can really do."

Graves shrugged. "I just got off the phone with the coroner—they're going to bump Lassiter up to the top of the list and process him tonight. We should hear something in the morning," Graves said.

"Okay, stay on top of that for me. I've got this phone call with the AG. He's going to rip me a new one."

Graves nodded. "How will that work—will we still be running the case?"

"I hope so," King said. "But I wouldn't be surprised if we got some 'help' from the State Police or Miami County. We look like a bunch of idiot hicks, letting him die like that. Did you see what happened?"

Graves shook his head. "I stepped out with Agent Shale—he went to call his office to see if they had any more information on the deed and property transfer. I went to call Detective Barnes to tell him to look out for any more financial documentation."

King nodded, staring at his desk. "Anything on the cameras?"

Graves shook his head. "Glitch in the system, they said."

"I'm just kicking myself—we should have taken his belt and shoelaces, at least."

"But that would have meant processing him into the system," Graves said. "You were trying to keep it casual."

King scoffed. "Fat lot of good it did."

Graves glanced out into the main room. "Where are Peters and Harper?"

King looked up from his notes—he had been jotting down what Graves had said about the coroner's office.

"I told them the same thing I told you—we need to find those girls. Immediately. If Lassiter had help, they'll be wrapping things up right now, tying up loose ends," King said. "I don't need to tell you what that means."

Graves nodded. "Jesus, I wish we could find those girls. At this point, I don't even care who Lassiter was working with—Nick Martin has been through enough."

King nodded.

"I'll let you know if they call in with anything—I saw them leaving together," King said. "Can you check in with Barnes, see if he found anything else at Lassiter's apartment? And check with the tip line. Now that the press has announced Lassiter is dead, maybe we'll get some calls about him and his activities."

Graves nodded. "Will do, boss. Just let me know what I can do to help," he said standing.

"Thanks," King said, getting back to his notes.

60

The sun was just setting. Peters was driving his squad car, making great time. He had the sirens going, and cars were slowing down and moving off onto the shoulder as the police car approached and passed. Frank didn't have to tell him to hurry.

It seemed like that, at each step of this case, they were always playing catch-up. But now, for the first time, Frank felt like they were in control. Ahead of the game, maybe. It was probably because he and Peters were keeping the information to themselves.

But Frank kept thinking about Ben Stone, driving alone down to Coral Gables. Had he had the same thoughts, driving to that dark part of town by himself, full of excitement and anticipation? Had he also assumed that it was better to work the case alone? Frank had Peters, at least.

They passed through a busy stoplight—Peters slowed, leaning on the siren and racing through the intersection, ignoring the red. He continued north.

"That's the turn for Troy," Peters said. "201 continues on for a bit, and then we'll be there."

Frank nodded as the car continued north, then turned off the main road onto smaller roads. Frank saw the large dairy farm he'd seen on the computer. Peters made a couple of turns, passing farms and country homes.

"OK, we're getting close. Let me call it in," Frank said. "And kill the siren."

Peters nodded and reached up, silencing the siren.

Frank took the radio handset and clicked it, calling in.

"Dispatch," the voice came back.

"This is Frank Harper—let me talk to Chief King."

There was a series of beeps, as the call was transferred over from the dispatch office to King's office. After a moment, King answered.

"Chief King here."

"Jeff, this is Frank," he said. "Just reporting in as requested—we've located the last known position of my vehicle."

"What?"

Frank looked at Peters, then spoke into the radio.

"Your cousin remembered that it had a GPS tracking device on it. The device isn't active anymore, but we were able to find out where the vehicle was last night. It's at a farmhouse north of Troy. We're heading out there now, ETA twenty-three minutes."

Peters looked over at Frank, curious.

King was quiet on the line for a moment. "Good news, but I don't like you out there alone. You need backup?"

Frank thought about it.

"Yeah, go ahead, but have them wait for us. And approach with caution," Frank said, shaking his head. "No sirens. Peters will text you the address. It's a long driveway up from the road."

"OK," King answered. Frank could hear the hesitation in his voice. It wasn't standard procedure, texting the address. But it was the only way to keep it off the police band, where anyone could hear it. Besides, nothing on this case had been standard. "Call in to the switchboard if you find the car."

"OK," Frank answered. "Otherwise, please limit traffic." That was code for not broadcasting any more than necessary.

Frank hung up as Peters turned again onto a smaller paved country road.

"Twenty-three minutes?" Peters said. "More like three."

Frank nodded. "We need the head start. Just in case someone was listening."

The kid knew where he was going, obviously, but Frank had no clue, so he grabbed the printed map again and found where they were. It was getting dark quickly, making it harder to see the road as it twisted between dark fields of dead corn. At least there was a moon—it was going to be very dark out in the country with no streetlights around.

They crossed a bridge—that was the river—and Peters slowed coming off the bridge, looking for a turn. "Good place to keep the girls—no one out here."

"At least no one could hear them," Frank said, agreeing.

They both scanned the trees ahead, looking for a break.

"Found it," Peters said, as a driveway came up on the right. Both sides of the road were lined with trees, and the driveway would have been easy to miss if you weren't looking for it.

Peters slowed the car and stopped on the shoulder. Frank was happy to see that Peters was smart enough to turn off his lights and pull off next to the road, not drive up the driveway.

They parked. Peters texted the address to his cousin, then looked up at Frank. "Now what?" Peters said.

Frank looked around, looking up the road they'd just driven. He could see back to the river bridge, but nothing beyond. It was getting dark quickly. If they were going to do this, they needed to hurry.

"Let's go," Frank said. "Close your door quietly."

Peters nodded, and they climbed from the car, quietly closing the car doors behind them. It always annoyed Frank when the cops in movies or TV shows would arrive at the scene of a crime and invariably announce their presence by driving up to the scene, lights blazing, sirens blaring. And they always got out and slammed their doors. It was like they were trying to warn the bad guys.

Peters waved Frank back to the rear of the squad car and pulled open the trunk. He took out a bullet-proof vest and handed it to Frank, then strapped on one of his own.

"Can't be too careful," Peters said.

Frank thanked him and strapped his on, pulling a CMPD windbreaker on over it. In his experience, it was never good to let the perps know you had on a vest. If they knew you were protected, they invariably went for the headshot.

Like with Ben Stone.

In the trunk, Peters also had brought a small arsenal of weapons—shotguns, handguns, and ammo. Peters took out two shotguns and loaded them, then handed one to Frank, who smiled. Frank also took out two small handguns with holsters, checking to make sure they were loaded.

Peters reached up and thumbed his shoulder radio. "Radio check," he said.

"Traffic clear," dispatch came back, and Peters adjusted the volume down.

Frank put his leg up on the bumper and strapped one to his ankle, and the other gun went on his belt.

"Okay, now stay quiet," Frank said, looking at Peters. "And stay with me. We have about ten minutes, probably, so let's keep moving. And don't get cute." Frank knew that the kid was good at getting coffee and walking Frank through who was who in the town to assist with the investigation. But he'd never been in a situation like this with a young kid like Peters. He didn't need the kid tripping over his own feet and shooting Frank in the back.

Peters nodded. "You lead, Frank. Don't worry about me."

Frank nodded and sighed, took one look back at the road, and started up the dark driveway.

61

The long driveway wound through trees into the dark. According to the map in Frank's pocket, the driveway ran up for a quarter mile, then came out into an open space that fronted the large farmhouse and a barn. Behind the farmhouse were a yard and that large fenced-in field. Beyond that, parkland, trees and the river.

Frank used his flashlight sparingly, flicking it at the driveway occasionally. Another thing they got wrong in the movies was cops running around, shining their flashlights everywhere. If you did that in real life, it would just show people where to aim. Instead, you pointed the flashlights down at the ground in front of you, or just ahead. Never up in the direction you were going.

They came out of the trees and he tucked the flashlight away. It was a big old farmhouse, three stories, sitting back from a large gravel parking area. The house had lots of windows, old-fashioned siding, and a huge front porch that wrapped around the entire front.

And, from what Frank could see, every single light in the house was blazing. Someone was home.

A rusty car sat in the gravel driveway in front of the home—an old Toyota Corolla, not the Mustang from the ransom drop. Frank thought about calling in the plates, but it really didn't matter at this point—the Taurus was here somewhere, or it wasn't.

Next to the home was the large wooden barn he'd seen in the satellite picture. Frank angled off toward the barn, moving parallel to the trees and skirting the edge of the gravel driveway.

"Stay off the gravel," he whispered to Peters, pointing at the ground. Peters nodded and fell silently in line behind him.

Frank moved in a semicircle around the parking area and approached the barn. It had two of those huge barn doors that slid horizontally. Frank tried both but found them locked. He glanced at Peters, who was keeping one eye on the house.

"Circle around," Frank whispered, pointing to another door in the south side, down from the large doors.

The smaller door of the barn was locked. Breaking and entering was frowned upon, obviously, but they had probable cause, so Frank set down the shotgun and got out his picks, starting on the lock. Peters covered him, the shotgun pointed at the gravel.

After a few seconds, Frank heard the lock click open. He put his tools away and picked up his gun, then nodded at Peters and slowly swung the heavy wooden door open, stepping inside.

Frank shined his flashlight around the interior space—the barn was gigantic. He could feel the open space over his head as he flashed his light around the interior of the barn, avoiding the windows.

In the middle of the barn, Frank saw his old Taurus.

"There it is," Peters said, nodding. Frank couldn't see his face, but he could hear the smile in his tone.

"Yup," Frank said, moving to the car.

It appeared to be undamaged—or no more damaged then when he'd seen it last. He shined his light inside—the CD player and discs were still sitting there on the bench seat.

"Phone?" Peters asked.

Frank shook his head and circled the car. He fished out his keys and quietly popped the trunk, but it was empty as well. Frank quietly closed the lid.

Something caught his eye, and Frank pointed the flashlight up. "Wow," Frank said. "That's a lot of pot."

"What?" Peters said, looking around warily.

Frank nodded up at the rafters, and Peters gave out a long, low whistle at the sight. Their flashlights illuminated scores of marijuana plants, hanging from every rafter and crossbeam.

"I think we better call it in," Frank said.

Peters nodded and grabbed his radio, keeping his voice down. "Dispatch, this is Peters," he whispered. "Requesting assistance. Vehicle located, residence occupied by unknown number of persons. Refer to Chief King for location."

Frank was looking around the interior of the barn.

"Dispatch here," the radio crackled. Peters turned it down even more. "Four units en route, ETA eighteen minutes."

"Must be Jeff, Barnes, and Sergeant Graves," Peters said, hanging up the radio. "Now what—do we wait?"

Frank shook his head.

"We need to scout," he said. "When more cops show, we'll lose the element of surprise. Our best shot at recovering the girls is now. They're most likely in the house, on the second or third floor, held separately. Or down in the basement."

"Dark and cold—secluded," Peters said.

Frank shook his head. "Now, don't you start believing that crap. She's a good guesser, that's all."

They left the barn, and Frank took a moment to close the door behind them, leaving it unlocked. Another thing they did wrong on cop shows was that they always left clues for any perpetrators that the cops were on scene. If one of the kidnappers happened to find the door standing open, they'd be alerted.

Frank made his way along the barn and then got into a position where he could observe the house for a moment.

Large windows, lights on—these people were not expecting anyone. The curtains were even open. He could see into several of the rooms—there was a front room, off the porch, then another room and a kitchen in the back. Beyond the back of the house, Frank could see a kid's swing set and a tall fence—it probably led to the back field. Based on what was drying in the barn, Frank had a suspicion that it wasn't a cornfield inside the fence.

Frank saw a young man walking through the house toward the front door, followed by an attractive young woman. Very attractive. They were arguing, or at least talking loudly, and unarmed. It looked like they were having a fight.

"That's her," Peters whispered from next to him. "From the ransom drop."

Frank nodded. "I'll bet that's the guy as well. He fits the general description and the age range."

"They're not very bright—what kind of idiot steals your car and then keeps it?" Peters said quietly. "Even if they don't know it's being tracked, it's still dumb to keep a stolen car."

Frank started to say something about how dumb people make the best criminals, but then he stopped when the front door opened suddenly, casting a long square of light out onto the front porch and the rusty Corolla parked out front.

The young woman came out.

"I'm leaving, George," she shouted. "I don't like this at all, and one of us needs to be gone when he gets here."

The young man nodded and picked up a large bag, handing it to her along with a fistful of keys.

"It's okay, Chas," the young man said with concern in his voice. "I'll meet you in town, as soon as it's over. By the big fountain."

She seemed to hesitate, then leaned in and kissed him. "You be careful, Georgie," she said quietly, but Frank was close enough to hear.

"Deputy, circle around the house—we need to know how many are here," Frank whispered, pointing toward the kitchen and rear of the home. "Be careful and look for any access to the second floor from the outside. The third floor looks like an attic—the girls could be on either floor."

Peters nodded and left, working his way through the darkness until Frank couldn't see him anymore.

A phone began ringing from inside the house.

While he was talking to Peters, the young woman had walked down to the Corolla and dropped her bags inside the open window. Frank cursed quietly to himself—if he'd been smart, he would have disabled their vehicle. Maybe he was slipping—

"Just stay for a second," the young man said loudly to the girl by the car. "That might be him."

She sighed loudly and crossed her arms, but stayed, and the boy walked back into the house. Frank thought about knocking out the girl, but that would give them away, and he had no idea how many more people were inside.

After a few seconds, the boy walked back out onto the porch. This time he was carrying a rifle.

"Chastity, come back inside," he said quietly.

She stomped her foot like a petulant child.

"No, Puddin'," I want to leave before he gets here—we talked about this! If we're both here when he—"

"It's too late for that," the young man said quietly, looking around at the trees, his shotgun up. "Chastity. Inside."

And Frank realized the young man knew the cops were here.

How?

Either the phone call or Peters had given them away.

Frank watched helplessly as the girl glanced around at the bushes and walked quickly back inside. The door closed loudly, and someone inside began closing all the curtains. Lights started going out.

Shit.

Surprise was out. That meant this was going to turn into a hostage situation in moments.

Frank shook his head and stood, making a decision that he would probably soon regret. He crossed the driveway and stepped up onto the wooden porch. Frank adjusted his shotgun and stooped over, looking in both windows before walking right up to the front door.

There was sudden movement off to his right. Frank turned and saw Peters emerged from the bushes next to the porch.

"There's only the two occupants, I think," Peters whispered. "And there's no ladders or anything—there's a tree, but it's too small for me to climb."

Frank thought about it for a moment.

"OK, we'll take the direct approach," he said.

Frank stood up, stepped next to the door, and rang the doorbell.

"What are you doing?" Peters hissed, incredulous.

Frank smiled.

"Go around back and get inside while I'm talking to them," Frank said. "Don't worry about anything except finding the girls. Get them out, or barricade yourself inside with them."

Peters nodded and slipped away.

"Who's there?" came a voice from the other side of the door.

"It's the police," Frank said loudly, standing off to one side of the door. No need to take one in the stomach if they took a shot through the wood. "You've got my car in your barn. Open up."

"Um, no," the young man said.

Frank shook his head.

"Look, I've got three cops with me and another dozen on the way. I know it's just you and the girl—I'm only interested in recovering Charlie Martin and her friend. You guys can leave, as far as I'm concerned."

It was quiet. Frank couldn't tell if they were buying it or not, but he could hear whispers inside. It didn't matter as long as the—

A loud shot rang out from the back of the house. Frank heard a scream and kicked in the door.

The doorframe exploded next to his head, and he ducked back outside. Two more shots rang out, missing him. One blew out a large front window, and the second shattered the side mirror of the Corolla in front of the house.

Frank ducked down and peeked in—he could see a foyer and stairs going up. Beyond was a long hallway—the rooms he'd seen through the windows were to the left—and beyond that, a kitchen.

Peters was down.

Frank could see him on his face on the floor of the kitchen, not moving at all. Blood was spreading out in a pool around him.

"Stay away from us!" the young woman shouted from somewhere on the first floor. She sounded completely hysterical. "Or you'll get it too!"

Two more shots followed, forcing Frank away from the front door.

He considered circling around, but it looked like the doors were all covered. With Peters down, he was outnumbered, and the element of surprise was gone.

Maybe a window.

He jumped the porch railing to the left of the door and worked his way along the curtained windows. The third one he tried was ajar. He slid it quietly up and climbed inside, being careful to not disturb the curtains.

In moments, he was inside the house, hidden by the thick curtain.

Frank parted the curtain slightly—he was in a formal dining room. A large table, surrounded by chairs, took up most of the room. He ducked down behind the table, trying to figure out where they were.

He saw them both in the hallway. The young man and woman were both watching the front door, and she was crying loudly, wiping at her face. They each had shotguns. Clearly, they did not expect Frank to swoop in from the side.

Frank knew this was his only chance before King and the others arrived and turned this into a long, drawn-out hostage situation.

He crept away from the table and stood next to the wall that separated the dining room from the hallway. Frank kept low and approached the man first—he was the closest. Frank would have preferred to incapacitate the woman first—she was the one who had started firing first, but she was farther down the hallway.

Frank stepped quickly from the doorway and hit the man hard on the side of the head with an open-palm strike to his ear. It was always a good opening strike—it surprised the victim with an amazing bout of instantaneous pain, but little actual damage. Cupping the palm made air rush into the ear canal—if done with maximum force, it could shatter the eardrum, knocking someone out of a fight immediately.

The man staggered away, a hand to his ear. Frank had expected the woman to fire at him, so Frank stepped around the young man, putting him between Frank and the woman. Instead, she screamed and sprinted away, running to the foyer and turning up the stairs.

Frank struck the wounded boy in the stomach and caught the shotgun as the young man dropped it. The boy crumpled to the floor, obviously in pain.

Go after the girls or check on Peters?

His instinct told him the girl would not harm the girls—but he could be wrong. Frank stepped over to Peters. He had been hit in the vest and shoulder. Blood was seeping from the shoulder wound. Lucky, but out cold.

Frank rolled him onto his back and grabbed a kitchen towel from the island, stuffing it into the shoulder wound and tucking it under the edge of the vest. It would at least slow the bleeding.

The rest of his mind was trained on the upstairs, straining to hear gunshots or the sounds of a struggle. In their desperation, kidnappers were sometimes known to execute their hostages just moments before capture. Frank tried not to think about it. He watched the stairs for the young woman and held the kitchen towel against Peters' shoulder.

Every fiber in his body told him to go upstairs, to find the girls and stop the young woman from doing something horrible. But King was coming, and Graves, and the ghost of Ben Stone kept reminding him to wait for backup. Ben's gun had still been in his holster. A fat lot of good his range rating had done him.

In the distance, Frank heard a siren.

62

Charlie heard a lot more shouting.

They had been fighting nonstop for the last few hours. Even when the man had brought Charlie her dinner, the woman had kept yelling at him from the bottom of the stairs. Yelling at him, calling him names that Charlie was not allowed to use. Bad names, mean words.

The man hadn't said anything, but Charlie could tell the mean names hurt him. He had tried to ignore the woman by telling Charlie another story, this one about a place called Griffith Park, a big observatory and museum that sat up on a hill above some place called Los Angeles. The story kept getting interrupted, but the man had kept with it until Charlie was done eating and he had left.

The woman kept yelling while the man fed Maya—Charlie didn't know if he told her stories as well, but Maya's English was pretty good.

After dinner, Charlie had waited a little while, just listening to the fighting. The woman wanted to leave, but the man didn't want to leave Charlie and Maya. The woman didn't care—she seemed to think that someone was coming to hurt her.

Charlie slipped out of the zip tie and tiptoed across the floor to the door, trying the lock. As always, it was bolted shut.

She was walking to the bathroom when she heard the first gunshot. It was so loud it rattled the glass in the windows. Another gunshot rang out, and another—they sounded like wood cracking, like when she'd been on the construction site with her dad, and the men would be building walls or cutting two-by-fours. They would have those saws with the spinning blades that cut right through the wood like butter, but sometimes the wood would snap off loudly instead of cutting cleanly.

If people were shooting downstairs, maybe the police had come.

Her father was on the City Council, and the police worked for him. He'd said once that the police were a little sore at him for taking away some of their money. Did that mean they didn't have enough money for bullets or guns? As the days had dragged on, Charlie had wondered if her father taking away the policemen's money meant that they weren't looking for her.

But her father also knew the Mayor and a bunch of other important people in town. He had even introduced Charlie to the Mayor once, a nice old gentleman that made models of buildings out of tiny wooden sticks. The Mayor had seemed nice, loud but nice. And he had clearly liked her father, with all the smiling and hand shaking. So there were people that liked her father and their family. She just hoped that the cops downstairs were ones that liked her father.

Charlie went to the window. She saw a police car coming up the driveway. So who was shooting, if the cops were just getting here? Maybe the young man and woman were fighting.

Charlie heard feet coming up the stairs.

She had only a moment to decide—get back into bed and pretend she couldn't get away? Or run?

The police were here. That meant she was going to be rescued. And staying inside the house seemed like a bad idea, especially if she knew she could get away.

Charlie ran to the bathroom and closed the door, then went to the window and slid it open. She stood up on the edge of the bathtub and climbed out. Charlie had thought about all the different things she could do, and she'd decided that the smartest thing to do was for her to escape and go get help, instead of trying to free Maya herself.

She pulled her way up onto the roof, walking the roofline. Her father always told her she would make a good gymnast. It must've been all those afternoons killing time around her father's construction sites, walking on planks of wood and two-by-fours and negotiating the tops of cinder blocks and basement walls.

Charlie scampered along the roofline and found the tree. Steadying herself, she ran and jumped. The half-second in the air was terrifying, but she caught the tree around the trunk, grabbing on tightly. She sighed and let out a quiet laugh, then began climbing down to the ground.

63

"Peters? Harper?"

Frank heard the police car come to a stop and cops approaching the front of the house. It sounded like Sergeant Graves. Frank wasn't sure why he'd used the siren, but Frank was glad he was there all the same.

Frank still had a hand on Peters. The young deputy hadn't moved.

"Back here!" Frank yelled from the kitchen. "One suspect, upstairs." The front door still stood open, and Frank could see the police lights out front. "There are two shooters—one female armed upstairs, and one male down, in the hallway. Circle around and come in through the kitchen!"

Frank heard someone walk in through the front door and down the wooden floor of the hallway. Sergeant Graves appeared from around the corner, wearing a bullet-proof vest.

"You okay?" he asked, looking at Frank, then down at Peters.

"I'm good," Frank nodded. "Peters took two from a shotgun," Frank said, nodding at the man's shotgun on the floor next to Peters. "One in the vest, but the other in the shoulder. It's a good thing we were both wearing—"

"The other one is upstairs?" Graves asked, cutting him off. He was looking around the kitchen.

Frank nodded.

"I'm assuming she's up there with the girls, if they're still alive."

"Good," Graves said. "Good you cornered her, so at least she can't get away. Backup and EMTs are on the way." Graves stood, picking up the young man's shotgun, checking the chamber. "Come help me take out the woman," he said.

"What about Peters?" Frank asked, his hand still on Peters' shoulder.

Sergeant Graves shook his head. "He'll be okay for a minute. Looks like you stopped the bleeding. We need to end this before something happens to those little girls."

Frank nodded and stood, grabbing his shotgun.

"Okay, let's go," Graves said, a shotgun in each hand.

They walked down the hallway to where the young man lay on the wood floor, still out cold. Frank checked his neck for a pulse, finding one, and then stood, starting up the hallway toward the foot of the stairs.

"The young woman went upstairs," Frank said, gripping his shotgun. "She's also armed with a—"

The shotgun blast caught him squarely in the back.

The power of the shotgun at such a close range hurled him nearly ten feet down the hallway. His back bloomed with burning pain that spread to every nerve in his body. He landed with a thud, hitting his face against the wooden floor, knocking the wind out of him. Frank slid nearly to the open front door.

The house went quiet. After a second, Frank heard someone yelling.

"You can come down now," he heard Graves call.

Every single part of Frank's body was screaming in pain. He tried to not move, tried to stay still. He concentrated on the voices, and looking out the open front door at the police car and the Corolla with the busted mirror and the trees beyond, splashed regularly with red and blue light.

He felt blood oozing from his mouth.

"Is it safe?" Frank heard the young woman ask from upstairs.

"Yup," Graves said quietly. He could hear him reloading the shotgun, sliding more cartridges into the bore. "There are more cops coming, so we gotta hurry. George is hurt—you better check on him."

He heard footsteps coming down the stairs.

"You get the other one?" It was a young woman's voice, the young woman Frank had seen. She sounded frightened.

"Yup, he's dead," Frank heard Graves say. "But more cops are on their way. I was already on my way, or they would've gotten here first."

Frank heard the young woman's feet on the wooden floor—she stepped down from the stairs, walked past Frank, and let out a little sound. She must have seen the young man. Frank heard her hurry down the hallway to check on the young man—

The next shot was much louder, filling up the entire world with sound. Frank heard the sound of a person crumpling to the ground.

"Stupid bitch."

Frank's mind was racing.

Graves was the leak, the cop, the kidnapper, in charge of the kidnappers, who made sure they got away. He had the duty roster, helped set the roadblocks, heard the call in to dispatch. He didn't need to call King to get the address. Maybe he did anyway, just to explain how he knew where to go. But Graves had the zip ties and knew about the second ransom. He was probably the one who jumped Frank, hit him over the head, and took the files and the money.

And carried him into the field to die.

Sergeant Graves also had been the last one in the room with Lassiter. The answers flashed through Frank's mind. There were all the answers, all in one place, falling into place like dominoes. And now Sergeant Graves was cleaning everything up. He'd been the first on the scene after the kidnapping. Graves had found the water bottle—or planted it. King had given him the lead on looking into who might be dirty.

Frank heard Graves start up the stairs.

The girls.

If they were alive, they wouldn't be for much longer.

He tried to move. At this point, playing dead just wasn't going to cut it.

Out the open front door, he saw the Corolla and the dark trees beyond. The broken side mirror hung crazily, the glass shattered.

Frank saw movement.

A little girl appeared near the car and glanced up at the house. She saw him on the ground, in the doorway.

Charlie Martin.

Frank lifted his head and looked at her. It took him a second to get enough breath in his lungs to speak.

"Run," he whispered as loud as he could. Blood sprayed from his mouth.

Her eyes went wide. She turned and disappeared from sight.

"Son of a BITCH!" Frank heard from upstairs.

He could hear Graves stomping around loudly, pissed off. Frank heard glass breaking. A loud thump, followed by more breaking glass—the man was turning over furniture. A shotgun blast went off, the sound muffled by the wooden floors.

"WHERE ARE YOU??!" Sergeant Graves was screaming.

Frank lifted his head and turned, looking to the stairs and the hallway.

George was sitting up now, eyes wide, holding his ear and looking at Frank. Their eyes met for a second, and then George crawled to Chastity and leaned over her, patting her gently on the back of the head. George's eyes were shiny as he pried the shotgun from her dead hands.

He stood and walked slowly up the hallway toward Frank.

Frank knew it was over.

At least he'd gotten to make up with Laura and meet Jackson and spend some time with them. He'd wanted more time with them, time to take Jackson to a baseball game or visit Laura at her new job. Time to see her happy. Frank wanted more time with them, more time to make up for the lost time he'd pissed away.

George stopped next to Frank. Frank got ready for it. He wondered if Ben Stone had felt like this, looking up at his killer.

George looked down at him, then slowly nodded and turned, starting wearily up the stairs. Walking away from Frank. The man's legs continued slowly up the stairs, finally disappearing out of view.

Frank felt a second wind rush through him, a temporary reprieve from the alarms of pain going off all over his back. Frank slid his arm down, trying to get to his belt holster.

Another shot rang out upstairs, and a second, then three more in quick succession. Two different weapons firing, back and forth. Frank could hear people walking around as well, stuttering movements and running, followed by another shot. He had no idea what was happening, but he managed to free the handgun and got his other arm under his chest, propping himself up.

Frank waited, watching the stairs.

He heard someone running on the second floor, the old hardwoods squeaking. Feet appeared on the stairs—it was Sergeant Graves, racing to get away. By the time he got halfway down the staircase, Frank could see he'd escaped any injury.

Frank shot him.

Graves screamed and fell backward, the shotgun clattering to the floor. Frank fired again. A red hole appeared in the man's neck. For a moment, he looked at Frank, Graves' hands going to his neck. Blood bubbled from between his fingers, and Frank thought of that cauldron of fake blood. Then the man slumped backward against the stairs.

He heard other people walking around upstairs. Frank smiled through the blood.

After a moment, the young man and Maya came down the stairs—she had been fighting him, slapping at him but then stopped when she saw the bleeding man on the stairs.

"It's okay, you're okay," George was telling Maya.

They walked gingerly around Graves. When they reached the bottom of the stairs, the young man pointed to Frank, who had managed to work his way up into a sitting position and was leaning against the door frame.

"You stay with him," the young man said. "He's a policeman, a good one. Not like the other guy. And help is on the way—Charlie already got out. You just stay here, okay?"

Maya nodded.

Frank watched as the young man walked back over to the woman and patted her on the back one more time, touching her head gently. It seemed like a very long moment, but it couldn't have lasted more than a few seconds. Then the young man stood, crying, and picked up two of the shotguns, hoisting them over his shoulders. His ear was still bleeding.

George walked over and looked at Frank for a moment, then stepped right over him and continued out the door.

Frank turned painfully. The young man put both shotguns into the Corolla, then walked over to Graves' police car and opened the doors, searching around inside for a few moments. He stood, taking out a green duffel bag, then pulled it open, smiling at the contents.

Frank couldn't see what was inside, but he could guess: it had to be the second ransom.

George walked back over and climbed into the white Corolla with the busted side mirror. He started the car, pulled on his seat belt and, with the curtest of nods in Frank's direction, drove down the dark driveway and disappeared into the night.

64

"And he just drove away?"

They were in his hospital room. Bright sunlight shone in the windows. Outside, the ground was littered with fallen leaves in a dozen different colors of red and yellow and orange. It looked like the rain was finally gone for good.

"Just stepped right over me," Frank said, nodding. "Kept on walking. Searched the police car and found the missing money—"

"Sergeant Graves had it?" Laura asked, leaning forward. "So he's the one that attacked you and took the money?"

Frank nodded and set down the Jell-O. It was the only part of his meager lunch that he couldn't stomach. Why did they always serve Jell-O in hospitals? He'd thought it was a myth from watching too many movies, but there it was on his tray. Green and slimy and not the kind of food he was looking forward to—Frank wanted a steak.

He leaned over gingerly and handed it to Jackson, who smiled and sat back down on the floor next to the hospital bed to enjoy it.

Frank turned to Laura.

"Yes, it was Sergeant Graves," Frank said. "Of course, I figured it all out too late, but he was in on it from the start. Helped Lassiter set up the whole thing and then 'managed' the investigation all the way through. 'Managed' Lassiter, too, right up to the end."

Laura shook her head.

"Geez, the guy sounds like a real piece of work," she said. "What about the young man—he got away?"

"Yup—George, the young man, was the one taking care of the girls," Frank said. "They put out a nationwide APB on him. Little Charlie was in yesterday to visit, and she said that he was the only one who was nice to them. Evidently the young woman, Chastity, helped out as little as possible."

Laura nodded and looked out the windows. A sturdy breeze shook the trees outside, which were painted with the fiery colors of fall. Most of the leaves had already dropped. Winter was right around the corner.

"I still can't believe it was a cop," she said. "It's horrible. It was no wonder those little girls got into the car with him. And then he was helping with the investigation? I can't believe Graves fooled everyone like that."

Frank nodded. "Peters and I were working from the 'inside job' assumption late in the investigation, like I told you. But we never figured out who it was, not until it was too late," Frank said. "He was clever, I'll say that much. While he wasn't running the investigation, he was close enough to influence it."

"Steering it?"

"Yes, to a degree," Frank said. "But he'd been dirty for a while. Apparently he'd been running a marijuana grow operation up at that farmhouse for years, growing the pot right out in the backyard. Between him being a cop and the high fences, no one ever found out."

"Why did he do it? Why be part of a kidnapping like that?" Laura asked.

"Money, I guess. Anyone can be tempted. The Chief also said Tyler Graves and Nick Martin had had a falling out a long time ago, back in high school," Frank said. "Nick was a football star back then. King wasn't sure what happened, but it had something to do with Glenda."

"Did they ever date, Graves and Glenda?"

"Not sure. The Chief is looking into it. Apparently there was a history of bad blood between them for a long time."

Laura nodded.

"Chief King is taking it worse than anyone," Frank said, looking down at Jackson working on the Jell-O. "He thought of Tyler as his right-hand man, really. The man had King completely fooled."

She looked out the window—it was a sunny day, warmer than usual for late October. The trees were moving in a breeze that dropped more leaves to the ground.

"Have you decided what you're doing with the reward?" she asked.

Frank nodded.

"Splitting it with Deputy Peters," he said. "He deserves it. He got shot twice as much as I did," Frank said, grinning.

Laura smiled. "You must feel better—you're making jokes."

"I am feeling better," Frank said. "I can't wait for the bruising to go down—it hurts every time I breathe. I just wish the food was better in here."

"I meant what are you going to spend your money on." she asked.

He leaned back into the hospital bed. "I'm not sure—probably a new car. Settle some debts." Frank looked up at her. "Maybe help you out with Jackson's school tuition—you said it was expensive."

"You don't have to do that," she said, looking down at Jackson.

He nodded.

"I'd like to help."

Laura looked up at him. "I'm glad you're thinking about getting a better car," she said, smiling at him. "Then maybe you can come visit more often."

Just the idea made Frank smile.

"How is Deputy Peters?" Laura asked. "Is he getting better?"

"Yup," Frank said, sitting up a little. His back was numbed up and itchy, but at least he could lean back and put pressure on it now.

"It was a good thing he had us both put on those vests," Frank said. "His vest blocked the shot to his chest, but the shoulder will take a little while to heal. It will be a few weeks before he's back on duty, and even then, he'll be stuck at a desk for a while," Frank said. "If I hadn't had my vest on…"

Laura looked at Jackson, playing on the floor. The dinosaurs were attacking the leg of one of the hospital chairs, ganging up and working together to defeat the piece of furniture. A T-rex and a Brontosaurus and a whole gang of smaller dinosaurs circled the chair leg and began fighting over the empty Jell-O container.

She looked up at Frank, her eyes a little shiny.

"I was just so scared when I heard you'd been shot," she said. "A policeman came to the house, and I was worried because of your warning. But then he said what had happened to you and I didn't know what to do. I thought he might be lying. He didn't use the word—"

He patted her hand. "It's okay."

"It's just...we were just starting to reconnect, and, for a minute, I thought it was all going to be taken away again." She looked out at the trees again. "I'm just glad you're okay," Laura said.

Frank smiled at her and took her hand, squeezing it. He looked down at Jackson, playing happily with the dinosaurs Frank had bought for his grandson, and then back up at his daughter.

"I'm better than okay," Frank said, smiling.

EPILOGUE

The setting sun was just touching the tops of the ocean waves, painting the edges of the water with reds and yellows. Beyond the beach, tall stands of pine guarded the rocky shore, long shadows stretching out behind the rocks and trees, blending together in a gathering darkness.

Sunset was coming to this quiet cove of salt and sand.

In the distance, a small boat plied the water, bouncing up and down on the gentle swells far out to sea, racing to bring in the catch before the sun set.

Closer to shore, sea birds dipped and soared above the surf, screeching in the twilight. Other birds scampered along the beach, stopping to dig at the sand with long bills, searching for food.

The beach was empty. The wooden lifeguard stand stood unmanned. It was far too late in the season, and far too chilly, for beachgoers to come out. Even if they braved the cold water, the setting sun would have chased them from the beach. The parking lot, often full in the summer, stood empty as the sun began to dip behind the watery horizon. Waves marched relentlessly toward the sandy beach, unwatched and forgotten.

A car approached.

The vehicle appeared from between the tall pines, winding in and out of the green, tracing a path down the curvy road that paralleled the rocky coastline.

It was a newer car, not more than five years old. As it approached, it looked somewhat worse-for-wear, but the engine sounded strong and true. Whoever maintained the engine did so with care.

The car slowed and turned into the empty parking lot, purring to a stop next to the sand. Birds skittered away and took flight, leaving the car alone.

The door opened.

A figure climbed from the car, a young man. He stood and stretched, his arms high above him. He stood and watched the water and the waves for a long time. The sun dropped closer to the waves, and the long shadowed stretched out even further.

The waves marched toward the shore, oblivious to the visitor.

After a minute, the young man leaned back into the car, rummaging through a green duffel bag, looking for something. The young man finally found what he was looking for and stood from the car, closing the door behind him with a solid "thunk."

George started his way across the darkening beach, taking his time, enjoying the rough sand and the hiss of the ocean. It was exactly as he had imagined it would be, and nothing like he imagined it would be.

He'd imagined someone by his side.

When he reached the water, George dipped his fingers in. The cold water lapped at his shoes, but he didn't care. Instead, he simply stood in the surf and stared out at the ocean. It was unclear if he was looking at the crests of water marching toward him, or the setting sun, or the distant boat. Perhaps he watched the birds diving into the tops of the waves.

The figure reached into his pocket and took something out. He held it up, looked at it for a long moment. It was the size and shape of a small apple, ornate and golden. George rolled the compact sewing kit in his hand, smiling. He looked at it for a long moment, then lifted it to his lips and kissed it.

"Chas, you made it."

He drew back and prepared to throw it as far as he could into the water, but hesitated.

George lowered his hand and looked at the golden orb. He looked at the waves around him, then back at the object in his hand. After a long moment, he slowly put it back into his pocket.

The young man stood unmoving, the water and waves crashing around him. The water hissed like snakes on the sand as it ran back to the sea.

And George patted his pocket and stared at the ocean, smiling.

CPSIA information can be obtained
at www.ICGtesting.com
Printed in the USA
LVHW041101260423
744961LV00003B/13